Also available by **E.V. Seymour**

THE LAST EXILE
THE MEPHISTO THREAT

E.V. Seymour lives in a small village in Worcestershire. Before turning to writing, E.V. worked in P.R. in London and Birmingham, then moved to Devon where, five children later, she began writing. E.V. has bent the ears of numerous police officers in Devon, West Mercia and the West Midlands – including Scenes of Crime and firearms officers – in a ruthless bid to make her writing as authentic as possible.

E.V. SEYMOUR

LAND OF GHOSTS

First published in Great Britain 2010.
MIRA Books, Eton House, 18-24 Paradise Road,
Richmond, Surrey, TW9 1SR

© Eve Seymour 2010

ISBN 978 0 7783 0343 5

60-0710

MIRA's policy is to use papers that are natural, renewable and recyclable products and made from wood grown in sustainable forests. The logging and manufacturing processes conform to the legal environmental regulations of the country of origin.

Printed in Great Britain by Clays Ltd, St Ives plc

ACKNOWLEDGEMENTS

I have never been to Chechnya and was, therefore, reliant on the published work of a number of writers and journalists. They are Arkady Babchenko, Yuri Felshtinsky, the late Alexander Litvinenko and Anna Politkovskaya. Politkovskaya's work was particularly invaluable as she spoke to both Russians and Chechens directly caught up in the last two conflicts. Much of it makes sombre reading. I also recommend the travel journals of Colin Thubron and Andrew Meier, especially for Meier's historical perspective on Russia. To gain an understanding of combat, I must make mention of *Sniper One* by Sergeant Dan Mills, a riveting narrative of fighting under siege in Iraq.

Personal thanks are due to Phillip Williams, Operations Manager, The Refugee Council, Birmingham, for giving up a morning in a very busy schedule to talk to me. Any views expressed in the book are entirely my take, and with poetic licence, and are not necessarily representative of the Council. I'm grateful to Jim O'Kane, formerly of the Mine Action Coordination Centre, who was assiduous in providing me with up-to-date information on mines and whose knowledge was key for a major scene in the novel. Thanks also to Eddie Todd, of VIP Helicopters, Doncaster, for entertaining me with hilarious tales of flying derring-do, and who provided the inspiration for Tallis's unconventional flight to Berlin. Huge thanks to Martin Rutty at Fly-Q, Leominster, for his generosity, humour and patience, more especially for introducing me to the thrills of flying at two thousand feet! Any technical mistakes in the text are my own, not his.

As always, I'm grateful to my agent, Broo Doherty, for her tireless enthusiasm and friendship, to Catherine Burke, my editor at MIRA, and, indeed, all the MIRA team. Ali Karim and Mike Stotter, of *Shots* magazine, deserve a special mention for rooting for Tallis from the very beginning.

Lastly, this was a difficult book to write. In common with many thriller writers, I study the news, apply the *what if* principle, add two and two and come up with five. Essentially, I write fiction and must make clear I have no political axe to grind, no side to take. Nevertheless, and inevitably, I found myself inhabiting some fairly dark places during the course of research. In short, I was not an easy person to live with. My husband, Ian, deserves a medal for putting up with my sombre moods without complaint or criticism, which is why this book is dedicated to him.

For Ian

PROLOGUE

Lubyanka Prison, Moscow, 1984

SHE was beyond terror. The drugs had seen to that. Hope, the last refuge of the desperate, had all but abandoned her, yet even now in her despair she clung to the belief that she had a chance, a last chance.

She'd seen and heard of places like this. Every Russian had. With its monstrous granite exterior, the Lubyanka, more than any other prison in Moscow, symbolised the might and ruthlessness of the State. For ordinary Muscovites, it held a morbid fascination. Walking within its shadow most days, it was at once familiar and alien to her. That she should now be incarcerated deep within the grey and crumbling construct remained a mystery.

Noise. She flinched, eyes straining through the cloak of darkness. She'd been kept for so long in solitary that even the slightest sound assaulted her ears. But, no, it was nothing more than the far-away cry of a soul in torment. Should feel sympathy, or fear or something, she thought, but she felt nothing other than gratitude it wasn't her.

It was bitterly cold in the cell. And damp. Spaced-out, she couldn't even move or control her limbs—unlike her thoughts, which tumbled, shrill and feverish. In a bid to find some mental foothold, she stared purposefully at the dripping walls, her mind tumbling back to memories of cool fresh air against her skin, snow on her boots, the reassuring voice of a colleague congratulating her on a job well done. A lifetime ago, it seemed. In here everything felt far-away, disjointed. Even herself. Since the time she'd spotted the surveillance officers—easy enough because of the shortness of their stature—and been followed, then picked up off the street, it was as if everything that had happened to her had really happened to another human being, another Malika Motova.

She shifted position and idly traced the line of bruises on her thigh—mementoes of where they'd held her down and injected her. However much she resisted, however much she fought against them the outcome was inevitable: mind-rape. Maybe that's why she felt so vacant, so physically disconnected from her surroundings. The only thing that felt even vaguely real was the insane beat of her heart inside her chest. In an obscure, desperate part of her she suspected that this odd physical symptom was what happened when the human spirit was pushed to the limit.

The air smelt of cold decay. She sniffed at it and wondered what hour it was, whether it was day or night.

During the early part of her incarceration she was left in a cement-coloured room, its only adornment a filthy mattress and bucket. A meagre ration of food and water was pushed through a grille. It was her only form of human contact. Other than that, she was simply ignored. Naturally she'd tried to assert her rights, to argue her cause. She was an intelligent woman with independent views. There had been a gross miscarriage of justice, a mistake, maliciousness at work. But it was no good. Nobody was listening. Swiftly, she became a non-person, a wraith, slipping into a limbo where no organisation was responsible for her, and nobody would admit to her existence. Sleep became a stranger, hunger a friend. This was the way the KGB worked.

She did not remember exactly when her anger had turned to despair. There had been no particular event or turning point. Hours and days alone in isolation had allowed her fear to build, to grind her down until every trace of her personality was ransacked, stripped away and eliminated. Clever really. By doing nothing those dry and dusty instruments of the State had convinced her mind to disintegrate and destroy itself. She wondered about its minions, those people who carried out its bidding. Didn't her captors have family and lovers, sons and daughters? Had they, too, been divested of their humanity?

Then they came for her.

She touched a hand to her face, felt the skin papery and desiccated. Is this me, Malika Motova? she wondered blindly.

There were two men, one woman. She was stripped, physically degraded and put in an isolator cell that measured eight by ten. Her questions, her cries, went unanswered. She could not rest for the constant light shining in her eyes and the screams in her ears from the interrogation units. During that terrible time, her fear had smelt stronger than the odour of her own urine. When the questions began they always followed the same pattern—analysis of her personal details, re-examination of her answers, her interrogators exhausting her, putting words into her mouth, dissecting her motives, making lies of the truth, truth of the lies. Interrogation assumed a brutal rhythm in her life. And always the same question: how long have you been spying?

Darkness, once an enemy, became a friend and on his shoulder she wept—for herself, for her friends, for her lover. She remembered Andrei's clean-shaven looks, those piercing blue eyes that seemed to stare right into her crowded imagination. She thought of his cool sophistication, a cover for the passionate soul beneath. Oh, if only he were here, if only she could get word to him, he alone would know what to do. He would make them see the mistake they'd made, the injustice they'd done her. He would set her free. But Andrei was working countries away, in London.

Noise again, this time closer. At the sound of the

bolts being shot, the lock being sprung, she cowered in the corner furthest away from those who came for her. Strong hands reached in and took hold, physically lifting her out. There was no point in resisting. She'd learnt that lesson early. Still had the broken teeth to prove it.

Corridors and doors looked the same. Overhead illumination. Dun-coloured walls. Dirt. Flaking paint. And everywhere that penetrating odour of desperation. At last she was brought to a room she had not seen before. Inside the light was a dull yellow glow. As she was escorted in she made out a table behind which sat a man she did not recognise. He was looking at a thick file, one hand resting lightly on a page. In front of the table was a stool on which she was ordered to sit. The others, her escorts, left. So it was just the two of them, her and her interrogator.

The man glanced up. He had dull features and tired eyes, his mediocrity typical of a person who worked for the State. Looking more closely, she saw that his hair was thin, his lips too full and red. Oddly sexless. That's when something strange rallied inside her. Even though she had no idea of his rank, she sensed that this time things would be different. She tried very hard to concentrate.

'Your name?' he said.

'Malika Motova.'

'Age?'

'Thirty.'

'Occupation?'

'Journalist.'

'You work for Izvestiya.'

'Yes.'

The man nodded. She was unsure whether she was answering well or badly. 'You live where exactly?' he said.

She'd been through this many times but she repeated what she'd told the others, that she lived in a faceless block of flats in the northern suburbs of Moscow.

'And you live alone?'

'No, I live with Filip and Lyudmila Korovin.' The apartment, in reality a cramped dwelling, was an oasis of sanity in a very mad world.

'Ah, yes, a poet and writer, I understand.'

'Yes, I—'

'And I gather you have many *artistic* friends.' It was enunciated as if he was saying she harboured a contagious disease. 'Olga Gusinsky for one.'

Olga, she thought, red-haired, green-eyed, wild and beautiful. Her mind spun back to what now seemed a lifetime ago, to the many nights they'd sat, all of them together, sharing food, drinking vodka, exchanging ideas, laughing at the absurdity of Russian life, ridiculing the frail old men in power. She had taken so much for granted, her freedom included. And what a painful illusion that now seemed.

Her interrogator was still talking. 'And, of course, we must not forget the Englishman.'

She blinked. Dark memory stirred within her. A faint smile played across the man's features. His lips looked redder than ever. He turned back to the folder, turning the pages, his finger tracing the text. 'I understand you and Edward Rose are close.'

'He is a friend, yes.'

'And you have many friends.'

'A few.' She licked the corner of her mouth.

'And lovers?' he said, glancing up.

'I…'

'Andrei Ivanov.'

She swallowed. What should she say? It was true but by agreeing with her interrogator was she denouncing Andrei? It took so little. An image of him being arrested at the airport on his return to Moscow streaked through her mind. All it would take was one wrong word, one misplaced gesture, one…

'Is this correct?'

She nodded dumbly.

'Speak up.'

'Yes,' she murmured.

'Yes,' he repeated, his full lips caressing the word. 'Ivanov works,' he paused, glancing down at the text, 'at the Tass News Agency.'

'In London,' she said, thinking, Thank God.

'And the Englishman, Rose, what does he do?'

'He also works for the media.'

Her interrogator studied her for several long moments. 'Do you know why you are here?'

'I know why you say I am here, but you have no evidence to support it.'

A sharp feral smile twitched across the man's flat face. At that precise moment the air in the room seemed to alter. The staleness of her surroundings was overpowered by the stench of something stronger, yet she couldn't identify it. 'You are a Chechen, I understand,' he said, polite, as though it were a matter of record.

'No.'

'No?'

'I am a Russian born in Chechnya.' She knew the State valued the importance of accuracy.

The man turned several pages, his small eyes raking the print. 'To a Chechen mother.'

She said nothing.

'It explains your blue eyes and dark hair.'

'My mother was a pro-Russian Chechen.'

'Indeed. And what would you say you are?' His look was searing.

'I am like her,' she said, remembering that her mother's blood ran through her veins, that a Chechen was known for courage and loyalty and honour.

'Is that so?'

She remained silent.

The man leant forward, resting his elbows on the table. He put his hands together in prayer, tips of his fingers touching his chin. 'Does Andrei Ivanov know that you sleep with the Englishman?'

She clenched her teeth. How could he possibly know? Nobody knew. Nobody, other than… Oh, Christ, she thought. Had she made a terrible mistake? Had she made a fatal misjudgement? The man behind the desk shuffled the papers in front of him. It sounded like the branches of a tree scratching against a windowpane in the night. In that gut-churning moment, she realised that her terror had only begun.

'You deny it?'

'I do not deny sharing a bed with him on one occasion,' she said, flushing at her confession.

'While your lover was away,' he said accusingly.

'Yes, but it only hap—'

'So that you could trade information.'

'That's absurd,' she gasped. 'I don't have that type of information to trade.'

'And what sort of information would that be?'

She wanted to put her hands over her ears, to scream and drown out the voice, the madness.

'You *deal* in information,' he said, hawkish. 'You're a journalist.' His tone suggested that this fact alone was proof enough of espionage.

'I am also a loyal servant of the State,' she said, her voice cracking with desperation.

'We believe otherwise. You are a spy.'

'You have no proof.'

'On the contrary.' The man swivelled his eyes to the door. It swung open. Rather than increase the illumination in the room, what little light there was receded. A figure stepped forward and took up a position inches from her.

'Hello, Malika.'

She recoiled in shock and horror. A chill cloaked her soul.

'What, no greeting?' He bent down, brushing her cheek lightly with his lips, an act that once had made her shiver with rapture.

'I don't understand,' she faltered.

'Nothing to say? That's not like you.' He slipped a packet of cigarettes from his jacket, taking one out and lighting it. Tossing the dead match to the floor, he looked down, met her terrified gaze. In that moment she understood that cruelty loitered beneath the skin, that his cool sophistication was nothing more than a complex disguise for his sadistic intentions. The eyes, which once had seemed Andrei Ivanov's most appealing feature, now belonged to the face of a fanatic.

'Right,' he said, voice dripping with menace. 'Let us start from the beginning.'

CHAPTER ONE

St Pancras International, London: present day

ASIM walked with a smooth and measured stride through the station concourse and up onto the upper level from where the Eurostar departed. Sexy and impressive though his surroundings were, he barely noticed them. As an experienced intelligence officer for MI5, his mind was on higher things: the defence of the nation and the curious reason Christian Fazan, a long-serving MI6 officer, currently based in Moscow, had requested an urgent meeting in the Champagne Bar. Inter-agency conferences were not a rarity, but unscheduled, top-priority appointments were.

Fazan was already inside, immediately identifiable by the *Financial Times* spread out in front of him, glass of champagne in hand. He hadn't changed so very much over the years he'd known him, Asim thought. His dark hair was going grey. With a naturally heavy build, he obviously worked hard to keep his weight down. Still had that rogue look in the deep blue eyes that made him so attractive to the opposite sex; Fazan's track record was legendary, although he'd never married. At Asim's approach, Fazan glanced up, smiled, raising his glass slightly in a gesture of conviviality. Asim slipped into the seat next to him. It was too early to drink, but he allowed Fazan to pour him a glass from the bottle of Dom Perignon already on the bar. Asim glanced around the chic surroundings. It wasn't that busy: middle-aged female shoppers clutching the spoils of war from Oxford Street, and travellers killing time. To be expected on a cold Monday in early February.

'I thought the Zoo would be a more likely choice of venue,' Asim said with a droll smile.

'Too clichéd. Anyway, since they closed the parrot house twenty years ago, it's not so much fun.'

'I was thinking more along the lines of endangered species,' Asim said. He was alluding to the fact that Fazan was the last of four MI6 officers or, as they were known now, secret intelligence officers, to be stationed at the Embassy. The rest had been chucked out by Moscow. Asim rated Fazan as the most senior, the equivalent of a station head.

'One down, three to go.' Fazan smiled, seeing the joke. 'I'm taking up a posting in Berlin.'

'Congratulations.' He didn't think Fazan had got him there simply to share the good news.

Fazan sipped his drink, fixed Asim with a cool look and dropped his voice a semitone. 'You're probably aware of the Russian situation here in London.'

'The fact that half Russia's diplomatic staff are involved in espionage, most specifically stalking Russian dissidents, actively hunting for military and political secrets and checking out any commercial endeavours likely to profit the motherland, or is there something else I should know?'

Fazan nodded another smile. 'Not to put too fine a point on it, a return to the days of the Cold War.'

That bad? Asim thought. He considered it more of a brief, steep drop in temperature. Asim reached for his glass, tasting the champagne, pleased that it was chilled to exactly the right degree. He hated champagne that was frozen.

Fazan continued to talk. 'I've lived in Russia for the best part of a decade. Believe me, there's a new authoritarianism abroad. Russia feels snubbed by the West and, as a result, wishes to prove that it can get along without us quite well. We have opponents of the regime slung into prison, ballot fixing, and the divide between rich and poor widening by the day. Need I say more?'

Asim shrugged. Old news, he thought. Russia was good at talking the talk. In spite of its upwardly mobile stance, the redevelopment of many landmarks in Moscow, the new elite, new money and the 'Europisation', the infrastructure outside the two central cities was crumbling. When states suffered domestic crises it was common policy to sabre-rattle, if not go the whole hog and march to war. It wasn't unique to Russia. The world had worked like that since time immemorial.

'They're heading for meltdown,' Fazan said glumly.

Asim wasn't at all sure he agreed but chose to keep his own counsel. In any case, the entire globe seemed to be heading for meltdown.

'When the Russians feel under threat,' Fazan said, 'they have a nasty habit of striking out and extending their rule.'

And the newly elected British government won't like that one bit, Asim reflected. Notwithstanding Europe's dependency on Russian energy, the government was determined to take a firmer line with the men in the Kremlin than its predecessors. New brooms and all that.

'Which brings me to the reason I asked you here,' Fazan said, a shrewd expression in his eyes. 'Chechnya.'

Asim's expression betrayed none of the surprise he felt. After ten years of bloodshed, the Russians had formally ended their war against the rebels in the region. Why on earth would they wish to reignite an age-old problem?

'It's feared that the warlords are making a play again,' Fazan said, a meaningful expression in his eyes.

'Did they ever stop?' To Asim's mind, Chechnya was a little like the troubled state of Northern Ireland: same heady mix of religion and politics, and same clamour for independence. Just when you thought things were sorted, a minority paramilitary group would flex its muscles.

'We're faced with a rapidly deteriorating situation,' Fazan said. 'Many hard-line rebels have set up camp in the mountains. Come April, it's feared they'll start a major offensive. Although Russian forces maintain overall control, the separatists are getting stronger and more assertive every day. Disappearances of civilians are on the up as is the daily killing of police officers and troops. You're aware of the recent spate of high-profile assassinations in Moscow?'

'Sensational murders take place in Moscow every day,' Asim countered.

'They do, indeed, but these victims share one thing in common.'

Asim arched an eyebrow.

'They were former military men and had less than savoury dealings in Chechnya's most recent conflict.'

'You're suggesting that Chechen terrorists are responsible?'

'They're certainly being blamed. It's why the Russians are going back in.'

'What's this got to do with me?' Asim said.

Fazan twitched a smile, clearly amused by the man from MI5's direct approach. 'As early as 1993, it was suspected that a key warlord had some rather surprising contacts. By the end of 2002, the Secret Intelligence Service was convinced of links to al-Qaeda. So convinced, we decided to try something rather innovative.'

Asim threw Fazan an expectant look.

'We put one of our intelligence officers into the field.'

Asim felt genuinely taken aback, although he was at pains not to show it. Sure, MI5 had successfully penetrated the IRA—Gerry Adams's driver was, in fact, a British spy—but this was in a different league. He considered how it had been achieved. Then another more pressing and ugly thought permeated his mind. The infamous attack on a school in Beslan took place in 2004. With a man in the field, had the Secret Intelligence Service received prior warning? Worse, there was a rumour abroad at the time, fuelled by the Kremlin, that foreign secret-service forces were at work in the Beslan siege. It was deemed that certain countries were trying to manipulate Russia.

'Heard of Akhmet Elimkhanova?' Fazan said.

Asim had. Elimkhanova had stepped into the power vacuum that had opened up after the warlord believed responsible for the school massacre had been killed. 'He's an *amir*,' he said, 'a leader of a seventy-strong group of warriors.'

'This is the group our man, Graham Darke, was sent to penetrate, which he did with a brilliance that is, quite frankly, beyond compare.'

'So what's your problem?' Asim said.

'He's gone missing.'

'Could have gone to ground.'

Fazan shook his head. 'Darke has been off the air for more than twelve months.'

Why had it taken the SIS so long to get onto it? Asim thought suspiciously. 'Why not use existing assets in the area?'

'Do you know anything about the topography of Chechnya? It's like looking for Osama bin Laden in the Tora Bora mountains.' Fazan glanced around again. The bar was now filling up with tourists and City traders. 'We think Darke's gone native.'

Fuck, Asim thought. Given the volatile situation, it wouldn't look good for the British to be seen to be meddling in Russia's internal affairs. Far more politically serious, what if Elimkhanova was linked to the assassinations in Moscow, thereby implicating Darke?

'Highly unusual, surely? Any clues in his background?'

Fazan raised a dark eyebrow. 'Apart from his Chechen blood ties?'

And, presumably, Asim thought wits sharpening, the reason Darke was able to successfully infiltrate in the first place. But the security services had also taken a risk. Inevitably, blood proved thicker than water. He decided to be straight with Fazan.

'Are you suggesting that Darke is orchestrating the assassinations in Moscow?'

'Something, as you'll appreciate, he is ably equipped to carry out,' Fazan said, his expression grave. 'Which is why it's imperative Darke is tracked down. I've heard on the grapevine you head a special unit.'

More like the Foreign Legion, Asim thought. In truth,

he ran a number of agents, off-the-books spooks, to carry out black operations. The advantage to the security service: if things went wrong, plausible denial could be claimed.

'We want someone from your unit to find him,' Fazan said.

Here we go, Asim thought, reaching for his glass, weighing up the possibilities. 'You want me to give one of my operatives a transfer, that right?'

'A secondment, on a temporary basis,' Fazan said, an astute look in his eye. That was what Asim had been afraid of. He feared that it might be very temporary indeed. 'You would, of course, remain in control,' Fazan added, lightly dusting a speck off the lapel of his jacket.

'You want me to head the operation?'

'Yes and no. You will act as liaison. I hear you've enjoyed spectacular results from a particular employee.'

Asim arranged his face into a picture of in-scrutability. He knew the exact man Fazan was refer-ring to, but wanted to find out how good his intel was.

'Paul Tallis is a decorated former soldier,' Fazan continued, 'an ex-firearms officer with an elite under-cover unit, and has been working off the books with your good self for a couple of years. He also has a talent for languages.'

'I'm impressed.'

'Don't be. Intelligence gathering is my stock-in-trade.' It was said without a trace of arrogance. 'His Russian is flaky but that doesn't matter. We want him to speak Chechen, a language with which we believe he is already familiar.'

How the hell did Fazan know that? Asim wondered. As for the mission, it was madness.

'And when your man is found, then what?' Asim said. 'Tallis would have a problem with assassination.'

Fazan gave a shudder of distaste and reached for his glass. Asim thought it a curious gesture. Fazan was no stranger to elimination. 'We simply want him to bring Darke back home.'

Asim's smile was thin. 'Are you serious?' Judging by the lack of expression on Fazan's face, he believed he was.

'It's not as difficult as it appears,' Fazan said smoothly. 'Paul Tallis and Graham Darke were school-friends.'

Asim still didn't buy it. It was one thing to put Tallis into what was effectively a deteriorating situation that might well escalate, quite another to expect him to bring an operative back, chum or no chum, who, by all accounts, had turned rogue agent. More thinking time required, he reached for his drink again. 'Is the Foreign Secretary aware of the details of the operation?'

'Certainly not. He's still catching up on his in-tray.'

Asim didn't like this one bit. If there was a serious risk of political blowback, the Secretary was usually informed. This was extremely irregular even by his standards. 'What about C.?'

He was referring to the head of the Secret

Intelligence Service. Fazan answered in the affirmative. That was something, Asim supposed. In the normal scheme of things, he would have followed it up, but the network he ran was no ordinary outfit. It was supposed to be secret. Few people knew of its existence. It meant that checking things out took a little longer. Again, Fazan's sharp intelligence seemed to spot his general reluctance.

'Look at it this way,' Fazan said, 'we're both running highly classified operations. Hence, not many are in the loop.'

'Yes, but—'

'The difference between Darke and Tallis and his like is negligible.'

Asim blinked. *His like?* Perhaps it was an unfortunate turn of phrase, but he didn't care for it. Asim had a burning loyalty to the men and women in his charge. 'I hate to labour the point but this business about your man going native.'

'Yes?' Fazan said, topping up their glasses.

'What evidence do you have, or is your supposition based on a dubious source?'

Fazan smiled, proof that he had taken no offence. 'Never turn down a tip from a dubious source, Asim,' he said lightly. 'I can see I'll have to work a little harder to persuade you.'

Damn right, Asim thought.

'Our source is trustworthy,' Fazan said.

So he did have one, Asim realised. 'Another Russian

oligarch who'd prefer not to be serving time on charges of fraud and tax evasion?' Asim's tone was less than complimentary.

Fazan deflected the implied criticism with a smile. 'Our last intelligence from Graham was that Akhmet Elimkhanova was planning to hold serious talks with fellow sympathisers outside Russia, possibly from the Middle East, identity as yet unclear. Our source, however, maintains that Akhmet is planning a spate of murders on selected targets in Moscow.'

'Something that Graham neglected to tell you?'

'Yes.'

Very worrying, Asim had to agree. The evidence, such as it was, was starting to stack up against Darke. 'And you suspect your military victims are just the start?' he chipped in, listening closely.

'We do.'

So this time the Chechens weren't being framed by the State. They really were responsible for the bloodshed. 'This source…' Asim flashed him another expectant look.

Fazan let out a sigh, clearly uncomfortable with having to disclose further information. 'We have an asset in the Moscow Police Department. Forensic evidence found at the scene of the first assassination implicates Darke.'

Unaccountably careless of him, Asim thought.

'Furthermore, our high-ranking source has somewhat more pressing information. Akhmet has someone on his hit list rather higher up the food chain. The man, in his eyes, who started the whole thing rolling.'

Asim frowned. Boris Yeltsin, the president who had originally ordered the army and air force into Chechnya, was long dead. He told this to Fazan.

'But not the man who orchestrated the campaign, who took over as president and is now prime minister.'

'Andrei Ivanov?' Asim said with alarm.

'Imagine the fallout if the British Secret Intelligence Service were seen to be responsible for the assassination of the most powerful man in Russia.'

CHAPTER TWO

No QUEUES, no waiting with the great unwashed, no sour-faced security, and no touting of airline scratch cards. Marvellous, Tallis thought as the Jet Ranger flew a final circuit before dropping down and coming in at a perfect seventy miles an hour to land.

Single-handedly, he'd flown a friend's helicopter from a helipad in Belbroughton, a posh West Midlands suburb, to a privately owned airfield at Reinsdorf. En route he'd refuelled with Av-Gas at L'Aeroport de Charleroi in Brussels, principally because the authorities weren't too anal about checking passports. From there, he'd flown directly to Berlin and was in the process of hovering over a grass airstrip that had formerly belonged to the Russians and now was owned by a laid-back German called Helmut. It was Tallis's idea to see if he could make the trip without first seeking normal permissions or going through official channels, including filing the all-important flight plan. Christ knew what he'd have done had he been caught but, by flying low and outside the zones, things had worked like Teutonic clockwork. Nobody had ordered him to land, and no jets had come up alongside, strafing and treating him like a terrorist. The entire rogue operation had been a blinding success.

Tallis removed his headset, and carrying out the post-landing checks, turned off some of the electrics, allowing the engine to cool down, then stepped out, feet crunching against the hardened ground. He flexed his tall frame in relief. For the past few hours, he had cruised at just under 140 m.p.h., initially in fairly lousy weather conditions, his surroundings leather-lined and luxurious. But he'd still been confined to what was essentially an oversized goldfish bowl.

He took in a brisk gulp of air and continued to survey the cold German crystalline scenery. In spite of sunlight filtering through a band of distant trees, the ordinariness of the cabins dotted around the airfield and the sight of Helmut striding purposefully towards him, he imagined an image of grey Russian MiGs, barbed wire and watchtowers.

'*Willkommen*, Paul,' Helmut said, slapping him clumsily on the back, his red, weather-beaten features stretched into a broad grin. In his battered leather jacket and open-necked check-shirt, Helmut exuded farmer-cum-Luftwaffe chic.

Tallis shook his hand warmly. '*Wie geht's?*'

'*Gut. Viel Arbeit, viel Essen, viel Sex, und beidir?*'

Fine. Plenty of work, plenty of food, plenty of sex, and yourself?'

'*Fantastisch,*' Tallis laughed.

'And how did you find the Jet Ranger?' Helmut cast an appreciative glance over the helicopter. The dark blue paintwork looked spectacular against the rather grey and muted surroundings.

'Virtually flew itself.'

'You were impressed?'

'*Sehr.*' How could he not be? The Jet Ranger was the helicopter of choice for many of the Bond films. 'Where do you want me?' Tallis asked.

'Here's good.' Helmut waved a stout arm, indicating a hangar a few metres away from where they'd landed. It was his for the next two nights. 'Come back to the office when you've finished. I want to hear all about it,' he added over his shoulder, striding off again. Tallis envisaged the next two hours spent drinking tea or something a good deal stronger while trading tales of aerobatics and brushes with the Civil Aviation Authority. Afterwards, he planned to order a cab and head off to his hotel, shower and change, and sample some genuine Berlin hospitality. Tallis had every intention of making the most of his forty-eight-hour stay. He'd never visited the city before and wanted to trawl the former Eastern Bloc, do the whole tourist thing, Brandenburg Gate, old bits of the Berlin Wall, Jewish memorials, the Reichstag, Checkpoint Charlie…

His phone rang, rudely interrupting his train of thought.

'Paul, it's Asim.'

Tallis had a sudden premonition that his history tour was about to be cancelled.

'Can you talk?'

'Give me a moment,' Tallis said, walking a short distance away, automatically checking his surroundings for potential eavesdroppers of which there were none. He glanced up as a Cessna flattened out, coming into land.

'Where are you?' Asim said.

'Berlin.'

'Alone?'

'Yes.'

'How long for?'

'A couple of days.'

'Whereabouts are you staying?' Asim said.

'A hotel in Alexanderplatz.'

'Is it possible for you to sneak away for a couple of hours?'

'Yes, I sup—'

'Meet me outside the Nikolaikirche, off Rathausstrasse tomorrow morning, ten your time.'

Tallis didn't have the chance to respond—Asim had already cut the call. He stood there for a moment, thinking. A consummate professional, Asim didn't usually go in for pleasantries, especially on a telephone. In person, he was good company, amusing, mischievous even. None of this had transmitted down the line. Not so surprising, yet for his handler to travel all the way to see him at such short notice was out of the ordinary. As an off-the-books spook for MI5, Tallis was inured to the unconventional, the quick change of plan, the downright unexpected. Even so, it could only mean one thing: this was serious.

Moscow: eight o'clock the following morning

Pavel Polyakova was a bitter man. That he, a Russian general, should be reduced to taking his kids to school was a source of profound humiliation to him. Not for the first time he screamed at them to hurry.

'Coming,' Leonid yelled back, pulling a face. Eyes fixed on his father, he hissed to his younger brother, who was struggling with a shoelace, to get a move on.

Polyakova surveyed his two young sons. He noticed the way they looked at him, registered the fear and loathing. He'd observed the same insolent expression on the faces of idiot soldiers he'd once had the misfortune to command.

'We want Mama,' the youngest whined, his mouth pulled down into an ugly expression, threatening tears.

'Well, you can't have her,' Polyakova growled back. *Mama*, dressed in skin-tight Diesel jeans and high heels, had left an hour ago to work for a friend who owned a new boutique off Red Square. Although the shop didn't open until later, Tanya was going in early to sort out the stock, or so she said. Since she'd taken the job, she kept the strangest of hours, often returning late, reeking of vodka. If questioned, she reacted with anger, waving a wad of notes under his nose and demanding to know who was putting food on the table. It was enough to raise a man's blood pressure to dangerous levels. Tanya might be a shining example of Ivanov's new vision for Russia, but she had lost all interest in the home, in the kids, and, Mother of God, in him. Mr Ivanov, in his wisdom, had created a generation of cuckolds.

Polyakova glowered at his broken-down surroundings, a rented dump of rust and exposed brickwork not far from the US Embassy. Not for him the gateway to the elite, the poplar-lined boulevards, the dachas, the three-storey affairs with maid service. Christ, he couldn't even resort to taxi-cabbing because his car was so old.

'Are you two ready yet?' he snarled, snatching up his car keys. Rush hour should be renamed death hour, in his opinion. Traffic jams were so intrinsic to Russian life it was quite possible to die in one's vehicle from boredom.

Leonid cast his father a sullen look from underneath a set of dark lashes. 'Boris has gone to the lavatory.'

Letting out a stream of expletives worthy of a military man, Polyakova turned on the worn-down heels of his boots and stormed out of the apartment. Outside lay a rabbit warren of concrete panel walls, shabby stairwells and non-existent lighting. Five flights down, he was still raging. As he emerged from the apartment block, fresh snow began to fall. Now God Almighty was against him, he fulminated, pulling up the threadbare collar of his jacket and banging his gloved hands together as he looked out at the vast expanse of streets and avenues. Freed from the old Soviet restrictions, the city felt horribly alive, he thought. Even at that time in the morning, it lay on its back like a whore, trading and bartering, selling itself to the highest bidder. Commerce was the new buzzword and, greased by the State, a new generation of entrepreneurs was stepping up to party in the playground of the rich. But not he: General Pavel Polyakova.

Stamping towards the parking lot, his beat-up Lada became the next recipient of his ire. First, he ripped off the tarpaulin and threw it into the boot then wrenched the driver door open, his large, dishevelled frame scrambling inside.

What was he to do? There were many impoverished military men like him slung onto the scrap heap. Naturally, he'd tried to call in favours. There had been mutterings of a governorship in Siberia but nothing had come of it. He'd offered his expertise in the fight against the latest batch of warlords but, apparently, he was deemed too out of touch—so much for doing his duty in the service of the motherland.

Unhappy men clung to former glory days with the same passion they reserved for slights. Polyakova was no exception. As he drummed his fingers on the dashboard, and with the snow tumbling about him, he found himself willingly transported back to Chechnya. It was 2002, weeks after the infamous Nord-Ost theatre siege. They had flown in from Moscow to Mozdok and then taken a helicopter armed with light-calibre shells. Like many helicopters, it doubled as a carrier for injured troops. Its interior smelt of dried blood, he remembered.

Following the line of the river Terek, they crossed over the Argun Gorge and landed near the village of Vedeno. The official line was that they were searching for Chechen snipers. In reality they were seeking revenge. He had a young lieutenant with him, Ivan, a man after his own heart, as hard working as he was hard drinking. They pitched down late afternoon when the sun was making its escape from the sky. With its grey fields, dirt roads, silent ruins and absent population, Chechnya was a godforsaken place. Always was. Always would be.

'Another trip to hell,' Ivan spat, as they pitched out of the helicopter.

As expected the 'dukh', or 'spirit', and military slang for the Chechens, had gone to ground. Those in evidence were old men with unwashed beards who stared at them with undisguised hatred. One of the conscripts lifted his rifle to a particularly gnarled specimen and threatened to shoot. Polyakova ordered the soldier, a former inmate of a prison in Ukraine, to lower his weapon, not because he was a compassionate man but because it would be a waste of a good bullet.

Underfoot, thick black mud. Up ahead, hills and peaks and mountains. Somewhere in the distance a stray dog barked. After a fifteen-minute trudge along a cratered road, they came to a group of mean little huts, clay-encrusted, that served as dwellings. The first two were deserted. Sticking to normal clean-up procedure, they burst in, checked the place for rebels and booby-traps then smashed the place to pieces before searching for spoils of war, jewellery, money and suchlike. It was a disappointing haul, nothing more than two necklaces, a diamond ring and a total of a thousand roubles. The last hovel, however, was a different matter. The last yielded gold.

They found the three occupants huddled together in one room: a babushka, a mentally disabled boy—by all accounts the old woman's grandson—and a dusky-skinned teenage girl. Polyakova felt himself harden in spite of the bitter temperature in the car.

That was the start of it all.

After turning the place over, Ivan trained a gun on the whimpering cretin.

'Please, don't hurt him,' the girl said. She had black hair, eyes so dark it was impossible to tell whether they were blue or brown. Polyakova noticed that she spoke Russian. He strode towards her, circled like a shark eyeing up his next meal, the leather of his boots making a cracking sound. He paused in front of her, and looked down into those deep, ensnaring eyes.

'What is your name?'

'Aimani.'

'And how old are you, Aimani?'

'I am fifteen.'

'At school?'

'No longer.'

'But you used to go to school, yes?'

'Yes.'

'And that is where you learned to speak the language of the motherland.'

Aimani said nothing. The atmosphere in the room was electric. And that was good in Polyakova's book.

'I will not hurt him,' Polyakova said, inclining his head in the direction of the snivelling boy, 'as long as you tell me the truth.' His smile was met with defiance. He transferred his gaze to her body. He could not help but notice the swell of the girl's breasts, the curve of her hips beneath her clothes, a mishmash of sweaters and cardigans over a long dark skirt. A mental image of her vulnerable and naked flashed before his eyes. 'Now, tell me, where are the men of the household?'

'They are out.'

'Where?'

His eyes were still on the girl. She opened her full lips to respond but instead the babushka answered. In halting Russian, the crone told him they had gone to gather firewood.

Polyakova spun on his heel. He viewed the woman's shrivelled features, the toothless gums and the hook nose. 'You lie, old woman.'

'Nyet...'

Polyakova nodded to Ivan who hit the boy across the head with the rifle butt. Letting out a loud scream, a wound opened up on his over-large head. Blood spurted and trickled down his face, dripping onto the dirt floor.

The old woman's gnarled hands shot to her face in distress. She began to cry, her sobs mingling with the cretin's. But the girl was different. She stood rooted, proud, dark eyes flashing, a mutinous look in her eyes.

'I will ask you again,' Polyakova said, speaking slowly, weighing each syllable. 'Where are the men?'

Nobody spoke. In the absence of an answer, the white-faced boy attempted to flee. Not so stupid after all, Polyakova thought as Ivan knocked the youth to the ground and swung back his boot to kick him.

That's when the girl made her move.

Pulling a knife from nowhere, she launched herself at Ivan, slicing at his arm. One-handed, Ivan caught hold of her, forcing the blade from her hand. 'We have a vixen here.' Ivan laughed, throwing her towards Polyakova. As the babushka scurried to the girl's aid, Polyakova calmly took out his pistol and shot the old woman in the face then turned his gun on the boy.

The girl's screams echoed in Polyakova's ears. He could still hear them, even now years on, in the freezing interior of his car. My, she'd been a sturdy one. Fought with the same ferocity as the Spetsnaz.

Where the hell are those kids? he cursed, wiping the steam from the window and peering out through a mirage of sleet and snow.

Naturally, he had taken the girl, taught her what it was to be a true Russian. He smiled to himself. He had kept a lock of her hair as a keepsake so that no matter how many times he washed, he could smell her skin, taste her sweat, hear her cries as she yielded to his demands. Unlike Tanya, he thought blackly, who yielded to nobody.

His eyes drifted to the window again. Leonid and Boris were still nowhere to be seen. My God, would he teach them a lesson, he thought, tooting the car horn angrily.

Afterwards, he'd smothered the girl. No point in leaving loose ends. He believed shepherds found the charred remains of her body several days later.

Out of the corner of his eye, he saw a flurry of activity. At last his sons emerged from the entrance, skittering in a fresh fall of snow, the youngest trailing behind as usual. Infuriated, Polyakova wound the window down. He was about to issue further admonishment, but Boris slipped over, hitting the ground hard with a yell. The child began to wail.

'Sweet Jesus!' Polyakova roared, switching on the engine, the last action of a condemned man.

As the car exploded into a fireball, and the young brothers dived for cover, the noise of the blast was heard several streets away.

Berlin

At the same time as Pavel Polyakova's head was detach-
ing from its body, Tallis was waking up. He'd slept
badly. It wasn't due to the room's close proximity to the
lift, the sound booming from the shaft suggesting that
he was sleeping in the hull of an old trawler. It wasn't
even as a result of the artificial orange light shining in
through the bedroom window, casting weird shadows
on the ceiling, or the absurd level of heat, or the fact
that construction workers outside and cleaners inside
had made an early start. Burning curiosity was responsible for his insomnia. He felt like a kid on the night
before Christmas.

Tallis took a hot shower, then shaved. He was not a
vain man but, through force of habit, he regarded himself
in the mirror. The scar over his left eyebrow, inflicted
during a childhood punch-up with his older brother,
looked less pronounced in spite of his naturally dark
colouring. Unlike a more recent scar on his cheek. The
woman responsible had been a Romanian murderess
who slashed her victims with a lethally sharpened fin-
gernail. His hair was still thick, no grey yet. Eyes might
have a couple more lines at the edges but this was a
matter of observation rather than interest or concern. Of
greater significance, his body was still in good nick. He
couldn't undertake his type of work without a high level
of fitness and at thirty-five years of age it was impossible
to wing it. Recently, he'd added weight training to his

workout. He briefly considered how many years he might have left in the game. Ten years, tops, he reckoned.

After taking a European-style breakfast in the conservatory, Tallis returned to his room, cleaned his teeth, checked his destination on the map and retrieved his leather jacket and gloves. As he stepped out into the corridor, a pretty chambermaid smiled and wished him '*Guten tag*', a greeting he duly returned. And it *was* a good morning, Tallis thought as he sauntered towards the lift. In spite of the urgency of the meeting, the danger he would ultimately encounter, he was intrigued by Asim's phone call. More than anything, after a break of a couple of months he relished the thought of being operational again.

The day was crisp and clear and, at barely four degrees, cold though not unpleasant. Turning right out of the hotel to avoid a group of workmen digging up the pavement, Tallis passed by a ten-storey block of flats, grey and granite, as grim a construct as anything he'd seen in the rougher bits of Birmingham. In front of the building, bins spilt litter onto a tiny scrub of land with a solitary scrawny tree under which two young teenage girls were standing smoking. They both turned, cupping their hands in the chill southeast wind, and looked at him, shuffling a little in their thin jackets.

At the end of the one-way street, Tallis found himself on a wide main road, shops one side and vast open space on the other. He crossed over, negotiating a tramline running between the two opposing carriageways and onto the square where the Marienkirche, or St Mary's Church, stood proud and alone in the shadow of the Fernsehturm, the television tower and the city's tallest structure. Rolling up the collar of his jacket, he passed a fountain of Neptune around which a gaggle of schoolchildren were crowding. Ahead lay the Rathaus, Berlin's town hall, an imposing red brick building, and another crossing, which took him down Rathausstrasse, past shops and cafés and boutiques. A man with white-blond hair and skin as pale as an albino approached from the opposite direction. He wore a dark trench coat with a white silk cravat at his throat. His smart, shiny shoes clicked as he walked along the pavement. Drawing level with Tallis, he minutely adjusted his designer sunglasses. Tallis registered the gesture, slowed down a little, quartering the street to check for surveillance, but there was nobody in sight. Nothing more than a fashion-conscious German, he thought, glancing over his shoulder, seeing the man disappear round the corner and from view.

Within seconds he reached Nikolaiviertel, a quaint quarter of cobbled streets on the bank of the river Spree. The place was crammed with bars and clubs, though none were open and all possessed a slightly addled, sleepy look. Few people were milling about. A lone chauffeur-driven Mercedes prowled down the street, a Japanese woman dressed in a fur coat seated in the rear.

Tallis walked on past a statue of a bear holding a

shield, a toyshop selling teddies, two souvenir shops and a high-class and exclusive gift emporium, no prices on the merchandise. Then he caught sight of the twin towers of the Nicholaikirche, the oldest, most sacred building in Berlin.

The door of the church was closed. Outside, a gravelled path on which a number of orange-eyed pigeons were pecking at the dirt. Underneath, a sign that said no football, no bikes, dogs welcome; a solitary bicycle was propped against a lamppost. To the right of the path, a grassy section with a single fledgling fir tree stood next to a large statue of a woman, half Boudicca, half pre-Raphaelite in style. Her naked foot rested on a helmet. Tallis gazed up at the church, a blaze of sunshine catching the leaded glass, then followed the path, passing the statue and a number of green garden seats with flaking, peeling paint until he came to a large half-moon-shaped bench hidden in a recess, secluded, cool and shadowy. Asim, wearing a dark cashmere overcoat and sunglasses, was already seated.

At the sound of Tallis's approaching footsteps, Asim neither turned nor flinched. Mysterious and inscrutable, he sat as still as one of the many statues Tallis had passed en route. Tallis slipped down next to him.

'*Bonjour,*' Asim said. '*Ça va?*'

'*Bien, merci,*' Tallis replied, slipping easily into French. This had to be a first, he thought. His conversations with Asim were usually conducted in English. He hadn't even known that Asim spoke French.

'I need you to travel to Russia,' Asim said without preamble. 'You'll be based in Moscow for a short time, building up your cover. From there, you'll go to Chechnya.'

Chechnya? An image flashed before his eyes. It was the same image that had taken the world by storm when the fighting had first broken out over a decade before: the picture of a woman in a headscarf, a bony hand clasped to her face, crying over the ruin that was Grozny. And things had just got sticky there again. Terrific, Tallis thought, shootings, bombings, and abductions. From Tallis's understanding, Chechen gangsters were like a high-octane version of the Sicilian Mafia. Winter in the mountains wasn't his idea of fun either. Many of them were mined.

'You speak Chechen?' Asim continued.

'I'm rusty. Why? I had a fr—'

'How long would it take you to become fluent?' Asim cut across. 'Could you do it in a week?'

'You must be joking.'

'Two?'

'Busting a gut, but, yes, probably.' Good job it wasn't Cantonese, Tallis thought.

Asim's dark head dipped slightly as though nodding approval. He explained the approach made to him by Christian Fazan, and that Tallis was to be temporarily seconded to the Secret Intelligence Service. 'I want you to locate an intelligence officer belonging to the SIS. The man was sent to penetrate a fundamentalist group loyal to a Chechen warlord, Akhmet Elim-khanova. The officer has been under cover since 2003. From my understanding, he yielded high-quality intelligence. For the past twelve months, nothing has been heard of him.'

'So it's basically a search and rescue, that right?' Tallis had the clear impression he was only being given edited highlights. There were too many gaps in the commentary. Best to stay tuned.

'It's a little more complicated than that,' Asim said, the hesitation in his voice so minor it would normally have passed unnoticed. Sitting next to him, however, Tallis spotted the body language, the slight twitch in Asim's jaw. 'We believe he's gone native.'

Gone native? Tallis baulked. A very different proposition to gone missing.

'It's possible he's responsible for a number of high-profile murders in Moscow.' Asim went on to describe the victims and circumstances of the killings.

Bloody hell, Tallis thought. If there was even a grain of truth in the allegation, the political consequences could be dire and would require a high degree of fancy diplomatic footwork.

Asim cleared his throat. 'We thought you were best suited for the job because the man you're tracking is an old friend of yours.'

'Oh?'

'Graham Darke.'

Christ. He hadn't seen Graham since he was fifteen.

They'd met in the last year at primary school in Herefordshire. He remembered a boy with sharp features, small for his age. Bullies made the fatal mistake of assuming Graham's stature indicated vulnerability. In Tallis's experience, it was often the short, wiry types who proved the most formidable opponents. Not too many tall and lanky members of the SAS. Graham proved no exception. He turned the tables in spectacular fashion one break-time. In the aftermath, two lads required hospital treatment, although neither could remember how they sustained their injuries. Tallis was the first to congratulate Graham. From that moment, they were firm friends, and went on to secondary education together. They'd also hit it off for another less obvious reason. Both had grandmothers on their mother's side who were foreign. Graham's gran was Chechen, Tallis's Croatian. It was the reason for Tallis's knowledge of both languages. But that was all a very long time ago. They hadn't been in contact since Graham abruptly left one night and moved with his old man to another part of the country.

Tallis glanced at Asim and did a mental recap. Graham Darke: an intelligence officer for the SIS. His mission: to penetrate one of the fundamentalist gangs roving the Chechen mountains and gather intelligence. Success rate: high, yielding good intel. Current status: Darke missing. Suspicion: Darke turned rogue agent. At this, Tallis frowned. Unless Darke had changed inordinately over the years, Tallis thought it unlikely, although was smart enough not to voice his opinion. When talking to Asim it was as well to listen more, speak less.

'I'm guessing Darke's suitability for the job was due to his Chechen roots,' Tallis said. Chechens, he remembered, were fiercely nationalistic people. They belonged to *teips* or clans, the system based more on land than blood. He was buggered if he could remember which *teip* Graham Darke's gran belonged to.

'Correct.'

'Are you suggesting that the killings are just the tip of the iceberg?' Where the hell did this bloke, Christian Fazan, Asim's contact in the Secret Intelligence Service, get his information?

'Which is why we require you to bring him back. This is no time for split loyalties,' Asim said in response to Tallis's sharp intake of breath.

Fucking cheek. Tallis bridled.

'What I meant,' Asim said, emollient, 'is that he'll be given a fair hearing.'

Oh, sure, and a lengthy jail sentence, Tallis thought. Or worse, he thought, Darke would be 'disappeared'.

'He's not the first agent to feel compromised.' The slightly smug note in Asim's voice hinted that he was, nevertheless, glad Darke was not one of his. But there was something else, a note of caution, perhaps? Asim normally conducted all dealings in comfortable, hospitable settings. By adopting this slightly over-the-top approach, was he showing his hand? Was he suggesting that the danger to Tallis was over and above what could normally be expected, and was he unconsciously trying to distance himself from the dirty work in which he was engaged? There was definitely something Asim wasn't telling him.

Tallis turned towards him. 'How much is at stake?'

Asim kept his eyes fixed ahead. 'A great deal. Should Darke follow through on his plans, he could help trigger World War Three.'

'What?'

'Darke has Andrei Ivanov, the Russian prime minister, in his sights.'

Jesus! 'You're absolutely certain?' This really didn't sound like Darke unless he'd lost the plot entirely. Then again, what did he know? He hadn't clapped eyes on Darke in nearly twenty years. An awful lot could happen to a man in that time—he should know. Being honest, Tallis couldn't escape the fact that a small silent part of him recognised he might be wrong about his old friend.

'That's my information,' Asim said.

Tallis wondered again about Fazan's original source but said nothing—it was above his pay grade to ask. Asim was speaking again. 'You know of nothing in Darke's background that could indicate his vulnerability?'

'Apart from the obvious fact he has Chechen blood flowing through his veins, which I presume the SIS has already looked into and discounted, no.' Then another thought struck him. 'If you're right,' Tallis said, 'what the hell makes you think Darke's going to come quietly?'

Asim turned his head fractionally. 'Nothing.'

Kill or be killed, was that the deal? Tallis wondered with alarm. And if he refused the job, what then? 'Is this a suicide mission?'

'You could decline the offer.'

That wasn't quite the answer he was expecting. A straight yes or no would have done. And if he did refuse, he might never work again. 'What do you take me for?' Tallis smiled.

'An intelligent man.'

Intelligent enough to know when to quit? Tallis thought. Was Asim warning him off? Was he saying he didn't rate his chances? 'No, I'll do it. I can never resist a challenge. Besides, there's a man's honour to defend.'

'Oh?'

'Graham Darke's,' Tallis said, bullish. Until he had proof, he refused to give up on his old friend. In many ways, Tallis realised, they worked in allied fields. As undercover operatives, both he and Darke were deniable and expendable. 'So what's the plan?'

'Meet me at the Brandenburg Gate in one hour. It will give you time to clean the bird shit off your jacket,' Asim flashed a smile. And with that, he got up and walked away.

'Great,' Tallis muttered, briefly surveying the foul green-yellow splodge on his shoulder, small comfort that it was supposed to be a sign of good luck.

* * *

Notwithstanding Asim's advice, Tallis stayed where he was, taking the opportunity to study his surroundings, a cover for what was really going on inside his head. He thought back to the Graham Darke he knew, a tearaway, and a ruffian. Tallis suspected that Graham's behaviour was a response to a childhood defined by neglect: he was one of eleven children. Although Graham at fifteen had been more prone to think first and lash out afterwards, his flashes of extreme anger spoke of a volatile temperament. What was not in doubt was Graham's sharp intelligence, a commodity, Tallis presumed, that served him well in his current occupation. It took courage to go undercover—he should know—but it took balls of steel to pass yourself off as a committed Chechen fighter. And what a terrifying way to spend the best part of a decade, Tallis thought. Strange, he'd often wondered what had happened to Graham Darke but never in his wildest dreams had he imagined this.

After cleaning himself up back at the hotel, Tallis headed off at a leisurely pace. He estimated it would take him no more than twenty minutes to reach Brandenburger Tor, the defining symbol of Berlin.

His immediate impression as he walked along Unter den Linden, the main street leading to the gate, was one of wide, open spaces, huge muscular buildings, perfectly proportioned, the sheer size mind-blowing. There was no visible litter, no dog crap. Culture oozed from every brick and column. And it was hard to miss the statues, which were in every conceivable place, lining bridges, staring down from rooftops, gracing every square and gravelled path.

Crossing to the next block, Tallis was delighted to find an entire row of car showrooms on opposite sides of the high street. With plenty of time to kill, he dawdled, face virtually pressed up against the windows of Ferrari and Bugatti, admiring the sleek lines and fast colours. For the tighter budget, there was also VW, Seat and Skoda, he noticed, quickly turning round at the sound of a minor spot of road rage—a lad on roller-skates pissing off a cab driver. Tallis smiled at the minor blow for freedom, and dragged himself away, continuing along the main thoroughfare until at last, up ahead, just past an S-Bahn station, he saw the familiar fluttering of embassy flags and then the gate itself with its fine neoclassical architecture and the four-horse chariot sitting on top, as magnificent and imposing as he'd expected. Evading a gaggle of Italian tourists who wanted their photograph taken next to a German soldier, Tallis cut towards Asim, who was standing in the square on the other side of the gate. At Tallis's approach, Asim turned on his heel and started to walk briskly west in the direction of the Tiergarten which, that morning, looked more wasteland than parkland. Tallis followed. A church bell tolled in the distance. Traffic whizzed by on three-lane carriageways. Cyclists tore down cycle-paths that seamlessly and confusingly adjoined the pavements. The sound of chainsaws buzzed his ears. A sign indicated that three hundred metres away and down a path stood the Reichstag in all its glory. Next, a huge monument commemorating the Soviet soldiers, over 300,000 of them, who'd lost their lives in the Battle for Berlin at the end of the Second World War. He looked neither right nor left, his eyes fixed on Asim's back, the way he walked sleek and feline and self-assured.

They were heading down Strasse des 17 Juni, named after the 1953 uprising—more reminders of Berlin's past. On they walked, towards Charlottenburg, once the centre of West Berlin until, without warning, Asim crossed the busy highway and stopped by a sign marked Potsdamer Place. There, he turned towards Tallis and stood with his arms folded, a wry smile on his face.

'What was that all about?' Tallis said, catching up.

'Checking for tails.' Asim said, this time speaking English. 'Shall we?' Asim said, indicating a path through the park.

They walked a little way along. Silver birch flanked both sides. The air felt cool and still, the atmosphere as tranquil as a Gregorian chant; the only people a middle-aged overweight jogger and a woman walking a German shepherd.

'Are you sure about this?' Asim said softly.

'Do I have a choice?'

'There are always choices.'

Tallis cast Asim a low, level look. 'And mine's made.'

Asim gave an *as you wish* nod. They walked on

again. 'You will be working under the cover of commercial interests,' he said eventually.

'About the only activity the Russians haven't stamped all over,' Tallis said.

Asim smiled. 'Those who have prospered under Ivanov are keen to hang onto their wealth and you are going to take advantage of it.'

'Go on.'

'Your newfound skill for flying helicopters is about to be put to good use.'

Tallis felt himself visibly brighten. 'Does this involve Shobdon, by any chance?' Shobdon was the small airfield in Herefordshire where he'd learnt to fly.

'It does,' Asim said. 'We've already talked to the owner of Tiger Helicopters and he's happy enough for you to use them as cover. I believe you know one of their employees.'

'Ginny Dodge?'

'Curious name.' Asim frowned.

It was. Tallis remembered her opening line. 'Dodge by name. Dodge by nature.' They'd got on like the proverbial house on fire. In fact, Ginny, slick and polished, wouldn't have looked out of place in Berlin, he thought.

'Ms Dodge is going to coach you in sales speak.'

Things were looking up, Tallis thought. 'You mean I'm going to be selling helicopters?'

'To the Russians.'

'Are they in the market? I mean, they've got their pick of ex-military choppers.' Tallis was considering how on earth he, a complete novice when it came to business, was going to fool some filthy-rich Russian oligarch.

'I think you'll find there's a certain cachet in buying from Britain.'

'If you say so,' Tallis said uncertainly.

'It's going to be your route in. With the recent troubles, Chechnya is closed to outsiders, even journalists right now, so you're going to have to get inventive to penetrate checkpoints and border controls.'

'I take it I'll be armed.'

'You'd be a fool not to be. The gloves are off on this one,' Asim said, plunging into silence as a jogger plugged into an MP3 player sped past, kicking up the gravel, followed by a group of workmen in yellow jackets carrying chainsaws. Tallis stared upwards, over the tops of the trees, catching sight of the massive Sony building, a construct of Perspex, steel and glass. Asim waited for the workers to pass by before he continued. 'There should be no problem picking up hardware once you're in Moscow. The place is swimming in weapons.'

Tallis nodded gravely. 'Where will I be based?'

'We're going to rent an apartment for you, details to follow. No trace to us, of course.'

'Of course.' Tallis smiled.

More footsteps. More silence. It was almost companionable, Tallis thought. 'And this bloke, Elimkhanova,' Tallis began.

'The warlord Graham's tagging along with. What about him?'

'Where do I find him?'

'The last report states he's somewhere near the mountain village of Borzoi. Think you can negotiate the terrain?'

'No problem.' Tallis expressed more confidence than he felt. It had been a long time since he'd tried anything like this—and he'd been a lot younger.

'This way,' Asim said, taking a detour, clearly clocking a woman cycling lazily towards them. She was swaddled in a hoodie, a white guitar case on her back. Tallis couldn't help but smile. What did Asim think—that she was going to dismount and produce an automatic weapon, Mafia-style? The woman flashed a *Guten morgen* as she ambled past.

They were in a maze of cobbled pathways that led to a monument, this time to musicians, including the greats—Beethoven, Haydn and Mozart. Beyond, and on the right, a small lake, and beyond this, where the leaves were stripped from the trees, a statue, green with verdigris, of a man on a horse. The place was unaccountably stark, the air chill, as if something dreadful had happened there years before; they fell into silence. It was some minutes before Asim broke it.

'Think you'll persuade Darke to return?'

'Depends on whether he's guilty or not.'

'Perhaps I should rephrase that. If he's guilty, will he come quietly?'

Tallis had pondered the same. 'I'd say the answer was no.'

'It's something you should be prepared for.'

Yes, he knew.

'With regard to brushing up on your Chechen,' Asim said, 'you must be able to speak the language as if it were your own. Your life could depend on it.'

He was well aware of that. He just hoped to God that Viva Constantine, an old friend of his, could deliver.

'We have plenty of linguists on hand to assist,' Asim said. 'Probably easier if you come to London.'

'Won't be necessary,' Tallis said.

'Oh?'

'I'd like to use one of my own contacts.'

'You know someone?'

'Yes.'

'Paul, we don't have much time.'

'I know, but I don't want to be coached by someone who only speaks the language. I need someone who's intimately familiar with the culture.'

'There is also the small matter of security,' Asim said, arching an eyebrow.

'I appreciate that.'

'So discretion is the name of the game.'

'Naturally.'

'I'll give you twenty-four hours on your return. If your contact lets you down, for whatever reason, you'll let me know?'

'I will.'

Together, they retraced their steps back onto the path and turned back onto the main road and into the shadow of the Sony building once more. Street sellers wearing fur hats with earflaps were out in force. Back at Brandenburg Gate again, Asim invited Tallis to join him for coffee, a transparent attempt to lighten the mood.

'I know the perfect place,' he coaxed.

Was this intended as a last act of a kindness to a condemned man? Tallis wondered. And why the hell had he agreed to do it? Easy, he thought. He needed focus, a goal, something to live for. He was also, frankly, curious. When he'd told Asim that he wanted to defend the honour of an old friend, he'd meant it.

The wind had dropped. Embassy flags flapped listlessly in the dead air.

'No, I'll head off. Start the ball rolling.'

About to extend his hand, Asim's mobile rang. He picked up. 'Yup?'

Tallis watched his expression, enigmatic and impenetrable.

'Right,' Asim said, closing the phone. He looked off for a moment, clearly digesting the news he'd received. Tallis looked at him in question.

'That call,' Asim said, dark eyes glinting.

'Yes?'

'A former Russian general has just been killed in a car bomb attack outside his house. Looks as if our man has struck again.'

CHAPTER THREE

TALLIS cut short his visit, the hurried journey back to the UK a blur. All he could think about was Graham Darke, the work ahead, the mission. And when he wasn't thinking, he lost himself in childhood daydreams—sitting on the branches of an apple tree, muddy-kneed, long-limbed and laughing, giving each other Chinese burns, talking low and long into the shadows, having his first fag in the woods and feeling sick, drinking Vimto outside the chippie, downing whisky in the park and considering what it might be like to get laid. All this to the accompaniment of Graham's throaty laughter in his ears. Sometimes, and always against his father's wishes, Tallis would go back to Graham's home, two council houses knocked together to accommodate the family. It was his first and only taste of domestic mayhem—kids everywhere, cats, dogs, cigarette smoke and meals on the run, and adults who liked a drink or ten and got up at noon. He had been mesmerised by it, and now, even with his memory blunted, he felt consumed by the desire to find his friend, to see how he'd turned out, to discover what had really become of him.

No sooner than he'd dropped the borrowed helicopter back at the helipad, he lost no time and drove straight to Viva Constantine's. He didn't even bother calling ahead.

Viva lived in Saltley, a suburb east of Birmingham, down a narrow terraced street largely populated by British-born Asians. Rasu, her partner, opened the door, his expression normally resigned and passive erupting into delight. Two years of living without the threat of being sent back to Iraq, his country of origin, had done wonders for him, Tallis thought. Rasu had filled out physically and lost the haunted look of a man banged up for a crime he didn't commit in a country that was not his own. Tallis had no idea how old Rasu was but, in the past two years, he appeared to have grown younger. Even his skin seemed less pitted, the features less sharply defined. The solemnity in his dark brown eyes was still there but they also shone with contentment. Must be love, Tallis thought, feeling envious.

'Come in, Paul,' Rasu said. 'It's good to see you again. Goodness, how long has it been?'

'Two years, got to be,' Tallis said, feeling faintly embarrassed he hadn't called sooner, not that Rasu was making a deal of it.

'Viva's not here at the moment,' Rasu said. 'She's at the Refugee Council on Thursdays.'

A grim monolithic building that wouldn't have looked out of place in Berlin, Tallis recalled. Dark and brooding, even when the sky was gilded with sunshine, the council sat opposite the police station in Digbeth, not far from the train station. Years before, he'd had reason to visit the place to interview a witness to a shooting. He remembered the stained green carpets, the numbered compartments (half post office, half Argos) the posters on the wall with warnings about sexually transmitted diseases, and rows of chairs, people sitting quietly, the embodiment of patience, their whole lives, it seemed, revolving around waiting and more waiting, like they were in scene from a play by Beckett. He remembered how surprised he'd been by the atmosphere of calm and good humour. He told this to Rasu, who flashed a smile.

'We try to do our best, and you'll be pleased to hear we've recently moved to Aston. Conditions for staff and clients have improved immeasurably.'

'I'm glad. So Viva works there as a linguist?'

'She works in Admin. We both do,' Rasu said, ushering Tallis into the kitchen, sweeping a pile of newspapers off a chair for his guest. 'Obviously, the fact we both speak languages is a major bonus. There are many Iraqis seeking asylum, Kurds in particular,' Rasu said. 'Our workload also includes those from Zimbabwe and Afghanistan. Unfortunately, at Birmingham we deal with what's called Section Four clients.'

Tallis cocked an eyebrow.

'People who are what is known as fully determined—they have already lost their claim to asylum. They tend to be single men in the eighteen to thirty-five age range. In reality, you're only ever in with a chance if you're a family.'

'Must be tough to deal with,' Tallis said.

'It is.' Rasu's smile was humble. And when it came to tough, Tallis thought, Rasu knew what he was talking about. As a Kurd in Iraq he had suffered terrible persecution under Saddam's regime. 'So was it Viva you came to see?' Rasu said, automatically filling the kettle.

'Both of you.' It was an honest answer. Tallis liked Rasu Barzani enormously. He was probably the most dignified individual he'd ever met. He was also highly intelligent, the kind of intuitive man who could deduce a great deal from very little.

'She should be back home for lunch any minute. You'll stay, of course.'

'Thanks,' Tallis said, glancing at his watch. 'And you, how are things, aside from work?'

'Life is good.'

'I see the elephants have been breeding.' Tallis laughed, his eye catching a dresser crammed with elephant ornaments. Viva, for reasons he'd never fathomed, had a thing about them.

'You should see the sitting room,' Rasu said. 'We're planning on opening a safari park. Tea or coffee?'

'Coffee, thanks.'

'And you, Paul. How's everything going? Still in

the same job?' Rasu and Viva were two of the few people who had more than an inkling of what he did, mainly because they had been involved in his first case.

'Yup.'

'And is this the reason you are here?' Rasu said. He had his back to Tallis but the smile in his voice was unmistakably genuine in spite of the direct nature of the question.

Tallis let out a laugh. 'You know me too well.' He was pleased somebody did. It made him feel less adrift.

Rasu said no more about it. Tallis watched as Rasu pulled various items from the fridge—hummus, salad, plump purple olives, and pitta bread. 'And, other than work, how are things with you?' It was spoken in a way guaranteed to be neither prying nor shallow.

Objectively, Tallis didn't really think about work much. It was easy to equate. He enjoyed the cut and thrust, the freedom. The scary situations in which he often found himself appeased the dangerous side of his personality, the part that revelled in risk. Solitary by nature, he was no stranger to loneliness and, although he didn't abstain from the company of women, since losing Belle he hadn't felt the urge to have a committed relationship, let alone settle down. Besides, it would only complicate things. So, yeah, life was fine. He told Rasu this and Rasu was smart enough to accept what he said at face value.

The coffee ready, Rasu put two mugs on the table and drew up a chair. 'Help yourself to milk and sugar,' he said, surveying Tallis in a way that was entirely solicitous.

Tallis stirred in two sugars. 'Can I ask you a rather weird question?'

Rasu lifted both eyebrows.

'Does Viva speak Chechen?'

'No.'

Damn. 'Anyone at the Refugee Council?'

Rasu shook his head with a smile. 'Apart from the manager, the staff are all bilingual, some speak more than one other language. In fact, there's an amazing guy who speaks about ten. Between us we must cover Eastern Europe, the Middle East, China and Europe, the Baltics but, sadly, not Chechnya.'

'So no Chechens seeking asylum?'

Rasu opened his mouth to speak. Viva's low voice stepped into the breach. 'Who wants to know?' She was leaning against the doorpost, her full lips drawn back in a big smile. Her coat was open, revealing a floppy dark brown roll-neck sweater over a long camel-coloured skirt. She had a handsome brown leather handbag slung carelessly over her shoulder. So far, so conventional. Her feet, however, were clad in what Tallis could only describe as suede pixie boots. They were an extraordinary shade of orange. Tallis had never quite got his head around Viva's dress sense. He turned and got up to greet her, kissing her on both cheeks. She looked well, too. Her brown hair was cut into a shorter style. Made her look sassy.

'And what brings the mighty Paul Tallis into town?' She grinned, peeling off her coat and kissing Rasu on the lips, giving his arm a tender squeeze. She wasn't what Tallis would call conventionally good looking. In a face that was full of character, her green eyes were almost too deep-set. Her mouth was probably her best feature, and there was definitely something compelling about her, more to do with her personality shining through, he suspected, than the way she looked. Viva could be challenging, and Tallis quite liked that. He found feisty women appealing.

Viva plumped down in an easy chair by the door, curling her legs up underneath her. Rasu made more coffee.

'There are several families of Chechens living in Scotland, if that's any help,' Viva said, picking up on the conversation again.

'But none in Birmingham,' Tallis said.

Viva and Rasu exchanged glances.

'I was telling Paul about the many languages we cover at work,' Rasu said, so obviously trying to get off the Chechen subject Tallis found it amusing.

'Sounds like the United Nations.' Tallis flicked a smile. 'So what do you do if someone shows up from some far-flung corner of the map for whom you don't have a suitable linguist?'

'We contact the Council in London,' Viva answered. 'There's a database of interpreters we can access. Sometimes we link up a conference call over the phone with a client, usually works quite well in an emergency. And, believe me, emergencies are our stock in trade.'

Tell me about it, Tallis thought.

'Occasionally we use an agency in Birmingham but, at fifty pounds an hour, it's not cheap,' Rasu chipped in. He was leaning against a work-surface, cup of coffee in hand, relaxed.

Tallis nodded, thinking he'd go for the curved ball approach. 'These clients, Section Four, you said.'

'The ones who get turned down,' Rasu said.

'Any of them Chechen refugees?'

Rasu opened his mouth to speak. Viva checked him with a classic look. 'One,' she said. 'But she won't talk to you.'

'Why not?'

'Because you're a man.'

'A very nice man.' Tallis shot Viva his most winsome smile, making her laugh.

'Why the interest?' Rasu cut in.

'I have to go to Chechnya for a job.'

Rasu nodded, his expression one of complete calm and thoughtfulness, unlike Viva's, which was suddenly bitter and spiky. Rasu indicated for Tallis to help himself to food, which he did. The hummus was so pungent with garlic it could have felled a dozen vampires.

'The Russian government has behaved deplorably towards the Chechens.' Viva let out a small hiss of anger, tossing the salad with vigour. 'They've virtually written off the refugees mouldering in Ingushetia. They've attacked civilians in Georgia. And now we have the latest crisis.'

'Which is why it's imperative I speak the language fluently.'

'I could give you the name of a linguist.' Viva shrugged, taking a decisive bite of pitta bread.

'Won't do,' Tallis said. 'I need to get a proper insight, know what I'm dealing with. My life may depend on it.'

Silence descended in the small kitchen. The clock ticked loudly in Tallis's ears. Everyone fell to eating lunch. Rasu, clearly uncomfortable, was first to talk. 'Are you intending to help the people there?'

'He's not an aid worker,' Viva scoffed. 'Sorry, Paul,' she said in answer to his arch expression. 'But you know what I mean.'

'I do and I don't particularly care for it,' he said without sounding too rancorous. Did he need to point out to Viva that had it not been for his help two years before, Rasu would be dead by now? 'Helping people isn't just about feeding and clothing them and dishing out medical supplies, important though that is. Like you say, the Chechens have had a raw deal. If I don't get out there in the next couple of weeks and work a bloody miracle, the Russian government is going to be the least of their problems. It's going to be *War and Peace* for real.'

Rasu's face creased with concern. He looked from Tallis to Viva. 'Perhaps we could talk to Lena?'

Viva pressed a little finger to her lip and began to

nibble the nail. She looked straight at Tallis. 'Leaving aside the literary comparisons, could you be a bit more specific about what's at stake here?'

'Can't,' Tallis said, draining his mug of coffee.

An uneasy silence prevailed, the only sound the clacking of cutlery and the continued slow steady grind of the kitchen clock. Tallis wondered how long it had been since Graham Darke had shared a meal like this at someone's kitchen table cluttered with yesterday's newspapers. He glanced across at Viva. Head bent, she was slowly pushing a piece of pitta round and round her plate. Yeah, he thought, she's torn.

'Heard of a place called Aldy?' Viva said at last, looking up.

'No.'

'Lena used to live there. It's a suburb of Grozny. In 2000, it was the scene of a massacre. Like most of the refugees, Lena headed to the mountains. Eventually, she made it to the independent state of Georgia and, after a circuitous route, half-starved and ill, she arrived in the UK in 2004.'

'*Two thousand and four?*' That's years ago, Tallis thought.

'It can take Immigration a while to get their act together,' Rasu said with a dry smile. 'To be honest, at the point where an asylum seeker is refused entry, the system breaks down. We've had clients hanging around for years existing in a state of limbo, sleeping on people's floors, living off handouts from friends.'

'There's a huge confusion in people's minds about genuine refugees and asylum seekers,' Viva explained in answer to Tallis's surprised expression. 'Contrary to popular opinion, they don't get handouts from the state. They have no right to benefits. They don't jump council waiting lists. Lena and hundreds like her live in a dark netherworld without rights or status. It's not a way to live, Paul,' Viva said, fluttering a hand in a gesture of despair.

No, it wasn't. 'What's her English like?' Tallis said.

'It's good,' Rasu said. This time his words went unchecked, a good sign as far as Tallis was concerned. He decided to push home the advantage. His appeal was to both of them.

'Could you at least mention me to her?'

Rasu looked at Viva. He was definitely on-side, Tallis thought. 'I could come to the Council, see her there.'

'No,' Viva said flatly. 'Too unorthodox. We have to respect client confidentiality—but,' she said in answer to Tallis's pleading expression, 'I'll talk to her, see what she says. I do want to help you, Paul,' she rushed on, contrite, not something that came easily to Viva Constantine, Tallis realised.

'It's all right. I understand; you want to protect her.'

'Someone has to.' Viva cast him a level look, her eyes deep sea green. 'Don't get your hopes up, Paul. She's been through a lot and, as you might expect, she's not the easiest individual to deal with.'

'Fair enough,' he said, glancing at his watch. In less than twelve hours he needed an answer. Now was probably not a good moment to push it.

CHAPTER FOUR

Russian air space outside Grozny, Chechnya

COLONEL FILIP LISAKONOV picked his teeth and stared down with contempt at the smudge of land below. More mud, more filth, more vermin, he thought. As deputy regiment commander of a platoon of conscripted soldiers and about to enter the Ethnic Republic of the North Caucasus, he believed that genocide of the Chechen nation should be a matter of state policy.

With all civilian flights suspended because of the recent upsurge in unrest, Lisakonov was flying in by helicopter for the forty-minute flight from Mozdok to Khankala. He had been drinking vodka for most of the trip, and was feeling foul—foul to be in the company of such a snivelling band of conscripts, *srochniki*, foul to be back in this godforsaken place. He fully expected to arrive in Grozny by nightfall. Grozny, he thought with disgust, flicking a fragment of fish from a lower molar. The very word meant terrible.

'You, soldier,' he said, eyeing a weak-chinned youth with fat lips and skin the colour of fresh Brie. The lad flinched, turned his dejected gaze from the floor to somewhere just over his superior's shoulder. Everyone knew that if you looked Lisakonov in the eye, you'd receive a severe beating for it later. 'Know what? I was part of 58 army during the last conflict.'

The soldier swallowed and nodded dumbly. The 58 had a reputation for extreme brutality. It was also well known that weapons were often stolen from the store and sold back to the Chechens, in other words aiding and abetting the enemy.

'Yeah, that's right.' Lisakonov's features fell into a grin, revealing a set of crooked teeth. Dark shadows lurked underneath eyes that appeared sleep-deprived. 'Back then, I could beat a conscripted soldier to death in minutes with a spade. My personal best was twelve and a half, know that?'

The soldier shook his head nervously, clearly wondering if he was going to be the next entry on Lisakonov's personal scorecard. With no escape, the youth's skinny body shrank into the interior of the hold. The others also shuffled position. If there was to be a scapegoat, let it be the next man.

'Mind…' Lisakonov grinned, taking another swig from a bottle of vodka '…sometimes they had their uses.'

Again the soldier nodded stupidly, his Adam's apple sticking out like he'd swallowed a gobstopper whole. The rest of his fellow comrades, pale-eyed and frightened, nodded in unison.

Lisakonov began to enlighten the lice-ridden lads under his command. 'Did a little buying and selling, see. Night was when the real trade began. Mainly weapons, nice lucrative sideline for Russian officers. What choice did we have?' he rolled his eyes, which were like two blue pinheads. 'Common knowledge we were starving. Lucky to get a tin of fish to last a week.' He scratched his head, momentarily losing his train of thought, took another gulp of vodka. 'Comes down to knowing your market. And the market then was for *soldiers*—rabble like you lot,' he added with a high-pitched peal of laughter. 'We sold them as slaves and declared them deserters. Christ knows what the Chechens did with them. Probably fucked them and slit their measly throats.'

The soldier to whom Lisakonov had been address-ing his speech made a small inarticulate noise.

'Chechens.' Lisakonov belched. 'We should have annihilated them years ago when we had the chance. Every Chechen is a Muslim and every Muslim is a ter-rorist. The Serbs have got the right idea with their ethnic cleansing.' He scowled, addressing nobody in particu-lar, leaning back, closing his eyes, a sudden weariness enveloping him. He knew he would not sleep, hadn't done for years now, not since…

Black dots and squiggles scampered at the edges of his consciousness. Sweat pooled underneath his arms and across his narrow shoulder blades. A sour taste filled his throat. In his imagination, he was back in the

mountains, the horrendous sound of men being cruci-
fied screaming in his ears. It was during the first
conflict. He had been an ordinary private then, not
much more than a boy. The older soldiers, even those
who'd fought in Afghanistan, had spoken of the exceptional brutality. 'At least in Afghanistan, you knew who
your enemy was,' one had told him. 'Here, it's like
fighting ghosts.'

The next day, when the barbarians retreated, they went
in to take their boys down. One poor soul was still alive.
Christ knows how. The others had all bled out. That's
what happened when your dick was scythed off.
Lisakonov was ordered to kill him, to put him out of his
misery. He hadn't wanted to but an order was an order
so, with tears streaming, he shot the young soldier at
point-blank range. He didn't think he'd ever forget the expression in the boy's dying eyes, that terrible look of
gratitude.

Seized by a sudden wave of anger, Lisakonov's eyes
popped open. 'When the fuck are we going to land?'
he slurred. In answer to his question, the rotor suddenly
stalled then stopped. 'What the…?' Lisakonov began
to speak, his words cut off as the helicopter dropped
soundlessly from the sky and forty-five seconds later
crashed into the Chechen countryside.

Shobdon Airfield, Herefordshire, England

'So never mind all this stuff about health and safety—
basically if the rotor stops working we're fucked.'

'Just time for a quick hug, darling.'

Tallis was smiling and remembering one of his early conversations with Virginia Dodge. He'd driven straight from Viva's after lunch to the airfield where Ginny had already been on standby. Turning off into the ten-miles-an-hour zone, and keeping well to the left and out of the way of incoming traffic, he also recalled her admonition to hang onto her rather than grab the controls should anything untoward happen.

'What sort of untoward?' he said, a cheeky grin on his face, for which he received a cute smile in return. He quite fancied the idea of grabbing hold of Ginny. She had shoulder-length dark hair, twinkly brown eyes and skin freckled from spending a lot of time outdoors. With a surprisingly athletic build for a woman of her age, late forties at a guess, she was definitely desirable and a lot of fun. And there was, according to her, no Mr Dodge.

Tallis parked the Boxster close to the airfield café and got out, relieved that he'd at last got round to replacing his battered old Rover with a car that was as practical as it was dashing. Even now he found the lapis-blue exterior, the upholstery in sand beige leather, the to-die-for six-speed gearbox irresistible. As for the handling, it was a superb example of German engineering. Beneath the glamorous image, the Boxster delivered at every level and, like it or not, image was all with the flying set. He'd never come across a breed like them. The helicopter and light aircraft business attracted people with determined aspirations and serious money—impossible to enter its holy portals without it. Simply learning to fly was synonymous with relinquishing eye-watering amounts of cash. As for the machines themselves, you didn't get much change out of fifty grand for the most basic two-seater second-hand helicopter. No, he reckoned, he'd got the better deal with his Porsche. And it fitted in with the rest of the cars dotted around the airfield—the Lexus, Audi TT, Ferrari and Jaguar convertibles.

Inhaling the cold clear air, watching as pencils of light fell out of the sky, illuminating the runway, he felt, as he'd done on previous occasions, like he'd passed through a time warp and found himself back in the 1950s. He couldn't really explain why except to say that the place, once a base for gliders during the Second World War, retained a strange enduring quality, as if whatever happened in the world Shobdon airfield would go on and on, remaining there silent and indestructible. Clicking his tongue for being so bloody fanciful, he walked past Ginny's handsome Mercedes SLK and over towards the hangars and the offices of Tiger Helicopters, automatically ducking a little as a bright green Agusta 109 Power Elite hovered overhead before landing.

Several police pilots from Kuwait, dressed in black jumpsuits, were hanging out at Reception. Sponsored by the Kuwaiti government, they were on an eighteen-month training programme with Tiger. Tallis exchanged greetings in Arabic with one of the pilots before darting upstairs to Ginny's office, which lay down a corridor off a main meeting room and kitchen area. Ginny was peering into a computer screen and talking briskly into her mobile. At Tallis's arrival, she turned, broke into a smile.

'So,' she said, cutting the call, 'mine is not to reason why but I've orders to turn you into a first-class salesman.' He wondered exactly what or how much she'd been told. Knowing Asim, not very much.

'Shouldn't be that tricky,' Tallis said.

Ginny placed a hand on her trim hip and elevated an eyebrow. She was wearing a pair of tailored cream linen trousers, a fitted navy sweater, which went in and out in all the right places, with a red silk scarf at her throat. It gave her a slightly nautical look. 'Let's hope not.' She smiled. 'Have you eaten?'

'I have.'

'Well, I'm starving,' she said, grabbing her handbag.

'No problem. Being the female of the species, you'll be able to eat and talk effortlessly at the same time.'

Ginny gave him a playful swipe with her sizable shoulder bag.

'Ouch, what did you do that for?' He laughed, putting both hands up in surrender.

'Didn't your mother tell you that talking with your mouth full is rude?'

As they got outside Tallis gave an involuntary shiver. The temperature seemed to have plummeted by several degrees in a matter of minutes due to the sudden onset of a bitter easterly wind.

'God help you in Russia,' Ginny said, swinging her hips as she walked.

'Who says I'm going to Russia?'

Ginny stopped walking and turned her stern brown-eyed gaze on Tallis. At times, she could be incredibly imperious, he thought. 'Credit me with a little intelligence. I've already got a deal in the offing with a businessman from Moscow. If it plays out, and the Russians I have to tell you are notoriously slow when it comes to meetings and negotiations, you, my boy, are going to handle the transaction.'

Not too slow, he hoped. 'This going to screw up your commission?'

Ginny's face lit up with a smile. 'Put it this way, I've been offered a very healthy incentive.'

Good, he didn't like the idea of her losing out.

'So, like I said,' Ginny picked up the pace again, 'you'll have no choice but to go to Russia. Only way to do business.'

The cafeteria, an old Nissen hut with floral plastic tablecloths on the tables, smelt of fried food and best-quality catering brew. It was already busy with late lunchers, mechanics and aircrew stealing a break, and the odd visitor out for an early afternoon pot of tea and cake. Ginny ordered egg and chips from a large-framed woman and two mugs of tea, which they waited for. It came out steaming and the same colour as well-fertilised soil.

With mugs in hand, they pulled up chairs near the window and sat down opposite each other. Ginny opened up her handbag, one of those large brown satchel affairs, and rummaged through it like a fox pillaging a dustbin. Aspirin, lipstick, tissues and Blackberry all piled out. Curious, Tallis picked up the Blackberry.

'How do you rate these?' The weight of it in his hand felt like a small firearm.

'Brilliant. Does everything.'

'Everything?'

She flashed him a reproving look. 'Combined email, computer, phone.'

'Next you'll be telling me it brushes your teeth, too.' Tallis knew it wasn't cool, but he wasn't much of a techno person—not unless it was the latest military hardware or satellite equipment. As far as espionage was concerned, in the field technology was simply an add-on. Technology left a trail. Electricity failed. Computers crashed and became prey to viruses. He still believed the human brain the most important component in any investigation. When it came to back-up, a firearm was all he required.

Ginny flashed him a grin then, businesslike, handed him a brochure. 'Read and digest,' she said. 'It will give you a flavour of the technical language so at least you sound as if you know what you're talking about.'

Tallis flicked through. Not unlike a helicopter version of *Top Gear,* same fact files, same performance ratings, same glossy photographs. He put it down. 'Anything I should particularly bear in mind when doing business Moscow style?'

'I'll come to that later,' Ginny said, leaning back as her plate of egg and chips arrived. 'Oh, bugger. I didn't ask for ketchup.'

'Hold on, I'll get it,' Tallis said, scraping his chair back and heading for the counter. He returned with one of those sauce holders in the shape of a plastic tomato. In his absence, Ginny had already nicked the brochure back and flipped it open to a page displaying several top-of-the-range helis.

'Thanks.' Ginny glanced up. 'Right,' she said, liberally dousing her chips. 'This is where we're at. See this…' She pointed with a manicured nail. 'That's what we're selling.'

Tallis took a look, eyes scanning the spec. 'Bit bloody bright, isn't it? Where did it come from?'

Ginny rolled her eyes. 'Limerick.'

'Is it the same Agusta 109 Elite that landed here this afternoon?'

'I had a mechanic put it through its paces.' Ginny speared a chip and put it in her mouth. 'We put an ad in one of the trade journals and received an enquiry a couple of weeks later from a Russian guy on behalf of an interested party.'

'You don't know who the party is?'

'Not yet but I will.' She gave a game grin.

Tallis had no doubt. Ginny was one of the most persistent women he'd ever come across. 'So it was a tentative enquiry, sounding each other out, that right?'

'Seeing which way the wind's blowing.' She jabbed a chip into a dull yellow yolk, causing a minor eruption. 'They go in for that a lot. I liken it to a form of elaborate courtship.'

'Can't wait.' He grinned.

She flicked him another of her reproving smiles. 'Several things worth remembering about the Russians,' Ginny said. 'They don't like to be railroaded, they respect pecking orders, preferring to meet people on a similar pay grade to themselves, and most importantly any business negotiation is viewed as win or lose.'

'With them in the winning seat.'

'You got it,' she said, devouring another egg-coated chip. 'Actually, you have a distinct advantage.'

'Yeah?'

'Ever been in sales before?'

Tallis shook his head and tasted the tea. It was a lot better than it looked.

'Didn't think so. Means you're not used to the typically British form of high-pressure sales tactics. That's good. Russians don't care for it. Patience is the name of the game.'

Not a commodity he had in abundance, Tallis thought, suddenly feeling glum. He wished he could just get out to Chechnya and be done with it. 'This call you received. What did you manage to glean?'

'The all-important budget.'

'Which is?'

'Between three and a half and five million.'

Tallis let out a long slow whistle between his teeth. 'Think he's serious?'

'Don't see why not.' She gave a shrug, pushing her plate towards Tallis, offering him a chip.

'Thanks,' he said, helping himself.

'A chip,' she said, smartly tapping the back of his hand with the knife, meeting his surprised expression with a flirtatious grin.

'You always had such a lively appetite?'

'Always.' She gave a sexy smile.

'I still don't really get why a stinkingly rich Russian wants to do business with Tiger—no offence,' he added, drinking some tea.

Rather than blowing him out, Ginny came up with the best argument he'd heard so far. 'Image,' she said. 'It's true the Russians have been producing helicopters for decades for both military and domestic use, but a lot of them are quite old and knackered. The point is it's no longer frowned on to be a capitalist—Ivanov is positively encouraging capitalism—so it's no longer bad form to buy from the West. In fact, the Agusta is perceived to be a status symbol—it says something about the man who's either flying or buying. And the Russians are hot on image.'

'This bloke you dealt with.'

'Our main man's engineer.'

'Does he have a name?'

'Kumarin.'

'Won't this Mr Kumarin think it odd you've dropped out of the negotiations?'

Ginny shook her head and reached for her mug. 'Goes back to what I was telling you about dealing with someone on the same level.'

'But I'm no more an engineer than you are.'

'But you're a bloke. When it comes down to the heavy-duty side, Kumarin will want to talk man to man and you can use Charlie, one of our engineers, to talk the talk. Look,' she said, pushing the plate away and leaning towards him, sending a fragrant mist of Dior in his direction. 'Buying a helicopter is not like viewing a house and putting in an offer. All sorts of things have to be gone through first.'

That was rather what he was afraid of. If the deal took as long as Ginny indicated, whoever had it in for Ivanov could already have assassinated him.

'So what are the moves?'

'If our Mr Kumarin bites, we invite him over and let him check the records. Basically, he's going to be looking at the airworthiness of the machine and, key, whether it's worth the money. With second-hand, he'll be looking at when or if it had a rebuild, whether it's got a proper service record, either every six months or fifty hours,' she added. 'Keep in mind he's looking for a deal.'

A bargain, more like. 'Which is going to be lose-lose for us.'

''Fraid so, but you can afford to take a loss, or so I understand,' Ginny said, a curious glint in her eye.

'Then what?' Tallis smiled, smoothly sidestepping further enquiry.

'You get to fly the Agusta over to Moscow, you lucky boy.'

'Nice,' Tallis agreed. Then another thought struck him. 'What if our Mr Kumarin cries off, or his boss doesn't bite?'

'We put another tiddler on the line and cast off.'

All very chancy, Tallis thought, briefly looking out of the window and wondering how Viva was getting on with persuading Lena to talk to him.

'Afternoon, Ginny. Aren't you going to introduce us?'

A heavy-set man dressed in a dark green fleece and jeans stood grinning like a meerkat at the pair of them. He had short dark hair plastered flat against his skull and blue eyes that bulged from his face as if they might pop out and land on the table at any second. His mouth was working its way round a wad of chewing gum.

Ginny flashed a cold smile. 'Blaine!' she exclaimed, the tension in her eyes evident. 'Blaine Deverill, this is Paul Tallis.'

Blaine stuck out a hand. Tallis rose to his feet, towering over the shorter man, and exchanged greetings.

'Haven't I seen you around?' Blaine said, eyes flicking in search of a free chair so that he could draw it up and join them. Ginny, very deliberately, took out her Blackberry and started checking for emails.

'Bound to. I took flying lessons here.'

'With Ginny?'

'That's right.'

'Good, isn't she?' Blaine smiled, clearly trying to curry favour. Ginny kept her eyes fixed doggedly on her gadget. 'Got your own bird?'

'Can't afford it.' Tallis gave a snort. He could but he wasn't up for disclosing his financial profile to a stranger—or anyone, come to think of it.

Ginny glanced up and gave Tallis a funny look then shamelessly clicked her tongue at Deverill, but Deverill was clearly not a guy to pick up a negative vibe, not even if it jabbed him on the arse.

'Know what you mean,' he said. 'Big boy's toys.'

'And you, Mr Deverill, enthusiastic amateur or in the game?' Tallis wished to hell the bloke would go away.

'Call me Blaine, please.' Deverill clicked a smile. 'Been flying since I was this high,' he said, gesturing with his hand, inferring that he'd become a pilot at the age of four. 'I've got a Squirrel.'

'Cool,' Tallis said, resisting the temptation to make a joke.

'Paul's our new sales guy,' Ginny said, without looking up, both thumbs tapping away.

'Really?' Deverill said, eyes alert with interest.

'Hoping to net a Russian deal,' Tallis said, glancing at Ginny who suddenly seemed to develop some difficulty in keeping a straight face. She was silently mouthing something at him, but he couldn't make out what.

'Good business to be had in Russia,' Deverill opined. 'Wouldn't mind a slice of the action myself. Things are so much better under Ivanov's influence. That man's managed to bring stability and prosperity to the country in abundance. Wealth is spreading from west of the Urals right across to Siberia. Plenty of money sloshing about and, as we all know, Paul,' he said in a worldly fashion, 'money is what makes the world go round.'

'Sure,' Tallis said vaguely. Ginny was still hissing like a viper at him, lips drawn back, revealing a perfect set of straight white teeth.

Deverill continued to spout on, clearly liking what he said and saying what he liked. Tallis had met plenty of blokes like him. The problem was, just when you thought they were talking bollocks, they'd say something mind-blowing.

'You seem to know a lot about Russia,' Tallis said, trying to stay focused. 'You lived there?'

Deverill dropped the smile, cast a cautious look around the café, and bent his head so close to Tallis's mouth Tallis could smell the pomade on his hair. 'Top secret,' he whispered. 'Twenty years ago, I served in the Special Air Service.'

Not The Regiment, Tallis thought, which was how its members usually referred to it. Tallis wasn't aware that the SAS had been on a mission in the Soviet Union but, then again, if it was Top Secret, why would he? Glancing across at Ginny, he suddenly realised what she'd been on about: *SAS*.

'Yes, well, Blaine, sorry to be a bore,' Ginny said, with emphasis, 'but Paul and I have got a stack of information to get through. Would you mind?' she said. 'Only it's warmer in here than in the office.'

Deverill broke into an embarrassed smile. 'Of course, forgive me,' he said. 'Nice meeting you, Paul. No doubt I'll see you again.'

Not if I see you first, Tallis thought.

'Christ!' Ginny let out, once Blaine was out of earshot. 'Should have warned you about Walter Mitty.'

'Does he tell everyone he was in the SAS?'

'Among other things, 'fraid so. Right, back to business,' she said, a schoolmistress look in her eye.

Tallis leant across the table. 'I love it when you're being dominant.'

Before he left Shobdon, Tallis contacted an old army mate. Monty or Jack Montague worked for the Mine Action Coordination Centre, an organisation dedicated to mine risk education training, including reconnaissance of mined areas and the collection of mine data.

'Monty, how are you?' Tallis began.

'Bloody hell, Tallis. Long time no hear. What are you up to these days?'

You don't want to know. 'Trying to make a living like the rest of us.'

'Tell me about it.' Monty laughed. 'The wife's just about to have our third. You married yet?'

'Do me a favour.' Tallis grinned.

'Your problem is you've never found the right woman.'

Oh, I did, Tallis thought, the shine disappearing from his smile.

'Anyway, this a social call or what?'

'Bit of both, really. Don't suppose we could have a chat, only I want to pick your brains.'

'I'm down your neck of the woods next week. Got a seminar in Birmingham. Would that be any good?'

'Perfect. Name a day and time and I'll be there.'

They agreed to meet up the following Tuesday.

'You going to give me a clue what this is all about?'

'Chechnya,' Tallis said firmly. 'I need country-specific information on the type of explosive munitions in the area, locations if you can establish them, in other words a complete rundown.'

'Any particular reason?'

'I have to go there.'

Monty didn't say a word—he was probably too surprised.

On his way back, Tallis visited a local gym and pushed some metal for an hour, arriving back home around eight in the evening, tired and sweaty.

The bungalow, his grandmother's bequest to him, felt derelict. Yes, it had all the modern trappings, the colour high-definition television set, the state-of-the-art computer, the squashy leather sofa and easy chairs, pictures on the wall. But there was something definitely missing—a woman's touch, perhaps. Occasionally, as an intellectual exercise, he wondered what it would be like to be in a settled relationship, to have someone to share his life with, or simply hang out with. But these were such rare fleeting hankerings he didn't trouble himself with examining the possibilities too carefully. He certainly didn't long for a partner on tap to take care of the domestic side of his life. Although the bungalow occasionally descended into abject disorder, he was tidy by nature, probably something to do with an early stint in the army, serving with the Royal Staffordshires. He'd always thought Graham would wind up in the forces. Sometimes it was the saving of a troubled boy; Graham, in his own way, had been as lost as he'd once been.

He showered, changed into clean clothes and, pulling bacon and eggs from the fridge, cooked and ate, the brochure Ginny had given him propped up against a bottle of beer. He was reading through the specifications for the helicopter again: 2005; thirteen hundred hours; sand interior; new green paintwork; price of £3.5 million.

After washing up the dishes, he put on an Amy Winehouse CD, switching straight to 'Back to Black', the haunting melody raw to the bone, drank another bottle of beer, and went to bed, his dreams filled with dark woods and mountains, of lunar landscapes and vivid sunsets, and two lads on the run.

The next morning, Tallis rose early, hung around the bungalow for a couple of hours, hoping to hear from Viva. With no word he was soon out in the open, heading down dual carriageways and fast roads, the rear spoiler automatically rising up out of the Boxster's body like an extra fin, wail and hum of the engine the only music in his ears. It took him a little over an hour to reach his mother's, a modest dwelling in a rural backwater. Since his father's death, he felt less threatened by memories there. With time, he hoped he could create new ones, happy ones, untrammelled by fear and conflict. Changing things around and stamping her own identity on the place, his mum had unwittingly gone some way to displace his troubled past.

Her eyes lit up with pleasure at his sudden arrival. That, too, signalled subtle transformation. There had been a time when she hadn't been able to abide surprises, or shocks as she'd referred to them. But that had been when his father was alive.

'Paul, I wasn't expecting you.' She smiled, wiping the backs of her hands on an apron, leaving a trail of floury marks.

'I'm not holding you up, am I?' he said, stepping over the threshold, the smell of newly baked cakes scenting the hallway.

'Don't be silly. Of course not. Just doing a bit of baking for the church bring and buy,' she said, trotting down the corridor, indicating for him to follow her into the kitchen. 'Put the kettle on while I finish these pies.'

'Tea or coffee?' he said, watching as she intently rolled out pastry to a fine, even depth.

'Second thoughts, coffee.'

Without a word, Tallis reached for a saucepan, filled it with milk. In posh circles this would be called a latte. His mother had been drinking latte for years, only she'd never realised it before.

'So what brings you out here?' she said, slicing off excess pastry from a pie lid and expertly crimping the edges.

'No reason.'

She gave him a short, sharp smile, her eyelids creasing. 'Paul Tallis, you always have a reason for doing things.'

'Well, I…'

'Come on, spit it out,' she said, elbowing him out of the way and reaching for the kitchen tap to wash her hands.

Tallis grinned and sat down. 'Graham Darke, remember him?'

'I'll say,' she said. 'The naughtiest boy in the village, not that you could blame the lad, what with that family of his.'

'They weren't that bad,' Tallis said, getting up to rescue the milk before it boiled over. He poured it out into two cups.

'I'm surprised they didn't all go down with tuberculosis or something, living the way they did,' she said, drying her hands. 'Much against your father's wishes, you two were as thick as thieves.'

They had been. There was nothing like it on earth, that kinship, that heady sense of doing anything to protect another, lying, ducking and diving. They'd been like blood brothers.

'Anyway, what about him?' his mother said, stretching over for the sugar.

'Do you know why he left?' Tallis had heard many stories as to why Graham had been there one minute, gone the next. At the sudden disappearance of his friend, Tallis had felt as if someone had hacked off his arm. In total shock, he hadn't consciously paid it close attention. To protect his sensibilities, he'd forgotten about Graham, willed him away, blanked him from his memory bank. Until now.

'Thought that was obvious. His mother was having another baby. Different father again,' his mother sniffed, disapproving. 'When Graham's real dad turned up, a lorry driver, I believe, Graham decided to join him on the road. It was too good an opportunity to miss. Dare say the lad needed an escape.'

Had it really been so simple? Tallis wondered. Had Graham been torn or even given him a second thought? 'And that's the last you ever heard?' Stupid question. It wasn't as if his mother was in touch with Graham's mother. She never had been.

'Yes, why do you ask?'

'No reason.' Tallis dipped his head slightly, flushing at his mother's amused expression.

The sky was a pale wash of blue, clouds tinged silver. It was noon, a bitter wind blowing, and he was sitting outside the primary school where he and Graham first met; his secondary school had been demolished and amalgamated with another as part of the New World Order. He believed the land on which once it stood had been used for a new housing development. Sitting there, engine running, heater on full blow, it was easy to imagine a ten-year-old Graham, scruffy in a tattered uniform handed down from at least three siblings, roaring round the playground, jumping off the walls, the original free-runner. Graham, Tallis remembered, had taken school meals. It had been the only difference between them and Graham had hated it, not because he wasn't hungry—he was—but because it made him different. And yet Graham *was* different.

They'd been like brothers-in-arms, setting things to rights, fighting all the small injustices of the world, or their world, to be more specific. And they really didn't care too much how they went about it. Always getting the blame for crimes they didn't commit, they didn't have much to lose. When a particularly aggressive games teacher, a bloke called Sadler, forced Graham to continue a cross-country run after Graham had twisted his ankle, vengeance was sworn. A few weeks later, Tallis and Graham hitched a lift to Sadler's house and, under the cloak of darkness, poured sugar into the fuel tank of Sadler's pride and joy, a Morgan motorcar, screwing up the engine. As Graham once quoted, 'If the cap fits, might as well wear it.' And was this what Graham was doing now? Running with the wolves, making a stand for freedom, fighting back on behalf of the underdog?

Once, Tallis remembered, Graham had talked about becoming a sniper.

'What, shooting people?' Tallis said.

They were about thirteen years old, sitting on the wall in the pub car park.

'Only bad people,' Graham said.

'Yeah, I know but…'

'Have to join the army, and that. Get myself properly trained.'

Tallis didn't say anything. It suddenly dawned on him that change was on the horizon, that they'd end up going their separate ways. He didn't like it.

'Got to be a good shot, like. Do you think you see their faces?' Graham frowned quizzically, turning to Tallis.

'I don't know.' What a horrible idea, he thought, not realising that he was destined to become a firearms officer. 'Can't you shoot them from a long way away?' His dad sometimes went out shooting, taking Dan, his elder brother, with him. They mostly shot rabbits and pheasants; taking pot shots they called it.

'Dunno,' Graham said, arching a bony shoulder.

'Bit like being a hunter, I s'pose,' Tallis said gloomily.

When Tallis's dad gave him a leathering, it was Graham Tallis fled to. Only with Graham could he let off steam, scream at the sky and plot revenge against his father—which was never taken. Graham was more of a brother to him than Dan. Graham was his mentor and mate. When Graham left, Tallis had his first unpleasant taste of betrayal.

Tallis headed back to the car, his phone feeling like a dead weight in his pocket. If Viva didn't get back to him soon with favourable news, he'd have no choice but to do Asim's bidding and travel to London and talk to someone who might speak the language but did not understand the power play, the political dynamics, the nuances of history that only a Chechen would understand. Lena, to his mind, was a far better bet.

Taking a big detour, he crossed over into Worcestershire, the Porsche letting rip, and headed for the small town of Upton-upon-Severn, a casualty of flooding some years before. Parking in the free car park on the periphery, he doubled back down the main street and went to a shop that sold maps. There was a slightly fusty smell, not unpleasant, as he walked inside. A map of Moscow was easy to acquire. Chechyna took a little more locating. The sales assistant spread the map out before him. His eye immediately went to the strange-sounding names, the range of mountains, the highest by 10,000 metres being Mount

Elbrus with its twin peaks. Chechnya, he saw, was a thousand miles south of Moscow straddled between the Black and Caspian seas. Reaching for his wallet, he wondered where Darke was exactly.

By the time Tallis returned home, he'd already had two missed calls from Asim on his mobile phone and it was getting dark. Wondering for how long he could keep his phone switched off and Asim at bay, he let himself in, the silence inside swallowing him whole. Unable to settle, he changed and went for a run, the illuminated strip on his sweatshirt glittering under the yellow glare of streetlights. A mile and circuit later, he returned home. More silence and still no word from Viva.

After an evening spent poring over his newly acquired maps, he decided to turn in. The call he'd been waiting all day for eventually came through as he was switching off the light.

'Lena says she'll talk to you.'

'Brilliant. When?'

'Now.'

Tallis glanced at his watch: 11:40 p.m. He was already getting out of bed. 'Be there in ten minutes.'

Rasu let Tallis in with a short smile and guided him through to the living room. With an imperious air, Lena Maisakov told Tallis to sit down. She, on the other hand, preferred to stand. Rather than him vetting her, Tallis thought, she was vetting him. He said nothing other than thanking her for seeing him, which she dismissed with a small wave of a bony hand.

Tallis did as he was told and sank into the nearby sofa. It gave him time to view what he was up against. He took some moments to study the razor-sharp cheekbones, dark, sallow skin and eyes like burning flames. Her black hair was tied tightly back from her face, giving her a haggard appearance. Gold hoop earrings dangled from both ears. She was wearing an old olive-green sweater and a long skirt, worn brown ankle boots on her feet. She was thin, very thin. It was impossible to tell her age. She could have been forty-five or fifty-five. She was, in fact, thirty-nine. He also found out that she'd once been a schoolteacher.

Viva charged the small fire with wood and coal and exchanged a wary glance with Tallis. Rasu had sensibly left them to it, said he'd go to the kitchen to make coffee.

'Why do you wish to learn my language?' Lena asked, eyes burning into his.

'Not learn exactly, more brushing up.' His Chechen was almost two decades out of date. Any other language would probably have evolved in that time, incorporated modern colloquialisms. With a culture entrenched in the past, Tallis wasn't sure if it applied.

'Learn, or brush up, as you say, my question remains the same.'

Tallis gave Lena the same answer he'd given Viva and Rasu: that he was going to help the people there.

Lena briefly smiled, a curt tilt of her lips. 'Help?'

'Assist,' he said, trying to sound vague but realising that she'd probably consider him a mercenary.

'You're clearly an idealist, Mr Tallis.'

'I'm not, actually.' He was polite but he hadn't expected philosophical debate, let alone this early in the conversation.

'Only idealists stay in Chechnya,' Lena said, unsmiling.

'I'm a realist.'

'That I doubt. If you were a realist, you would know that your mission is doomed to failure.'

'I think I'm the best judge of that.' Tallis kept his voice neutral, his expression unreadable. It was a trick he'd perfected years ago when questioning a criminal. They could be going off the deep end, cursing him with expletives, and still he retained a mask of cold professionalism.

'You're wrong,' Lena said.

'Fine, I'm wrong,' he said evenly.

'You cannot afford a mistake.' Her tone was biting.

He met and held Lena's gaze. He really didn't warm to this woman even if her English was impeccable. 'Touched as I am by your concern for my welfare, Mrs Maisakov, are you prepared to help me, or not?' He ignored Viva's warning expression.

Like a practised politician, Lena interposed a question of her own. 'Are you a Muslim?'

'No.'

'Are you familiar with the Koran?'

'No.'

'So you know nothing of our culture.'

'That's why I'm here,' he said.

'What makes you think you can learn?'

'Because I have a gift with languages and I'm a willing pupil. More than that,' he said, eyeing her, 'I'm determined.'

'You're very sure of yourself, Mr Tallis.'

And you're bloody impossible, Tallis thought, calmly standing up, heading for the door. 'Thanks, Viva. Sorry I've wasted your time. Give my warmest regards to Rasu. Goodnight, Mrs Maisakov.'

'Surely—' Viva began, spreading her hands.

'If you run away so easily from a woman,' Lena cut in, a mocking note in her voice, 'I rate your chances of survival as zero.'

Tallis whipped round on his heel. In spite of Lena's sallow skin there were two high spots of colour on her cheeks. His attempt to leave had been a calculated move that had paid off: Lena had called his bluff. Time to play his ace. 'You know,' he said, 'there's no real difference between Chechens and Russians. No difference at all. You're all proud, stubborn as mules, all hell bent on knocking the shit out of each other. And for what?'

Viva opened her mouth in protest but Tallis wasn't done yet.

'Because you're both full of pride. You care more about so-called honour than a future for the next generation.'

'Paul, I…' Viva began helplessly.

'You think yours is a unique situation,' Tallis said, looking straight at Lena who stood rooted, colour bleeding from her cheeks, 'but it isn't, and one day, like it or not, you'll call a truce, sit down at a table and do a deal with the devil, if that's the way you want to see it, because your children are dying and your young men are being butchered in their beds. And then you'll live alongside one another in what passes for peace.'

Lena met and held his gaze, her stare incinerating. The atmosphere was electric, like Tallis had thrown a grenade into the room and everyone was waiting for it to stop rolling and explode. Rasu walked in with a tray, caught the vibe, and walked back out again.

'Do you know our history, Mr Tallis?' Lena said quietly, the challenge diminished if not exactly absent from her voice.

'No,' Tallis said softly. 'Why don't you tell me about it?'

And with that they both sat down.

It was like sitting around a campfire in the woods again, Tallis thought, legs spread out. He was listening to Lena's strangely hypnotic voice, and watching the last dying embers. A sucker for history, he was transfixed as Lena guided him through two hundred years of conflict, starting with Catherine the Great's expansion plans for the Russian Empire and the fierce resistance with which her Russian army was met. Later on, in the next century, another spat broke out that lasted thirty years, thirty years of trying to tame the mountain people, thirty years of savagery on both sides. Then came the greatest betrayal of all, Lena told him darkly. During the Nazi invasion, thousands of Chechens fought the Germans. However, a small, independent minority decided to take the opportunity to lay claim to independence. As the war came to a close, Stalin's revenge knew no bounds. Entire villages were razed to the ground and half a million Chechens were displaced and deported.

'And a nation of outcasts was created,' Viva said sombre. She was curled up like a cat on the floor in front of the fire.

'It is the way with us,' Lena said sadly. 'Many are punished for the sins of the few. Most Russians believe that Chechens bear collective responsibility for the actions of individual criminals.'

Tallis leant towards her. The firelight was playing on her hair, colouring it red, catching her face, throwing a ghostly hue over her features and revealing a level of pain.

'In the early 1990s, there was a move towards national independence,' Lena said in a way that neither seemed to support nor oppose it. 'By then the Russian regime was already in some turmoil. A decision was made, some say by the FSB, the newly branded KGB, to return to old values. In order to validate that return, and get the Russian people onside, it was necessary to deliberately inflame the criminal situation in Russia.

Chechnya was the first casualty of that decision. By 1994, we were at war.

'The Russians were unsuccessful. Fighting subsided but by now the warlords, some of them fundamentalist, had taken to the stage. You have to understand, Mr Tallis,' Lena said, her shoulders bowed with anxiety, 'most ordinary Chechens couldn't have cared less about politics, or about gangsters and the warlords of this world—we simply wanted security, to earn a decent wage and be able to put food on the table for our families, to live in peace. It was not to be,' she said sadly.

'In September 1999, a series of explosions ripped through Moscow. It was rumoured that the FSB were behind them.'

'What, they killed their own people?' Tallis said, aghast.

'A necessary evil,' Lena said, a thin smile on thin lips. 'They blamed Chechen terrorists. It was the excuse to go to war again.'

'Hold on,' Tallis cut in, 'Who would give the order for something like that?'

'Ivanov,' Viva said, her voice still and small from the fireside.

Again Tallis remembered Asim's assertion that the prime minister was top of the hit list. He felt cold fear, bright and metallic.

Lena nodded. 'The second war was bloodier than the first. I suppose you can say Ivanov won.'

Nobody spoke for some minutes.

'Would you choose to go back?' Tallis said.

'To what? There will never be freedom.'

'Never?'

'A generation of young people, sons and daughters who have lost fathers and brothers and families have grown up hating the Russians.' Her voice tailed off. An eerie silence settled on the room again like a shroud.

'Tell me what happened at Aldy, Lena,' Tallis said finally. He could almost hear his breathing, and the sound of blood trickling through his veins. Viva stirred. Lena pinched the bridge of her nose, sat very straight in the chair, shoulders back, gathering herself.

'They came on the fifth of February, 2000,' she began, her voice strangely detached. 'Before the first war I taught at School No. 39. There were many children there. By the end of 2000 there was no school, and no children and our houses had been reduced to rubble. There was nothing to do except collect the dead and prepare them for burial.

'By now, the fighters had abandoned Grozny and gone up into the mountains so there was nothing left to fight for but still the Russians shelled the village. You couldn't sleep for the sound of bombs being dropped, missiles being fired, mortars howling like rabid dogs. It got so bad that some of the men of the village decided to take action. Carrying sheets as flags of surrender, they went to plead with the Russian commander leading the attack. They wanted to reassure him that they were not harbouring terrorists, as the Russians claimed. But it was no good,' she said, her skin parched and drawn, so that she resembled an old woman.

'Shots were fired from the Russian positions. The first villager killed was an ethnic Russian.' A bitter smile flashed across her lips at the lunacy of it all. 'The next day a delegation of troops arrived, youngsters. You couldn't help but feel sorry for them. They were dirty, hungry and exhausted. Some of them had running sores on their hands and, yes, like us, they were frightened. They told us that if we knew what was good for us we should leave. 'Don't hide in your cellars,' they warned. They said that others were coming, bad men, they said.

'But where were we to go?' Lena spread her hands, appealing to Tallis. 'It was February. It was cold. There was snow on the mountains. We hadn't eaten, or slept properly for months. So we stayed,' she said heavily. 'Seven hundred of us.'

'The next morning was thick with mist. We crept out of our cellars and basements to pray and were greeted by the strangest thing, something we hadn't heard in years.' She paused, raising a hand, pointing an index finger to the ceiling. 'Silence,' she whispered.

'At first, we thought this was a good sign. We thought they had listened to our plea. Some of the men set about making running repairs to homes damaged by the shelling. Myself, I was trying to melt ice to boil water. That's when they came for us. That's when the mist proved a friend to me, an enemy to others.

'I heard them before I saw them,' Lena said, her voice wavering. 'I ran back to the house, grabbed Asya, my little girl, and we ran for our lives, and kept on running. Within minutes soldiers and armoured vehicles and trucks surrounded the village. If you hadn't already got out, you were finished. The place was sealed off. A few managed to escape with me and together we fled to higher ground. Each time we stopped to rest, we…'

Lena stopped, her mouth sagging, eyes bruised and wide with remembered horror, the skin underneath blue in colour. She put the heels of her hands to her eyes. Viva got up to comfort her but Lena shrugged her off. With the same iron will that had aided her survival, she moved her hands away, cleared her throat and battled on.

'The soldiers, shaven-headed, bare-chested, tattooed, they came with Kalashnikovs and hunting knives. They came for sport,' she said, with a sudden burst of anger. 'We threw ourselves to the ground, covered our ears against the sound of shots and screams until we could bear it no longer. You understand,' she said, eyes perilous and unfathomable, 'we had to watch, to bear witness so that others would know what was done that day.

'We saw men we'd grown up with taken out and killed, and they were the lucky ones, believe me. We watched as grenades were hurled into homes, the doors barricaded so that there was no escape. We saw women and children lined up against walls. We saw young girls raped, old men and the simple-minded shot in the face, their passports and papers clutched worthlessly in their hands. Then came fire. At first we saw only flames then vast plumes of smoke until the cold winter air was black and acrid with the stench of heat and burning flesh. It was late afternoon before the soldiers left. And still there were screams, the screams of women who'd lost husbands and children, children who'd lost parents, neighbours who'd lost friends.

'Afterwards, the government called it a necessary evil, a *zachistka*.' Tallis was familiar with the word. It meant clear-up operation, a polite way of saying ethnic cleansing. 'But it was a lie,' Lena said, her shadowed eyes filling with tears.

'And you and your little girl?' Viva's voice was soft, hesitant. Tallis realised that even Viva had not heard this story before, in all its vivid, tragic detail.

'Asya stepped on a mine in the mountains. My little girl died.'

CHAPTER FIVE

Outside Moscow State University
Friday morning: 8.00 a.m. Moscow time

PROFESSOR ALEXANDER Tertz was taking a stroll before lectures and smoking his second cigarette of the day. It had suddenly turned exceptionally mild for the time of year but it was of little consolation to him. He preferred bright sunshine to unremitting grey. And, my God, was it grey. Even the trees in the park looked fed up.

He inhaled, drawing the smoke deep into his lungs, enjoying this small, vital pleasure, and returned to a favourite grievance. How could it be that university lecturers, revered by international peers abroad, remained unappreciated at home? As a teacher of economics, he had no status and his government-paid salary was lousy. It was a scandal that Russia's new economy did not include the likes of him.

'You should have gone into politics,' Galina complained in a rare, talkative moment. Since his return from the war, his wife could hardly bring herself to look him in the eye let alone speak to him.

She was right, of course, Tertz thought, narrowing his vision against a thin stream of smoke. Politics was the natural home for retired senior soldiers—if one could grease enough palms.

He walked on, feeling a spit of rain against his face, and wished he'd brought an umbrella. In the distance he saw a handsome-looking couple walking a Rottweiler, a tall imposing dark-haired fellow and a petite blonde-haired beauty with the palest skin. There were also two figures jogging, an absurd occupation to his mind. The fact it might be considered pleasurable was equally bizarre to him. These days his only solace was in vodka, which he poured liberally each night. Only then could he escape, dream, and reminisce about the old times.

He had worked at Chernokozovo, a prison turned filtration camp. Many, many Chechens passed through its doors. They were brought in chiefly by the OMON, *Otryad Militsii Osobogo Naznacheniya* (police unit of special designation) or the riot police, as they were known. Some prisoners he could do business with, buying and selling, but most were snivelling wrecks who were only good for venting one's spleen on or exercising one's desires. He reckoned that was why Galina steadfastly refused his advances. She could spot perversion and betrayal in his eyes.

Sometimes the guys from the FSB would show up, sociopaths the lot of them, Tertz thought with disgust. They'd arrive with their cheap leather jackets, their superior manner and tell him how it was going down. He had no choice but to turn a blind eye. And what did it matter to him if they liked nothing better than to film him and his men gang-raping a *dukh*? Luckily, there was a timber mill nearby, handy for the disposal of bodies, and essential for covering up evidence. Apparently, the resulting videos were distributed to the boys at the front, to toughen them up, put fire in their bellies.

One of the joggers pounded slowly towards him, hood up against the wind and rain, feet hitting the ground with a heavy tread, disturbing Tertz's thoughts. Tertz went to sidestep but they both moved foolishly in the same direction, the jogger stumbling heavily into him. 'For Christ's sake,' Tertz barked, feeling a sharp stab of pain in his thigh.

The jogger ran on without regard. Tertz scowled, rubbed his leg, which hurt like hell. No doubt he'd have a nice bruise, he thought, glancing up at the statue of Lenin, and silently saluted his hero.

Two minutes later Tertz started to feel unwell. Heat was spreading through his body like an uncontrollable forest fire. Insides loose, a terrible nausea gripped him, vice-like, and his bruised leg was causing him considerable and an unusual amount of pain. By the time he reached the university building, his vision was blurred and he was running a fever. As he crashed through the doors, yelling for help, he had no idea of the lingering suffering that would precede his death three days later.

Tallis climbed blearily into bed around five that morning. Hardened to tales of tragedy, he felt shaken to the core by Lena's story. Who could blame Darke if he'd gone native and joined the armed struggle? Suddenly, the intelligence handed to Fazan and passed on to Asim seemed credible, he thought as he closed his eyes and drifted off to sleep.

Three hours later, Tallis's alarm sounded. He got up and called Asim.

'We're on,' he said, relaying the arrangements. He'd no idea why Lena had agreed to the plan. As a devout Muslim woman, it must have gone seriously against the grain. Perhaps it was because she had nowhere else to go, because she was desperate, because she hoped that Tallis was genuine in his desire to help her people. Whatever her motivation, that evening Tallis was to acquire a house guest. He just hoped Immigration didn't turn up and rudely cut short his language lessons. He mentioned his worry to Asim. 'Think you can pull strings?'

'No way.' Not after the previous dust-up with Immigration two years before, Tallis remembered. 'You'll have to keep her hidden and pray they move at their usual snail-like pace,' Asim added.

'But if they get the bit between their teeth, there's no

stopping them. She could be put on the next flight home.'
The Home Office, as Viva had once pointed out to him,
was not known for its bleeding heart. And what was one
lone foreign female against an entire organisation?

'Let's hope not, then,' Asim said, breezy. 'By the
way, I'm having an up-to-date photograph of Graham
Darke couriered to you.'

Tallis thanked him. It wasn't simply a practical con-
sideration. He was genuinely intrigued to see how
Graham had turned out.

'Other than the spectre of the immigration authorities, you feel reasonably comfortable with the set-
up?' Asim said.

'Fine.'

'And you've teamed up with Virginia Dodge at
Tiger?'

'Everything's in place.'

'Good. Keep up the pressure. We need to get you out
to Russia soon as.'

Tallis spent the next two hours clearing out the spare
room and cleaning the bungalow, preparing for Lena's
visit. The courier arrived as he was depositing another
bin liner of junk into a dustbin. He took the envelope,
signed for it and went back indoors.

It was a head-and-shoulders shot, front on. Like most
mug shots, it wasn't particularly flattering but he could
definitely identify traits of the boy inside the man.
Graham had retained the same well-defined cheekbones and jaw line, although they had broadened out a

little with age. The thin lips and aquiline nose were un-altered, his colouring a couple of tones darker, but it was the expression in his eyes that troubled Tallis. The mischief had translated to something more cold and dangerous. It seemed as if hostile and unbridled energy lay at the core of the man. Tallis looked on the back of the photograph. It was dated July 2005.

Slipping it back into the envelope, he put it with the rest of what he called his 'gear to go', a rucksack of es-sentials should he be suddenly asked to drop everything and be somewhere else at short notice. After that he returned to the kitchen and wondered what to cook for his guest that evening. It occurred to him that half his staple diet would be unsuitable to Lena and set about chucking out every pork product he could lay his hands on, including several packs of ham and bacon. Throw-ing everything into a bag, he nipped round to his next-door neighbours. Jimmy, as Tallis had nicknamed him, opened the door. Seventeen years of attitude and bel-ligerence stood before him.

'Oh, it's you,' Jimmy said, half of him playing the cool guy, the other half, Tallis suspected, wetting himself. Thanks to Tallis, Jimmy had narrowly missed being on the receiving end of a gun the previous year.

'Well, hello, and it's lovely to see you, too.' Tallis flicked a smile. 'Here,' he said, 'thought you'd like this.'

Jimmy scowled, took the bag and opened it. 'Bacon?'

'That's what it's usually called. What did you expect—used tenners?'

Jimmy cast him a piteous look.

'Knowing your fondness for bacon butties, thought you might enjoy it.'

Jimmy bent his head, sniffed the contents warily. 'Is it alright, like? I mean it's not past its sell-by date, or nothing?'

'It's fine,' Tallis said. 'I've got a friend coming to stay. She doesn't eat pork. She's a…oh, never mind, long story.'

'Normally are with you,' Jimmy said, closing the bag. 'I'll give it to my mum. Nice motor,' he said, making to go back inside. 'No wonder you look smug as fuck,' he added, shutting the door.

Tallis was returning from an emergency trip to the shops for fresh provisions when his mobile went. It was Ginny.

'Hi, handsome.'

'You sound in a good mood.'

'I'm always in a good mood,' she chirped back. 'You'll be pleased to know that our Mr Kumarin has expressed an interest. I gave him your number. You should be hearing from him any moment.'

'Brilliant. What's the drill?'

'Suggest he gets a taxi from Heathrow to White Waltham Grass—Heathrow's far too expensive. You can meet him there and fly him back to Shobdon. Should take you about forty minutes. Then Kumarin can check the records, talk to the mechanics, and check out the helicopter for himself.'

'Fantastic. Thanks, Ginny.'

'You'll let me know how you get on?'

'Will do.'

'Good luck.'

Kumarin's call came through in the middle of Tallis stowing the shopping. Kicking a cupboard door shut and lobbing a packet of cornflakes onto a worktop, Tallis reached for his phone.

'Mr Tallis?' Kumarin said, in thick, heavily accented English.

'A pleasure to talk to you. Miss Dodge has filled me in on the details. How can I help?'

'My client wishes me to travel to Shobdon to inspect the helicopter.'

'Great news. When would you like to come?'

'Next week. Friday would be good for me.'

'Perfect. I'll clear my diary.' He told Kumarin about the suggested transport arrangements at the UK end.

'This is good,' Kumarin said. 'I will let you know the time of my arrival then you fix the cab for me.'

'No problem. Look forward to hearing from you.'

Tallis clicked off and punched in Ginny's number. It went straight to voicemail. He left a quick message, keeping her in the loop, and suggested that they run through his presentation one last time. He suggested Monday morning for a meet.

That afternoon, he spent studying maps, locating

Borzoi in Chechnya, tracking some kind of route from Grozny, the capital.

On the hour, he switched on the radio, tuning into the news. Chechnya and the fast disintegrating situation there ranked as the number one news item.

By the time Viva dropped Lena off, Tallis felt unaccountably nervous. Other than the off mate kipping for the night, usually after too much to drink, he'd never had someone stay before, not even Belle. Lena stood in the idle of the room, staring with wary eyes. She looked so small and lonely, he thought, nothing like the arrogant and feisty woman of their first meeting.

'Where's the rest of your stuff?'

She swung the rucksack from off her shoulders and onto the floor. 'This is it.'

He stared. *That was her life?*

'You'll be alright, then,' Viva said, her expression dubious.

''Course.' Tallis winced at the hearty sound of his own voice, which was way too loud. Lena, seemingly rooted to the spot, nodded.

'If there's anything you need,' Viva said, touching Lena's arm, 'call me. Mind how you go,' she muttered to Tallis, more warning than concern as she left.

'Right.' Tallis turned to Lena. 'Guided tour.' He took her through the sitting room and opened the door to what would be her bedroom for the next few weeks. He hadn't thought beyond that, which, he guessed, was pretty stupid of him.

Lena walked inside and touched the bed gingerly, then ran her roughened fingers lightly over the dressing table left to him by his grandmother. For an odd moment he thought she was checking for dust, but the gesture seemed too reverent. At a loss, he indicated the en suite bathroom. 'It's only a shower. This is how you work—' He broke off, knowing instantly from the misted look in her eyes that something was wrong. 'Is it alright?' he said anxiously. 'If you like, we can swap rooms. I can easily—'

'No,' she said, shaking her head, swiping at her face with angry hands. 'It is very nice and you are very kind.'

'It's nothing,' Tallis said, bewildered. Dear God, he'd never understand women as long as he lived.

'In Moscow,' Lena said slowly, 'there are men who live in secret cities, deep in the forest, in *cotedgi*, huge houses of marble and gold, while my people are forced to live in the grimmest places—in industrial zones, beneath power lines, in slums. They have lost everything, you see, a place to live, jobs, even the most menial form of employment, and there is no social welfare. Last, they lose their dignity. It is a slow way to die, Mr Tallis. This,' she said, surveying the room with wonderment, 'makes me feel guilty.'

Tallis shook his head sadly then smiled. 'Feel lucky instead.'

At Lena's insistence, and after a degree of wrangling, they agreed house rules: after their first meal together only Chechen would be spoken at home, and the housework and cooking was to be divided between them. Tallis was unhappy.

'You're my guest.'

'I'm your teacher,' Lena countered. The inference was that he would do as she said.

Tallis looked up, noticed the shine in her eyes, the hidden smile. He laughed and caved in. What was the point of argument? Her mind was clearly made up. Between Lena and Ginny, he felt surrounded by bossy women.

Dinner was French onion soup and lamb tagine. Tallis offered a small prayer of thanks to Nigella Lawson.

'What would you eat at home?' Tallis said, keen to put Lena at ease.

'We eat lamb, beef, goat maybe. We grow fruit and bottle it for cakes and desserts and cordials. We eat cheese and drink milk. I had a small orchard of apple trees before the war broke out. We had a cow but she was killed by a shell.'

Tallis nodded in understanding. When a person experienced tragedy firsthand, it became the only context in which to place events, but he didn't want to get too personal. Not tonight.

'And you,' Lena said. 'Have you always lived here?'

Tallis told how he'd acquired the bungalow. He told her about his life, all the simple, easily understood bits like family, work (heavily edited). To his ears, it sounded like someone else's story.

'And there is no woman in your life?' It was asked in a very fact-gathering way. Not for one moment did Tallis have the sense that this was either a chat-up line or naked intrusion.

'No.'

'She left you?'

'She died.'

She had eaten slowly and sparingly, like a bird.

'How would you say Chechens are best defined?' Nobody said he couldn't discuss Chechen culture and national psyche over the coffee. Besides, he wanted to fit as much in as he could before the hard graft started.

Lena put down her cup and thought for a moment. 'Courageous, fearless, proud and vengeful. It is a point of honour to avenge the dead of one's family. If you do not, you are shamed.'

Pretty much fitted with what he already knew.

'And, believe me, we have long memories.' She paused, as if sensing that she was perhaps not painting her people in an attractive light. 'But they are the best people in the world, too,' she said, sudden passion in her eyes. 'They are the most hospitable. Walk into a Chechen's home and you will be given everything that is theirs, they will guard you with their very lives, and we have a strong tradition of looking after our old people. Unlike the Russians, who hide their elderly in homes, or leave them to rot, we take care of the most vulnerable in our society. It is not unusual for a family to take in orphans or the simple-minded.'

Tallis nodded his approval. 'And how in general should I behave towards a Chechen?'

'Show respect and be servile.'

Tallis pulled a face. He didn't do servile.

Lena leant across the table, her dark eyes trapped by candlelight. 'You realise you will never be trusted.'

'I can earn it.'

Lena shook her head. 'You are not one of us. You will always be treated with suspicion.'

'Does that mean you don't trust me?'

'This is different,' Lena said, picking up her cup again, tilting it to her lips.

What she meant was that, in a position of weakness, she had no choice. Tallis waited a beat. 'How can I demonstrate my worth?'

Lena met Tallis's eye, inclined her small dark head. 'Prove yourself in battle.'

He found it odd to share his home with another, particularly a stranger, particularly a woman. He felt as if he'd lost his normal spatial awareness. Overnight he'd become clumsy. He couldn't even calm his nerves with a drink for fear of causing offence. The bungalow seemed to breathe differently with Lena in it, he thought, lying in bed, face staring up at the ceiling, Lena yards away in the room next door.

The entire weekend was spent steeped in speaking

Chechen. His voice was his new instrument—contorting it, creating with it, practising, mimicking, and tuning it to Lena's. He'd forgotten the sheer mental agility required for remembering a dictionary's worth of vocabulary. Although Lena was an excellent teacher, by Monday morning he felt stewed, glad to escape to Shobdon.

Hardly out of the drive, his mobile rang. It was Kumarin. Tallis glanced at his watch: nine here, noon in Moscow.

'My plans have changed,' Kumarin said lugubriously.

Fuck, Tallis thought. He said nothing, decided to let the other bloke do the talking.

'I intend to fly to London on Saturday.'

'This Saturday?' Tallis looked at his watch, worked out the date. Marvellous, he thought.

'That is correct.'

'I'll arrange transport.'

'And you will confirm?'

'I will.'

Tallis closed the phone, tapped his fingers on the dash. He looked back at the bungalow and saw Lena's anxious face at the window. He waved, smiled, stuck the car in gear and tore off up the road to Shobdon.

Ginny dropped two frisky kisses either side of his cheeks in greeting. She'd done something freaky with her make-up, creating a vampish look that reeked of artifice. He couldn't decide whether he liked it or not.

'A minor alteration, Kumarin's arriving on Saturday.'

'I'm not surprised.'

'No?'

'Par for the course, in my experience. Their schedules always change.'

'Having a laugh?'

'I wouldn't put it quite like that,' she said, delicately lifting an eyebrow. *You have a lot to learn,* her expression seemed to say.

They went straight to the meeting room. While Ginny made coffee, Tallis ran through his notes. Apparently, Russians liked long and detailed presentations, including a history of the subject.

'Remember,' Ginny said, plonking a mug of instant in front of him, 'this is a sounding-out exercise on Kumarin's part. The whole point of the initial meeting is to determine whether he thinks you're credible or not.'

'He's not going to travel all this way just to see whether he likes the look of me.'

'He hasn't travelled here yet. He may well change his mind again.'

'Thanks for the vote of confidence.'

Ginny leant forward, rested her chin in her hand and grinned. 'Off you go with your presentation. I'll pretend to be Kumarin.'

Tallis started with a brief word of welcome, a potted history of Tiger Helicopters, ethos and work practices, and then launched into the history of the Agusta 109, describing it as a multi-role helicopter developed by Agusta Westland in Italy. He ran through its various versions, pointing out that it was originally developed as an ambulance and rescue helicopter for use in Switzerland. After moving on to a complicated discourse on technical specifications, he pointed out its practical applications and versatility.

'Naturally, we'll be in the hangar and I'll have the machine in front of me so I can point out the specific advantages,' Tallis added as an aside.

'Pretty good,' Ginny said, when he'd finished. 'Remember, when you pick up Kumarin, he'll want to be schmoozed. Russians love to chat, to get to know you, to talk about anything other than business.'

'With or without vodka?'

She broke into a smile. 'Without for you,' she said. 'No fun flying when you're pissed.'

'Is this the voice of experience talking?'

'It is, and you don't want to know.' She flicked a skittish smile. 'As for Kumarin, there aren't many Russians who turn down the offer of vodka.'

'Could make things tricky for me.'

'Not if you tell him you're an alcoholic. It's about the only way you can refuse a drink without causing offence.'

'How come you know so much about it?'

'Stuff I've picked up.' She shrugged, wrinkling her nose. 'Something else, the man Kumarin is negotiating for.'

'What about him?'

'Remember that all Russian businessmen are Geminis.'

'You don't believe that rubbish, do you?'

'Bet I know what you are,' she said, flirting mercilessly.

'Oh, yeah?' he challenged her.

'Dark-featured, reckless, very secretive, odds on you're a Scorpio.'

'Only reason you know is because you've seen the date of birth on my CV.' He let out a laugh. 'And what the hell's this got to do with our mythical Russian Gemini?'

'Geminis have two faces. Behind every upright executive there's a crook.'

Tallis scratched at an imaginary itch on his chin. 'I'll bear it in mind.'

'What are your plans for the rest of the day?' she said, touching his elbow, steering him towards her office.

Talking Chechen. Studying more maps. Getting into the national zeitgeist. 'Why?'

'You're not supposed to answer my question with another.' Her voice was low, seductive, and she still had her hand on his arm.

'Nothing in particular.' He smiled, more to see what she'd actually say.

'Fancy coming to Wellesbourne for the day?' Wellesbourne was an airfield in Warwickshire. It was fun, friendly and generally a nice place to hang out. Her fingers were unconsciously stroking the weave of his jacket.

'Are you flying there?'

'Uh-huh.'

Tempting. He looked full into her eyes. They had the same unpredictability as a tiger's, he thought. 'Better not,' he said, watching the smile fade from her face. 'Another time, maybe.'

And so he prepared to return to Lena to talk, to repeat, to correct, to learn.

Tuesday and his meeting with Jack Montague, his friend who worked for the Mine Action Coordination Centre, crept up on him with surprising speed, mainly because he was enjoying the cut and thrust of improving his language skills. He liked the sound of Chechen on his tongue, in his voice. Although there were similarities with Russian, it was quite distinct. Sometimes it felt more akin to an Arabic dialect.

He'd already explained to Lena that he had to pop out to see a friend.

'This is good. It will give me time to clean up.'

'Clean up what? The place is fine,' he said, feeling irrationally put out. He didn't welcome Lena going through his cupboards, tearing down his cobwebs, rearranging his stuff. He didn't fancy the intrusion. 'Why don't you read a book or something?'

'You don't want me to clean?' Now it was her turn to look put out.

'No, I don't,' he said as pleasantly as he could, snatching up the keys for the Porsche and making a fast exit.

Tallis drove to Brindleyplace in central Birmingham and parked, the journey to the international and anonymous Hyatt Regency Hotel a short walk away.

Monty was bang on time. Apart from losing a bit more hair on top, he hadn't altered one bit, Tallis thought. Always a snappy dresser, Monty wore a beautifully cut grey pinstripe with a pale pink shirt and iron-coloured silk tie. His shoes shone to army-style perfection. With his dark brown eyes and even features, he was an exceptionally handsome man. Had he been a foot taller, he'd be male model material, Tallis reckoned.

Monty beamed at him and extended a hand, clapping Tallis on the back like an old mate.

They sat in the lounge, ordered coffee and, because Monty was on a time limit, got straight down to business. Monty pulled out a sheaf of papers from his briefcase.

'I've printed out some stuff, but basically the overview is this: Chechnya, in spite of some mine clearance carried out by a humanitarian demining mission in early 2007, and military clearance by deminers from the federal forces to allow for troop movements, the place still contains a large quantity of both mines and IEDs.'

Improvised explosive devices, Tallis thought, remembering the jargon.

'Problem you've got is that both rebels and Soviet forces are responsible for the mayhem: the military predominantly lay anti-personnel mines with the aim of protecting facilities and places like military installations, power plants, communication masts and strategic high ground. The rebels, anywhere they can thwart Soviet forces.'

'I'm assuming you're talking about mines laid in large numbers rather than singly?' Tallis said.

'Yup, the idea is you set off one, you set off a load more. There are three specific types, which I've itemised,' Monty said, pointing at the top sheet. 'You've got your anti-personnel fragmentation mine or stake mine, as we call them. Basically it functions by pressure on a trip wire. They tend to be placed on the surface, either left visible to create a barrier or camouflaged with vegetation.'

'What's the lethal hazard area?'

'About ten metres, but fragmentation can be projected out to a hundred,' Monty said, lifting a cup to his lips and taking a quick gulp of coffee. 'Then you've got your anti-personnel bounding fragmentation mine. Again functioned by tension on a trip wire, or command-detonated by an electrical charge sent to the mine. On initiation, a small charge propels the mine into the air normally to about waist height.'

'Nice,' Tallis said dryly.

'The joker in the pack is that the main charge then sends out fragmentation, increasing the hazard area.'

'How do you identify it?'

'It's normally buried with the fuse mechanism visible above the surface,' Monty said.

'The last type is an anti-personnel blast mine, a PMN. It injures the victim using just the explosive content but it also causes fragmentation from the ground—rocks, earth, stones—resulting in these being driven into the victim by the sheer explosive force.'

'ID?'

'Usually placed on or just below the surface—I've included some pics,' Monty said, pointing at the folder again. 'At depths greater than 40 millimetres, the fuse may be too well protected by the soil to operate reliably.' Let's hope so, Tallis thought. 'Again, it's activated by pressure on the top surface of the mine,' Monty continued. 'Normally by some poor bastard standing on it. Most are intended to cause serious injury rather than kill, although this rather depends on the size of the charge, but a typical AP will destroy a foot or leg and cause multiple lacerations from casing fragments and debris.'

'Lethal for a child, then,' Tallis said, thinking of Lena's daughter.

'Lethal for anyone if you don't get the necessary medical help in time. You could easily bleed to death.' Monty drained his cup, viewed Tallis with watchful eyes. 'None of my business, mate, but are you sure you know what you're getting into?'

Tallis flashed a no-worries smile. Along with his Chechen, his skill for lying had improved enormously.

By midweek he was able to talk with a great deal of fluency. Settled, Lena had lost much of her early reserve. She became cheerful, less intense and on occasions displayed a sense of humour. Against his wishes, she did rather more in the home than he'd intended. Washing curtains and cleaning down paintwork was not his idea of a good time, but it gave Lena purpose so he left it at that. He never made reference to her previous life, to her family and what she'd lost and, so far, they'd only briefly touched on Islam, and that had arisen from her questioning him about his own beliefs.

'Brought up a Catholic,' he said. 'Although I don't follow the faith any more.' Funny how people like him got turned off God because of the terrible things he'd seen while others, like Lena, as a result of their dreadful experiences became more religious. She didn't make a deal of it but he knew that she prayed five times a day, that her only source of reading was the Koran.

Their existence assumed an easy pattern—rise early, talk, eat, talk, shop, talk, walk, more talk, and eat again. Sometimes they would sit in silence, mainly because he was too knackered to crank his brain into gear, and occasionally he'd imagine a knock on the door, officialdom in full flight, the final push from Immigration.

The more she learnt to trust him the less strident her views. In his experience, it was always those most fearful and insecure who bandied about extreme opinions. Having said that, he also discovered that his initial impression of Lena was nearest the mark. A firebrand by nature, it took very little for her to ignite on certain subjects.

'How can you say such a thing?' she demanded, eyes flashing. They were in the kitchen, preparing a meal, or rather Lena was preparing a meal and he was sitting at the kitchen table, drinking coffee, brain working at full tilt.

'I'm simply pointing out that Britain has hardly been accommodating in extraditing certain Russians. It plays both ways, Lena.'

'And do the British government respond by sending hit squads to Moscow?' she said, a withering note in her voice. 'No,' she said, jabbing a kitchen knife in the air to make the point. 'Russian security services have always maintained departments dedicated to assassination.'

No different to former Iraqi hit squads, the Mossad and countless other government-sponsored institutions, Tallis thought, deciding not to pursue it. Never wise to argue with a woman holding a knife in her hand, even if it was ostensibly for the purpose of chopping onions.

It was early Friday night, the evening before he flew to London to collect Kumarin. He'd spent much of the day, when not conversing with Lena, reading up about mines: how to spot them and how to manually clear an area should he be unfortunate enough to find himself in a minefield. The key words were look, feel and prod.

Lena was talking about oil, the reason, she said, for the blackness of the earth in Chechnya, although Tallis suspected it had more to do with humus, an organic constituent of soil.

'You can buy home-refined petrol at any crossroads.

It's big business,' she said. 'Unfortunately, it also attracts criminal gangs.'

'Seems to me anywhere in Chechnya provides a haven for armed thugs.'

Lena conceded with a weary shrug. 'The Russians have a vested interest in exporting criminality to the Caucasus.'

Tallis said nothing. Notwithstanding everything he'd been told, he was starting to tire of the Russians as bad guys argument. Life was never that simple. 'This mission of yours,' she said, a tentative note in her voice. 'You will be leaving soon?'

'Hopefully. But there's no need for you to move out,' he said, in quick response to the unsettled expression in her eyes. 'You can stay as long as—'

'I'm permitted,' she cut in with a tight smile.

'You're welcome to stay was what I meant.'

She nodded again, staring at the hearth, her face thrown into stark relief by the firelight. Features fused in concentration, she was clearly turning something over in her mind. Tallis wondered whether she was remembering her flight through the mountains, the cold and the dark, the gut-churning horror when the mine had exploded and claimed the life of her daughter.

'When you travel, are you flying to Moscow, or will you be going in through the back door?'

She meant through Finland or Estonia or one of the many other borders. It had puzzled Tallis that Asim hadn't ordered him to go straight in, no messing about, but he guessed Asim had his reasons for what seemed to him an elaborate subterfuge. 'I'll be spending some time in Moscow.'

'That's good,' Lena said. She never told him why and Tallis didn't ask. That came later.

CHAPTER SIX

FABULOUS weather, Tallis thought as the helicopter lifted and soared heavenward—bright, crisp sunshine, wind speed light, soft puffy clouds in a watercolour sky. For maximum impact, it had been decided that Tallis would not fly the Agusta to collect Kumarin, but wait and unveil it, *ta-da*, the other end. Instead, he was in the ditzy two-seater Robinson 22. Everything would have been perfect had it not been for the sour-faced, sour-breathing Russian travelling in the passenger seat close beside him. Apart from his typically Slav appearance—short stature, flat rectangular face, washed denim blue eyes—he seemed to defy everything Tallis was told to expect, notably that Russians were friendly and big on chat as a preliminary to getting down to business. From the moment Tallis met Kumarin, he was virtually expressionless and monosyllabic. At first, Tallis thought this was through sheer disappointment—the R22 was a tiny, fun machine but a little crowded for two men, but on the contrary he was assured that the

Robinson was perfectly fine—or that there was some language difficulty, but even a quick burst of Russian elicited a flatline response. For the entire flight back to Shobdon, Tallis was subjected to the silent treatment, his questions answered by either a straight *nyet* or *da*.

Desperate measures, Tallis thought, showing Kumarin into the meeting room and whipping out a bottle of vodka. At once the man's hardened features softened. His mouth actually formed half a smile. Thank Christ for that, Tallis thought, pouring Kumarin a healthy measure, which he tossed back with gusto.

'You're not drinking?' Kumarin said, wiping the back of his hand across his mouth.

'Afraid not,' Tallis said. 'I'm an alcoholic.'

'Me, too,' Kumarin said deadpan, gesturing for Tallis to pour him another. 'So how long have you worked here?' Kumarin said, putting his briefcase on the floor and parking his stocky frame on a chair.

Tallis fed him his cover story and handed him a carefully crafted business card, the flip side displaying Tallis's impressive list of bogus credentials. It had all been carefully scripted in Russian using Cyrillic text. Now that they were on a comfortable footing, largely thanks to Smirnoff, he felt himself relax. A convivial hour later, Kumarin asked to use the *tualet*. Tallis opened the door from the meeting room and indicated the lavatory down the corridor. When Kumarin returned Tallis escorted him downstairs and into the hangar housing the Agusta. At once, the Russian's eyes danced with light. He walked around the helicopter, surveying, one hand on his chin, a gleam in his eye suggesting naked admiration, then opened the pilot doors, and climbed inside.

Contrary to Ginny's advice, Tallis kept his mouth shut, and let the helicopter do the talking. Let Kumarin set the pace. When Kumarin was satisfied, he climbed back out and they returned to the meeting room where the Russian requested the logbook and records. Afterwards, he politely asked to be left in peace. 'I will be some time.'

Tallis read the sub-text. In Russia certain items were three times more expensive to the tourist than to the Russian. Applying that same logic, Kumarin would try and find reasons to bring the price down. 'Can I bring you anything to eat or drink?'

'No, but leave the vodka,' Kumarin said, a sly smile touching his mouth.

Tallis left, shutting the door behind him, and walked down the corridor to Ginny's office, which she shared with one of Tiger's pilots, the man in charge, as she called him.

'No Ginny?' Tallis said.

'Not in today,' the guy said, stretching in his seat, making the creases in his crisp white shirt rustle. 'Got a cold, or something.'

Tallis wondered if Ginny's absence was deliberate, whether it was connected to him giving her the brush-off. No, of course not, he thought. She wasn't like that.

Deciding to catch some fresh air and a sandwich from the tearoom, Tallis bowled down the stairs, slapping straight into Blaine Deverill.

'Just the man,' Deverill said, all smiles. Tallis wasn't sure whether Blaine was a natural fool or one of those exhausting individuals who constantly seek to please—he found the always-happy routine irritating. 'How's that Russian deal of yours shaping up?'

'Still shaping,' Tallis said, making for the exit, Deverill falling into step beside him.

'Heading that way myself. Fancy a coffee and a bite to eat?'

With no escape, other than to hang around the mechanics and drive them crazy, Tallis reluctantly agreed.

'Enjoying it here?' Deverill said, once they'd ordered, taken their drinks and were settled at a table.

'How could I not?' Tallis said, noncommittal.

'Know what you mean. Flying gets under your skin. If you can turn a hobby into work, bloody marvellous.'

'So what do you do when you're not speeding through the skies?' Tallis said, spooning sugar into his mug.

'Bit of this, bit of that,' Deverill said, elliptically. 'I'm an engineer by profession, first-class degree from Caius, Cambridge, for my sins.'

'Right,' Tallis said, feeling seriously cheesed off. This was going to be one hell of a boring coffee break.

'You a university man, Paul?'

Tallis shook his head.

'Worked in industry for many years, but that was after I'd done my stint with the Hereford Gun Club.' A pseudonym for the Special Air Service, Tallis knew.

'Right,' Tallis said, barely listening. A practised liar himself—necessary for the job—he could sniff one out at a hundred paces. And Deverill was telling fibs. Probably never set foot in Cambridge let alone been in the SAS.

'You look like a forces man, if you don't mind my saying,' Deverill said in a nudge-nudge fashion.

'Me? No. Humble plod, that's all. Well, used to be.' That was the other thing about telling convincing lies— it always paid to mix in a pinch of truth.

'That so?' Deverill said. 'Where was your patch?'

'Nowhere very exciting—West Mercia,' Tallis lied. 'Decided to escape after I was left a bit of money.'

'Got you,' Deverill said.

Mercifully, their food arrived, sausage and chips for Deverill, BLT for Tallis. He fell on it, hoping that Deverill would shut up and follow suit. He didn't.

'How do you rate the lovely Miss Dodge?'

'Rate?' Tallis frowned.

Deverill began to laugh, shoulders pumping. 'I didn't mean like that,' Deverill said, wheezing slightly.

'Like what?'

'You know,' he said, rolling his eyes.

'No, I don't,' Tallis said, drinking his coffee.

'She's quite a sharp one, isn't she?'

'If you say so,' Tallis said, noncommittal.

'Not without guile.'

'That right?'

'Razor-sharp brain. Got her wings years ago before women really got into flying.'

Two words to that, Tallis thought: Amy Johnson.

'Asked me out a couple of times,' Deverill continued, droning on.

Here we go, porkie time again. If Ginny Dodge had asked Blaine Deverill out, Tallis reckoned he'd run round the airfield naked. 'We had quite a thing going.' Yeah, yeah, Tallis thought. ''Course we had to cool things, what with her old man showing back up on the scene.'

Tallis made a pantomime of looking at his watch. 'Hell, is that the time? Sorry, I promised my Russian client I'd be back in twenty minutes. See you around, Blaine,' Tallis said, standing up. 'Thanks for the chat. Been interesting.'

For the next two hours, Tallis went to ground, Kumarin finally emerging half an hour before they were due to fly back to White Waltham. Tallis wondered if it was a tactical move. On the other hand, it would be Kumarin who missed his flight, not him.

'I am generally pleased with what I've seen, but there are a number of shortcomings.'

'Oh?' Tallis said, sounding casual.

'My client is a distinguished businessman.' That's not what Ginny thinks, Tallis thought. 'He trades in international circles. He has a reputation to maintain. Do I make myself clear?'

No, not really, Tallis thought.

'The leather seats, for instance, they are sand-coloured. My client likes tan, and there are no gold fittings, no drinks cabinet.'

No problem. 'I'm sure we can arrange to meet your client's specific requirements. Naturally, it will cost.' He did the maths: another fifty thousand, at least.

'Cost *you*, yes.' Kumarin shrugged.

'I'm not sure I can authorise that.' As soon as the words had left his mouth Tallis knew he'd messed up.

'Then I would like to speak to someone who can,' Kumarin said, grit in his voice.

'What I mean,' Tallis said, trying to recover some ground, 'is that *I'm* unwilling to authorise such a deal.'

'Then we have no deal.' Kumarin tipped his short frame forwards, bending down and picking up his briefcase.

'That will be a pity,' Tallis said, bullish.

'Indeed,' Kumarin said, equally bullish, straightening up.

'Naturally, in the interests of international relations, I'd like to come to a mutually favourable arrangement.'

The glint in Kumarin's blue eyes, the slight twitch of his wide nose, suggested he'd scented weakness.

'Which is why I'm prepared to compromise,' Tallis said.

'Not a word I like.'

'Concession, then.' Tallis arranged a warm smile on his cool lips.

Kumarin sat back down and gave a silent nod for him to continue.

'We will cover half the cost. I will also personally fly the Agusta to Moscow to an airfield of your client's choosing.'

'Half, you say?' Kumarin said, rubbing his smooth chin.

'Half,' Tallis said, pointedly looking at his watch.

Silence. It seemed that Kumarin was hell-bent on playing hardball. Finally, he spoke. 'We pay twenty-five per cent. You pay the rest.'

'I'll send the contract,' Tallis said, knowing the Russian would further modify it to his advantage. 'And you'd like me to deliver?' Tallis said, pressing home the point.

'But of course,' Kumarin said, getting to his feet, his final words on the subject.

The journey back was a lot more fun. Kumarin seemed genuinely interested in Tallis, and Tallis was surprised to learn that Kumarin was a keen collector of Russian artefacts. He briefly wondered whether it was legitimate, or part of a mean trade in stolen art.

'I am also a keen painter,' Kumarin announced proudly. 'I have supplied one of your galleries here.'

'What, in the UK?'

'Moreton-in-Marsh, you've heard of it?'

'The Cotswolds, yes,' Tallis said, expressing genuine surprise. 'What sort of work?'

'Women.' Kumarin glanced across at Tallis, a lusty note in his voice.

After dropping Kumarin back to his taxi to Heathrow,

Tallis returned to Shobdon. By the time he'd wheeled the Robinson 22 into the hangar, it was already dark, which probably explained why he noticed the lights on in Ginny's office. Naturally curious, he decided to investigate.

Moving silently, he went up the stairs, crossed the meeting room, softly opened the door into the corridor and heard the sound of a lavatory flushing. Tallis paused. The door swung open and Blaine Deverill came out.

'Caught short,' he said, with obvious embarrassment.

'Right,' Tallis said, moving along, listening as Deverill's footsteps receded down the stairs.

When he went into the office, the lights were off, nobody there.

The contract was returned four days later with predictable edits, namely that Tiger would cover the entire cost of the refit. In fact, the SIS was picking up the tab. A subsequent phone call to Kumarin confirmed that the Russian position was immutable. Tallis decided to play the good loser. Kumarin revealed that his client was a man called Orlov.

'How soon can you deliver, Paul?'

'I'll need to file a flight plan…'

'Not necessary. Mr Orlov can ease any permissions you will need. He has connections.'

In Tallis's mind, Orlov was bear-like, grey-haired,

urbane and sober-suited, with a taste for the finer things in life. 'Yes, but I'll also need to apply for a visa.'

'This can also be taken care of.'

Friends in high places, Tallis thought. He called Asim straight away and delivered the good news.

'So you could be out there in a few days?'

The reality of the situation suddenly hit him. Truth be told, he'd got used to having Lena around. He'd taken her shopping for clothes. A pair of jeans, new shirt and a sweater knocked a decade off her. At last she was starting to look like a product of the twenty-first century instead of several before.

'Don't see why not. Method of contact?' He had visions of dead-letter drops or being asked to stand at a certain time on a particular street with a particular newspaper, an SIS operative waiting and watching in the shadows, ready to pass on information.

'Phones in Moscow. You'll be on your own in the mountains.'

If only it were true, Tallis thought. From warlords to FSB officers and soldiers, the mountains would be crowded, and everyone in them a potential enemy.

'Something you should know,' Asim said.

'Uh-huh?' Tallis picked up on the warning tone.

'A professor at Moscow State University is feared to be the latest victim.'

'Feared? Don't you know?'

'Different modus operandi. The man was killed with poison, maybe ricin, although that hasn't been confirmed. Before he collapsed he was in collision with a jogger in the grounds of the university. It's believed the runner was the assassin.'

'No description?'

'None that's filtered through.'

Tallis felt relief. He didn't want to know that it was Darke. 'And don't tell me,' he said. 'Our professor was a bad boy in the Caucasus.'

'A prison guard with deviant sexual tastes.'

Lena seemed restless. Tallis had not yet told her that the following morning he was leaving. He believed that, by some sixth sense, she already knew.

'Tell me about the music of your people,' he said, in a bid to divert her.

A sad smile touched her lips. 'Every Chechen knows how to sing and dance. It is in our blood,' she said, pointing to her heart. 'Laments, wedding anthems and religious chants, music celebrating human endeavour and redemption.' Suddenly, her voice broke into low tremulous song, tribal, raw and defiant. It was a song of the mountains, a poem of respect for the dead and those who had trodden there before. Tallis imagined a ring of men and women, beating time to the music with shouts and drums, silhouettes dancing slowly around a campfire. As Lena's voice rose in strength and pitch, Tallis felt the hairs on the back of his neck rise and stand erect. Long after she'd finished he sat mesmerised, watching the early evening shadows at play.

'When I think of my country,' Lena told him, 'I think of a symphony in black.'

Much later, with the last pieces of wood burning from red to white, Lena asked a favour of him.

He thought it might be money to tide her over while he was away. 'Sure.'

'Will you find my son?'

'Your son?' Lena had never mentioned a son or even a husband before. 'I don't understand,' he said, bewildered.

Lena disappeared to her bedroom, returning with a battered-looking photograph. She pushed it into Tallis's hands. The lad looked to be around twelve, maybe thirteen years of age. He had the same dark, edgy features as his mother, same slightly pinched nose and chin—a bleak version of a young Graham Darke. 'This is Ruslan. It was taken ten years ago.'

Tallis refrained from immediately saying that it was out of the question. On top of what he already had orders to do, he didn't have the time, didn't have the energy. It would mean being seriously sidetracked. He should simply say no.

'For our survival we decided to split the family up,' Lena was speaking quickly, rushing along, railroading him. 'It was Sahab's idea.'

'Sahab?'

'My husband. You see, all males from the age of ten to seventy were considered potential terrorists so he thought that it would be safer if I stayed with Asya in the village while he and Ruslan, my son, went to the mountains. At first, we could get word to each other, but after I fled, I lost contact. You have to understand I had no documents, they were destroyed in the shelling, and without documents you are lost. You cannot register. You cannot get food aid. If you have money, you can survive. I had no money,' she said simply.

Tallis looked up, saw the wildness in her eyes, saw the exhaustion in her face, saw the incredible decision she'd been forced to take: her possible survival and that of her daughter weighed against the questionable survival of her husband and son. What kind of choices were those?

'I heard through someone recently that Ruslan was living in Moscow.'

'And Sahab?' Tallis said.

She shook her head, two snatched movements. He'd known Lena long enough to know when to ask and when not to push a question. The angularity of her limbs, the way she was holding herself said *Don't go there.*

'Where in Moscow?'

'I do not know.'

Dear God, this was all he needed.

Seeing his reluctance, Lena grasped the sleeve of his sweater. 'Go to the worst places, to the ghettoes, the prisons. Look for the people with their pockets sewn up.'

'What?' he said baffled. There was a frightening, un-checked expression in her eyes.

'So that the police cannot plant drugs or detonators on them.'

'Lena, I don't—'

'Please, Mr Tallis, *please*.'

CHAPTER SEVEN

THE Agusta was a dream to fly. From Shobdon, Tallis had flown to Groningen Airport and then on to Szymany in Poland. On coming into land, he felt as if he'd entered a novel by John le Carré. The airport, cloistered at the end of a potholed country lane that ran through dense forest, trees dripping with rain, had a shabby control tower that looked out over a long runway.

After refuelling and sleeping the night in a nearby hostel that stank of badly aired laundry, he flew on to Zelenograd, a town forty kilometres north of Moscow, to the Sheremetyevo international airport, where he was to meet Grigori Orlov, Kumarin's client. The trip had taken him three days.

Following Orlov's specific instructions, Tallis stowed the helicopter safely in the hangar and made his way through a less than congenial arrivals hall. The place looked as if it could do with a lick of paint. Passport control was light on welcome, bordering on indifference, but with no interference he headed into an open area where a stringy, pock-faced twenty-something was holding a piece of cardboard with his name on it, spelt incorrectly. Tallis approached the bloke and smiled.

'*Zdrastvuyte.*' Hello, he said in greeting.

Immediately, two other men who'd been idly smoking nearby jumped to join the welcoming party. One had a squat frame, the other was the same height as Tallis but blond, with green lazy-looking eyes. All three men bulged with weaponry.

'I was hoping to meet Mr Orlov.' Or Kumarin, he thought, surveying the arrivals hall. He addressed the remark to the Blond, who viewed him with slow eyes.

'We are to drive you to his house.' His expression and the too casual way he studied his nails suggested that he had delivered far more important people than this miserable Englishman standing in front of him. Tallis lightly commented on Kumarin's absence. The Blond shrugged, waved his hand dismissively. 'He has an important meeting.' More important than you, he inferred. 'You will come,' he added with emphasis.

Not much choice, Tallis bristled, puzzled that Orlov, a man who'd just shelled out a ton of money, should not be present to view the goods.

Outside, snow was falling, making the surrounding scenery bleak rather than enchanting. This was certainly no Winter Wonderland, Tallis thought.

The waiting car was a Saab. There was a blue light on

the car roof and Tallis wondered whether the guys playing
escort were actually moonlighting police officers.

The blond-haired guy climbed in the front, exchanged an OK with the driver, Tallis in the rear with the
other two heavies on either side. It was pretty clear they
were trying to do a number on him. Fuck them, he thought.

Conversation was non-existent and Tallis didn't bother
trying. He looked out at a grey and forbidding urban
landscape with buildings and warehouses that looked as
if they should have been pulled down a long time ago.
The guy's driving style resembled that of taxi-drivers
he'd come across in the Middle East: pedestrians deemed
as sport and to be accelerated towards at all times.

As they reached Moscow, the traffic became dense,
the roads clogged. Tallis saw block after block of drab
housing complexes that he imagined would be cramped
inside. He saw no evidence of city gardens. At the
blond-haired guy's command, their driver switched on
the blue light. The effect was magical: vehicles swerved
out of the way and pulled over, and the route opened
up in front of them. Within a kilometre, Tallis was
cruising down wide poplar-lined boulevards, granite
avenues with historic and stately-looking architecture.
He was given an impression of wealth, of commerce;
it really didn't tally with any ideas he already had. On
they drove, past small parks and embassies, the road
snaking west, leaving the city. He could see birch trees
and parkland, great five-storey houses with gates and
guards and fortifications. The scenery changed again:

pine trees and forest. They were heading down a road flanked by tall fences, CCTV strategically placed. The road became a lane then a track. Tallis had a sudden image of his body in a ditch, a single bullet to the head.

At last, they pulled up outside a set of gates. A guy with a crew-cut hairstyle and an AK47 slung over his shoulder popped out of something resembling a sentry box, exchanged a greeting with the driver then opened the gates and waved them on. Had the drive been paved with gold, Tallis couldn't have been more surprised. He'd seen English stately homes before, been a guest at one on a couple of occasions, but nothing had quite prepared him for this. Set in magnificent grounds with sweeping lawns and several lakes surrounded by trees, here was an example of the *cottedgi* Lena spoke about.

Tallis stared up at an almost too perfect example of Regency architecture: verandas and balconies with ornate decorative cast-iron work, elegant Ionic-style columns and terraces. He could have been in the middle of Cheltenham, he thought, except this particular pile had a few additions: bronze lion heads on either side of the marble entrance, statues to Greek gods in the gardens; chandeliers visibly hanging from upstairs ceilings.

The doors of the Saab flew open. Everyone got out, Tallis included, then the minders wordlessly dumped his luggage and climbed back into the car and drove away down the drive, gravel spitting. Tallis briefly turned to watch them depart, his attention caught by the man he presumed to be Orlov bounding down the steps to greet him, his hand extended, a silver-grey-coated Weimaraner at his side. What was it with wealthy men and their dogs? Tallis thought.

In build, Orlov was exactly as Tallis had imagined, a bear of a man, reminiscent of the former President Boris Yeltsin but without the height. He had a shock of white hair that curiously looked dyed, and laughing brown eyes. His suit was also white, Tallis suspected to better display the tan and the profusion of gold jewellery slung around his neck. Tallis also caught sight of an eyewateringly expensive Breitling SuperOcean watch on the man's wrist. On his feet, Orlov wore a pair of flat black leather slippers. His thick-knuckled fingers were festooned in gold, something Tallis discovered when Orlov held him in a bone-crunching handshake.

'Mr Tallis, *dobri dyen*. Your journey was good?' He patted Tallis lightly on the back, gesturing with his free hand for Tallis to go inside.

'Fine, thank you.'

'And my merchandise is in perfect condition?'

'Of course.' Again, he wondered why the big man hadn't come to see for himself. Then it dawned on him. The drop-off instructions, the collection by Orlov's heavies, the silent drive, was part of the power play.

They were standing in a hall the size of a swimming pool, one side flanked by a vast marble fireplace surrounded by a cluster of leather sofas, the same tan colour Orlov had insisted on for the helicopter. There were three doors off, all closed. At each, a young man in liveried uniform stood to attention. Tallis was starting to wonder if he was dreaming. At a click of Orlov's thumb and finger, the nearest moved forward, taking Tallis's bag and jacket and handing him a pair of buckskin slippers.

Tallis stared at them, mystified.

'Your shoes,' Orlov said, pointing at Tallis's feet. Penny dropping, Tallis duly changed his footwear. Oddly, the slippers fitted his feet perfectly. Picking up the conversation again, Tallis said, 'I'm a little surprised neither you nor Mr Kumarin came to view the helicopter. I might have flown in a different machine.'

Orlov wagged a finger as if he were addressing a naughty child. 'That would have been most unwise.' His expression hadn't altered but there was a hint of menace behind the smile. Tallis now had the definite impression Orlov was making plain who was calling the shots. 'As for Boris, most unfortunate. He had some pressing family business to attend to. Please accept my sincere apologies on his behalf.

'You must be tired after your journey,' he said, clicking his fingers again. As in a carefully choreographed ballet, one of the doormen disappeared, reappearing with a tray bearing a bottle of chilled Flagman vodka and glasses. Another plumped up the cushions on the sofa and charged the fire, which was already burning half a forest's worth of wood by the look of it.

'Kumarin tells me that you are a reformed alcoholic,'

Orlov said, a shrewd gleam in his eye, 'or is this the English way of keeping a clear head when doing business?'

'You're very astute,' Tallis said, genuinely impressed. 'No offence was intended on my part.'

'And none taken.' Orlov flashed a grin.

Tallis sat down and accepted a drink from Orlov, toasting their success. The vodka tasted strong and delicious. He imagined it creeping into his bloodstream, primed for attack later. Pleasantries over, Orlov offered Tallis a fine Havana cigar from a box, which he refused. Orlov selected, prepared and lit one then launched into a graphic history of the construction of the house, which, he informed Tallis, had been built only five years before.

'I am also working on a construction in Voronezh, my home town. It is not a good place, full of pollution, very poor, dirty, stuck in the Soviet era,' Orlov said, with what Tallis thought was surprising candour. 'And dangerous,' he added. 'Many of the city's youth are out of work. But,' Orlov said, brown eyes twinkling amid a cloud of blue-grey smoke, 'construction is, how do you say, the *name of the game*. There is much scope for the developer.'

'You certainly seem to know what you're doing,' Tallis said, looking around him, polite.

'I love the English architecture,' Orlov said with fervour. 'My next project here will be in the Georgian style. After that, Queen Anne, I think.'

Orlov gave a signal and one of the liveried men hurried forward, removing the vodka and replacing it with a bottle of opened red wine from Georgia and fresh glasses. 'Everyone thinks we Russians drink nothing but vodka,' Orlov said, pouring out two generous glasses and handing one to Tallis. 'In truth,' he continued, in a slightly professorial tone, 'the more elevated among us drink it only for toasts.'

Before Orlov strayed onto quizzing him about his own taste in architecture—how would he rate bungalow-chic?—Tallis asked Orlov whether he'd been involved in any projects during the rebuilding of Chechnya.

'Good money to be had in the early days after the second conflict, but now, with the latest unrest…' Orlov shrugged '…it is not a safe place to travel, too many factions. You know they call it the FSB's workshop?'

Tallis cast Orlov an enquiring smile.

'It is well known that the FSB has been infiltrated by various criminal groups. No better place for them to cut their teeth than in Chechnya. Not that I am a defender of the Chechens,' Orlov stated.

'No?' Tallis said.

'Barbarians,' Orlov said, chucking out another great gust of smoke. 'The place has turned into a no-go area for ordinary, law-abiding Russians.'

'Are there any no-go areas in Moscow?'

'There are certain places where it is unwise to travel, but that is the same the world over. Where are you staying?' Orlov asked him, taking a gulp of wine.

'An apartment in Tverskaya district.' Asim had handed him a key several days before.

Orlov shrugged. 'Expensive, soulless but safe. This is OK. Now finish your drink and I will show you my collection of art.'

The art, according to Orlov, mainly consisted of works seized by the Red Army as part of Stalin's 'cultural reparation' against the Germans. Tallis didn't like to point out that Stalin's 'trophy brigades' acted in revenge and that the art in question originally belonged to victims of the Holocaust. He doubted Orlov could care less about either the politics or the provenance. He probably viewed them as justifiable spoils of war.

'The Pushkin Museum in Moscow and the State Hermitage in St Petersburg house the finest pieces,' Orlov said, with a knowledgeable air as they gazed at paintings by Titian, Matisse and Botticelli.

Several glasses later, events moved at a staggering pace. Orlov announced that he was throwing a party that evening and invited Tallis to stay as his guest. Protest would not only have been rude, it could possibly be dangerous to his health, Tallis thought so he beamed and smiled, and thanked Orlov as he was shown by yet another young man in breeches to a lavish guest suite.

An hour later, refreshed, suited and booted, he was introduced to Orlov's squeeze, a stunning leggy blonde from Siberia, called Svetlana. In her mid-twenties and possibly twenty years younger than Orlov, she wore a shade of killer-blue eye shadow that matched the dress she was wearing. A cigarette drooped louchely from her fingers. She wore a perpetual expression of disdain. Like Orlov, she had a thing for jewellery.

'I like your English friend,' she drawled, ruffling Tallis's hair, her accent thick and tarry.

'Not too much, I hope,' Orlov said, slipping his hand around her waist and giving it a proprietorial squeeze.

She bent her tall frame slightly and deposited a kiss on his forehead. 'Never as much as I like you, Grigori.'

Orlov cast Tallis a knowing grin. 'Svetlana is being nice because she wishes to spend more of my money in Petrovka Street.'

Tallis moved away and mingled. Since Ivanov had come on the scene, it was no longer standard practice for Russians to speak English in polite society. A kaleidoscope of sounds sizzled Tallis's ears.

By now the place was filling up with Orlov's pals—men in shades and suits, women in furs and stilettos—the atmosphere vibrant and dramatic. Kumarin, wearing a black tuxedo, strode towards him and greeted him effusively. Tallis felt the heat of alcohol coming off Kumarin's breath in waves.

'Paul, so sorry to miss you this morning. Fyodor is not such an agreeable companion, no?' he grinned.

Too right, Tallis thought, smiling politely.

'But I understand from Mr Orlov all is well.'

'Fine,' Tallis said.

'This is good. I believe you will be asked to test-fly the Agusta tomorrow.'

'You'll be there?'

'Maybe, maybe not. Depends on Mr Orlov's wishes.' Kumarin's eyes fell to the glass of champagne in Tallis's hand. 'A word of advice, Paul.' He winked. 'Next time you'd do better to—how do you say—"oil the wheels". You might pull off a more successful deal.' And, laughing loudly, he headed off to refill his glass.

The heavies Tallis had met earlier at the airport, including the blond-haired Fyodor, were circulating, wordless, among the guests. Several more were posted outside, talking into radios, watching out for signs of trouble.

They ate in a vast banqueting hall, the epitome of architectural showbiz, plates piled high with caviar, *shchuka* pike, beef topped with cheese (a Siberian dish, Svetlana later informed him) Russian-style ravioli stuffed with pork, and *shashlyk*, meat kebabs. There was also a rich array of Georgian cuisine, food influenced by the Middle East and Mediterranean. Tallis found himself sitting next to a big-boned Russian woman called Marina. Her rich chestnut hair was piled in a mass of curls on top of her head and she wore a low-cut white chiffon dress edged in claret-coloured satin. She also had an impressive décolleté. It was like having dinner with a woman from the Napoleonic era.

Marina was one of the new kids on the block, apparently. Ambitious and dedicated, she did a mean trade in importing clothes and carpets from Turkey. She was already planning on buying property in the form of a number of retail outlets.

'It is a good time for women,' she said, tasting the wine, Saperavi, a rich full-on red produced from grapes of the same name. 'We have freedom,' she said, rolling her r's. 'We have stability, at last, after years of economic chaos. We are divorcing our husbands and getting into business, something unthinkable a decade ago. Yes,' she said, a pragmatic gleam in her eye. 'Life is sweet. And you, Paul? You like doing business here?'

'I do,' Tallis said. 'I thought it might become tricky.'

'Tricky?' Marina frowned at him with big green eyes.

'Difficult—with the disintegrating political situation.'

'Oh, that.' She beamed. 'Most of us are not very interested. You go into a nightclub in Moscow, the talk, my English friend, is not of politics, international or national, but of the best places to eat, to buy clothes, to make money.'

'So Ivanov has been good to Russia?'

'I *love* the man,' Marina said. 'Without Ivanov we would be fucked,' she said, clipped, 'and it is good that we have someone strong to lead our great nation, to stand up to the rest of the world, even your country,' she said with a sudden impish smile. 'A tip for you, Paul. Art and business thrive even when our leaders do not like each other very much.'

Later, Tallis drifted onto one of the many balconies to clear his head. After the formal dinner, there had been a number of toasts—to wealth, to health, to life, to love, to business, even to Orlov's dog. Timur, a thin-faced, urbane-looking man from St Petersburg, was also taking the air. He introduced himself and offered Tallis a cigarette, which Tallis declined.

'You are the British helicopter man.'

'Paul Tallis, that's right.'

Timur nodded slowly and lit his cigarette, inhaling deeply and blowing out a perfect smoke ring. King of Cool, Tallis thought, identifying something very contained about the man. Without knowing anything about him, he recognised the type: this guy was a loner. Tallis also wondered whether he was a loser. 'So another little bit of Western democracy exported to the East,' Timur said.

'I wouldn't put it quite like that,' Tallis said affably.

Timur, pensive, fell silent.

'So what's wrong with Western democracy?' Tallis decided to rattle Timur's cage for no better reason than he'd had more to drink than was good for him. They were both leaning over the balcony. From there, a fine view of the grounds, lit by flaming torches, Olympic style, gave the numerous statues and bronzes a ghostly sheen.

'What's *wrong*?' Timur laughed, deep-throated. 'The United States and the West, that's what's wrong. You want nothing more than political overthrow. Look what you've done in Iraq, Afghanistan, how you oppose the Serbs, how you expand and position NATO members to further threaten our great nation. And the hypocrisy,' Timur sneered. 'You tell us to behave one way and then you act another. You

British: warmongers every one of you. How you love to patronise us, to tell us in what way to behave. I tell you, if you don't stop lecturing us, we will become your enemy.'

That's rich, Tallis thought. Russia had not that long ago invaded South Ossetia and recently taken a number of liberties with foreign air space. He suspected it was simply because they wanted to try their luck, test the reaction, and see whether they could get away with it. Now he thought it was a way of flexing their military muscle. 'Sounds like a threat,' Tallis said mildly.

Timur let out a snort and took another drag of his cigarette.

'So what do you do when not engaged in political debate?' Tallis said.

'I work for the State,' Timur said flatly.

Tallis glanced across at him. Timur's face shone green and chiselled in the moonlight. The State, meaning the FSB? Tallis wondered. He didn't push it. There were plenty of people who worked for the State, some professional killers.

'Does your work take you to Chechnya?'

'Sometimes,' Timur said, taking another drag, his thin cheeks hollow. 'Why do you ask?' he said, suspicion in his eyes.

'Interest.'

'You think the situation there is cruel?'

'All conflict is cruel.'

Timur agreed. 'But sometimes a necessary evil.'

'In Chechnya,' Tallis said, 'I'm not clear what the goals are.'

'To subdue the enemy, to bring them to heel,' Timur said, as if it were blindingly obvious. 'We cannot have a united Russia with these religious madmen waging a guerrilla campaign in our own backyard. It is the same as you British have in Northern Ireland.'

Actually, Tallis thought, it was quite different but refrained from saying so.

'I will tell you something,' Timur said darkly. 'Men love to war. It is an addiction more powerful than sex or love. And the Chechens, my friend, are junkies. But war is not their only addiction: they are also hooked on religion. To feed their habit, they must convert the rest of us to their perversions. You know what the Chechens do to captured Russian soldiers?' Timur did not wait for a reply. 'They gut men as easily as a fisherman guts a pike. They even use their own intestines to strangle them.'

'You mean the fundamentalists, the warlords,' Tallis said, struggling to restrain the images of epic cruelty taking shape in his mind. He hoped to God Graham Darke was not involved in such practices. But, Tallis also recognised, it would be hard for Darke to separate himself from the barbarism around him. His was a straight choice: go along to complete the mission or blow his cover and be killed. A question of ends justifying means, Tallis thought, and sadly something he had experience of.

'I am talking about every one of them,' Timur said, eyes reptilian.

'You can't believe ordinary people share those beliefs. They simply want to live in peace.'

Timur shrugged. 'They are guilty by default. They shelter terrorists. They hate the motherland.'

'They do now,' Tallis said, aware that he was treading on dangerous ground. 'The wanton destruction of towns and villages, the killing of hundreds of innocent people, has produced the next generation of malcontents. For that, your government has to take some responsibility, surely?'

'You do not know what you're talking about,' Timur said, cool. 'They must never be allowed to triumph.'

'You can't kill them all,' Tallis said with an easy laugh.

Timur said nothing. Dropping his cigarette on the floor, he ground it with the heel of his boot. 'It is important to maintain stability,' he said softly. 'It is what the Russian people need and want.'

'At any price?'

'Whatever the cost,' Timur said, walking back inside.

CHAPTER EIGHT

TALLIS awoke with a monumental hangover. Timidly, he opened one eye, trying desperately to focus on his surroundings. Gone the thick carpet, the heavy damask drapes at the windows, the works of art and marble, and extravagantly expensive bedroom furniture. Instead he was met with plain white walls, oatmeal-coloured curtains and newly renovated furnishings, Western style. For a brief, terrifying moment he wondered if he'd wound up with Marina, but a quick recce told him that he was entirely alone and that there was no evidence of another.

He went into the bathroom and took a leak. Events of the previous twenty-four hours cut into his consciousness with all the precision of a scalpel. So maybe he hadn't been as drunk or relaxed as his body now seemed to suggest. Nevertheless, as he trawled his memory, his recollections appeared to be laced by a particular brand of alcohol.

Each nuance of every conversation, in particular with Orlov and Timur, sliced through his brain: Orlov affable and generous; Timur cold and mean-spirited. He remembered eating a meat-heavy dinner followed by tooth-shatteringly sweet pastries, all washed down with sugary Georgian wine. He recalled the vodka toasts and, Christ, the *konyac*. 'Brandy from the Caucasus,' Orlov had told him, and no doubt the reason for the concentrated level of pain behind his left eye. Somewhere, in a temporarily misplaced part of his mind, he pulled out the idea that Orlov had promised to take him to his *banya*—a bit like a sauna only more extreme—that very same day. Lastly, he had a fairly strong image of getting into a taxi and having one of those strange conversations that you had with taxi drivers all over the world. This conversation had not been exceptional, typified as it had been by the long-suffering gloom and doom displayed by most ordinary Russians.

After a hot and cold shower in a weak effort to flush some of the alcohol from his vital organs, he dressed in the clothes he'd already packed and brought with him. A more detailed inspection of the four-roomed apartment yielded more clothes to fit his muscular physique, including mountain trekking gear, a healthy stash of roubles—money to bribe by—and a false passport and press pass stating that he was a freelance Russian journalist by the name of Nikolai Redko. The kitchen was large and well equipped, although Tallis had no intention of spending any time in it other than for a quick refuel. From the apartment, which was in Spiridonovka Ulitsa Street, he had a fine view of

Pushkin Square and the high walls enclosing the Kremlin.

After forcing down a mug of coffee with painkillers, he left the apartment and went out onto the street. It wasn't as cold as he'd expected, which was a pity. A lot of the snow had begun to melt, replaced by dirty-coloured slush. Avoiding the smart and expensive shopping avenue, Tverskaya, the equivalent of New York's Fifth Avenue, Tallis soon found himself among a gathering of hawkers and *babushkas* selling all manner of goods in the open air. Business appeared brisk; the capital's desire for commerce and trade reminded Tallis of a recent mission in Turkey.

Walking along, his gaze flittered and came to rest on a number of disparate people. He observed a lone middle-aged man giving away a free newspaper under the watchful and intimidating eye of a couple of police officers. Teenagers gathered on street corners, smoking, mucking about, as in any other international city, and there were kids zooming about on rollerblades like he'd seen in Berlin. All signs, he noticed, were in Cyrillic so the average tourist was entirely stuffed because they wouldn't be able to read them. Moscow, he reminded himself, was home to over ten million people. Roads, which were vast, flowed with cars, trucks and trolley-buses, the noise of traffic deafening. He decided to go with the flow, to keep on walking. He had an intuitive feeling that if he could find Lena's son Ruslan, he would find Darke. Or perhaps it was simply the line he'd sold himself. In truth, Ruslan was a side issue. Finding Darke was his main objective.

Walking towards the Kremlin, the seat of power, he skirted east past Red Square and headed out towards Lubyanka, stopping briefly to gaze upwards at the grey-walled former prison and currently new home and headquarters of the FSB. An involuntary shiver travelled up his spine at the thought of the innocent victims who'd been incarcerated within its forbidding exterior.

Many streets on, past an amazing amount of construction work, eventually negotiating a dimly lit underpass near Komsomolskaya, he came across two young Russians sitting on a threadbare blanket, drinking vodka, begging. He threw some coins into their bowl and squatted down on his haunches in an effort to talk to them, but their piss-off expressions told him that he'd come to the wrong place for conversation. Taking out a thousand-rouble note from his wallet, he waved it in front of the two lads. Both sets of eyes shifted his way.

'There is more,' Tallis said, in Russian.

The lad who looked to be the eldest spoke, 'I'm Vladimir. This is Viktor.' Vladimir had straight brown hair that fell over his face, thick eyebrows and a prominent chin. He'd made an unsuccessful attempt to grow a beard. 'What do you want?'

'Information.'

'You a spy?' Viktor let out a laugh. He had several missing teeth in an otherwise fine-featured face. His hair was spun gold and he had penetrating blue eyes. Tallis didn't like to apply the phrase pretty to a youth, but Viktor definitely fitted that description.

'No. I'm looking for a Chechen by the name of Ruslan.'

Viktor's mouth dropped open. His face turned grey and a sheen of sweat suddenly coated his brow, in an instant turning his fringe of gold to brown. It was as if he'd aged forty years in a second. Tallis recognised that look, the apathy of the brutalised. Vladimir cast his friend an anxious look. 'Why?' Vladimir said sharply. Tallis looked from Viktor to Vladimir, knowing that the wrong answer would finish further conversation no matter how much money he offered. He wondered what their story was.

'To kill him,' he said, keeping his voice low.

Viktor stirred, vital signs returning. He licked the corner of his mouth. Some of the colour was reappearing in his cheeks. At that exact moment Tallis's mobile rang. Cursing, he sprang to his feet, walked away a little and answered the call. It was Orlov.

'Good morning, Paul. I trust you are well.'

'Perfect,' Tallis winced. The painkillers were starting to wear off and the collective pain had dimmed to a dull agonising throb.

'Top-notch,' Orlov said, much to Tallis's amusement. Along with architecture, out-of-date vernacular was another example of Orlov's obsession with all things English. 'I am calling to firm up arrangements.

I shall collect you from your apartment shortly after two.'

'Fine. I'll be there.'

'Make sure you have your papers with you,' Orlov added, cutting the call.

When he turned round Vladimir and Viktor had gone, and so had his money. Tallis cursed, unable to believe his own crass stupidity, especially at such an early stage in the game. Fucked over by a couple of vagabonds, he was going to have to seriously sharpen up his act, he told himself grimly.

At ten minutes past two, a red Maserati Spider pulled up outside the apartment block, Orlov in the driving seat. Tallis went downstairs and slid in next to him.

Orlov issued a wide smile. 'You like?'

'What's not to?' As the 4.2 litre V8 engine kicked into action, the thrust sent him flying back into his seat. He imagined the considerable amount of oomph piling out of the quartet of exhaust pipes.

Orlov zipped up the gears, six-speed F1 shift. 'What do you drive at home, Paul?'

'A Porsche Boxster.'

'Good car. I have a 911 Turbo,' Orlov said. You would, Tallis thought. Everything Orlov did was turbo-charged. For a bloke of his age he had a terrific fund of energy. 'But my favourite is the Bentley.'

'Really? Which one?'

'The Arnage. For me, it is so English.'

'I thought Bentley was owned by the Germans.'

'It is still essentially English craftsmanship. You must ride in it some time.'

Tallis wasn't sure whether Orlov simply enjoyed showing off or whether he had a genuinely weird obsession with all things Anglo-Saxon. Whatever the truth of the matter, Tallis had the obscure feeling it might play to his advantage.

Orlov drove to Zelenograd. Fyodor, the blond-haired heavy, was there to meet them. No sign of Kumarin. Perhaps he was surveying another machine for Orlov's empire, Tallis thought.

'Take the car back to the estate, and don't scratch it,' Orlov warned.

Their papers scarcely looked at, they went to the hangar where the Agusta was stowed.

'Very nice,' Orlov said, running his fingers smoothly over the paintwork in the same way a man stroked the flanks of the woman he was sleeping with. It was Orlov's intention for Tallis to fly them back, no more than a short fifteen-minute hop.

It was starting to spit with sleety rain when Tallis climbed in, Orlov next to him. Tallis pressed one of two buttons in the roof panel to the left, just above his ear, in order to start the engine, followed by a second button for the second engine. After checking the controls and fuel gauge, and maintaining visual contact, they took off, flying west and high to make the most of the tail wind.

In the air, Orlov resumed his favourite topic of conversation: himself.

'Who'd have thought it? Me, a poor boy from Voronezh and now I'm being flown in my own helicopter.'

'Don't get too used to it.' Tallis laughed. 'I can't stay in Russia for ever. I have to go back to the UK. You should take some lessons, learn to fly.'

'It is not my way. I prefer others to do the hard work. You know, Paul, I'd like to do more business with you. Kumarin said that you have a very nice outfit back at Shobdon.'

'Well, it's not exactly my outfit,' Tallis said. 'That's why I've decided to start up my own sideline.'

'Sideline?'

'My own business.'

'This is very good news.'

'I've got a couple more Agustas in the pipeline, flying them over from Ireland for a strip-down and refurb,' Tallis said, deciding to get creative.

Orlov nodded vigorously. 'It is as well to be your own boss. That way nobody tells you what to do,' he said paternalistically. 'Should you need any help while you're here, you only have to ask. I know many, many people. I can get you anything.'

'Anything?'

'Introductions, contacts, *false* papers,' Orlov said, a sly lilt in his voice.

'False papers?'

'Nobody gets anywhere these days without, how do you say, cutting corners?'

'How many corners can you cut?'

'Why?' Orlov said. There was a definite note of mischief in his voice. This guy, Tallis thought, loved a challenge, especially if it meant screwing on the other side of the tracks.

'Can you get me a firearm?'

Tallis glanced across at Orlov to see how his question was received. In spite of the impassive and unperturbed exterior, Orlov's eyes were alight. Furthermore, there was no shock. 'There are many illegal weapons in circulation in Moscow alone.'

'I know, but that wasn't my question.'

'I do not have access to such things personally.' He was heavy on the *personally*. What Orlov really meant was that he had the necessary contacts. For a brief moment in time, Tallis was reminded of the late Johnny Kennedy, a crime lord he'd come across in the Midlands. Kennedy had had involvement in dirty dealings that he'd kept at arm's length. Tallis wondered if Orlov was fashioned in the same mould

'You disappoint me, Grigori,' Tallis said, tongue in cheek.

'But I know someone who does. Leave it with me, and I will look into it for you.' And with that Orlov changed tack and disclosed his plans for the rest of the day. 'This afternoon we will share a *banya* and this evening you will stay as my guest for dinner, a private affair.'

'That's very kind of you,' Tallis began, 'but you've already been so—'

'Not at all.'

'Yes, but—'

'I have a very good surprise for you.'

Tallis flicked an enquiring smile. He didn't like surprises. And he had important work to get on with.

'We are being honoured by a special guest,' Orlov said, rolling his eyes.

'Yeah?'

'*Da,*' Orlov said, a big grin on his face.

The *banya* rated as one of Tallis's more painful experiences. It made the Turkish equivalent appear feeble. The heat was too hot, scalding in fact, the obligatory beating with birch branches too severe, the *basseyn*, or ice-cold pool, too damned chilly. The only positive result was that, by the third time, his hangover disappeared immediately, presumably evaporating in a burst of eucalyptus-infused steam.

Spread out on a bench and covered in sheets, Tallis fell into easy conversation with Orlov. It wasn't long before Orlov was on the boast again. He had plans, apparently, to buy up a plot of land in St Petersburg and develop it.

'Timur is from St Petersburg, isn't he?' Tallis said, neatly massaging the conversation.

Orlov agreed with a grunt.

'Interesting guy,' Tallis said. 'Gather he works for the FSB.'

'Is that what he told you?' Orlov said with a low laugh.

'Perhaps I made a mistake.'

'Not really,' Orlov said, a cunning light in his eye.

Tallis said nothing, waited for Orlov to fill in the gap. He didn't. The conversation took a completely different turn.

'Timur mentioned that you were interested in the Chechen situation,' Orlov said. 'Is this connected to your desire for a firearm?'

'What would you say if I said yes?' Tallis's manner was light to underplay the immense but calculated risk he was taking.

'I would say you are a fool. And, Paul, you must understand that in Russia loose talk costs lives.'

Tallis adjusted his position. 'Are you threatening me, Grigori?'

'Of course not. I'm offering good advice. Anyway, what does an Englishman want with a group of terrorists?'

If this was the view of the average Russian, God help the British government if word ever got out about Graham Darke. 'Not every Chechen is a terrorist, Grigori. Even you know that.'

'What do I care?' Orlov shrugged. 'Jews, blacks, Chechens. They are all the same. You cannot trust any of them.'

'Is that so?' Tallis said, quietly trying to contain and extinguish a sudden flare of anger.

'It is,' Orlov said, 'and, Paul, whatever your views, you must put them to one side, at least for this evening.'

'Why, is Timur coming to dinner?'
'No, his boss is.'

Dinner wasn't quite the intimate affair Tallis imagined it would be. The State Room, as Orlov referred to it, was like a banqueting hall. Running down the centre was a vast table as shiny as an ice-rink, laid for thirty, chandeliers hanging from the ornately designed ceiling. Whoever the honorary guest was, he or she certainly commanded a high level of security. A Mi-8 helicopter hovered overhead. Supplementing Orlov's company of heavies were six men with mean-looking faces and even meaner-looking haircuts. They spent several hours talking into their cuffs and checking the estate for intruders and anything untoward. Tallis had heard somewhere that the Spetsnaz recruited from a ready pool of Olympic-grade athletes. Any one of the guys striding round the complex fitted the profile.

Guests started to arrive shortly after seven. A flurry of activity followed as coats were taken, drinks dispensed, champagne the preferred choice. Kumarin, Tallis noticed, was conspicuously absent. He found it odd, filed the information away. A small orchestra of musicians, including a pianist who played with such shivering brilliance Tallis would have happily listened to him all night, played romantic pieces by the composer Edward Elgar.

Abandoning her veneer of listlessness, Svetlana, dressed in a ruched green silk dress with thin shoestring straps that accentuated her long, sloping shoulders, acted the perfect hostess, nodding and smiling, only the slight moving of her blue eyes revealing that she was more concerned with the impending arrival of the guest of honour than in what was being spoken. Indeed, everyone had half their attention focused on the wide double doors. The atmosphere in the room sizzled with intrigue. At last, the orchestra of musicians switched to a stirring piece by Dmitri Shostakovich: 'The Assault on Beautiful Gorky'. Conversations sputtered into silence. Orlov, dressed in a white tuxedo, virtually tripped over himself in his desire to rush to the other end of the hall before the doors flew open, revealing his mystery guest. Then the man himself strode into the room, his minders at his side, the air encircling him electric. All heads swivelled, Tallis's included, as Andrei Ivanov, the Prime Minister and most powerful man in Russia, eyes bright with fire, made his entrance.

Tallis watched the obvious warmth between the two men, each patting each other on the back rather than the more formal handshake. Orlov then fell into a cringing eulogy of welcome, Ivanov listening politely before returning the compliment by thanking his host for such a generous invitation. A round of applause followed then, at Ivanov's signal, the guests resumed their conversations, the lilt and chatter of human voices cranking back into gear. Tallis stood mesmerised. Ivanov was taller than he'd expected, his sober, beautifully cut dark blue suit emphasising his lean, muscled physique. His face was better looking and was remarkably unlined for a man in his forties. He had extraordinary eyes that appeared to miss nothing, a residue, Tallis suspected, from his former life as a spook.

Twenty minutes later, they were seated, Tallis, to his amazement, six place settings away and within perfect earshot of Ivanov. With one ear listening to the droning voice of his next-door neighbour, a fat man from Kursk, he eavesdropped as Ivanov chatted to Orlov about his latest acquisition, a chateau in the Cote D'Azur. From the tenor of the conversation, it became clear that Orlov had been instrumental in its renovation. Nice work, Tallis thought.

'And that small problem with the indoor pool has been fixed?' Orlov said.

'Perfectly. I am hoping to spend more time there in the summer,' Ivanov said, picking up his knife and fork, a signal for everyone else to start eating, 'but I fear my influence and therefore my time will be needed in the Caucasus again.'

'Indeed,' Orlov said, glancing nervously in Tallis's direction.

'Especially with this latest round of murders in Moscow.'

'An outrage,' Orlov agreed, flicking Tallis another warning look.

'More than an outrage. It's a base attempt to undermine Russia's stability.'

'Forgive me,' Tallis said, addressing Ivanov directly.

'I was a former police officer in Britain so mine is more of a professional interest, but I presume you have evidence that the murders are linked?'

Orlov, his cheeks drained to the colour of frozen snow, began to noisily protest at the interruption, but was halted in mid-sentence by Ivanov.

'And you are?' Ivanov said imperiously.

'Paul Tallis.'

'He is the man I was telling you about,' Orlov said, eyeing Tallis angrily while trying to recover some composure for Ivanov's benefit. 'He sold me the helicopter.' It sounded like an accusation.

Ivanov nodded. Tallis wondered whether Ivanov secretly disapproved. If he did, he certainly concealed it well. 'A man of many talents,' Ivanov said, with no hint of condescension in his voice. 'You sound more like a journalist than a police officer, Mr Tallis. And I have to say I care little for either breed.' He laughed lightly, turning to Orlov who broke into a nerve-fuelled titter. 'What were you, a detective?'

'A firearms officer.'

Orlov turned a paler shade. Ivanov delicately elevated an eyebrow. 'A highly skilled job. You have my admiration. Your new friend is a very interesting man, Grigori. Where have you been hiding him?'

'Well, um…' Orlov mumbled.

'But to answer your question,' Ivanov said, returning to Tallis, 'our police officers are one hundred per cent sure that the murders are linked. Moreover, they have forensic evidence supporting the view that the killings were carried out by a single assassin.'

'With a varied modus operandi,' Tallis said.

'A skilled individual, for sure.'

That was exactly what Tallis was afraid of. 'But why the Chechen connection?' Tallis persisted. 'I thought they were a rather undisciplined lot.'

A pulse in Orlov's temple twitched. Ivanov, on the contrary, seemed to enjoy the opportunity to educate the Englishman. 'And you would be right, Mr Tallis.'

'So?'

'It comes down to history and motive. In the North Caucasus the people have always been rebellious. There is nothing new about this except we have an additional component: terrorism. And, after the dreadful bombing in London, I'm sure I do not need to lecture you on the consequences of ignoring religious fundamentalism. Terrorists are responsible for every criminal act that takes place in my country. We must not tolerate another Beslan, another Nord-Ost. I've spent years of my life working to ensure economic and political stability for Russia. I will not have that undermined by a band of religious savages.'

'So you're saying the hits were politically motivated?' Tallis said evenly.

'Absolutely.'

'Then the logical conclusion is that your life and that of the President is also in danger.'

Ivanov smiled, snake-eyed. 'As you can see,' he said,

with a regal wave of his hand, 'I am very well protected.'

'I hear Elimkhanova is gathering support in the mountains,' Orlov said tentatively, darting Tallis a nervous look that said, *Keep your mouth shut*. Akhmet Elimkhanova, the Chechen warlord Darke had been sent to infiltrate, Tallis thought, holding his expression steady.

'Yes, and when they strike,' Ivanov said darkly, 'we will be ready to crush them.'

After that, the discussion went off on a tangent concerning Gazprom. Tallis got dragged into a conversation on taxation and unemployment in Britain, the influx of migrant workers a particular point of interest. After dinner and a number of toasts, he got stuck with the tubby man from Kursk. 'Vodka is recession proof in Russia, and even if you can't afford it, you can make your own,' he was saying, the half-closed lids indicating that, single-handedly, he'd done his bit to stave off any slump in the economy. But Tallis had eyes and ears only for Ivanov. So engrossed was he in watching the man, he didn't notice Orlov coming up behind him, gruff and glowering.

'Fortunately, Ivanov has accepted your bleeding-heart attitude. In fact, he was quite taken with you.'

'A man of taste,' Tallis grinned.

'I am not certain I would have been so tolerant,' Orlov said sternly.

'As well you're not the prime minister, then.'

Orlov continued to scowl then flashed a sudden smile and punched Tallis hard on the shoulder. 'You English,' he said, weaving his way through assorted guests to where Svetlana was holding court.

Tallis left several hours later, long after Ivanov, amid much glad-handing, had made his exit, and by which time Orlov had recovered his sense of humour.

'Thank you,' Tallis said. 'I'd no idea you had such elevated connections.'

'And I'd no idea you were a policeman who shot people for a living.'

Tallis winced. A long-ago image, a little faded now, floated into his mind: *black girl, midnight eyes*. He flicked it away. 'That's not how we do things in Britain,' he said. 'Our job is to save lives, not take them.'

'You'd do well to remember that the next time you bring up the Caucasus.' Orlov laughed.

And with that piece of advice boxing his ears, Tallis made his escape.

But he didn't go back to the apartment. He asked the driver to drive north and drop him off on one of the main roads out of the city. It was four in the morning and freezing, the weather plummeting to minus eight degrees. The ground, covered in a spectral coating of frost, creaked and crunched underneath his shoes. He was glad he was wearing a thick overcoat to conceal the smart suit he wore beneath. By any measure, he was a mugger's dream victim. And there were plenty of potential candidates. He'd never seen so many young people off their faces on booze. Even seasoned binge-drinking young Brits would struggle to keep pace. Vagabond throngs punctuated every street corner, the atmosphere thick with threatened violence. Tallis hurried on and away.

He drew close to one of the prisons known as a SIZO, a large pre-trial and remand institution, and even though it was dark and badly illuminated, the hinterland felt different. Dwellings were downtrodden. You couldn't call them homes. Concrete and lichen grew through the stone. Litter lay piled in the gutters. The air even at that time in the morning smelt of sickness. He remembered that tuberculosis and HIV was rife in Russian prisons, along with extreme brutality dished out by prison staff. Tales of random beatings and broken bones were commonplace in a Russian institution. With such serious overcrowding, prisoners were forced to sleep in shifts with only the most basic of toilet and washing facilities. He also knew that it was possible to be banged up for years without having your case heard. No wonder the place smelt of desperation. Lena's words echoed in his mind. *Go to the worst places, to the ghettoes, the prisons. Look for the people with their pockets sewn up.*

At once he heard footsteps behind him. He could tell from the gait that this was no mugger, nobody who had something to hide. On the contrary, this sounded like officialdom in action. Tallis turned. A torch was shone into his eyes, momentarily dazzling him. Tallis put his arm up to his face. The man flashed an ID card in front of his nose, but it was so fast Tallis couldn't catch the name, let alone the guy's rank, or to what organisation he belonged. He sensed that this was not the time to ask.

'Papers,' the man said in Russian.

'I'm English,' Tallis said, spreading his hands. 'I don't speak Russian.'

The officer repeated the order, this time in stilted English.

'I don't have them with me.'

'You have no passport?' The man's eyes narrowed.

'Yes, of course, but, like I said, not with me.' For which Tallis knew he could be fined.

'You have committed a crime.'

Act dumb, Tallis thought. 'I'm sorry, how?'

But the guy was having none of it. 'Have you registered with the police?'

'Well, no, but—'

'Your name?'

Tallis told him.

'Where are you staying?'

Tallis told him the truth.

'What are you doing here?' Now that Tallis was up close, he could see that the man was wearing a leather jacket and jeans, and a holster. Tallis could also smell alcohol on his breath. Time to adopt the cover of hapless Brit abroad. Tallis knew three things about telling a successful lie: keep it plausible, and keep it simple. Most of all, *believe* it.

He looked the man straight in the eye. 'I'm lost.'

'Lost?'

'Yes, I had a problem sleeping so I thought I'd take the air. Stupidly, I wasn't looking where I was going.'

The guy, quite rightly in Tallis's opinion, stared at him with open disbelief.

'Look,' Tallis said, 'I'm a tourist who made a silly mistake. I can easily come to Tverskoy police station later and show you my passport.'

The man seemed to consider this for a moment then began to speak of a possible fine.

'Fair enough,' Tallis said. Fine, bribe, what the hell did he care? 'How much do you want?' he said, taking his wallet from inside his overcoat.

The man looked at it greedily. 'I think we can come to some arrangement,' he said.

Josef Petrova, the man who'd encountered Tallis near the prison, felt immensely pleased with his night's takings. As a former military intelligence officer charged with recruiting spies from the Chechen population, he had recently found a new home and new role with the FSB. His current job was similar in style: it involved trawling prisons to recruit criminals. In return for freedom, they were armed, told to follow their instincts and let loose in Ingushetia and neighbouring Chechnya to shake up the civilian population. Occasionally, they were given specific goals: the abduction, ransom and murder of foreigners, Brits and the

Dutch the current favourites. The idea was to smear the warlords' reputations in addition to making money. The British fool he'd stumbled across on his way home in the early hours of that morning didn't realise quite how lucky he was.

Petrova walked on through charmless streets made drab in the morning light, his destination Butyrka. Conditions there were brutal, a perfect breeding ground for the specific type of man he was looking for: someone who wouldn't wince at putting a bag over a youth's head, or choking and beating him to death, or think twice about cutting a man's throat. Slicing through a windpipe was not as easy as it seemed. There was skill attached. Men could be surprisingly resistant to dying.

A chill wind lifted the hair on his head and Petrova instinctively rolled the collar of his jacket up. He enjoyed this part of the day when people were stirring, pottering about their business but without the shake and clatter.

Taking a short cut through an alley, he paused to extract a packet of cigarettes, and felt the comforting weight of fresh money in his wallet. So pleased with the world he didn't notice the silent tread of an assassin behind him. So surprised he didn't react as his head was wrenched backwards.

'What the…?'

A flash like quicksilver cut off his speech. Collapsing to the ground, blood pumping from a severed jugular vein, Petrova had no time to consider the level of expertise required for his own murder, or that his death was just another in a series of politically motivated killings.

After a few hours' sleep, Tallis attempted to return to the area around the prison. It was a risk, foolhardy even, but Lena's advice to search the ghettoes for her son was like a nagging refrain in his ears. Tallis was also aware that time was running out. He was concerned that the assassin responsible for the Moscow murders might strike again, and further destabilise the political situation in Chechnya. Tallis knew that he needed to get out there quickly. It was essential to find Darke. Hard though it was, Tallis had one opportunity to find Lena's son Ruslan, and if he failed he'd simply cut his losses and move on.

On his way, he swore he was being followed, the dying echo of someone else's footsteps a constant in his ears, but however often he turned to look for a tail, the alleys yielded nothing.

A few streets away from his destination, his passage was stopped by a crowd of angry protesters, their rage contained by a phalanx of stone-faced riot police with shields held close to their torsos, batons in their hands. In among the crowd, people with give-away faces were trying to escape. Tallis noted the dark looks, women with hawk-like features and gold hoops in their ears. He asked the nearest person to him, an elderly Russian guy in a tattered coat, what had happened there.

'An FSB officer had his throat cut early this morning. Every day, another murder,' the old man complained, balling his fist and shaking it at the sky. 'Filthy Chechens,' he added, spitting into the gutter.

Tallis decided to retreat. After buying a bottle of Stoli, a cheap brand of vodka, he returned to the underpass near Komsomolskaya. A busker was playing an accordion and singing a heartfelt Russian ballad, the kind of music to slit your wrists to, Tallis thought. Vladimir and Viktor, the lads he'd encountered the previous day, were in the same spot, sharing smokes, looking belligerent. Neither appeared alarmed nor surprised by his arrival. Wordlessly, Tallis handed the bottle to Vladimir. Vladimir's hand shot out. 'Killed any *dukh*, Englishman?'

'Not today.'

'Pity,' Viktor said, his eyes red-rimmed already from drinking. He was wearing clothes that looked too big for him. With his helmet of golden hair he looked half street urchin, half angel.

Tallis squatted down. Vladimir unscrewed the cap and offered the bottle to Tallis, urging him to drink.

'Thanks,' Tallis said, taking a swig, feeling the heat and sweetness on his tongue. Christ, any longer in Moscow and he'd turn into an alcoholic.

'You said *dukh*—that's a military phrase, isn't it?' Tallis said, handing the bottle back.

'I was a soldier,' Vladimir said.

Tallis expressed surprise. Vladimir didn't look old enough. He told him so.

'That's what war does.' Vladimir laughed without mirth. 'Either it makes you old or arrests your development. I was nineteen when I was sent to the front line in 2000.'

'Where exactly?'

'Novye Aldy. Shit place. Shit people. And I'm not just talking about the *dukh*. You know what a Russian soldier's life is worth? Nothing. And the military for all their fucking badges and medals are nothing more than a bunch of drunken sadists. To be honest, I was more scared of my commanding officer than the Chechens.'

'That bad?'

'That bad,' Vladimir said, sullen. He took another snatch of vodka, wiped his mouth with the back of his hand, and passed the bottle to Viktor. 'They call it *dedovschina*.'

Punishment, Tallis remembered.

'It's meted out for the most minor violations, lack of respect mainly. There was one guy, a real hard-faced bastard. He liked nothing more than to beat us with spades. He'd fuck you if he had the chance. Some of the guys couldn't take it. They'd wind up hanging themselves. You'd see the bodies carried out night after night.'

Christ, made the tit-for-tat shootings in London suburbs seem like child's play, Tallis thought.

'Tell him about the *zindan*,' Viktor said, eyes glittering and strangely alive.

'*Zindan?*' Tallis said, not understanding the phrase.

'A hollow torture pit faced with brick,' Vladimir explained. 'It had an earthen floor. You could be kept there for days. No food, no water, nowhere to piss or shit. That kind of stuff does weird things to you,' he said, his voice momentarily trailing away. 'And most of us were ill, dysentery, TB, foot-rot from the rubber boots we were forced to wear. As for food, there wasn't any. Hunger is as much a soldier's enemy as brutality if you're Russian,' he said, taking another swig of vodka. 'That and the fact nobody actually trained us to shoot, let alone protect ourselves from machine-gun fire. In the summer, the temperature could soar to fifty degrees centigrade. In the winter, you'd be freezing your nuts off. Could even drop to minus ten. As for the *dukh*, they'd often leave little goodbye presents.' Vladimir smiled thinly. 'Mines and boobytraps in abandoned apartments, the type that blow your balls off. Oh, yes, Englishman, if you kill a Chechen, think of me.'

'And you, Viktor?' Tallis said quietly. 'Were you a soldier, too?'

Viktor froze. Vladimir looked at him, searched for and met his gaze, seeking some sort of permission, it seemed. After a few seconds, Viktor nodded, a quick flick of his head, and took a snatch of vodka.

'Viktor was taken hostage when he was twelve,' Vladimir began. 'His parents were quite rich, you see. They owned a house near Grozny.'

'They were Chechens?'

'Russians,' Vladimir said with emphasis. 'It was there, during a holiday, that he was taken.'

'By whom?'

'Chechen gangsters. He was tortured,' Vladimir swallowed, glancing away. 'His parents were desperate and went to everyone they could think of for help. They offered everything they had in an effort to get him back. Lots of promises were made. Time passed. Nothing happened.'

'And these gangsters were kidnappers? They kept in touch?'

Vladimir nodded. 'They used intermediaries to demand eight hundred thousand dollars.'

Tallis glanced at Viktor, who was sitting motionless, tuned out, still as statuary.

'They sold everything they had and gave it to anyone who said they'd help, including the police, a gangster said to have close ties with the kidnappers and the republic's branch of the FSB. They lost everything to find their son.

'What they didn't know was that the very people said to be looking for him were in conspiracy with the kidnappers. You see, it's hard to tell who is working for whom in Chechnya. Fortunately for Viktor, having been bought and sold several times by certain Chechen faces, he managed to escape one night when his captors had more to drink than was good for them.'

But Viktor's torment had only begun, Tallis thought, looking at the boy, feeling hollow.

'Last month, he was briefly detained for punching a young Chechen's lights out.' Vladmir smiled, putting an arm around Viktor's shoulders, giving him a hug, Viktor's response to reach for the vodka.

'Where was that?' Tallis said, casual.

'Ryazan Prospekt.'

'Slums,' Viktor muttered.

Tallis stayed another half an hour with the boys. When he left he gave them money, told them not to spend it all on booze.

Viktor was right, Tallis thought, looking about him. After taking an age to travel across the city, even on the Metro, he was standing on a street in the middle of an industrial zone populated by crumbling five-storey dwellings and derelict workshops. The entire area looked as if it had been subject to looting, the grinding atmosphere one of depression punctuated by paranoia. You could see it in the faces, in the body language. Here, it seemed people lived a vagrant-style existence, constantly suspicious, always looking over their shoulders.

And there was something else, Tallis thought. Where were all the young men? It seemed to him then that Chechens had become the new Jews. They had effectively been ghettoised. As such, they got the blame for everything.

He walked on down a raddled-looking street where great lumps of masonry had fallen off the buildings. A woman dressed in a long coat and scarf, her face parallel with the ground, scurried past. Tallis took out the photograph of Lena's son from his jacket and, speaking to the hurrying woman in Chechen, explained that it was an old photograph but did she know of a Ruslan Maisakov? At first the woman shrugged without looking.

'Please,' Tallis said, pushing the photograph into her hand. He watched her face, the pinched, tired features that were so similar to Lena's, the hollows in her cheeks, saw the light of recognition in her eyes. Then the woman's expression turned to one of suspicion. 'Who are you?'

'A friend. His mother sent me.'

She stared at him for several moments.

Come on, Tallis thought, sparking. He knew that she knew, but would she talk? Could she be persuaded somehow? He returned her stare, intense.

'I know of Ruslan,' she said at last. 'He was taken this morning.'

'Taken where?'

'Vykhino police station on Sormovskaya Street.'

'Why?'

The woman briefly smiled. 'Don't you know that all Chechens have been redefined as criminals?' And then she went away.

A wad of cash to a police officer at Vykhino police station confirmed that Ruslan Maisakov, along with two others, had been taken, following interrogation, to Moscow State Prison. Tallis's heart sank. There was no way he was about to knock on doors and draw further attention to himself. Defeated, he headed back to the apartment block. He was standing outside when his phone rang. It was Orlov. 'That matter we discussed,' he said elliptically. 'I know someone who may be able to help.'

'Sounds good to me,' Tallis said, glancing at his watch: one o'clock.

'I will get one of my men to pick you up. Be ready in half an hour.'

Orlov was as good as his word. Fyodor collected him in silence and drove in silence. Tallis couldn't have cared less. He had nothing to say to him.

It soon became clear from the direction in which they were travelling that they were heading for the estate. As soon as they arrived, Fyodor dropped Tallis off at the helipad where Orlov was already waiting.

'What sort of space do you need to land one of these things?' Orlov said, pointing at the 109 and brandishing a map.

'A clear one,' Tallis said. 'No power lines, not too many trees, about the size of a tennis court.' He'd landed in tighter areas but he wasn't going to admit that to Orlov. Knowing him, he'd have him land on a roof somewhere.

'Good,' he said, showing Tallis where they were heading, a dacha between Kaluga and Tula and on the river Oka. Tallis knew better than to ask Orlov whether he'd filed a flight plan. In reality, Russia was quite different from the UK. As long as you'd initially filed a large enough plan covering a big enough radius, stating

the reason as *training in the area*, you were pretty clear
to fly when you wanted.

This time it was Tallis's turn to show off, flying low,
tracking the river at about six hundred feet. Orlov was
in his element. 'We travel fast, no?'

'It's only perceptual,' Tallis said. 'The lower you fly,
the quicker it seems.'

Orlov's enthusiasm was undiminished. 'This is like
in the film, *Apocalypse Now*,' he cried excitedly.

Wagner's 'Flight of the Valkyries' immediately
flashed through Tallis's brain. 'This contact we're going
to meet,' Tallis said. 'Who is he?'

'Yuri Chaikova, a former soldier and good friend of
mine. Yuri will get you anything you need. During the
Chechen conflict, he was charged several times for
selling arms.'

'What, to the other side?'

'A man has to make a living.' Orlov gave a lugubri-
ous sigh. 'He has many, many contacts.'

Tallis smiled. That's exactly what he'd hoped for. It
wasn't the weapons he was interested in but the fixer
supplying them.

After a minor hiccough on landing—bracken was not
ideal for a tail rotor—Tallis climbed out and was greeted
by the extraordinary sight of beautifully landscaped
gardens with flowering fruit trees and vegetable patches,
all carefully cultivated and nurtured, unlike the actual
house, which, although big, wasn't particularly attractive. It reminded him of a broken-down German schloss.

A bloke with a shaved head and massive features resembling a banned breed of dog sauntered towards
them. Tallis imagined this was Chaikova's heavy. He
bet underneath the clothes the guy was covered in
tattoos.

'Grigori,' the man said, clapping Orlov on the back.

'Yuri,' Orlov exclaimed in return. Tallis stood back,
feeling faintly embarrassed. When they were done, he
was introduced. Up close, Tallis saw that Chaikova's
face bore a number of scars.

'Look forward to doing business with you,' Chaikova said in a nasal voice, his cool blue eyes fasten-
ing onto Tallis. 'Grigori tells me you were a firearms
officer in the UK.'

Grigori would, Tallis thought. 'A long time ago,'
he said, thinking on the next occasion he'd keep his
mouth shut.

'But one never forgets,' Chaikova said shrewdly.
'Tell me, when you went in for the kill, did you do it
the Russian way?'

Tallis hiked an eyebrow. 'Going in for the kill'
sounded more akin to illegal fox hunting.

'The *kontrolnyi vystrel*. It means several shots followed
up by the control shot,' Chaikova said, eyes gleaming.

'You mean a double tap,' Tallis said.

'Ah, that is what you call it,' Chaikova said, making
a pistol shape with his hand. 'Bang, bang!' He laughed.
'I think you will appreciate what I have to offer you,'
he continued, as if he were about to host a wine tasting.

Tallis was shown to the house, an impression of large rooms and doors off, modestly furnished. The arms were kept in a wood-panelled room off a main living area. 'This is my study,' Chaikova said with a laugh. Except there were no books on show, only guns. Tallis stared at racks and racks of them. The shelves included Bren guns, Minimis—250 rounds, fired in bursts of twenty—Magnums and Armalites. Orlov, meanwhile, had made himself comfortable in the only easy chair in the room.

'What was it you were after?' Chaikova said, taking out a bunch of keys, presumably to open one of the glass-fronted cabinets that housed pistols and revolvers. Tallis spotted a couple of hefty Desert Eagles. The only time he'd seen this much gear had been in the armoury at the National Firearms School. Not even Johnny Kennedy, the former Mr Big he'd come across in Birmingham on his last mission, had had weaponry on this scale. Tallis reckoned half the Russian haul was stolen; the other half spoils of war. 'How about a Makarov for starters?'

Chaikova nodded, went to one of the cabinets, opened it, took out the gun and handed it to Tallis. 'Modelled on the Walther PP,' Chaikova said. 'Perfect for a hit.'

Tallis felt the weight of it in his hand. 'Anywhere I can test it?'

'Later,' Chaikova said. 'You choose what you want then we take the firearms to the range.'

Tallis put the gun down and walked towards the rack nearest him, reached out and touched a Heckler and Koch SA80. 'This takes me back,' he said affably.

'You were a soldier in the British army?' Chaikova said.

'Before joining the police.'

'See any action?'

'First Gulf War.'

Chaikova grinned, seemingly impressed.

'Tallis here is interested in our own little war,' Orlov said, stretching his legs out expansively. 'Chaikova could tell you a few tales.'

'Yeah?' Tallis said, indicating to Chaikova that he'd like to check out the H&K MP5K.

'I used to run a business taking people to places they were not supposed to be,' Chaikova said.

'What sort of people?'

'Journalists, mostly, the ones who could not get the necessary permissions from the Kremlin to travel. At the time, flights were temporarily suspended to Grozny so there was plenty of work for people like myself.'

'Sounds interesting.'

'Sounds stupid and dangerous,' Orlov said bluntly, his voice reverberating from the bowels of the soft leather armchair.

Chaikova inclined his head towards Orlov and, looking at Tallis, laughed. 'As if he would know.'

'There are less dangerous ways to make money,' Orlov huffed. 'Anyway, thank God you've packed it in.'

Chaikova flashed him a grin and handed the MP5K to Tallis. 'You like?' Chaikova said.

'Very much. Used this a lot. Particularly like the telescope,' Tallis commented. Not all models had them. Some had adjustable iron sights. 'Probably my favourite submachine-gun.'

'It's versatile, yes?' Chaikova said. 'Good for concealment.'

That's what he was banking on. 'So why did you pack it in?' Tallis asked Chaikova. 'Because of the recent unrest?'

'Market forces,' Chaikova said crisply. 'The price on a Western journalist's head has recently tripled. They do not wish to go. I have nobody to take. Not even the Russian press wish to take the risk.'

Tallis nodded. So it wasn't a case of being afraid, he thought. 'I'll take these, and can you find me a Glock?'

'Model?'

'Seventeen.'

'Good choice, and you can interchange the cartridges with the Makarov.'

Bullshit, Tallis thought, and said so. 'They might be nominally the same size but they aren't interchangeable,' he added.

Chaikova broke into a smile and turned to Orlov. 'He's good, your man.'

The range turned out to be a flat piece of land adjoining one of the many vegetable plots. Targets were laid out at different intervals. A broken-down building at the far end was rigged up as a practice area for hostage retrieval. Putting all three guns through their paces, he struck a deal with Chaikova, and to seal it drank several toasts: to business, to Orlov's personal connections; to Chaikova's resourcefulness and daring; to Tallis's ballistic skill. After that, things got interesting.

'And what are you going to do with all this weaponry?' Orlov said. 'Take the guns back to Britain and sell them on?'

'I'm not that kind of a businessman,' Tallis said mildly.

'He's a soldier.' Chaikova grinned, the scars on his face joining up and forming an interesting curve.

'Yes,' Orlov said, in a knowing way that told Tallis he was putting the pieces together. It seemed the best moment to indulge in a little misinformation.

'You guessed.' Tallis smiled, watching as Orlov's dark eyebrows shot up and met his bleached hairline. 'I'm on a bit of a mercy mission. You see, back in the UK I met a Chechen lady who has a son here. She asked me to pass on a message for her. Well, more than that. She asked me to see that he was OK. Now, I know what you both think,' Tallis said, meeting their mystified expressions, 'but she's a nice lady and what harm could it do?'

'You need guns for that?' Chaikova said, his eyes narrowing.

'Not exactly,' Tallis fudged. 'I had this idea of taking him back to Grozny.'

'Madness,' Orlov snorted. Tallis noticed that Chaikova said nothing at all.

'Trouble is, it turns out this guy was arrested this morning and carted off to Moscow State Prison. Any ideas how I can spring him? I'm willing to pay.' Tallis looked from Orlov to Chaikova who, in turn, looked at each other for a long moment. A sly smile crept across Orlov's face. Tallis got the feeling that another business proposal was in the offing. 'How much?' Orlov said.

'Whatever you want.' Tallis hoped that the SIS had deep pockets.

'Kumarin mentioned you picked him up in a Robinson 22.'

'Yes, that's... Wait a minute,' Tallis said. 'You mean you want me to get you one?'

'*Give* me one. It is a fair exchange,' Orlov said, sounding very reasonable about something that was entirely *unreasonable*.

Tallis let out a sigh.

'Second-hand,' Orlov said.

The equivalent of sixty, maybe seventy thousand pounds, Tallis thought. 'Alright, but can you do it?'

Orlov licked the corner of his mouth, nodded slowly. 'I have a friend who is Chechen. He could help.'

A *friend*? Tallis thought. He thought Orlov hated the Chechens. He kept his gaze steady. One thing he was beginning to discover about Orlov was his moral inconsistency.

'Who gives a fuck about one lousy Chechen?' Orlov

shrugged, rolling his eyes, as if this explained the ambiguity in his thinking. 'Medved,' Orlov said with emphasis to Chaikova.

'You mean Medved, the second-hand car dealer down the road?' Chaikova grinned.

'Not sure I follow you,' Tallis said. 'If this guy's a Chechen, how the hell can he help?'

'His brother-in-law is Russian and he works in Moscow State Prison.' Orlov winked. What Orlov meant was that, for the right price, he could be persuaded to spring Ruslan.

A short journey in Chaikova's Land Cruiser led them to Medved's yard. Broken-down-looking cars with dents in their flanks lined one side of a perimeter fence, vehicles for sale, mainly Ladas, Volvos and Zaz Tavrias the other. Medved was the Russian word for bear. A hefty-looking man with a grizzled beard and thick, fleshy features, he suited the nickname.

'My brother-in-law, Ilya, is a piece of shit,' Medved growled, 'but for the right price he can be organised.' Tallis was already doing the maths: a helicopter to Orlov, a bung to Medved and a bung to his brother-in-law. *Ouch!*

'What about the police, the FSB, the—' Tallis broke off as three pairs of eyes swivelled and trained on him.

'This is Russia.' Orlov grinned. 'And in Russia all things are possible.'

CHAPTER NINE

ORLOV was right. Twenty-four hours later, Tallis received a call. Ruslan Maisakov was to be released from prison at eleven o'clock sharp. Before he left, Tallis made contact with Asim and gave him edited highlights of events to date.

'Ivanov seems pretty well protected for someone who's no longer in the limelight,' Tallis said.

'Never underestimate the role of the Prime Minister. He may no longer be President, but he's generally regarded as the power behind the throne. Our killer needs only to get lucky once. And there are plenty of opportunities to strike. The opening ceremony of the World Newspaper Congress takes place in less than three weeks. Traditionally, the President takes part, but the role could also fall to the Prime Minister.'

'Can't you issue a covert warning?'

'Too risky. This arms dealer, you think he's your in?'

'Fairly certain. I thought I'd leave it a day and contact him, see if he'll play ball.'

'Don't leave it too long. Things have gone scarily quiet.'

'I've been thinking about that. Do you honestly believe that Darke would risk coming all the way down from the mountains, across the Caucasus to Moscow, to carry out the hits?'

'He's certainly capable of it.'

'Then why am I looking for him in the mountains? Why not here?'

'Because we have no intelligence to suggest he's actually living in Moscow. His last known address—'

'If you can call a terrorist training camp an address,' Tallis chipped in.

'Is somewhere near Borzoi.'

Not for the first time, Tallis wondered about Asim or rather Fazan's source of information. 'Something else,' Tallis said. 'I think I might have gone seriously over budget.'

Asim let out a laugh. 'For once I can honestly say that's not my problem.'

The prison surroundings were much as Tallis had imagined, daylight giving it, if anything, a more dismal and threatening appearance. The same could be said for Ruslan, Tallis thought, watching as a tall, pale-skinned young man wearing nothing but a threadbare jacket and baggy trousers slowly emerged from the eighteenth-century entrance. In spite of his bruised face, this was still recognisably and without doubt an adult version of the serious youngster in the photograph, but the aspiration and hope evident in the child's expression had long been extinguished.

As Ruslan shuffled past, Tallis spoke. 'Ruslan?'

Ruslan turned slowly. He had sad, angry eyes, much like his mother's. 'Do I know you?'

'It's OK,' Tallis said softly in Chechen, raising both hands, palms facing. 'I'm a friend.'

Ruslan's laugh was dry. 'I don't know who the hell you are. Leave me alone.'

'Your mother sent me.'

Ruslan scowled, his face a picture of suspicion. How many times had he been tricked? Tallis wondered as Ruslan shook his head, turned on his heel and made to go.

'No, wait,' Tallis said, catching at Ruslan's sleeve, the fabric oily in his fingers. 'Here,' he said, pressing the battered photograph into the young man's hand.

Ruslan stopped in his tracks, uncurled his dirt-streaked fingers, ran a grimy nail over the print, staring, it seemed, at another soul, another life. 'My mother gave you this?' He looked up, awe-struck.

'Lena, yes.'

'And she is alive, she's well?'

'She is living in England.'

'England?' Ruslan said, bewildered. 'And my little sister, Asya?'

Tallis saw hope flare in the young man's face. 'Look,' he said, 'I don't know about you, but I'd prefer we had this conversation somewhere quiet and warm.

I'm staying in an apartment in Tverskaya. We can talk there. It will be safer.'

'Nowhere is safe,' Ruslan said. This time the smile was genuine.

'Well, it's the best I can do,' Tallis said, a sudden feeling of elation sweeping over him. Ruslan was a sign, an omen, even the key. Now that he'd found him, he knew, in his bones, Graham Darke would follow.

Ruslan hesitated, briefly looked behind him then back at the prison walls. 'Alright,' he said, 'but walk slowly.'

The reason for Ruslan's sluggish gait soon became apparent. Back at the apartment, while Tallis dug out a set of clean clothes, Ruslan took a bath from which he emerged, a towel wrapped around his waist. His thin body and legs were a mass of bruises the colour of fresh aubergines.

'Jesus!' Tallis exclaimed.

'Prison brutality is normal in Russia. You have no idea what prisoners endure. If you're like me, well…' His voice petered out, a lost expression on his face.

'I'm surprised they didn't break anything.'

'One of the lucky ones.' Ruslan flicked a smile, stiffly pulling on the clothes while Tallis made coffee. 'Now, tell me about my mother and my sister,' he said when they were sitting down.

So Tallis did, breaking the news about Asya as best he could. When he finished there was a long, painful silence. Finally, Ruslan spoke. 'You say my mother will be deported?'

'Eventually, yes.' Except what had Rasu said? *In reality, you're only ever in with a chance if you're a family.*

Ruslan thoughtfully stroked the stubble on his chin then turned his full dark-eyed gaze on Tallis. 'I'm not clear why your paths crossed. You must have some reason.'

'I do. I need to find someone.' Tallis got up, retrieved the photograph of Graham Darke from his backpack, handed it to Ruslan. 'He's a British guy. He's gone missing in the mountains.'

Ruslan stared at it, shook his head sadly, handed the print back. 'He's probably dead. People disappear all the time. And now, with the new offensive...' His voice petered out.

'I have to try.'

'You're crazy. You don't understand.'

No, you don't understand, Tallis thought. How could you? 'It's not negotiable.'

Ruslan leant back in the chair. 'You're paid to find him?'

'Yes.'

Ruslan nodded. Tallis could almost see the word *mercenary* flashing up on Ruslan's forehead. 'Then I hope you were paid a lot of money,' Ruslan said. 'Not only are there mines in the mountains but Mafiya, and soldiers, the type of guys who resent being back there again and who would kill simply because they've run out of vodka. There's only one way to do it and that's to find a fixer.'

Tallis nodded.

'And you'll need false papers.'

Tallis nodded again.

Ruslan inclined his head. 'If you know all this, why are you here?'

'If *you* know all this, why are *you* here?' Tallis smiled.

Ruslan let out a cold laugh. 'Where do you think I'd find that kind of money?'

Tallis leant towards him. 'Would you go back if you could?'

'Of course. It's my home. I still have family there.'

'Really?' He didn't remember Lena mentioning anyone.

'My aunt Katya, my father's sister. She lives in the suburbs of Grozny. Perhaps, one day, I could find a place for me and my mother there,' Ruslan said, reflective.

'Then come with me.'

'You're mad,' Ruslan half laughed, not quite certain whether to take this Englishman seriously.

Tallis flashed a grin. 'I know.'

Tallis gave Ruslan a bed for the night. First light, while Ruslan was kneeling and saying his prayers, Tallis was up drinking coffee in the kitchen, studying the photograph of Darke, trying to work out whether Chaikova, the arms dealer, would play. He took Chaikova for being a calculated risk-taker. He could read it in that

scarred face of his and in his eyes, and although Tallis
didn't particularly relish him at close quarters, he
reckoned he'd be a really useful bloke to have on board.
Cool and unflappable and used to things getting down
and dirty, he'd provide a decent piece of muscle should
the need arise. In fact, Chaikova probably enjoyed dis-
pensing damage and, like it or not, Tallis thought it
might be necessary. If Chaikova could get him and
Ruslan to Grozny, Tallis could make the rest of the
journey into the mountains alone.

One phone call to Orlov later, Chaikova was on the
line. Tallis explained what he wanted him to do.

'To Grozny, you say?' Chaikova said, in a considered manner.

'Yes.'

'One way?'

Tallis hoped not in the literal sense. 'Yes.'

'After that, you are on your own,' Chaikova said.
'And you say there are two of you?'

'That's right.'

Tallis hesitated. Chaikova was quick to pick up on
it. 'And?'

'He's Chechen.'

'As long as he doesn't tell me what to do, so what?
Grigori will fix papers for a price.'

'Fine,' Tallis said with more confidence now that
he'd been given official clearance from Asim.

'The route,' Chaikova said, 'it is probably better I
decide. I know the checkpoints.'

'Fair enough. Vehicle?'

'Four-by-four is best. There's a lot of mud this time of year. Where are you staying?'

Tallis told him.

'I will get things organised then visit and collect the money. I will also bring extra firepower.'

Tallis had an image of Dragunovs, AKs and hand grenades. 'The papers,' he said. 'How quickly do you think Orlov can get hold of them?'

'Soon as. I will talk to Grigori personally.'

'That's very good of you. I appreciate it.'

'No problem,' Chaikova said. 'Life is dull. It is some time since I enjoyed an adventure.'

The next two days were a whirl of activity. Any reservations on Ruslan's part were swiftly overcome in the light of reports of a heavy-handed clampdown in the ghettoes. The simple truth was that the journey home provided him with a goal that had long been absent from his life.

Tallis bought enough suitable clothing for the boy. A Russian-style Cossak hat, pulled well down over Ruslan's head, helped take some of the focus off his bruises, which were now fading to a paler shade of green. As for Tallis, he cleaned his weapons, checked and double-checked basic equipment—compass, knife, map, backpack, including a down-filled sleeping bag, all-important water and vacuum-sealed food supplies. He noticed that someone had thoughtfully added field dressings to the kit and several phials of morphine and a syringe.

Knowledge was power, particularly when it came to route planning. Although Tallis thought he could trust Chaikova's judgement, he and Ruslan studied the maps in detail.

'Most people used to fly from Moscow straight to Grozny. With the flights suspended you could still travel by road. The troops used to come in via Mozdok, a front-line town on the border. The headquarters of the combined forces of the North Caucasus are based there. Failing that, they'd fly by helicopter to Nazran.'

'And now, which would be the best way?'

'The best meaning safest? Travel by road to Rostov-on-Don.' Probably what Chaikova had in mind, Tallis thought.

'How far?'

'Seven hundred and forty-four miles.'

Depending on mode of transport, it could take the best part of three very uncomfortable days, Tallis estimated.

'But whichever way…' Ruslan pointed out on the map '…there's a main checkpoint here beyond Nazran, and beyond that the OMON, or riot police, are stationed at the village of Assinovskaya. 'This friend of yours,' he said, looking up. 'He must be worth a lot to you.'

'Yes,' Tallis said simply. 'He is.'

As it turned out, Ruslan was right about the route, but

not the method of travel. Chaikova called round two evenings later bearing false papers. He was wearing khaki-coloured pants and a camouflage-style jacket. He also sported a pair of aviators. Tallis thought he might as well have *Come and Arrest me* painted on his shaved head.

'Change of plan,' Chaikova announced. 'We're going by train tonight.'

'What?' Tallis said. 'If we travel by train we can't take any weapons with us.'

'No problem,' Chaikova said, a phrase that Tallis suspected was going to drive him nuts. 'I know a man in Rostov who will supply.'

'And how are we going to travel after that?' Tallis said, trying to tame his growing exasperation.

'Rostov has a huge car market,' Ruslan pointed out.

Chaikova nodded. 'We will easily pick up a set of wheels.'

'It's a good plan,' Ruslan said, studying the papers that told him he was a Russian-born administrative assistant. He showed the papers to Tallis. 'Administering what?' Tallis frowned.

'Doesn't matter,' Chaikova said loftily, 'it will do.' The way he was eyeing Ruslan, Tallis half wondered whether it was a trick but, then again, if one went down, they all did.

They caught the Metro to Komsomolskaya and walked to Kazansky, a vast draughty train station. The train they were catching was bound for Vladikavkaz,

capital of North Ossetia. En route it would stop at
Rostov-on-Don. Chaikova had booked tickets in a
second-class carriage with a sleeping compartment.
The train, which was warm and cosy, was busy with
families and single men saying goodbye to lovers. Tallis
didn't sleep much that night.

The next morning it seemed that they were stopping
at every station along the way, the train constantly
filling up with and emptying its cargo of passengers.
The atmosphere on the train was strangely electric. A
spirit of bonhomie prevailed that simply didn't exist in
Britain: people shared food and drink as well as conversation. Some stations were busy thoroughfares, providing goods for sale, men and women rushing to the
windows to trade anything from bottled fruit and sweet
pastries to whole fish wrapped in newspaper, and bags
of beetroot; others looked empty and forgotten, a little
like the bleak Russian steppes, Tallis thought. Neither
he nor his travelling companions talked very much:
Tallis because he feared that one of the numerous
female officials stomping up and down the corridor
might overhear; Chaikova because it was a way of demonstrating his dislike, on principle, of Ruslan. Despite
that, they all ate well in the dining car—soup and
pirozhi, savoury meat pies, washed down with coffee
in plastic cups. By the second evening they were pulling
into Rostov-on-Don. Herds of their fellow passengers
disembarked. Here they met their first obstacle: OMON
patrols.

'Stay cool,' Chaikova said, taking out a pack of cigarettes, walking calmly in front, papers at the ready.

'Cigarette?' he offered an officer as Tallis and Ruslan surged forward, averting their eyes from the granite-faced policemen, the patrol entirely unable to cope with the sheer volume of people.

'Thanks,' Tallis heard the officer say behind him as Chaikova pushed his way through to join them.

'Which way?' Tallis muttered.

'Here.' Chaikova led the way, crossing over and turning immediately into and down a road lined with nineteenth-century red-brick houses. A few narrow streets on and they were in a less salubrious part of town where they were booked into a dispiriting and dilapidated-looking hotel. Tallis soon got the picture: hookers outside; cockroaches inside. He was too tired to pay much attention to either.

As soon as they were shown to their room, a barren chamber furnished with three single beds with dubious-looking bedding, Ruslan fell to his hands and knees to pray. Chaikova yawned and stretched. 'A man must have his enthusiasms, I suppose,' he said cynically. 'Say one for me while you're at it.'

'I'd be here all night, then,' Ruslan flashed back, with more humour than Tallis thought Chaikova deserved. Ruslan's magnanimity was rewarded by a deep throaty laugh from Chaikova.

The next morning, after a vile breakfast of sour yogurt and stewed coffee, they headed for the market. The nearest Tallis had ever come to visiting a place like it was one of the big markets outside Birmingham where you could pick up a battered Fiesta for two hundred quid. This was full of Ladas, Volgas, Mercedes, Land Cruisers, and museum pieces that he'd never seen before in his life. Chaikova had his eye on a Soviet-style 4x4 that had seen better times. Tallis preferred the look of a Nissan 4x4 but, as Chaikova had offered to do the buying and driving, he graciously deferred. Driving the vehicle to the nearest petrol station revealed a number of strange-sounding noises from the exhaust and clutch, although none seemed particularly terminal.

'Nothing like travelling in style,' Ruslan said dryly.

'As if you'd know,' Chaikova shot back. 'At least it's quicker than a tractor.'

'What are you suggesting?' Ruslan said, edgy. 'That Chechens are all peasants?'

'Far too glamorous a description.'

Ruslan let out a slow hiss of anger. 'I guess that's to be expected from a foul-mouthed, pig-eating Russian.'

'Oi, boy,' Chaikova growled. 'Remember, I'm doing you a favour here.'

'Really? Well, I'll act grateful if you act nice.'

Chaikova twisted round and blew Ruslan a kiss, a naughty grin suddenly plastered across his face. 'Nice enough for you?' At which Ruslan then Tallis burst out laughing.

After they'd filled up, Chaikova announced the next stop: his friendly arms dealer.

'Drop me here,' Tallis said. 'I'm going in search of a decent cup of coffee and something to eat.'

'You don't want any weapons?' Chaikova said, mystified.

'No need,' Tallis said, pointing at the backpack positioned down by his feet. 'That's why I wanted the Kurtz, remember?' And the Makarov, he thought.

Chaikova broke into a big smile then his expression darkened. 'What about the Chechen? Does he want guns?' Chaikova gestured with his thumb at Ruslan, who was sitting in the back.

'Thought you were supposed to be polite.' Tallis looked across unsmiling. 'Why don't you ask him?' He had no time for backbiting between them. It could cost them their lives.

Chaikova, chisel-faced, swivelled round, raised an eyebrow. 'I'd be grateful.' Ruslan nodded, ironic, squeezing a grudging smile from the Russian.

'He'd better go with you, then,' Tallis said, opening the door and hopping out with his backpack. 'Meet me in a couple of hours back at the dump,' he said, alluding to the hotel, and walked away. He quickly found himself in wide tree-lined streets with nearby parks. Rostov-on-Don, the entrance to the Caucasus, was, in fact, a much nicer regional city than he'd first imagined. Although it was cold, slashes of sunlight filtered through the trees, dappling the pavement, giving the illusion of spring. It hummed with people and, like a little Moscow, the buzzword was trade.

After a while, the parkland dried up and he found himself in a quieter area with far fewer people. He seemed to be in a maze of brick railway arches and back streets with tired-looking homes, the only inhabitants an old woman pulling a shopping trolley, muttering obscenities and a couple of teenage boys off their faces on hard liquor. Nobody paid him any attention. Nobody posed a threat.

Feeling hungry, he went into the first café he came across, off a side street full of lock-ups, close to a road where the river Don ran through the city. In Russian, he ordered coffee and pizza. Both arrived promptly and he ate and drank, savouring the solitude. He was so lost in thought he almost missed the two leather-jacketed men who entered the café, one a typical Russian— short, stocky with fair hair and blue eyes—the other taller, heavier featured with pouched cheeks. They were talking softly to the female proprietor. Something in her tense expression triggered Tallis's alarm bells. When she glanced anxiously in his direction he thought it time to decamp. He scraped back the chair and got up slowly, working a smile onto his face and thanking the owner as he left. The two men immediately stopped talking and glanced away. There was something too studied about them, Tallis thought as he opened the door and slipped outside. If they were professionals, he knew they wouldn't immediately follow so he hacked down the narrow street, darted into a darkened doorway and, taking the Makarov from his backpack, loaded a magazine, attached a silencer and released the safety.

Sure enough, the Russians came out of the café, looked both ways then, as if by a sixth sense, headed in the direction he'd just taken. Tallis could almost feel the air part as both men walked past. Counting to five and knowing that as soon as they hit the main street they'd realise his trick, he moved back into the alley and walked swiftly in the other direction, body hugging the wall. He'd gone no more than a few metres when the sound of footsteps hammered in his ears. That's when he knew he was clean out of options.

He turned in time to see the stocky guy move for his weapon, the taller of the two already taking up a typical shooting stance, legs apart, knees slightly bent, a deadly PSM blow-back pistol in his hand. Without hesitation, Tallis squeezed the trigger, taking down the tall guy first with a head shot, then let off a second round, felling the man's colleague. Two follow-up shots reduced his ammo to four rounds. Pulse hammering, Tallis looked around him. Other than a dog bolting past, the alley was empty. He couldn't do anything about the blood, but he could remove the bodies. Breaking into the nearest lock-up, he lifted both men inside, careful not to leave a trail. A quick trawl through their wallets revealed nothing other than their names: no organisation, no rank. Reversing his jacket to conceal a bloodstain on the sleeves, he pulled the door closed.

Rolling up his collar, he set off down the street, leaving what he hoped seemed nothing more serious than evidence of a drunken brawl behind him, and returned via a circuitous route to the seedy hotel entrance. Why the two guys had singled him out, he hadn't a clue. And that worried him. Could it be connected to the FSB man he'd run into when he'd been checking out the prison, and who'd later wound up with his throat cut? Could Orlov be playing fast and loose? But, then, why would he compromise the safety of his friend Chaikova? The trouble with working in a strange land was that it was difficult to tell who was the enemy.

Nodding a good morning at the blowsy-faced proprietor, Tallis crossed the lobby and went up the stairs to the room he shared with the others.

Chaikova was in his element. Wearing a shoulder holster, he was examining the goods: the latest Browning, derived from an earlier high-power model; and a SIG P226. For heftier weaponry, Chaikova had gone for an Uzi sub-machine-gun, not the standard pray and spray but the more diminutive model, the Mini-Uzi, smaller in every dimension bar the calibre. Ruslan had settled for the thirty-round Steyr SPP.

'I told him it was good for a two-handed hold,' Chaikova said.

'Look,' Ruslan said, imitating a typical shooting stance, more American gangster than British firearms officer.

'Bang! Bang! That's my boy,' Chaikova said appreciatively, immediately colouring on realising the inadvertent warmth of his remark. Spotting weakness, Ruslan grinned and winked at him.

'Fine.' Tallis sincerely hoped Ruslan wouldn't need the advice.

'And I got us these,' Chaikova said, producing three Kevlars.

'Good idea.'

'Everything alright?' Chaikova frowned.

'Cool,' Tallis replied.

They left the next morning before first light. It took them eight hours to drive south along the main three-lane highway in the direction of Stavropol. On the way a news report hissed and crackled out of the radio. Tallis strained to pick up the gist, fearing that it would reveal the killing of two men in Rostov-on-Don. It didn't. It concerned a Chechen terrorist attack at Nalchik.

'What do you say to that?' Chaikova said, an ugly note back in his voice, the remark clearly aimed at Ruslan.

'I say there are terrorists on both sides,' Ruslan said, staring out of the window. 'I don't agree with either.'

Chaikova gave a snort. Tallis was wondering whether Darke had had any involvement.

The journey was punctuated by numerous check-points. So far their luck had held out. After cursory examination of their papers by jumpy and undernourished-looking soldiers, they were waved through. Tallis understood the sub-text. Another crackly news report had talked of the possibility of suicide bombers. Whether this was the Russian government's method of ramping up the fear factor or whether it was based on genuine intelligence, you could hardly blame the average soldier for being scared. Suicide bombers were difficult to defeat. It really was a case of Russian roulette. Fortunately, the threat was working in their favour. Nobody wanted to invite the opportunity by stopping them and poring over their papers.

Tallis, in the front, his cheek against the glass, spent the time contemplating the ever-changing landscape—fields of maize and sunflowers lining tributaries, surprisingly green pastures with cows and sheep, the odd shepherd's hut, finally hints of shadowy peaks that haunted from a distance. It wasn't so much what he could see as what he could sense, as if the land beyond spoke another narrative: of impending violence and hatred and dissent.

By the time they were drawing into the outskirts of Pyatigorsk, the light was starting to fade. Tallis stared out at a dense thicket of trees, their branches broken, the 4x4 slowing, rattling along a road slippery with mud and cratered with potholes, another checkpoint ahead. Usual four-man combo—one to flag them down, one to cover him, one sentry forward and one at the rear. This time they weren't so lucky.

'Registration number,' the guy doing the talking barked.

Chaikova gave it.

'Where's your spare wheel?'

Chaikova smiled, yawned and told him. Had he got

the answer wrong it would indicate that the vehicle was stolen, Tallis registered, trying to calculate whether the soldiers were going for a quick search based on nothing at all, or whether they'd been tipped off and were working up to a thorough going-over. As Chaikova had passed their little test, Tallis hoped that they'd be waved on.

'You, get out,' the soldier ordered, waving his rifle in Tallis's direction. Not a good idea, Tallis thought. Once he was out of the vehicle anything could happen. He stayed put.

The soldier barked the order again. Three others gathered round, weapons raised. Tallis had a sick image of the vehicle peppered with bullet holes, three metal-riddled bodies spilling out of the wreckage. He blinked. He could feel Ruslan's hot breath on his neck. Chaikova, cool as mint julep, stared ahead, lazily chewing a wad of gun. Against every instinct, Tallis got out, nice and slowly, acting as easy as possible. He smiled at the officer, who had a face like a graveyard, and spoke to him in Russian.

'Papers,' the soldier said, one hand shooting out.

The night crackled with tension.

Tallis hesitated, knowing that whichever set he relinquished could be a bad move. Problem was, he had to act one way or another. Remembering Chaikova's comment that journalists no longer travelled to the region because of the high price on their heads, he decided to go with his British helicopter guy identity. When they cocked their weapons he did as he was told.

'You British?' the soldier said, looking up.

'*Da.*'

'Businessman?' The word was spat out.

'*Da.*'

The soldier fired a volley of Russian, too fast for Tallis to catch. Another soldier standing next to him burst out laughing. Tallis was handed back his papers and waved away as if he were no more than a speck of dirt underneath the soldier's boot.

Tallis walked slowly back to the 4x4, climbing into it as lazily as he'd climbed out. Chaikova started the engine, depressed the clutch and jolted down the road. Tallis let out a breath. A kilometre later he asked Chaikova what had been said. Chaikova kept on chewing.

'Well?' Tallis said, impatient.

Chaikova turned to him, briefly taking his eyes off the road. 'He said you are a dead man.'

Leaving Pyatigorsk, one of those sprawling places that looked as if it had previously enjoyed more refined times and could currently do with some money being spent on it, they travelled south along the M29, along the last of the flatlands, and headed towards Nalchik, in the central Caucasus, and roughly one hundred and thirty miles west of Grozny. Chaikova was reluctant to spend the night there due to the recent terrorist attack. Tallis took the view that if the place was a recent target it was unlikely to come in for a repeat performance any time soon. After a frank exchange, in which Tallis gained the upper hand, they booked into an unassuming hotel in the centre—another win to Tallis as Chaikova had favoured a more elegant hotel in the wooded suburbs.

According to Ruslan, Nalchik was a spa town known for its fine mineral water. Not that any, either mineral or plain tap, was in evidence that evening or any evening at Hotel Rossiya, something Chaikova took great pleasure in pointing out. It wasn't that extraordinary; water had a habit of being switched off in Russia and its satellite states. Later, with no ill will, Chaikova produced a bottle of *konyak* and offered to share it with Tallis, Ruslan already being asleep in bed.

The two of them stood out on the balcony overlooking the street, the cold against their cheeks, the only sound the howl of a stray dog and the noise of small-arms fire in the distance. The night was as black as any Tallis had seen. As if someone had switched all the lights off, it felt compressed, with silence and fear.

'You know Timur?' Tallis said, feeling the alcohol zip through his veins.

'Timur Garipova?'

'I'm not sure of his surname. He said he worked for the State. Grigori invited him to one of his dinners and we got talking. I had the impression he was connected to the FSB. Quite a cool customer.'

Chaikova let out a slow gurgling laugh. 'I know the man. Part of the new criminal elite.'

'What?'

'You're right,' Chaikova flicked a smile. 'He does work for the FSB.'

'And?'

'In a rather specialist unit.'

'Oh, yeah?' Tallis took another drink. Chaikova wasn't being coy. He was enjoying the chase.

'It's a secret department dedicated to extra-judiciary killings.'

'Assassinations?' Tallis suddenly felt quite sober.

'Among other things.' Chaikova shrugged.

'What other things?'

'Abduction, terrorism, provocation.'

Tallis took another drink, trying to think. Could Timur have engineered the incident in Rostov-on-Don? Had he ordered his execution? Then his mind leapfrogged in another direction. What if all this stuff with Graham was a blind? What if Graham Darke and his merry band were fall guys? What if Chechen terrorists had had absolutely nothing to do with the hits? His mind travelled back to Lena's remark. She'd claimed that the FSB were behind a series of explosions that had ripped through Moscow as a means to discredit Chechen terrorists and provide the motivation to go to war for the second time. Trash or truth? And were they doing it again?

'To black night,' Chaikova said, raising his glass and toasting the sky. 'The time for trade in bullets and booze.'

The next morning the air was thick with low swirling cloud that clung like shrouds. They left Nalchik and

followed a tributary of the Terek, the river running cold
and stark beside them. Mountain peaks faded in and out
of the gloom, colours bleeding out. Eventually, they
branched off towards the infamous town of Beslan,
scene of a school massacre. The place was silent.
Kestrels wheeling overhead, hemmed in on all sides by
ridges and peaks, the slow earth descended into dirt
track, the perfect terrain for mines. Tallis spent the next
hour feverishly scanning for tripwires, the tell-tale
stakes denoting the presence of the POMZ-2M, and the
flat, circular-shaped pieces of metal common to the
PMN. He suggested they get off the slip road and follow
a main route, pressing on towards Nazran. It would
then only take a couple of hours to drive from there to
Grozny, but Chaikova said it was too dangerous. 'You
want to make that OMON guy's dream come true?'

'He's right,' Ruslan said, his voice travelling from
the rear. 'I can get by. Even that big lump in the front,'
meaning Chaikova, 'can wing it. You stand no chance.'

And this time Chaikova didn't protest or disagree.

And so they dropped down towards Vladikavkaz, the
capital of North Ossetia and the ultimate destination
had they stayed on the train instead of getting off at
Rostov-on-Don. The road became steep and wild, hills
and high mountain peaks rising up out of the murk.
They turned off and followed the Assa River towards
Achkoi-Martan, skirting the foothills of Samashki and
on to the houses of Alkhan-Yurt, staying clear of the
Federal Highway. The village, only a kilometre from

the outskirts of Grozny, was once, according to Ruslan, the scene of a massacre. 'Russian soldiers maintain a fierce battle took place here even though there was no sign of Chechen fighters and the victims were all civilians,' he added dryly. 'At first they came with planes,' he said, 'and then they sent in federal forces.'

Tallis looked around him, saw a belt of trees chopped down.

'Mosques were destroyed, homes flattened, the bodies of the dead and dying left lying in the dirt,' Ruslan said, his voice a chilling commentary. Chaikova, shaking his head in pity, drove on.

The village was deserted apart from a couple of amputees who stared at them with empty eyes. In spite of the rebuilt minarets, the homes with double-glazing and pretty courtyards, Tallis pictured something else: corpses; scavenging dogs; and destruction.

'Where have all the people gone?' he said.

Chaikova pulled up. Ruslan hung out of the vehicle, asked one of the men, dark-skinned and deep-eyed, what had happened.

'Up into the mountains,' the man said, pointing with a crutch. 'They fear another onslaught.'

The cloud lifted. The sky was the colour of mercury. On they drove, dipping and looping through conflicting scenery: forest one side—providing perfect camouflage for troops of either denomination—marsh with tall rushes and ducks the other, the flood plain extending to the foot of the mountains. It was here, where the trees clung to black shale and they stopped for a moment to relieve themselves, that Tallis was seized with the weirdest sensation, as if these surroundings had absorbed past events. It was in the trees, in the soil, and in the rocks and crevices. The stony ground beneath his feet felt poisoned with fear and the spilt blood of too many young men. He'd felt the same sense of waste and hopelessness on the Normandy beaches and on a bleak visit to Auschwitz. In spite of not being particularly cold, he felt chilled to his bones.

From Alkhan-Yurt, they bumped along and, again after several checkpoints, made it to Grozny. When they finally arrived, Tallis was struck by the utter normality, the newness and modernity. It was evident in the buildings, the hotels and mosques in particular, the sidewalks and tree-lined avenues. Paradoxical was the word that sprung to mind. He felt as if he'd travelled from one country and into another. Ruslan was even more impressed.

'The new Chechen president might be a Russian puppet,' he said, 'but, my God, he's transformed this city. Only a few years ago this was nothing but rubble.'

Driving down the block and past Minutka Square, Tallis saw a group of teenagers chatting on mobiles. Kids like these were barometers of political and social stability, he thought. They looked happy, oblivious, more connected than their Moscow counterparts, and yet…

There was a definite Russian military presence and, out of the corner of his eye, he saw the glint of metal

as four plainclothes men with raw features lounged
outside a café, automatic weapons at their sides. 'Local
officials,' Ruslan murmured.

'Not your usual choice of accessory for the office,'
Tallis said, meeting the heavy-eyed, silent gaze of one
cold-looking individual as they cruised past. Were they
looking for someone? A man who'd killed two others
in broad daylight, perhaps? He swatted the thought.

'Nothing more than bandits,' Chaikova growled. 'As
for your president,' he said addressing Ruslan, 'he's
nothing more than an illiterate thug. Paramilitary units
in his own government form the rule of law here, and,
whatever our Russian Prime Minister says, he's hated
by lots of people in Moscow. It's only a matter of time
before he goes. You wait and see. Once Ivanov fades
from the scene, that Chechen rebel you call a leader will
disappear.'

'If he does, all hell will break out among the clans,'
Ruslan said.

And that's what Tallis was afraid of.

Ruslan's Aunt Katya lived on the outskirts to the east
of the city. Dotted between block after block of new
housing complexes and sites under construction were
some of the old-style properties that had miraculously
escaped destruction in the two previous conflicts.
Typically each dwelling had a walled courtyard garden
with wooden fences and fruit trees of apple and pear,
and shrubs of flowering jasmine. Years before, they'd
have provided terrific cover for men with murder in

mind, Tallis thought, imagining them scooting over the walls, clambering among the trees and taking up positions. Perhaps they would again.

'This is it,' Ruslan said, his cheeks coloured with excitement.

Chaikova pulled up. Ruslan got out. It was unspoken but this was Ruslan's moment so Tallis and Chaikova stayed where they were. Tallis watched as Ruslan went in through the gate, his shoulders back, his head held high, a lilt in his step as he walked up the short path to a dwelling no bigger than Tallis's bungalow back in Birmingham. He briefly thought of Lena, wondered if she was alright, hoping that Rasu and Viva would keep an eye on her like they'd said they would, wondered if Lena's sister-in-law had the same parched features, the same...

Tallis craned forward almost the same time as Chaikova, Tallis twisting his head to get a better view. He was transfixed. He didn't believe in love at first sight, lust certainly, but it wasn't that either. He literally felt his heart explode. Unlike Lena, Katya was blonde, her skin, without make-up, fine textured and the colour of buttermilk. Her eyes, pools of electric blue, shone with vitality yet the slight downturn at the edges revealed fragile vulnerability. She had a small straight nose and her mouth was small, too much so some might say but, to Tallis's mind, it was utterly kissable, and when she smiled, her face lit up.

Moments later, and with introductions over, of which

Tallis remembered nothing, they were standing near the stove, in Katya's tiny kitchen area, the rest of the room part sitting, part dining room. As the kettle boiled for tea, conversation between aunt and nephew rattled along. It gave Tallis the opportunity to perfectly study and commit each detail of Katya's face to memory. She really was astonishingly beautiful.

Her voice, he noticed, was low-pitched, more oboe than flute. A cheap dark green shawl hung across her slim shoulders. Underneath, she wore a loose-fitting shirt tucked into a pair of slim-hipped worn denim jeans and boots. Her hands, ringless, fluttered like doves each time she made a point. When she looked at Ruslan, her expression was full of warmth and pride and concern.

'And Lena, your mother!' Katya exclaimed. 'You say she escaped to England?'

Ruslan nodded and explained Tallis's connection.

'You met her?' Katya said, her eyes wide and enchanting.

'That's right,' Tallis said.

'And Asya?' She beamed.

'Aunt,' Ruslan intervened, darting an anxious look at Tallis. 'So many questions. Come, the kettle hasn't boiled yet. We can make tea and then we can talk and I will answer them all.'

The way she moved, unstudied, fluid, it was quite clear to Tallis that Katya had no idea how beautiful she was, or how attractive to the opposite sex. In spite of her Chechen blood, Chaikova also gawped at her, stupefied.

Finally, the tea made, the conversation returned to family and took a painful downward curve. Ruslan first broke the news about his father, Katya's brother.

'We were near Shatoi,' Ruslan said, making Tallis's ears prick—Shatoi was not far from his final destination. 'When we were ambushed by reconnaissance troops heading into the mountains. They thought we were rebels. Dad said that if we went to them and explained, everything would be alright. I tried to dissuade him,' Ruslan said, his voice cracking. Katya fluttered a hand towards him, letting it rest on his arm.

'But, well, you know,' Ruslan said with a sad smile. 'He was always convinced that with reason, justice would prevail.'

'He believed that people were ultimately good,' Katya said, her voice low and strong so that Tallis could tell she shared the same view.

'Well, I don't.' Ruslan's voice was resistant, hard and petulant. 'I went one way. He went the other. And they shot him.'

'You saw this?'

'With my own eyes.'

She sat stock still, acceptance in her expression, as if somehow she'd already known. Then the shock kicked in. A hand flew to her breast, her mouth falling open very slightly. Her luminous skin turned the colour of ash. Tallis felt uncomfortable. He didn't think he should be there witnessing the grief of someone he didn't know, and though a part of him badly wanted to put his arms around her in a simple gesture of humanity, he knew it wasn't his place. He stood, bowed his head, as Ruslan gently guided a mug of hot sweet tea into her hands. Some traditions spanned both East and West. Tallis shifted his weight from one foot to another, and made a move for the door, muttering about getting some fresh air, half dragging Chaikova with him.

'Jesus, what did you do that for?' Chaikova growled.

'What are you, a voyeur?' Tallis rounded on him. 'For God's sake, the woman's entitled to some privacy. We don't belong in there.'

'You certainly don't, for sure.' Chaikova scowled, dragging out his cigarettes. He took one out, tapped the end against the pack, plugged it into his mouth and lit up, blowing two long streams of smoke out through his nostrils.

'What do you mean?' Tallis's tone was ugly. He knew it. Chaikova knew it.

'I saw the way you were looking at her.' Chaikova leered. 'Not that I blame you. I wouldn't mind giving her one myself.'

Cold anger shot through him like a lightning strike. 'Know what, Yuri? You've got about as much sensitivity as an elephant's foreskin.'

'Elephants have large dicks, no?'

Tallis glared at him. Chaikova burst out laughing. Tallis shook his head, began to laugh in spite of himself, the tension between them instantly broken. They waited until Chaikova had finished his cigarette and went back inside. Ruslan nodded quietly. 'My aunt says it is fine for you to stay.'

'No, it's—'

'Fine,' Chaikova said firmly, darting a mischievous look in Tallis's direction.

'Not too Chechen for you?' Ruslan said, lifting a dark playful eyebrow. Chaikova's embarrassed reply was cut off by Katya's reappearance from the cellar where she'd been rooting for bottled fruit and tins of meat and fish.

'Here,' Tallis said, 'let me take those for you.'

'Thank you.' She smiled, shy. When his hand lightly brushed hers he felt as if he'd been shot.

The evening took on a festive atmosphere. They ate a glossy-coloured tomato and lamb stew with carrots and rice, followed by bottled cherries and sour cream. Ruslan, talkative and witty, was a different man in the company of his own flesh and blood. For one brief moment in time Tallis forgot the mountains and the mission. After dinner Chaikova, to Tallis's amazement, insisted on clearing up. Katya, meanwhile, said she was going upstairs to find bedding for them all, in spite of Tallis's protests that they'd brought sleeping bags.

'My nephew will sleep in a proper bed tonight.'

'Then let me help you,' Tallis said.

Katya nodded graciously and Tallis followed her upstairs to a narrow landing, one room off on either side. Katya opened the door to the right. Inside was a single bed, a large bookcase stuffed with books, some piled one on top of the other, and a wardrobe filled with linen. She pulled out sheets and blankets and pillows.

'You're not what I expected,' Tallis began.

'No?' She wrinkled her nose.

'I thought you'd be like Lena somehow.'

'Ah, you mean in looks. We're not all descended from Mongol hordes.' She laughed.

'No, I didn't mean—'

'It's fine,' she said, throwing a sheet to Tallis who shook it out and covered the mattress. 'Most of us are pretty indistinguishable from the Ingush, jointly known as the Vainakh. Farming people, we're the result of decades-ago migration and war and, although the Russians don't like to recognise it, we've been around for six thousand years. Some of us are rumoured to descend from the Crusaders.'

'Hence the blonde looks.' Tallis smiled. 'What do you do here?'

'Exist.' She twitched a dry smile.

'Oh, I'm sorry. I—'

'No, I teach like Lena.'

'Is that why you stay?'

She puffed up a pillow, placed it on the bed with care. 'Suffering this kind of tragedy either turns you into a committed terrorist or pacifist.'

'And you're a pacifist?'

She thought, nodded. 'But I don't blame those who have chosen another path,' she said. 'I don't condone it,' she added quickly, 'But I understand. Before the

Russians marched in and messed with us, most Chechens' desire for independence was secular. Because of the conflict Islam has won many converts. Religion is the natural home for those who seek an identity.'

Tallis understood, at least, that much. The same could be applied to a certain strand of young British-born Asians back home.

'Children need to know that there's another way to live,' Katya said. 'All of the kids in my care have lost family in previous conflicts. There's a whole generation out there waiting to wreak revenge. Unfortunately, the latest turn of events doesn't make my job, or the prospect of long-term peace, any easier.'

'Aren't you afraid?'

'Often,' she said simply. 'Although not like before. Then I really thought I might die.'

'What was it like?' Tallis said, leaning his tall frame against the wall.

She thought for a moment. 'You like fireworks?'

He smiled.

'Think of all those tiny glittering sparks littering the sky then imagine every spark as a fragment of metal. Envisage it raining down on your head.' He knew only too well the damage inflicted by grenades and mortars on the human body. 'I felt then as if I had the lifespan of an insect: from chrysalis to bug to full maturity and death in a matter of days.

'There are no definitions in war, no meal times, no routines, no full stops or commas to the day. Everything goes to hell. It's the uncertainty, the endless passage of time, not knowing whether you might suddenly be caught up in events beyond your control. Things can change with surprising speed in these parts.

'So,' she said, smoothing down the bed sheets. 'What are you doing here?'

Keep it simple. 'Looking for someone.'

She inclined her head. He half thought she was going to say something. Instead, with a smile, she suggested they return to the others.

Midnight. Katya and Ruslan were still talking. Outside was the sound of baying dogs and random gunfire. Chaikova and Tallis were bent over a map. Both planned to leave the next morning in different directions. Tallis traced a line down through the Argun Gorge towards Shatoi.

Chaikova shook his head. 'You will be passing through the triangle of death.'

Tallis looked up. 'This folklore or informed opinion?'

'He's right,' Katya said. 'The area between Shali and Kurchaloi is dangerous.'

'It's all dangerous.' Tallis shrugged. His passage was going to mean a keen divide between speed and concealment. He knew that to leave at night might better obscure his movements, that his sense of smell would be more acute, but the journey would be tortuously slow, especially in unfamiliar terrain. At night, sound was louder, shapes and distance distorted and, if there were mines, he ran the strong risk of triggering an explosion and seriously injuring himself. On balance, he opted for speed.

'Which is why I need to say this,' Katya said, turning to Ruslan, suddenly cupping his chin in her hands. 'You know I love you.'

'Yes, Aunt,' Ruslan said, two points of pink appearing on each of his high cheekbones reminiscent of Lena.

'Then you know that what I'm about to say next is because I love you.'

'What?' Ruslan said, squirming with embarrassment, drawing away.

'We have enjoyed peaceful times, but I fear for the future,' Katya said. 'Things are changing.'

'But—'

'Listen,' Katya said softly, stroking his face with one finger. 'Moscow is nervous. You know we are being blamed for bad things that have happened there. I know, I know,' she said in answer to Ruslan's *whatever* expression, 'it is the way with us. We are the whipping boys. But it's rumoured that the rebels are planning a new offensive. They've changed their tactics, Ruslan.'

Underneath Tallis's impassive expression, his brain was spring-loaded. What change in tactics?

'There are fewer head-on collisions with federal forces,' Ruslan argued.

'That's true,' Katya conceded, 'but the guerrillas are

fighting on their terms now. More ambushes, hidden bombs, targeted attacks. Don't you see, the situation cannot continue? The Russian government will respond the way it always does, with a crackdown. We've already seen the signs—more military presence in the streets, checkpoints, spot checks. You know all this for yourself.'

'What are you saying, Aunt?'

She looked up imploringly at Tallis. 'Go back with this man. He will look after you.'

Tallis opened his mouth to say that it was out of the question. Ruslan beat him to it.

'No, absolutely, definitely—'

'It's for the best,' Katya said. 'Perhaps you could get to England, to be with your mother.'

Ruslan was adamant. 'No. This is my home.'

'Your home is where you make it,' Katya said, an urgent expression in her eyes.

Ruslan jerked away, angry. 'Then come with me.'

She shook her head.

'Why not?' he said, grabbing hold of both her hands.

She didn't answer. Her gaze fixed on Tallis. Christ, he could willingly drown in those eyes. 'You'll take him, won't you?' she said, beseeching.

I'd willingly take all of you, Tallis thought wildly. 'I'm sorry. I can't.'

'Please,' Katya said, a pleading note in her voice.

'I already told you,' Tallis said elliptically, aware

that Chaikova's eyes were boring into the side of his face.

'Oh, that.' Katya let out a sad laugh. 'A foolhardy mission.'

'Maybe, but—'

'Danger is everywhere.'

Tallis looked at Chaikova. Chaikova stared back, shrugged his large shoulders, and rubbed a paw of a hand over his grey-stubble jaw. 'I'll take him back if that's what you want,' he told Katya gruffly.

'Stop it!' Ruslan shouted, his voice more child than man. 'I am not going back.'

'Ruslan,' Katya began, but Ruslan was unyielding. He turned to Tallis. 'I'm coming with you into the mountains.'

Katya put the heel of her hand to her forehead. She looked anguished. 'No,' Tallis said. 'That's not a good idea.'

'I can help you,' Ruslan argued, his voice hard and grainy. 'I know my way through. I've been there many times before. You won't make it without me. Not now.'

'I travel alone,' Tallis said, firm.

'You don't understand,' Ruslan said, drawing himself up to his full height. 'The mountains are like no other place on earth. They are greedy. They will devour you.'

'The answer is still the same,' Tallis said. 'I'm sorry.'

The rap at the door came at three in the morning. Tallis, who'd been asleep on the narrow landing, stirred in time to see a glimpse of naked thigh as Katya dragged on a robe over her nightshirt. Ruslan, too, was out of bed, Chaikova snoring open-mouthed, oblivious, on the floor.

'Soldiers,' she hissed, putting a finger to her lips, and motioned for Ruslan and Tallis to hide in the cellar.

'What about Chaikova?' Ruslan whispered.

'It's OK,' Tallis said. 'Give me two seconds.'

'We don't have two seconds,' Katya said, anxious.

Undeterred, Tallis roughly woke Chaikova, and whispered hurriedly in his ear. Chaikova rubbed his eyes, then grinned and nodded. 'OK. Let's go,' Tallis said, at the sound of more banging on the door.

The cellar consisted of two chambers that extended across the perimeter of the house. One side was full of gardening implements, the other, further along, food provisions. Tallis and Ruslan hid in the furthest part. For good measure, Tallis dragged a sheet of garden netting over the pair of them to break up their body shapes should anyone enter. Both fell silent. Tallis suddenly remembered Lena's account of the massacre at Aldy, the grenades thrown into the cellars. He wondered what he'd do in such circumstances: stay and be blown to pieces in an orgy of torn flesh, or run into a waiting wave of machine-gun fire. He could tell from Ruslan's expression that he was thinking the same. The atmosphere ratcheted up several notches.

Tallis craned his ears, listening for sounds of trouble. After the first barked orders, he heard nothing more.

Seconds thudded by, then minutes. Ruslan looked at Tallis with a questioning expression. Tallis shook his head. At last, a peal of laughter followed by the sound of a door banging shut. Minutes later, the trapdoor opened and they were released.

Katya was smiling broadly. 'Your friend deserves an Oscar.' She laughed, glancing from Tallis to Chaikova who looked almost punch-drunk with glee.

'It worked, then?' Tallis said, wishing he didn't feel so pissed off.

'Like a charm,' Chaikova said.

'Would someone tell me what's going on?' Ruslan scratched his head.

'I'm your aunt's new Russian lover,' Chaikova announced proudly. 'As part of the new offensive, I, in my official capacity as an officer belonging to the Central Intelligence Directorate, am familiarising myself with the enemy.'

'And they believed you?' Ruslan said, astonished.

Chaikova flashed a grin. Then he turned to Tallis, his expression cool and muscular. 'The soldiers also delivered a warning.'

'Yeah?'

'Two intelligence officers were killed in Rostov-on-Don two days ago.'

'Really?' Tallis said. 'Extraordinary coincidence.'

'Both were shot.' Chaikova said. 'Looked like a professional job. Someone who really knew what they were doing.'

Silence briefly invaded the room. 'Like Katya said…' Tallis glanced at her with an easy smile '…danger is everywhere.'

CHAPTER TEN

FIRST light.

Tallis headed east towards Khankala, keeping strictly to the main road. He'd already spotted anti-personnel mines in a ditch running alongside. Cold, sleety rain filled the air. That was good, Tallis thought. It would deaden the sound, deepen the shadows, and obscure the vision of anyone with evil intent. He didn't think about the young man he'd left behind, still less about Katya. He couldn't afford to. His focus now was on Darke.

Khankala, in the rear of both wars, possessed all the hallmarks of a place that had grown: new three-storey dwellings; cafes and restaurants. As he walked through unnervingly quiet streets, he found it hard to believe that during the first conflict rebels had shot a helicopter to pieces there, that during the second wave of hostilities fleeing refugees stormed military helicopters to hitch the forty-minute ride to Mozdok and what they hoped was freedom.

With each step events loomed from the past to haunt the present so that when, in a blast of bitterly cold wind, he eventually dropped down to Argun, skirting a canning factory and military detention centre, he could almost smell the burn of human flesh when a decade before a truck filled with explosives had been driven into the barracks where police officers were stationed.

By early afternoon, he was tracking alongside the winding road, close to the Argun River, the ground shale and stone beneath his feet. Mud built, virtually windowless dwellings spotted the landscape. Barns with bushes and rushes growing out of the roofs huddled together. The contrast between the capital and the outer region couldn't have been starker.

There were few people. Those he saw were women, gypsy-like, dark and flashing. There were no men, apart from several oldtimers with crevassed, wind-burnt faces. There were no children. He wondered about the disappeared, about the twenty-to-thirty-something men his age, who'd covered the same terrain, walked where he was walking. Maybe they had made it as far as Urus-Martan, a place where there were frequent ambushes, according to Lena and Ruslan, only to be picked up and stamped out as though they'd never existed. Except to those who loved them.

With the wind whispering in his ears, he continued through cheerless villages, mountains gathering ahead, and on towards Chiri-Yurt, in the Shali district, the foothills below the Argun Gorge. Rocks and grass underfoot, he briefly travelled through a thick forested area before swiftly cutting back onto a more cultivated track after spotting an arms cache that contained a number of anti-personnel mines, including a PMN-2 with fuse, the sort that would propel the surrounding boulders and earth into the victim by sheer explosive force. Beyond the woods, he found many scratching a living in the shale, refugees from mountain villages, refugees from life. They paid him the same attention they'd have bestowed on an elephant walking past. Here was a single man, a foreigner, walking alone, but nobody spoke, nobody asked questions. With every pace, he wondered if he was going to receive a bullet or a blade in the back. The adrenalin was coursing so hard it hurt.

Stopping to rest in a nearby cemetery on the edge of the village, his back against the gnarled bark of a tree, he was suddenly aware he had company. Slowly, he slipped his hand inside his jacket, took the Glock from his shoulder holster then looked round, and cursed.

'I told you I travel alone.'

'You need someone to watch your back.' Ruslan had a mutinous look in his eye as he squatted down next to him. He had some colour in his face as if he'd run through the wind. His eyes danced with fire.

'You followed me all the way?' Tallis was seriously afraid he was losing his powers of observation and that was worrying.

'Not exactly. Chaikova gave me a lift.'

Tallis shook his head and smiled. Yuri Chaikova was even more of an enigma than Grigori Orlov. Somewhere in that rough old frame of his beat a human heart.

'The road ahead is extremely dangerous, full of troops in vehicles,' Ruslan said. 'It's rumoured there are soldiers in the village. I will take you to where you need to be then I will return.'

Tallis let out a sigh. He could see that argument was a waste of energy. Ruslan interpreted his silence as a good sign. 'Here,' he said, rummaging through his backpack, 'I brought you these.' He handed Tallis a plastic bottle filled with water and a neatly wrapped parcel. Tallis took them, drinking the water straight off. Inside the paper was a meat pie, freshly made by the look of it. Suddenly ravenous, he broke off a piece and ate. It was excellent. He wondered whether Katya had prepared it. My God, he thought, what would she say when she discovered Ruslan gone? He posed the question.

Ruslan shrugged. 'It will be alright. She will forgive me.' A slow smile spread over his face. 'Especially when I return.'

By the time they started off again, the rain had settled to a slow steady patter. Skies and earth, tree and leaf were grey. And there was mud. Thick, humus-rich, it sucked at his boots. As they skirted the river, a badly bloated corpse floated face down in the water. Christ, Tallis thought, giving a start. Originally he'd mistaken it for a piece of junk until he'd made out the clothing and a pair of putrefied hands. Neither he nor Ruslan passed comment or exchanged a word.

The landscape here was one of jagged silhouettes with trees clinging to cliffs and rocky outposts. At every turn they faced peaks and gorges, forests and jutting edges. The spectre of the mountains, hovering in black, was all around them. Tallis understood then Ruslan's remark about the voracity of their appetite, their need for fresh blood. This strange, rebellious land of baying animals and women with avian faces, their menfolk gone, felt as foreign to him as anything or anywhere he'd ever known. He felt as if he was walking through a land of ghosts.

Without warning, the chop-chop sound of rotors hammered his ears. Tallis looked up and saw two Mi-8Ts, military-transport helicopters, hacking through the sky. Grabbing hold of Ruslan, he dragged him into the trees and waited for them to pass over.

Night fell quickly due to the increasingly appalling weather conditions. With it came the sound of repeated automatic gunfire. Tallis decided he needed a change in balance: concealment was called for. Although he was happy to keep moving at a reduced pace, he could tell that Ruslan, although a decade younger, was flagging— a major reason for Tallis wanting to travel unencumbered.

Taking out a pair of night-vision binoculars, he looked about him and saw a solid shape ahead with what looked like a fence around it. He pointed it out to

Ruslan. It was a shepherd's hut and it was deserted. Had been for some time, Tallis thought, clocking the log fence around the perimeter, as he stepped inside. It had an earth floor, one window. Against the walls, which were a maze of rat holes, a single broken spade rested. It wasn't the Ritz but it was dry and sheltered. While Ruslan dropped to his knees to pray, Tallis took out his sleeping bag and removed his wet-weather jacket, spreading it out on the ground, leaving his holstered Glock in place. Then he heard a noise, brief, in the distance, like the sound of tyres on mud.

'What?' Ruslan said, his eyebrows arching in surprise.

'Noise.'

'I didn't hear anything.'

Tallis put a finger to his lips. The air hummed with silence. Forty seconds later, he heard it again, nearer this time. It was coming from the direction of their destination, from the mountains. Ruslan craned his ears, shook his head.

'You didn't hear it?'

'No.'

Tallis grabbed his night-vision binoculars and the Kurtz. 'Stay here.'

'Wait…'

'Stay here.'

Tallis went outside, creeping low, keeping his body parallel to the fence to break up his body shape and obscure visibility, the pouring rain providing extra cover. As he suspected, they definitely had company. Two beams of light were bumping along the track, the engine note denoting a 4x4. Maybe they were people passing through like him, but a strong gut feeling told him otherwise. Why else was the place deserted? *Because it wasn't safe to stay.*

Switching the combined safety and fire selector down one notch to single shots, he dived across the track to the relative safety of a patch of trees and, putting the binoculars to his eyes, watched, listened and waited. The noise increased. Gone the on/off jerking sound. This was more of a slip and judder. As feared, the vehicle, an ugly-looking Nissan, came into view, slowed, skidded a bit, and came to a bumpy stop. It was right outside the hut. Three doors opened. Three men got out. They were all dressed in tracksuits and running shoes. None of them appeared obviously armed but it was hard to tell. One, the driver, walked a couple of metres away, let his pants down and started to take a leak while the other two went to the back and pulled out a box, obviously heavy, judging by the way their bodies strained and heaved. And, oh, God, Tallis thought, they were heading inside the hut with it.

Shouts broke across the night sky. The driver, who had finished his pee, dashed towards the hut. Within seconds Ruslan was dragged painfully outside on his knees, the three of them starting in on him with questions that didn't require answers. Next came fists. Ruslan started to protest but it was no good. Tallis had seen this over and over again—in kids of fifteen, young males and sometimes young women, the pack in action, cowardly and self-serving—and it sickened him to his bones. Using the commotion as cover, he scooted back towards the fence. By now Ruslan was on the ground, his body balled, hands over his head, grunting as the boots went in. The blokes were laughing, jeering, high on cruelty, their intention clear enough—they wanted to kill him. When the driver stood back and pulled out a weapon, Tallis took aim and fired the first shot, dropping him. Two more shots followed, slotting each man so fast neither had time to process what was happening, let alone react. Tallis ran over, checked for vital signs in all three targets: none.

Ruslan let out a long groan as Tallis pulled him to his feet. His face was bleeding and swollen and his clothes were spattered with blood and bone from his assailants.

'Come on, let's get you cleaned up,' Tallis said, hauling him back inside. 'Who the hell were they?'

'Gangsters,' Ruslan spat, losing part of a tooth.

'Russians?' Tallis reached into his backpack for some medi-wipes, which he handed over.

'Chechens,' Ruslan said, dispirited. He dabbed at his face, tentatively exploring his injuries, spat out another gobbet of blood. 'What are we going to do with them?' he said at last.

Chuck them in the river, Tallis thought. As for the 4x4, it was probably worth commandeering, but maybe not. Frankly, he was more interested in what was in the box. It didn't take long to jemmy it open, revealing a bumper pack of automatic rifles and sub-machine-guns, grenades and bullets. Useful.

Half an hour later, they'd dragged the bodies of the three men to the side of the river and pushed them into the water, Tallis removing every trace of their existence by raking over the ground with the broken tip of the spade. The weaponry he decided to keep for a rainy day. Using the tree as a marker, it took him a couple of laborious hours to bury the box, the soil sticky and unyielding. By the time he staggered into his sleeping bag, he was exhausted. Graham Darke, he thought, plunging into sleep, you'd better be bloody worth it.

The next morning they awoke to a sky of cerulean blue and the sound of songbirds. There was no wind. 'This is what I came back for,' Ruslan said, gazing out wistfully across the countryside. 'The land here is beautiful. It's what men do to it that makes it seem so ugly.'

Tallis nodded and took a gulp of liquid from his water bottle. Privately, he thought it a perfect day for snipers. 'The future lies in your grasp, Ruslan,' he said, resting a hand lightly on the boy's shoulders. 'This place needs people like you.'

Ruslan gave a big sigh as if the responsibility was too onerous and daunting for one man. 'Perhaps, with the help of others, and God willing, we may be able to change things.'

After covering the fresh earth with stones, they drove

for no more than six kilometres, the vehicle running out of petrol near the verdant pastures of Chishki. Abandoning it there, and with no time to remove their traces, they went on foot, and set a course for the mountain village of Shatoi.

The higher they climbed, the more intimidating the scenery. The road had become a track then a path. Tallis felt his temple pulse with concentration, his entire focus on the ground beneath his feet and on the lookout for tripwires. Venturing into the mountains felt as if he was entering Tolkien's Mordor in *The Lord of the Rings*.

Eventually, the path opened out again and back onto a potholed road that crested a thickly wooded ridge. Rebellion hardwired into the topography, the forested mountains lent the best possible cover for resistance.

He started to breathe more easily. More stone dwellings. More grim-looking villages, clinging for dear life, it seemed, to the cliff edges. In spite of the sunshine, the place echoed with sadness. It was in the earth and in the air.

'Shit,' Tallis said, stopping dead in his tracks.

Ruslan looked up. He was out of breath, wheezing slightly. 'Checkpoint,' he muttered.

'And they've seen us,' Tallis said, slowly walking towards the soldiers, silently counting: four scared and jumpy-looking boys, probably no older than Ruslan, and one hard-faced bloke who was prematurely grey and had the strutting gait of a rooster. Tallis reckoned he was their commanding officer. The closer he got, the clearer the view of the badges the man wore, including one of a Scorpion that Tallis thought was only worn by the Russian Special Forces, the Spetsnaz.

'Leave them to me,' Ruslan murmured, pulling his hat down over his face and striding past Tallis before he could stop him.

Ruslan pulled out his papers, flashed them under the nose of the older man. Jerking his thumb in Tallis's direction, his voice riddled with disdain, Ruslan spoke in Russian. 'I am charged with bringing this man into the mountains so that he can witness the rebels' attacks on the motherland for himself.'

The older guy handed the papers to one of the young soldiers and looked Ruslan in the eye. He's not buying it, Tallis thought. He's seen the cuts and bruises and knows that Ruslan's lying. Tallis drew up alongside.

'You have the necessary written permission from the Kremlin?' the officer said, addressing Ruslan.

'We do.'

'Let me see.'

'Unfortunately, we were jumped by Chechen gangsters,' Tallis intervened, 'They stole some of our papers.'

'But not these,' the officer said, thrusting Ruslan's papers back in his hand and snatching up Tallis's, including the press pass for one Nikolai Redko.

He barely looked at them but he looked at Tallis. Tallis looked straight back. He didn't like the coldness in the man's eyes. Something in them reminded him of

Timur, the FSB guy and State assassin. The officer's eyes travelled down to Tallis's wrist. 'Nice watch.'

The four inexperienced soldiers, *srochniki*, conscripts, had picked up the mood. All fiddled nervously with their weapons.

'Have it,' Tallis said, undoing the clasp and handing the watch over.

The man pocketed it without looking. 'Go,' he said, his dry red lips curled with contempt.

'Thanks,' Ruslan said.

Both of them started to walk away. The road ahead was empty. The air hung thin and still. Sun was shining. Sky was blue. An eerie silence descended. Exactly what Tallis most feared. Instinct kicking in, he pulled the Glock from his holster and wheeled round a split second after they opened fire, the first burst of machine-gun tearing through the air, ripping up the ground beneath his feet and singeing his hair. Everything slowed. Ruslan went down. The officer, his pistol smoking, shouted to his men to spread out. Bullets whizzed haphazardly. An intense flash of pain caught Tallis under his ribs, almost lifting him off his feet. Gasping with shock, Tallis shot the commanding officer in the face, blowing half of it away, his body jackknifing in the dirt. The trauma of losing their boss turned the soldiers into headless chickens. Two began to run for their lives. The remaining two took off, then turned, letting off another round of machine-gun fire that went high and wide. It was the biggest mistake of their short lives. Two shots later, both were dead. Tallis, ignoring the pain in his side, sprinted to Ruslan, whose legs below the knee were peppered with bullet-holes. He was bleeding profusely. Tallis grabbed both his legs, making him scream, and held them in the air to try to limit the blood flow. That's when he noticed the wound in Ruslan's chest from where the officer's bullet had made its exit.

'You weren't wearing your Kevlar.'

'I thought it would frighten Katya,' Ruslan grunted, wincing with pain. 'That's why I left it behind.'

Fuck, fuck, fuck, Tallis thought, diving into his bag for dressings, knowing it wasn't enough.

'I'm dying,' Ruslan said, his eyelids fluttering.

'No, you're not.'

'Leave me here,' Ruslan said. In seconds, his face had become as white as a sheet. 'You can't carry an injured man through the mountains.'

'I'm not leaving you. I'm taking you back. I'll get help.'

'No point. I won't make it,' Ruslan said, his breathing scratchy and laboured. 'If you go back, they'll arrest you and you will never find your friend.'

He was right. But what choice did he have? If he took Ruslan into the mountains, the lad stood no chance of survival. 'We're in this together,' was all Tallis could think to say.

Ruslan smiled, already, it seemed, looking into the angel face of his sister. Tallis did his best to patch him up. It had been too long since he'd worked in battle conditions. He thought about giving him morphine, then decided against it—it would be the quickest way to kill him. And though it might be kinder in the long run, he couldn't bring himself to do it.

'I'm cold,' Ruslan complained.

'Soon get you warm.' Tallis picked Ruslan up as gently as he could, the pain in his side searing from where a bullet had torn through his jacket and bounced off his Kevlar. No doubt he'd have an ugly bruise on his ribcage, but that was all. As he put the injured man over his shoulder, Ruslan groaned, then went quiet.

Straightening his back, Tallis moved east in a big detour, his sights set on Haracoj. He tried not to think of the two soldiers he'd allowed to get away, the inevitable raised alarm and subsequent pursuit by soldier and tracker dog. And the trail of blood he was conveniently leaving behind for them to follow. All his thoughts were directed at the injured man on his back. Against all the odds, he willed Ruslan to survive. Somehow, he promised, he would find help.

For several kilometres, Tallis moved forwards. It was slow going and arduous. The weight on his back grew heavier and heavier, and the sun, which had up until then been his friend, was starting to burn a hole in his head.

On he went, his feet slipping and sliding. The smell of the river was strong in his nostrils and he knew at some stage he'd have to get across. He seemed to be in a no-man's land, the ground ahead unpopulated and barren, without life. Part of him was afraid to stop. He didn't want his worst fears confirmed. But when he could go no further, when his vision was starting to blur, he decided he had to. At last, up ahead, he spotted a lean-to for animals. It would be an obvious place for the soldiers to look, but…

He did the calculation: the most efficient time for them to send out their trackers would be that evening or early the following morning when the sun was low. Added to that, they wouldn't necessarily think that he'd adopt a contradictory route. It was a gamble but one he was prepared to take. He reckoned he had a couple of hours to rest before moving on.

Tallis set Ruslan down gently on the charred ground. The young Chechen's trousers and sweater were soaked in blood where it had oozed through the dressings. Remarkably, he was still breathing, just, but his pulse was weak and erratic. Tallis knew then that it was only a matter of time.

He took out a bottle of water and, cradling him in his arms, gently put it to Ruslan's cracked lips. The dying man's eyelids fluttered. Water trickled down his chin.

'You were right, Tallis. You travel alone.' Then Ruslan's eyes rolled up into his head and he was still.

You're wrong. I travel with ghosts, Tallis thought sadly.

CHAPTER ELEVEN

WITH a heavy heart, Tallis replotted his route and resumed his journey. He decided to bypass Shatoi altogether. The way for now had flattened out a little. Footholds were easier to see. The sky was the colour of a large open wound and the sun was setting. With it, the temperature dropped fast. He listened hard for signs of a pursuit. After another few kilometres of tracking, and picking his way through stony ground, eyes skinned for booby-traps, he decided to pitch up for the night in the relative safety of some woods on the leeside of a hill. He was tempted to light a fire but didn't want to risk exposure and alert others. Instead, he made a shallow depression in the ground and, dragging some broken boughs over it, settled himself into the makeshift burrow with his sleeping bag. After a hasty meal of dried rations, he fell asleep, exhausted.

The next morning he awoke to sunshine filtering through the leaves of his shelter, casting a fine net of light over his makeshift bed. He rose, took a leak, and listened for the sound of human activity. Other than his own, there were none. Next, he took a compass reading then, after eating once more, he started off again, his destination Borzoi.

After a time the sun rose high in the sky, the temperature, too, starting to soar. He found himself in a belt of green pasture, an alpine hinterland. Two shepherds herding a flock of sheep trundled past and nodded in his direction. He nodded back, a snatch of normality in the prevailing madness. On he went, ears alert, eyes scanning the horizon. Suddenly the track on which he walked widened out and he was brought up short by the sight of scorched earth and dead vehicles, including a burnt-out tank on which someone had painted 'Russians Are Pigs'. He strode on, not stopping, to where the land briefly dipped into a half-farmed valley then rose, stark and sheer.

Out in the open again. The further he travelled, the higher the climb, birds of prey and mountain goats the only signs of life. At last he reached a peak and the landscape changed again. He was on the edge of a wooded area. He held back, took out his map. The band of trees signified the most direct route to Borzoi, but they also offered the possibility of mines. The road, easier terrain, meant people and vehicles, checkpoints and soldiers. Breaking his own rules, he opted for the forest.

It was time-consuming travel. Most mines were found simply by observation. Knife in hand, Tallis scanned the ground for protrusions and surface fuses, for earth mounds and craters, for signs left by others: crossed sticks; cairns of rock and rubble, bottles and cans placed on the top of stakes; lines of painted rocks. He had no choice but to adopt a slow, leisurely gait, the mantra of look, feel, prod repeated on a loop in his head. Then he saw it, gleaming white in the sunshine, a metre away, gaping up at him. He stopped in his tracks, a metallic shiver travelling up his spine, making the hairs on the back of his neck stand erect as he processed the information, and stared at a human skull. Chechen or Russian, he thought, and what the hell did it matter? Somewhere a mother had lost a child.

He scanned the forest ahead: nothing untoward. About to walk on, he heard a crack behind him. No falling branch, no animal scurrying through, it was a sound he recognised only too well—the sound of a rifle cocking. Very slowly, he turned round, arms up. A thin-limbed boy emerged from behind a tree. Eyes glittering with malice, he resembled a wicked wood sprite from a fantasy tale. His skin was the colour of a pecan nut. He had a long face, the features off centre and sharp. He wore filthy combat trousers and a torn jacket. His boots, army issue, rubber-soled with the laces missing, looked too big for his thin legs. He carried an astonishing array of bullets across his chest and he was holding a Tikka-M65, a sporting and hunting rifle made in Finland. Designed for precision shooting, the target more usually big game, Tallis didn't feel inclined to call the boy's bluff. He was put in mind of child soldiers.

They could be as ruthless as they were unpredictable. At any second he could be cut down. The only way to prevent certain death was either to attempt to kill him or appeal to the child's venal nature.

'I'm worth more to you alive than dead,' he said in Chechen.

The boy smiled. That means nothing, his expression inferred.

'I have money,' Tallis said.

'And weapons.'

Tallis felt surprise. The boy spoke with a young man's voice, yet he only looked about twelve. He also spoke Chechen with a Russian accent. He pointed at Tallis to remove his holster and throw over his backpack. Tallis did both. Yes, he could have pulled out the Glock and shot him, but he had an unspoken rule about youngsters. He didn't think he could live with himself even if it meant saving his own life. Now what? he thought. Would this sprite-child kill him there and then?

The boy dropped to the ground, sat cross-legged, and rummaged through Tallis's belongings like he was going through a Christmas stocking, each new find an added source of delight.

'I'm a Westerner,' Tallis said, 'English,' he added, this time speaking in Russian.

The boy looked up and beamed. 'This is good,' he said, reverting to Russian. 'I know someone who will pay a lot of money for you.'

* * *

Tallis led. Sprite followed. 'No tricks,' the boy warned, his untamed eyes glanced ominously at his loaded weapon just so Tallis knew he wasn't fucking about. Tallis swallowed, walked on, feeling like the human equivalent of a mine detector. Having already spotted several tripwires on either side of the track, he half expected to be blown to kingdom come at any moment. Either that or it would be a bullet in the back. In this strange land the danger played to its own twisted beat.

From the way the light was falling, Tallis estimated it was approaching three o'clock. With storm clouds gathering, it would soon be dark. Tallis tried to engage the lad in conversation by asking his name. When he didn't answer, Tallis briefly turned back.

'I have no name,' the boy said darkly. 'Now, walk,' he added, raising his weapon.

An hour further on, they were clear of the forest and on land that peaked sharply. Tallis expected to track along what appeared to him the nearest and less demanding route. Sprite had other ideas. They were moving up, vertical, high into the mountains where the air was thin and the going tough.

It began to rain, sheeting down like a fusillade. Every so often, Sprite would order him to stop, not to rest, but so that he could listen and smell the air. It seemed the boy had highly developed senses. Once he called out a warning as a piece of cliff edge plunged past, crashing down the mountainside, missing Tallis by centimetres, and once he picked out a hidden stream from which they drank the water. Tallis had tasted nothing like it. It was clear and bright and thirst-quenching.

Darkness fell like a curtain. Tallis became seriously worried. He couldn't see a damn thing and the path ahead was savage. Suddenly the night sky lit up with tips of red and yellow tracer. There were reports of small-arms fire. He wondered if Darke was there in the thick of the action.

'Rebels,' Sprite said matter-of-factly. 'They are trying to draw the Russians' fire.'

Tallis saw the logic. Whoever held the higher ground had the advantage. It was probably the rebels' best card.

On they climbed until Tallis stumbled, Sprite overtaking him, the boy's sense of direction acute and unerring. It was as if he had another sense: night vision. After that, Sprite set the pace: fast and ferocious. Tallis had no intention of turning tail and making a dash for it. Either he'd fall in the dark or be shot, neither prospect appealing.

Finally, they arrived at Sprite's destination: a lonely ledge underneath an overhanging cliff. It wasn't a bad place for a shelter, Tallis thought, feeling his way around, conscious that Sprite was scampering about his den like a stray dog. Flicking on the torch he'd stolen from Tallis's backpack, Sprite shone it in a wide hole in the rock, plunging one hand deep inside and pulling out a filthy sleeping bag which he threw to Tallis. The boy obviously intended to enjoy the spoils of war by commandeering the belongings of his victim.

Tallis wasn't that bothered. After two nights out in the open, he smelt like a hyena. Might as well live like one.

Wriggling inside, he lay down on the rock. Sprite did the same. Then the questions started.

'Your papers say that you are Russian yet you say you are English.'

'I am English.'

'Then what are you doing here?'

Tallis thought. Whatever he said could prove disastrous. 'I've come to join the fight.'

Sprite let out a squeal of laughter.

'What's so funny?'

'*You* fight the Chechen when you cannot even fight a child?'

Tallis froze. Words, which seemed a lifetime away, reverberated through his head. In an instant he was back in Birmingham, in Viva Constantine's cosy sitting room, Lena standing there with an arrogant look in her eye. She'd accused him of running away from a woman. And now, with Ruslan dead, what else would she accuse him of? An image of Katya, blonde and beautiful, floated before his eyes. He blinked her away. 'I haven't come to fight the Chechen. I've come to fight the Russians.'

Sprite sat up a bit at that. Tallis could hear him rustling in the darkness.

'Why?'

'Because I think the Chechens have had a raw deal. I think this time they're in serious trouble.'

'What do you care?'

'My grandmother on my mother's side was Croatian.'

'Ah,' Sprite said knowingly, 'you hate the Serbs so you hate the Russians, too.'

'And you?'

'I have no loyalties to anyone other than myself.'

'Isn't that dangerous?'

'Only if you're stupid.'

'So what are you exactly?' Tallis said, pushing it. 'You speak Chechen but with a Russian accent.'

'I am unfortunate,' Sprite said with no hint of self-pity whatsoever. 'I am an ethnic Russian born in Chechnya. I belong to no one.'

Tallis woke the next morning with a boot in his rear. 'Get up!' Sprite shrieked.

The weather was dire. Thick mist shrouded the mountains. It was bone-crunchingly cold. And it was still raining. Tallis was ordered to climb. Thin air punched him in the chest. On he climbed until joyously they were cresting the peak and heading back down. Tallis adopted a sideways motion, using his inside hand to feel his way, feeling for mines. According to Sprite, the Chechens were fond of setting tripwires.

Bit by bit, the fog started to clear. Tallis could smell water again. The ground flattened out into a wooded valley, sunless, trees dripping with moisture, a river running through. Up ahead, round the next spur, barely visible, was a rough wooden bridge.

'We go over,' Sprite said.

Below, deep and wide, the river boiled and hissed barbarously, like a wounded sea-snake from Greek mythology.

The other side was a plain with a narrow road running through it, surrounded by more mountains, their tops mislaid in the mist.

'This way,' Sprite said, striding on. He was growing more animated, more talkative, his speech, half tour guide, half professor, a jabber. Tallis couldn't reconcile the boy inside the man. Sometimes he seemed a kid, other times a guy in his twenties. Maybe his was a genuine case of arrested development. Or maybe he was simply a sad casualty of war.

On they walked. 'See,' Sprite said with glee, taking off, Tallis bounding after him, watching in horror and amazement as Sprite leapt onto the burnt-out shell of a tank, a prominent white transverse cross marked on the remains of its turret.

'Watch out!' Tallis cried. 'It might be booby-trapped.' He could almost feel the boom, smell the terrible stench of burning flesh and entrails, but nothing happened. Nothing at all.

'It's fine,' Sprite said. 'Look.' He danced up and down then dropped into a squat, kicking his legs out like a mad Cossack.

'How the hell did that get there?'

But Sprite had taken off again, too busy running up and down the thing. Suddenly, he stopped dead.

'What?' Tallis said, clambering on top, his boots crunching on the blackened and twisted metal. He drew alongside Sprite and followed Sprite's gaze. Ahead stood a lone figure, frozen, as still as statuary. Sprite took out Tallis's binoculars and lifted them to his eyes. In that brief, unguarded moment Tallis knew he could take the boy. One swift, accurate blow to the back of the neck and it would all be over.

'It's Bislan,' Sprite said, handing them to Tallis. 'He has strayed into the minefield.'

Tallis looked for himself. The boy, thirteen or so judging from his physique, was standing, his back towards them, roughly forty metres away in a grassy area off the road. God knew why. The tank, with its white cross, had served as a warning, Tallis realised. For some reason the kid had disregarded it. Tallis didn't know the terrain but it looked from the rigid way the lad was standing that he'd either realised his mistake too late or had actually stepped on a mine that had failed to detonate. Tilt mines, the type that explode once the pressure was released, were rare in that area. Could be remote-controlled, Tallis thought, scanning the landscape.

Then again, why hadn't the operator simply got on with the job? The slimmest chance of all was that Bislan had, indeed, stepped on a mine that had failed to engage. Sometimes, in a PMN, a type of anti-personnel mine, if the fuse was too well protected by the soil, this was exactly what happened. But that didn't mean to say that there weren't others, undetected, waiting, and ready to strike. Whatever the real state of affairs, Bislan was doing what any sane individual should do: freeze and wait for back-up.

Sprite jumped down from the tank, twisted his rifle round, and lifted it.

'What the hell are you doing?' Tallis said.

'It will be better this way,' Sprite said, chambering a round and looking down the sight.

Tallis leapt and landed square in front of Sprite. 'No.'

'What do you mean, no? You want to see him torn limb from limb?'

'I can rescue him.'

Sprite's expression darkened. 'You are no use to me dead. I need you alive.' He sounded petulant.

'I'm not going to die. Christ, I've got this far,' Tallis argued. 'Who is this Bislan anyway?'

'He is Akhmet's son.'

'Akhmet?' Elimkhanova? Tallis wondered, hoping against hope that it was the warlord whose gang Darke had been sent to infiltrate.

'The man who will pay good money for you.'

'Won't he pay more money for the life of his child?'

Sprite's features sharpened. '*Only* if you succeed.'

'And I will.'

Sprite thought about it, ran a hand over his hairless chin. He's weakening, Tallis thought. 'Think how you will look in Akhmet's eyes.'

Sprite stood, stared, reflective. He looked like a gambler weighing up the odds. Tallis said nothing, fearing that one wrong word would force Sprite to abandon Bislan. Finally, Sprite nodded, giving in.

'Good. Now, let me have my knife back.'

Sprite grinned and shook his head. 'You will try to kill me.'

I could have tried to kill you on two separate occasions, Tallis thought, grim. 'I won't. You have my word.'

'Your word?' Sprite mocked.

'Fuck's sake, I can't save him without it. You want your friend to die?'

Sprite seemed to consider this. 'Alright,' he said, reluctantly swinging the rucksack off his back, taking out the knife and handing it to Tallis.

'And tape,' Tallis said. 'There's a roll of white tape in the bag,' he added in answer to Sprite's puzzled expression. Again, Sprite obliged.

'I will hold onto this,' Sprite said, catching the rifle round the stock and waving it in the air.

'Do what you like,' Tallis growled, the prospect of what he was about to do making him break out in a cold sweat.

Together they moved forward across the road. 'Talk to him,' Tallis said. 'Tell him I'm coming to help. Tell him to stay absolutely still.'

Sprite did. The only visible sign of movement was a slight tension in Bislan's jaw. That was good, Tallis thought. The last thing he needed was a reactor or panicker. That way they'd both get fragged. He dropped to his knees on the road, stuck the knife between his teeth, roll of tape in his pocket, and, leaning over onto the dirt, ran his fingers over the earth in front of him, centimetre by centimetre, inching forward. *Look, feel, prod,* he repeated, fingers feeling for fuse mechanisms and any buried mines. It took ten minutes to establish that the ground was safe enough to take the width and length of his body. As soon as he'd done that, he took out the tape and marked his passage.

'You will be here all day,' Sprite carped from the sideline.

Tallis ignored him, repeating the process. *Look, feel, prod. Look, feel, prod.* He had moved a couple of metres, no problem, when, to the right, he noticed a tripwire. Didn't say a word, just marked the spot and changed the angle of direction, clearing the ground anew. Slowly did it. *Look, feel, prod. Look...*

'Shit,' Tallis let out, his fingers hitting metal.

'What?' Sprite called.

Tallis gently eased the soil away with the knife, revealing a disc shape in the ground. 'Partially buried mine,' Tallis called over his shoulder.

'Fuck it,' Sprite cursed.

'Shut up,' Tallis snarled, flaring with anger.

The device was an anti-personnel blast mine. Although the size of the charge varied, it was most intended to maim rather than kill. A typical blast would destroy a foot or leg and cause multiple lacerations from casing fragments and surrounding debris. It was a weapon often used to slow down enemy troops. Not nice, Tallis thought, another wave of sweat breaking out across his brow, praying as he marked the spot so that he would avoid it on the journey back. *If he made the journey back.*

'I'm looping round,' he shouted, changing direction, fingers moving over the soil as if he were reading Braille. Ten minutes later the area to the left of the mine was cleared. Again, Tallis marked his trail with tape, feeling like a latter-day Hansel and Gretel. Off course a bit, he'd moved to within twenty metres of the lad. Doing fine, he told himself, calm down, keep focused, *look, feel, prod.*

About to feel the way again, his temple pulsing in concentration, he caught a movement out of the corner of his eye and froze. Jesus, he thought, minutely turning, seeing not one figure but several, all dressed in black fatigues, bandannas on their heads, AK47s slung over their shoulders, their grizzled features giving them the appearance of pirates. Were they responsible for the mines? Tallis thought feverishly. Were they about to set the bastards off?

A volley of shouts broke out, anxious, fearful and angry. Sprite shouted back, told the men what was happening. Some called Bislan's name. 'Keep quiet,' Tallis barked in Chechen. A chill silence settled on the land. Taking a deep breath, Tallis continued his lonely odyssey, inching forward again, nearer and nearer.

Fuck, another tripwire right across his path. He looked up, caught the boy's haunted gaze. He'd seen it too. In a strange way the tripwire had saved his life. Had he stumbled on, he'd have set it off and bled out by now. 'It's alright, Bislan,' Tallis told the boy. 'I'm going to mark it then I'll double round behind you. You're doing fine. Just keep still for me, there's a good lad, and I'll have you out of here in no time.'

Slowly, slowly, mark, avoid, and move on, Tallis told himself, edging his way round. The pulse in his temple was hammering now, and sweat was pouring off him in spite of a chill wind. He was vaguely aware of a crowd gathering on the nearest hillside, but his focus was aimed on the ground, the dirt, the sick jokes it might reveal. Seconds and minutes thudded by. He was utterly in the zone. Every sinew in his body strained. *Look, feel, prod...*

Eventually, and by a tortuous route, he reached the child, his eyes continuing to scan the ground. There were no obvious fuses, no metal plates. 'Are you actually standing on anything?'

The boy shook his head. Tallis stretched out a hand, touching the backs of the boy's legs, felt the rigidity in the muscles in the calves. A great cheer went up from the hillside.

'I'm going to make sure the ground around you is safe, Bislan,' Tallis said. 'Stay put for a little while.'

'Okay.' It was the first word he'd spoken.

Fingers spreading over the earth, Tallis cleared an

area measuring roughly half a metre around. 'Now turn very slowly on the spot so you're facing me.'

The boy did as he was told. In spite of his dark colouring, he was ashen-faced. Even his jet-black hair looked grey in the half-light. 'That's good. Now, move onto your hands and knees.'

Bislan did as he was told.

'You alright?' Tallis smiled, eyeball to eyeball. Critically, he needed to make eye contact, to make sure the boy fully understood what was being asked of him. It was imperative he gain the boy's trust if they were to crawl out of there alive. Bislan nodded silently. 'Good. I'm going to stand, turn around and get back down. As soon as I start crawling forward, you follow in my tracks exactly. You don't stray or move outside the line, got that?'

'Yes.'

'Okay. Here we go.'

Tallis got to his feet slowly, muscles straining, each movement tiny. Back down on his knees and facing the right way round again, Tallis moved off, edging his way, inching along the marked-out trail. A crowd of fighters assembled close to Sprite, watching the final extraction, two women among them. One man, massively framed, head and shoulders above the rest, stood intent, his dark eyes ablaze.

Tortoise-like, they moved in tandem, metre by painful metre, until, finally, Tallis emerged triumphant, crawling onto the hard surface, clearing it and collapsing onto the ground, Bislan safe behind him. Gunfire exploded into the air. An almighty cheer and cries of 'Allah Akhbar' ricocheted off the mountains. Tallis looked up, caught Sprite's eye and grinned. Sprite grinned back until he realised the trick he'd been played. With the boy safe, there was no way Akhmet was going to buy Tallis, or make him a hostage to fortune. By his small act of courage, Tallis had made himself priceless.

In seconds, Bislan, dazed and speechless, was held aloft like the prodigal son, several Chechens breaking into spontaneous dance around him. Tallis, meanwhile, was pulled to his feet by one of the female fighters. He noticed that she wore fingerless gloves, the type that snipers used. As his gaze travelled up, she smiled. Her hair was the colour of an old teddy bear. She had weathered skin and her blue eyes were framed in a heart-shaped face. 'My name is Irina,' she said, her Chechen accented. Russian, Tallis noticed, wondering if he'd ever get the hang of all these split loyalties.

'And I am the *amir*,' a resonant voice said.

Tallis looked up into the face of the man who had been standing apart. He had a long beard, no moustache and the kind of mesmerising eyes that burned into you. He wore a military-style cap on his head. It took a while for Tallis to work out that the man was smiling. It looked as if he was baring his teeth.

'The *amir*?'

'The leader. My name is Akhmet Elimkhanova.

These are my warriors. And Bislan is my only son,' he said, taking a step forward and putting an arm around Tallis in a half-hug. 'I am indebted. You have my greatest thanks. Come, we will eat and feast and you will tell me what you are doing here in the mountains.'

Out of the corner of his eye Tallis saw Sprite scowling. He registered that the boy, cheated of his prize, would remain a danger to him. Of Graham Darke, there was no sign.

CHAPTER TWELVE

THEY travelled along a steep, gravelled road, past mountain goats and sheep, in a fleet of old 4x4s. Nobody travelled more than fifteen miles an hour, the road so furrowed it sometimes seemed unpassable. The hero of the hour, Tallis rode with Akhmet and Bislan. As a mark of respect his weapons were returned to him. Tallis felt ambivalent. Against such a range of firepower, one man alone was hardly going to save himself should things cut up rough.

Now that his son was safe, Akhmet's relief turned to anger. In stern parental tones he gave Bislan the father of all talks about the stupidity of straying from home, the dangers lying in wait, from Russians as well as explosive devices.

'I have already lost a daughter and a son to the infidel. I have no desire to lose another child. Think what it would do to your mother,' Akhmet said, his tone deep and sonorous.

'Yes, Father. I am sorry,' Bislan said, contrite. Out

of immediate danger, the colour was returning to the boy's cheeks. He was a handsome child with strong features like his dad, Tallis thought. He had the same mesmerising expression in his dark eyes, too. Bislan couldn't thank him enough for saving him.

'We've received reports of soldiers being killed at a checkpoint outside Shatoi,' Akhmet said to Tallis.

'That was my work. Unfortunately, two escaped.'

'You were lucky to meet Aslan, then.'

So he did have a name, Tallis thought. Lucky wasn't the description that easily sprang to mind.

'Had it been another of my men,' Akhmet continued, 'they would have killed you without asking questions. So, Englishman, why are you here?'

Tallis told Akhmet what he'd told Sprite. Aslan might be his real name, but it was a bit too C. S. Lewis to Tallis's mind. Sprite suited him so much better. It suggested a degree of wilful malevolence. Tallis added that although he had not fought in any of the training camps, he had served as a firearms officer back in the UK so he could more than a handle a gun.

The *amir* nodded silently. If Akhmet disbelieved him, he didn't say so.

The compound, which was high in the mountains, was a fortified mound of stone, planks of wood, corrugated iron, razor wire, netting and sandbags, the equivalent of a British army sangar.

Inside were many dwellings, simple and basic. In common with many Chechen homes, the living area doubled for eating and cooking. Latrines were to the rear of the camp. Washing facilities were plentiful but basic.

Tallis counted in excess of forty men left behind to man the hilltop fortress; the entire fighting force in the region of seventy. In addition, women, dressed in hijabs, all with rifles close to hand, went about their daily routine, some cooking *shashlyk* over campfires and baking flatbread, some washing, others looking after children, a mass of domestic activity. There was even the equivalent of a parking lot with each 4x4 assigned a particular slot.

Bislan was swiftly returned to the loving arms of his mother, a plump, dark-haired woman with eyes like a raptor. Word of his lucky escape from the jaws of death had torn through the camp with the rapidity of a forest fire. Everyone gathered around. Everyone had smiles for the tall dark-haired foreigner.

Except one.

Tallis hardly recognised him. His hair was short, unlike his beard. In common with many of the fighters who'd stayed behind, he wore a beany hat on his head, fatigues on a body that was as wiry as ever. But it was his face that transfixed Tallis. A deep scar ran from the corner of one eye in a diagonal motion, across the bridge of his nose, across his left cheek, tailing off in a ragged mess of scar tissue. There was nothing about Graham Darke's stance or demeanour that suggested he recognised his old friend. Tallis hardly expected a warm welcome, but there was not even the faintest glimmer of recognition. Have I changed that much, Tallis wondered, or was Darke simply protecting his cover and, maybe, even Tallis's? Tallis sincerely hoped so.

'Who the hell is this guy?' Darke said to Akhmet, black fury in his eyes.

'This is the man who has saved the life of my only son,' Akhmet said, glancing at Tallis, his bare-teethed smile full of gratitude.

Darke's suspicious expression didn't alter. 'He's a Westerner. What's he doing here?'

'He has come to join the fight, as you did all those years ago.'

Darke spat on the ground. 'But I am Chechen. What is this man?' His narrowed eyes never left Tallis.

'A man who hates Russians,' Tallis said, staring hard back hard.

'He has already killed three soldiers down near Shatoi,' Akhmet threw in.

'So he says. Did anyone see?' Darke's voice was granite. He looked around at the others. All slowly shook their heads. Some fingered their rifles. The air crackled.

'You calling me a liar?' Tallis snarled.

Darke shrugged. 'I do not care whether you lie or not. I care only for our protection.' Once more, his eyes grazed those who gathered around, including Sprite, who danced from one foot to the other as though he had a hornet in his pants. 'How do we know you're not a spy?' Darke accused Tallis.

'Had I been a spy, I would either have killed Bislan or left him in the minefield.'

It went dead quiet, the silence broken by the noise of birds of prey wheeling above their heads. Darke stiffly asked for a private audience with Akhmet. Akhmet nodded. As both men walked away, one of Akhmet's warriors, a short, swarthy-faced individual with pitted skin, looked at Tallis and, in a typical Chechen gesture, drew a finger underneath his throat and smiled. Tallis smiled back. Always good to be able to identify the enemy, he thought, only wishing he had a better handle on Darke.

Five minutes of kicking the dirt gave Tallis time to think. Of one thing he was absolutely certain: Darke was highly regarded by Akhmet, his loyalty without doubt, his position almost that of second-in-command. He'd obviously done a first-rate job at infiltration, but at what price? He'd been under cover for so long, perhaps that was where his loyalty lay. Perhaps he had nothing to return to. Perhaps he no longer knew to whom he owed his allegiance.

Ultimately, Tallis felt he had to consider the possibility that the intelligence was correct, that Darke had, indeed, gone native. Tallis wondered how long ago Darke had sustained the injury to his face. Had it been his only injury? Had his mind been affected as well as his body? Could that be the reason he'd gone off the radar? Maybe he'd spent months flitting in and out of consciousness left to the primitive ministrations of a less than basic field hospital. Maybe, during a period of convalescence, he'd had a chance to reconsider his situation, re-evaluate his priorities, and change loyalties even. Whatever he believed, one thing was now very clear to Tallis: Darke could not have personally orchestrated the hits in Moscow. Someone, somewhere would have remembered a face like that. His scarred appearance would definitely have given him away. But that didn't mean he hadn't choreographed the murders. Tallis knew it was critical to get Darke alone. He had to talk to him, find out what the hell was going on.

Tallis looked up as Darke walked towards him, Akhmet watching from a distance with wary eyes. Jesus Christ, what had Darke told him? 'I'm to show you the sights,' Darke said, not exactly looking ecstatic about it. 'What did you say your name was again?'

Tallis inclined his head. 'Tallis, Paul Tallis.'

Not even a flicker. 'Right, then, Tallis, step this way.'

The camp was extraordinarily well organized, with separate tented shower blocks and dozens of mud huts within the fortress providing living accommodation for warriors and their families. Each had sleeping bags and beds and kerosene lamps, some powered by knackered-looking generators. Darke's commentary was straightforward and impersonal. It was delivered in the manner of an army sergeant showing a young recruit around. There were several opportunities when Darke could have whispered a word to him, but he said nothing, and

Tallis, for the moment, held back, biding his time, trying to suss him out. When they entered what Darke called the hospital wing, a hut with makeshift beds and stretchers, Tallis asked Darke about his injury, the closest so far he'd got to a personal question.

'Mortar fire,' Darke said crisply. 'Fortunately, I've got these people well trained. They've watched me set bones and pick out shrapnel. I've even performed the odd amputation without the patient bleeding out or dying. Not easy when your only painkiller is omnopon.'

Shit, Tallis thought, the equivalent of strong aspirin. 'So, basically, they knew what to do.'

'They saved my life.'

Next stop was the armoury. Tallis gaped at dozens of assault rifles, RPGs and Fly rocket launchers, a weapon, Darke pointed out, that if it didn't kill on impact would cause death later.

'It ruptures vital organs, lungs and liver mainly,' he said, matter-of fact.

There were also sniper and assault rifles, some worn-looking handguns and AK-47s with grenade attachments, several Soviet-made Dshke heavy machine guns, formidable against the enemy and designed to bring down helicopters. And, bloody hell, Tallis thought, one five-inch-calibre Barrett sniper rifle, a blow-your-bollocks-off weapon. He found himself drawn helplessly towards it. Not only could it disappear the enemy, it could be used to detonate explosive devices from a safe distance. It had an accurate range of 2,000 metres—and with the right ammo was capable of taking out armoured vehicles.

In addition, there were dozens of boxes of cartridges and grenades, bullet belts and bayonets, mortar rounds and dynamite. Tallis's eyes alighted on a quantity of C-4 military-grade plastic explosive. 'Where the hell did you get this lot?'

'Mostly off the Russians,' Darke said, unblinking. 'Every man has his addictions. With the Russians, it's usually vodka, weed and cigarettes.

'Before I arrived…' Darke allowed himself a rare smile '…Akhmet's men were an undisciplined rabble. And that's what gets people killed. You won't find any Rambos here,' he said, the smile gone, looking pointedly at Tallis.

Tallis nodded, met his eye, unsettled. Was this Darke warning him off? Did it amount to an admission that he knew who he was? Tallis wondered what was going on behind those pale, risky-looking eyes. He glanced around. Nobody was within earshot. Now could be the time to reveal his mission, ask Darke about the hits in Moscow, and whether he'd orchestrated them. Tallis hadn't fought his way here to play games—the body count had been too high—yet with Darke proving so illusory, he was wrong-footed. The ugly truth was that Tallis posed a threat to Darke and that meant he was in great danger. 'So what's the immediate strategy?'

'Akhmet will tell you,' Darke said, dismissive.

Tallis tried again. 'I'm impressed by the scale of

murders in Moscow. Quite something to hit the enemy in its own back yard.'

'I don't follow.'

'Prominent Russians who took part in the last two conflicts. In other circumstances they'd probably be identified as war criminals.'

'What about them?'

'They're being bumped off, one by one.'

'Serves them right.'

'Nothing to do with you?' Tallis studied Darke's expression very, very hard. If not Darke, who the hell had compiled the hit list? And who had passed on the intelligence to Fazan?

'Have you any idea how far it is from here to Moscow?' Darke glowered.

'Yes, I know th—'

But Tallis was interrupted. Darke, or Musa, as the Chechens called him was wanted elsewhere. 'You can sleep there.' Darke pointed to an open yard with an awning jutting out from a lean-to affair, not unlike Tallis's carport back home. This one consisted of three walls of stone, one side exposed to the mountain air. 'Don't forget to wash fully before prayers,' Darke warned, stalking away.

Tallis spent much of the afternoon waiting and watching and listening. Free to move where he wished, he saw many fighters busily cleaning their weapons. Tallis was familiar with the drill of stripping down, wiping every surface, cleaning out any dirt, oiling and wiping, reassembling and finally testing to see that the weapon worked. And these guys had clearly been properly trained. Others, with binoculars, patrolled the makeshift parapets while another section carried out running repairs on vehicles. Darke, he noticed, spent time coaching two female fighters, including Irina, in the art of firing a Dragunov. 'Remember, when you're working in pairs, number one checks out the position while number two is responsible for getting number one on target.' Both girls hung on his every word, Lula, a dark-eyed Chechen, in particular. Every time Darke spoke to her she blushed.

Everywhere Tallis went he was told what a great guy Akhmet was, devout and loyal to his men, a true warrior of Allah. Musa's standing was almost as high. He was a great warrior in battle, they said. His compatriots took it as a huge compliment that the man had returned to honour his bloodline. If only they knew, Tallis thought. Or was he the one who was fooled?

He was astonished to find a number of Russians among the group. As one explained, 'I served the motherland and what did I get? Cruelty and starvation, that's what. Even if you survive the fighting, you get no allowances or compensation, not even if you're injured.' Tallis remembered Vladimir, the former soldier now begging in a Moscow subway.

'I deserted and took my chances,' a tall, well-built Russian called Alexander told him. 'Akhmet is a better leader than anyone in the Kremlin.'

Tallis was introduced to several of Akhmet's family members, including his aged mother, a bent old lady with a weathered face as creviced and cracked as the mountainside. She told Tallis that her husband had fought alongside the Russians against the Germans in the Second World War and that, for his pains, they were banished wholesale to Siberia until their son decided it was time to return and reclaim their land.

Tallis was struck by the degree of reverence paid to old and young alike, including a simple-minded lad called Salman whose family had been killed in the second conflict. Against this rather cosy Waltons-type view, he heard breathtaking tales of savagery that did not exclude their own people if they were caught drinking or stealing or engaging in premarital sex. The warrior who'd performed the finger under the throat gesture, a guy called Lecha, was particularly vocal in his disapproval concerning such sinful activities. 'An insult to Allah,' he maintained, 'and worthy of great punishment.' Tallis was also shown 'the factory'. His Chechen escort, built like an all-in wrestler, was a man called Sultan.

'This is where we keep our guests,' he said with a big black-toothed smile, reminding Tallis of an eighteenth-century pirate. Sultan indicated a window-less dwelling at the rear of the compound, close to the latrines. Shooting the bolt, he opened a door, the sudden stench of excrement and fear strong in Tallis's nostrils. Sultan nodded for Tallis to enter. Adjusting his vision to the dark, Tallis saw on either side of a main walkway what could only be described as holding pens. Inside were three occupants, chained by one ankle, all boys, teenagers probably, their wretched faces hollow with exhaustion, their bodies emaciated from malnutrition. He'd seen better accommodation for battery hens.

'Who are these people?' he managed to get out.

'Hostages.'

Tallis nodded blindly.

'Go in, if you want. They won't hurt you,' Sultan said, as if he were talking about his pets.

Tallis did, not out of curiosity, not even out of pity. He wanted to see how easy it would be to liberate these poor bloody unfortunates. Judging by the chains around their ankles, no simple task. Out of the three only one strained close. He had a long jaw, blue enquiring eyes, blond matted hair, which he scratched distractedly, most likely due to lice. The boy opened his bloodied mouth, muttered something and then grew confused. Jesus, Tallis cursed. Two of the fingers on his right hand were bloody stumps. It took all his self-restraint not to punch Sultan, grab his weapon and set the boys free. But he couldn't. Not yet. And what the fuck did this sorry sight say about Darke?

In addition to this blatant atrocity, he saw little kids encouraged to pose with weapons.

'The children of Chechnya are growing up strong and ready to fight,' Irina told him, introducing her sidekick, Lula, the young woman whom Tallis had already spotted, mainly because her gaze seemed to be constantly focused on Darke. While Lula was short and olive-skinned, Irina was tall and athletic looking. The girls worked together. They were snipers, they told him proudly.

'And you are Russian?' he said to Irina.

'St Petersburg, yes.'

'And you, Lula—Chechen?'

Lula, doe-eyed, nodded.

'My girls.' Akhmet beamed, striding over. 'Did they tell you they specialise in the rose shot?'

A shot to the temple, Tallis thought. At the point where the bullet makes its entry, the wound blossoms like a flower. However much Akhmet glowed with pride, Tallis doubted Irina and Lula a match for a true professional.

'You like my operation here?' Akhmet said, slapping a paw of a hand onto Tallis's shoulder and manoeuvring him away.

'Very slick.'

'We have Musa to thank for much of the way we do things. Before I came to rescue my people I was a humble market trader. I knew nothing of fighting.'

Or strategy, Tallis thought. 'Musa mentioned you have plans in place. Sounds mysterious.'

Akhmet's eyes shone. 'Attack is the best form of defence, no? And surprise is the best form of attack.'

Tallis blinked. Akhmet reminded him of his late dear old gran. She'd had a habit of speaking in platitudes. It was about the only thing about her that used to drive him crazy.

'Were you responsible for the attack at Nalchik?' Tallis asked.

'We were,' Akhmet grinned, proud. 'And now we have another plan. We are about to take the war right into the enemy camp.'

'How so?'

Akhmet leant towards him, his massive frame towering over Tallis. 'We are going to ambush a police station and take down a military convoy. And you,' he added, a sinister light in his eyes, 'will fight with us.'

CHAPTER THIRTEEN

THE police station was close to the village of Komsomolskoe, south of Grozny. The Russians maintained that it was all under the control of federal troops. According to intelligence received, the reality was different: the station was woefully undermanned. Tallis gleaned this during the feast the night before. Against a backdrop of magical music and epic song, *illi*, they ate and danced round a huge fire, faces a sparkle of light and laughter. The only beverage was black tea, sweet and strong. As a devout Muslim, alcohol in Akhmet's camp was strictly prohibited, any infringement severely punished.

During the festivities Tallis tried to corner Darke.

'Akhmet told me of his plan.'

'Really?' Darke's eyes flicked from side to side. Tallis picked up on it. Was he looking out for danger, or was it borne of years of guerrilla warfare?

'I think it's crazy.'

'Why?' Darke's voice contained a surly note.

'Armed police, for example? Soldiers?'

'It's not the police we're after.'

'That doesn't really answer my question.'

'Akhmet has a good working relationship with them.'

'You mean they supplied the intelligence?'

'They won't present any problems to us,' Darke said with a slow, cold expression. 'As for the convoy, we'll use overwhelming force to deal with them. Our priority targets are six FSB guys who are visiting the station. One is believed to be a Chechen who defected to the other side.'

Tallis swallowed. He knew that they reserved the greatest punishment for such people. And what the hell was he thinking? The last thing he wanted or needed was to get involved. It would only massively complicate things, quite apart from the small fact that he didn't have the stomach for it. He was supposed to be saving lives, not taking them. His only consolation was that with Darke virtually under his nose he stood more chance of uncovering any plan to assassinate Ivanov, the Russian Prime Minister. He glanced around. Lula was standing close by, her gaze, Labrador-like, fixed on Darke.

'Don't worry,' Darke said, turning his cool gaze on Tallis, 'you'll be with me.'

Tallis stared at him. Ideas flickering through his mind, he suddenly and horribly got the picture. To eliminate the threat, Darke was going to dispatch him in the moment of battle.

An uneasy silence descended. Fireflies danced through the night. Laughter gilded the air. The strains of a balalaika drifted through the woodsmoke, its melody haunting.

'I have to check in with the sentries, ensure we're protected,' Darke said, tight-lipped, striding away.

'About the plan,' Tallis called after him.

'Tomorrow,' Darke said over his shoulder. 'We'll talk tomorrow.'

The day began early. After an uncomfortable night with a bitter wind stinging his face, Tallis woke to the sound of the call for prayer. It was barely light as sixty bare-footed silhouettes knelt down in neat rows and gave morning thanks to Allah. More ominously, they prayed for deliverance. Tallis, joining them, followed suit. Afterwards, he ate a simple meal of flat bread and mutton soup. They all did, eating slowly, as if it might be their last. That's when Tallis understood. So today was the day, Tallis thought, hardly able to believe the bad round of cards he'd been handed. Never had he felt so unprepared for what was about to take place.

After they'd eaten, and the women had cleared away, Darke spoke to the fighters. 'Remember, we go in quiet, hit hard and fast, disengage and initiate a swift with-drawal. Our aim is to undermine and eliminate as many as we can in as short a time as we can. It will require daring and decisiveness. You all know which groups you're in and it's vital that you move as a group, spread out, like we practised, putting fast and accurate fire into the enemy position. If you get split up, remember the drill—dash, down, crawl, observe, fire.

'Lula and Irina,' he said, addressing the girls. 'Don't forget that as snipers you are the most feared of all. Whatever opposition we encounter, your job is to remove strategic targets. Got that?'

Both girls nodded, Lula slavishly. Darke smiled. '*As-salamu alaikum*—peace be with you.'

Then Akhmet came and stood among them to ready them for the fight, his presence compelling and magnetic.

'My warriors, today we go into battle against a colonial power, a power that has repeatedly put our people to death, a power that states it wants constitutional reform. Let me tell you that what Russia really wants…' Akhmet raised a finger, shaking his dark head 'is the elimination of our way of life, our culture, our values and our religion. Be under no illusion, our fight today is not for independence and freedom. Our fight is for Allah.'

A murmur of agreement trickled through the camp.

'And with Allah on our side, how can we not win?' Akhmet's voice soared. 'Some accuse us of being ter-rorists. What does that make the Russians? What do you call those who kill thousands of innocent Chechen women and children and old people? What words do you find to describe those who rape and murder a heavily pregnant women and the baby in her womb? How many of you have lost loved ones, brothers and sisters, mothers and fathers, daughters and sons? Remember this, if you remember nothing else: we fight today to defend our people.

'Do not forget that the Russians are running scared. They are so frightened of us they lie to their own citizens about our victories in battle. Our ambushes are explained away as mines, or booby-traps, or roadside bombs, and when a Russian soldier is killed, his death is blamed on an accident, a road crash or the mishandling of a weapon. Sometimes a death is not mentioned at all. This is the Russian way,' he sneered. 'What must the mothers think, that their sons were taken away by evil spirits?' Akhmet let out a derisive laugh, his fighters joining in until he finally called for quiet with a raised hand. Silence fell soft like a cashmere blanket. Nobody moved. Nobody stirred.

'Do not spare the enemy, but be careful where there are civilians. We do not want to hurt our own. Remember that we live in equality. We respect the rights of others. We live free and equal like wolves.'

Then his tone became grave. 'Some of you today will not return,' he said. 'To those who go to Paradise, I say think of us as we will surely remember you. Keep in mind that to die in battle is a magnificent thing. Remember this also: this is our land. It belongs to us. It will always remain our land.'

'Ready?' Darke said, eyeing him. He wore grenades in his webbing, a pistol on his belt, Kalashnikov in his hands. His stare was icy.

Tallis nodded, grabbed his Kurtz and six mags, thirty rounds in each, and followed. He had no choice.

They moved in a slow convoy down the other side of the mountains while the mist was still creeping among the trees. The track was stony and rutted, eventually widening as they dropped down into the foothills. With several fighters in their vehicle, Tallis had little option but to go along with what was being asked of him. If this ever got out, he wondered how the SIS was going to square two Brits fighting alongside Chechen warriors against the sovereign forces of Russia. And it made him feel queasy.

From the moment they reached flatter ground, they moved on foot, in single file, two metres apart. The way was wooded, giving excellent cover. They advanced in a rough arrowhead formation with Sultan as point man, Darke following as leader, Tallis behind him to cover, with two flanking warriors carrying machine-guns and grenade launchers, and two men behind them, including the Russian, Alexander. They formed the small advance party to secure a temporary base, the remaining fighters split into groups of four sixteen-man units some distance behind, the rear led by Akhmet. Lula and Irina alone were given a roving commission, their job to spot and kill.

They were in a forest, thick with leaf, the mist swirling like smoke through the trees. Several dozen metres ahead lay the police station, its occupants sleepy and unaware. Sultan stopped, scanning the horizon, ears attuned for sound of the enemy—and that meant anyone who fought against them. Silently giving a thumbs-up, he motioned for the other sections to advance, which they did by fanning out, the team to the right charged with setting up base plates without which the aim would prove inaccurate for the mortars.

The military convoy was timed to pass that way in less than half an hour. Explosives had already been put in place to bring the convoy to a halt. Akhmet and his men planned to take the convoy and the police station simultaneously from all four sides in an overwhelming show of force. Surprise was key. The enemy might set the time, Tallis remembered from a piece of military fieldcraft, but the attacker sets the place. A lot would depend on the incompetence of the opposition. And, in his book, no matter the intelligence, it didn't pay to underestimate the enemy. Never mind what Akhmet had said in his call-to-arms speech, Tallis felt immediate concern for the homes nearby and the villagers who could easily be caught in the crossfire. He mentioned his worry to Darke but was assured that, with the sudden surge in fighting, most had fled the area.

Darke's party, or assault team, was charged with opening fire on the halted vehicle and those soldiers leaving it, their escape routes cut off by the three other groups with machine-gun fire and mortar shells fired directly into the killing zone. Irina and Lula's job was to kill the occupants of the police station. If all went according to plan, it would be a bloodbath. Tallis fingered his weapon nervously, considering how long he could last without firing a shot, wondering also how long it would take Darke to attempt to slot him. Nerves and tension, he reminded himself coldly, equalled mistakes.

Twenty-eight highly charged minutes passed during which Darke made one radio transmission, telling Akhmet to stand by, the message, in the normal scheme of things, picked up by the commanders of the other two groups. There was no response. At once Tallis saw a fatal flaw in the plan. Foliage and mist could have seriously adverse effects on radio communication. He looked, questioning, at Darke. Darke opened his mouth to speak but stopped at the sound of an engine, the note heavy, denoting a truck. Tallis's ears became keen as the noise grew louder, confirmation, at last, of a military vehicle approaching.

All seven men hunkered down. The truck swung into view barely visible through the shrouds of morning fog. Tallis watched and waited for the explosives to detonate and bring the vehicle to a halt. Any moment now, he thought. Seconds ticked by. He could feel Darke tense next to him, body wired, finger on the trigger, all senses on high alert. Still they waited. The truck drew to a halt. No explosion. Silence, the damp air swaddling their ears. Tallis was reminded of another piece of military law: when it goes quiet the enemy is up to something. No sooner had the thought taken form in his brain than he heard a scream and whistle followed by the howl of descending mortar rounds as they flew from two directions, from the left and from the right, red-hot metal fragments slicing into two of Akhmet's units simultaneously, the yells of those already cut down around them ringing in their ears. At the same time, men in the station were letting loose with a terrifying volley of automatic fire. Next, the familiar whine and hiss as rocket-propelled grenades flew through the air, parting Tallis's hair as a barrage of bullets whizzed past. Christ Almighty, Tallis cursed, realising the trap they'd walked into. Momentarily shocked by the sudden onslaught, a zillion thoughts pounded through his mind, notably that whoever occupied the building retained the high ground. In an instant the odds had spectacularly reversed against them.

He dropped flat onto the ground to try and work out what was going down, a storm of bullets flying over his head in all directions. The Chechens were outmanoeuvred, the Russian attack planned, highly organised and therefore predictable: they were going to draw them into the killing zone, outflank them and cut off their escape route. It was imperative they melt back into the landscape, and quickly. To their advantage, the fog, as long as it remained, would aid their flight, and the Chechen were masters at taking advantage of the local terrain. It's what made them expert at guerrilla warfare. At least, that's what he'd been led to believe. From where he was lying, it was hard to tell. Some, he could make out, had sprinted for cover. Most had become detached from their units. It was every man for himself.

'Come on,' Darke said. 'I'll go first. You cover.'

'Like old times, then.' But Tallis's voice was lost in the clamour of arms, the pyrotechnics of battle, the smoke and dust and shouting.

Both of them spread out, creeping low, laying down a burst of suppressing fire at the same time as the military vehicle discharged a seven-man crew of black-clad soldiers letting off magazines on full automatic.

Darke darted forward with a grenade, pulling the pin, waiting two seconds while it 'cooked' then lobbing it. Tallis, instinct kicking in, followed up with a short burst of fire, killing three, heads exploding like coconuts at a funfair. The drawing of enemy blood seemed to have a morale-boosting effect. Within seconds, the girls, the snipers, had lined up and taken out one of the Russians' mortar guys, giving the remains of Akhmet's mortar men time to fire an accurate shot with which they hit a unit of Russian soldiers. With awesome courage, one young Chechen rushed forward and fired an RPG into the police station, only to be cut down in a fusillade of bullets as bits of the building shattered and collapsed. Of those who escaped, many Russians were picked off. A loud cry of victory went up from the Chechen gunmen.

Then, to his horror, Tallis spotted more soldiers coming from the east, from the west and from the north. The fact he could even see them meant that the curtain of mist was lifting. All they needed now was an air strike and they'd be finished. 'Fuck's sake,' he cursed aloud, suddenly seeing a grenade hurtling in his direction. Letting out a shout to Darke, he flung himself down onto the ground, putting his hands over his ears. First there was silence then a terrific boom as the thing exploded, shrapnel spraying into a man metres away, at waist height, shredding his body to pieces, guts and intestines spilling out, hot and bloodied on the ground.

Temporarily deafened, and with the smell of freshly mutilated body parts strong in his nostrils, Tallis staggered to his feet, a storm of bullets smacking into the dirt around him. It felt as if it was raining steel. He exchanged glances with Darke, who was slightly in front, both falling into a well-choreographed pattern of laying down suppressing fire and covering the other while withdrawing, other fighters who'd managed to escape valiantly taking care of arcs of fire on the flanks.

Men fired at long range and at close. Some Chechens, including Sprite, Tallis noticed, had taken to hand-to-hand combat at which they excelled, the scare factor alone enough to rock and seriously undermine an inadequately trained soldier's morale. Tallis glanced in awe as Sprite tore through a Russian's windpipe with a hunting knife. But whatever valour the Chechens displayed, they were overwhelmed by sheer volume of numbers.

Then, from out of nowhere came a mighty roar, like the sound of a pride of lions. Tallis felt his bones vibrate, the blood pump in every vein and vessel of his body. Lights flashed. Tracer rounds ripped through the forest behind him, tearing down trees, shredding anyone in its wake. He knew instinctively that a large-calibre cannon had been discharged, scorching the way back, razing the ground, turning it into a dead zone. Darke let out a gasp. 'Whoever sold us out, I hope he's happy with his thirty pieces of silver.'

With the way behind open to another round of cannon fire, they moved forward again, each covering the other, heading for the remains of the police station yet trying to avoid the killing zone. Leaping in front of Darke, Tallis heard the deadly hiss of RPGs, the dull crump of mortar, the chatter of machine-gun fire, and everywhere the sound of wounded and dying.

At last they came to the remains of a house. Mortared in the crossfire, it was just a collection of walls and rubble. Apart from the dead, the place was empty. Both men fell against the nearest pile of stones, glad of the obscurity. Tallis loaded another mag into his weapon.

'This way,' Darke said, scooting along, keeping low, Tallis in full flight behind. As they turned a corner, they found Sultan beating a Chechen in a leather jacket with the stock of his automatic, what was left of the man's face a bloody mess.

'The hell are you doing?' Darke said.

'He's with them,' Sultan spat, his face a collection of dark edges. 'He works for the FSB.' Sultan took out a long knife from his belt. 'I'm going to gut him.'

'No, let me,' Darke said, reaching for his own knife.

A terrible moan came from the man on the floor, snot and blood oozing from a hole in his face. Tallis froze in horror then blinked in astonishment as Darke whipped the pistol from his belt and emptied two shots into Sultan's head.

'Say nothing, or I'll kill you.' Darke swivelled round, his cold eyes level with Tallis's, the pistol still in his hand. 'Now move it.'

It was chaos. With smoke grenades launched to mask their retreat, the only way left to them was to flee back into the mountains where the fog hung still and in heavy folds. Out of the seven men in their group, only three were left—Tallis, Graham and the Russian, Alexander. Of the other three groups, the casualties were hard to estimate. Everywhere Chechens were in retreat. At one point it was rumoured that Akhmet had been killed, until word on the ground confirmed that he was safe. What couldn't be denied was that they'd been hammered.

And one among them was a traitor.

CHAPTER FOURTEEN

'It was him,' Lecha said, his voice spiked with malice, pointing an accusing finger at Tallis.

They were counting their losses. Of sixty-eight men who'd gone out to fight, twenty-five returned, two dying on the fierce retreat through the mountains. Of those twenty-five, ten were injured, three seriously and not expected to last the night. Women keened for their lost husbands and sons. Children cried for their fathers. Everywhere there were women with empty eyes. The mood in the camp was sombre. And there was anger.

'How can it be him?' Lula said, drawing a shape in the earth with the toe of her boot. 'He only just arrived. This has been planned for days, if not weeks.' She glanced at Darke, who was also standing with them. For a second Tallis wondered if Lula suspected something.

'Doesn't mean he wasn't involved,' Darke said, casting Tallis a stony look.

Thanks very much, Tallis thought. He understood Darke's desire to protect his back and his cover, but he didn't need to sell him out to do it. As for what he'd witnessed on the battlefield, he hadn't yet fully processed it. Darke's behaviour was a paradox. Just when Tallis thought he had a handle on it, that Darke had, indeed, turned native, Darke acted in a way that didn't fit. Spy or rogue? Tallis simply didn't know. Akhmet, his fury contained under an ominous cloak of silence, was of the opinion that the informer was a police officer. Tallis was not fooled. The cold look in those dark eyes told a different story. No way had Akhmet ruled out that there was a traitor among them.

That night there was no celebration, no dancing. The dead were washed and prepared for burial, their bodies dispatched to the ground on a grassy slope to the east of the compound with a speed that left Tallis breathless.

Many hours later, as the night manacled the moon to a cloud, Tallis made his way to Darke's quarters, a low dwelling of stone and corrugated metal. Nudging the door open, he slipped inside. A kerosene lamp burnt in the centre of the room, casting shadows over Darke's living quarters. It took Tallis two seconds to see that Darke was not in bed.

Two seconds too long…

The blade felt cold and sharp against his throat. Darke, shorter in stature, was wiry and extremely strong, the muscles in his bare arms rope hard. His voice was a low growl.

'You've got thirty seconds to make your pitch. You

screw up and either I'll denounce you as a spy and hand you over to Akhmet's tender mercies, or I'll slit your throat here and now.'

'I've been sent to find you and bring you back.'

'Who by?'

'The SIS, the people you work for, or had you forgotten?' The blade grazed his throat, making a tear in the skin. Fuck, it hurt. Tallis tried to control his breathing.

'Keep talking.'

'They say you've dropped off the radar, that you've made no contact for months.'

'I nearly died, for fuck's sake.'

'Alright,' Tallis conceded. 'Thing is they have intelligence that you're directly involved in a number of murders in Moscow.'

'Bollocks.'

'They have forensic evidence.'

'Bollocks again.'

'They think you've defected.'

'Absolute crap.'

'Is it? It would be understandable.'

Darke wrenched at his throat hard, almost throttling him. 'Have you forgotten what I did on the battlefield?'

'Maybe you did it for show,' Tallis rasped, 'to impress me, seeing as I was the only witness.' Christ, Tallis thought, he was taking a risk. An image of Sprite cutting a Russian soldier's throat, animal and gory, raced through his mind, but he had to be clear about which master Darke served.

'And maybe they sent *you* for show,' Darke sniped back.

So you do remember me, Tallis thought.

Darke was still arguing. 'If anyone else had seen, we'd both be dead. These murders…' he said, relaxing his grip a fraction.

'What about them?'

'I can't be answerable for the entire Chechen nation.'

'So you had no involvement?'

'How could I?'

Easily, Tallis thought. You could have trained the killer. 'You know nothing about a plan to murder those involved in the last conflict?'

Darke let out a low laugh. 'Now I know why they sent you. You always were a fool, Paul. It would be suicidal for the Chechens to do such a thing,' Darke said, cold creeping back into his voice.

'Pity they didn't remember that when they stormed Beslan.'

Tallis felt a blade of fear pass through Darke's body and into his own. 'That was different.'

'Was it?'

'It was a grave mistake and I wasn't involved.'

'You mean you didn't actually take part?' Tallis said, his voice scathing. 'Isn't that what the guards said when they herded the Jews into the death camps?'

'How fuckin' dare you?' Darke snarled. 'You think I like what I do? Think I enjoy it?'

So it wasn't exactly a denial, Tallis thought.

Something cold slimed in the pit of his stomach. 'It's well documented that although many terrorists were killed at Beslan, some escaped. Were you one of them?'

Darke suddenly yanked Tallis back. Tallis closed his eyes. This was it, he thought. He was going to die like a dog in a strange land. Then the grip eased and he was free. He turned, faced Darke's gimlet eyes. In that brief moment in time Tallis understood how the years of living a lie, with death hounding him from every corner, had taken its toll on his old friend. He suddenly looked ancient.

Darke let out an anguished sigh, put the heel of his hand to his forehead. 'I tried to send warnings, but it was hard to get word out. Believe me, I'll carry the guilt of what happened at that school to the grave. But you have to understand that Beslan and many other atrocities were gifts to Ivanov. They handed him his *raison d'être*, both with his own people and with the West. It wasn't the bombing of terrorist camps but the wanton destruction of cities and villages, the killing of hundreds of innocents, that produced the state of terror that will take generations to rectify.'

Exactly how Lena had described it, Tallis recalled. 'You sound like a sympathiser.'

Darke shook his head. 'I'm telling you how it is. Ivanov is on a mission. He won't rest until he's subjugated the Caucasus, even if it takes him to the day he dies.'

'Which might be a lot sooner than you think.'

'What?'

'You've no idea about any plan to assassinate him?' Tallis's expression was searing.

'Christ, they sent you all this way to ask me that? They actually risked your life and mine? Unfucking-believable.'

'Obviously not,' Tallis said with a dry smile. 'And if someone kills him and it's discovered that you've been working alongside the rebels, imagine the political fallout.'

Darke cast him a hard look. '*If*. Have you any idea of the personal risks I'm taking? Do you know what would happen to me if Akhmet got even a suspicion that I'm a spy?'

Unfortunately, Tallis could.

'So you go back, tell our masters I'm clean, and, while you're at it, you can pass on the latest piece of intelligence.'

'What intelligence?'

'You think I'm just going to come out with it?' The haughty, distrusting note had crept back into Darke's voice. Was this the hallmark of a man who'd spent the best part of a decade trusting nobody but himself, or did it signify something else? Tallis wondered. 'How do I know I can trust you?' Darke said, with narrowed eyes.

'Because I came through the mountains to find you. Because I remembered a lad who cheered me up, who made me laugh, who stuck up for me when nobody else did, and whom I missed when he left. And because seven men have died on your account, including a young Chechen I couldn't save. You don't own the monopoly on guilt, Graham.'

'Graham.' A smile touched Darke's mouth. 'Haven't heard that name in years,' he said, momentarily dreamy, his pin-sharp eyes losing their intensity, drifting off to some far-away and forgotten place. 'Alright,' he said, collecting himself. 'Akhmet is planning a meeting with a bloke called Hattab.'

'The same Hattab who wants to overthrow the Algerian government and set up an Islamic state?'

Darke nodded. 'He bears allegiance to a number of jihadist causes and movements. It's thought he has close links with al-Qaeda.'

'And Akhmet's going to do business with him, you say?'

'It signals more bloodshed to come.'

For which ordinary people like Katya will be deemed culpable, Tallis thought. 'Can't do it,' he said. 'I've express orders to bring you back.'

'Says who?'

'Christian Fazan at the SIS.'

'You work for Fazan?' Darke said, amazed. 'He sent you?'

'I'm on secondment to him. I've been working for Five for the past couple of years. Before that, I was with West Midlands police as a firearms officer.'

Darke thoughtfully stroked his beard. 'And Fazan believes that I've gone native, that I'm working with the rebels? That I orchestrated the hits in Moscow?'

'And that you have the prime minister and former president in your sights.' He suddenly remembered Asim's fears for the opening ceremony of the World Newspaper Congress. Time in the mountains seemed to work in a different vortex. He wondered whether it had taken place or not, whether it had, in fact, passed off without incident.

'Where did Fazan get his information?' Darke scowled.

'I wasn't privy to his source.'

Darke didn't say it but Tallis knew what he was thinking. *Something isn't right.* 'What's this Fazan bloke like?' Tallis said.

'Experienced, dedicated, been in the service for a good many years.' Darke shrugged.

'Think someone is trying to frame you?'

'Or him?' Darke smiled. 'I don't know. Chechens get the blame for most things.'

Had the Russians somehow pulled the wool over Fazan's eyes, too? Tallis wondered. But they didn't know about Graham Darke so what had led Fazan to be so specific? And then another more ugly thought entered his head. What if Asim had been set up? What if Asim was in some kind of danger?

'I've got to get word to my contact,' Tallis said urgently.

'Not going to be easy. Especially after what happened this morning.'

'What was your usual method for communication?'

'Going down into the foothills and making contact

with a Russian commander who is also working for the British. Last time I went there was no sign of him. Might mean something, might not.'

'If you try to sneak away now, it will look like you had something to do with the ambush going wrong and the trap laid. Any thoughts on that?' Tallis said.

'Two. I don't believe Akhmet's contact in the police snitched. I do believe we have an insider. And it wasn't me,' he added in response to Tallis's challenging expression.

'Think it's me?' Tallis gave him a level look.

Darke smiled. 'Not unless you've changed.'

'People do,' Tallis said mildly.

'Not people like you.' It was the closest he'd come to a good-natured smile. Tallis smiled back, a mask for a misshapen thought flitting through his mind. Why *you* and not *us*?

'Look, maybe I can talk to Akhmet,' Darke said, 'try and persuade him that we need to scout out the surrounding area, see how many Russians are heading for the mountains.'

'Think he'll buy it?'

'Don't see why not. Then you could give me the slip.'

'Dangerous. Much better if you come with me. Clear your name.'

Darke thought for a moment. 'Leave them all behind?' He sounded almost wistful, Tallis thought. 'No, it's more valuable if I stay.'

'But I have my orders. For Chrissakes, Graham, someone out there is killing an awful lot of people. The President and the Prime Minister could be next. Whatever your personal thoughts about the people in the Kremlin, I need your help. You've got to come with me.'

'I'm not coming back,' Darke said, eyes flashing, immutable.

Loyalty or treachery? Tallis wondered.

CHAPTER FIFTEEN

THE next few days, lost days as far as Tallis was concerned, were taken up with regrouping, nursing the injured and burying those who died from their wounds.

Akhmet, statesmanlike, talked to his men, comforted the widows, promised that their needs and those of their children would be met. He complained bitterly that the Russians had used elite FSB commandos disguised as Chechens. Tallis wasn't sure how Akhmet could have been that certain. It was hard to distinguish one from another in the mist. In spite of Akhmet's brave talk, suspicion hung over the camp like a black cloak. Nobody trusted the man sitting next to him. Already a young Chechen had been disciplined by being cast into a pit. His crime: he had not acquitted himself well in battle. Sprite, Tallis noticed, took a perverse delight in watching the unfortunate boy's suffering.

'He's lucky,' Sprite said, with his weird long-faced smile. 'In the height of summer the temperature can reach fifty degrees Celsius.'

'And in winter, minus ten,' Tallis countered.

Two hours later, after Darke finally intervened, the boy was released. While he had Akhmet's attention, Darke put forward a proposal.

'I've been thinking about the attack. Obviously, like you say, someone has talked. It's imperative we stop the leak of information. If we don't, the campaign for the summer is compromised.'

'What are you suggesting?'

Darke looked at Tallis. 'We send him down the mountains to gather intelligence. He speaks fluent Russian,' he said, ignoring Tallis's startled expression, 'and he's not known as a fighter.'

'But he killed three soldiers at a checkpoint,' Akhmet said, sharp intelligence in his eyes.

'If I shave my beard, I won't be recognised,' Tallis chipped in helpfully.

'And I could go with him,' Darke said, 'and ensure he does as he's told.'

Akhmet said nothing. He looked out across the camp, his eyes scanning the sorry remains of his band of warriors. Lula and Irina were standing nearby, cleaning their rifles. Akhmet smiled at them. 'My girls,' he said softly. Then he turned to Darke, the smile fading. 'No,' he said, and walked away.

As Tallis passed Lecha, who was drawing water from the well, he swore he heard his voice trickle with laughter.

Moscow: 09.00 a.m.
Opening ceremony of the World Newspaper Congress

'Ladies and gentleman,' the President of the Congress began. 'My apologies for the delay of this the eighteenth World Editors' Forum. As you're all aware,' he said, looking across an auditorium of nearly two thousand newspaper executives, 'security procedures are particularly tight, and we've had to reschedule our programme due to the President being unable to attend after he was suddenly taken ill last night. It's nothing too serious, I'm assured, and we all wish him a speedy recovery. However,' he said, 'it's my pleasure at very short notice to introduce the Prime Minister of the Russian Federation, Andrei Ivanov.'

At once, a gasp went up from the crowd. People rose to their feet, straining to see the figure walking up onto the stage, clapping and whistling applause. The ovation lasted a full three minutes in spite of a cry of dissent from a small vocal group of protesters complaining about the lack of press coverage on the newly emerging situation in Chechnya. As they tossed leaflets into the air, armed security officials swooped, heavy-handed, rounding them up, dragging every one of them out.

Apart from one who lay in wait.

Abzo Gaziev watched the Prime Minister with awe and fear. A doctor, Gaziev was not naturally a violent man. His mission in life was to save it, not destroy it—unlike the man soaking up the adulation on stage. My, this was something of an unexpected turn of events, Gaziev thought. He didn't know whether it would play to his advantage or not. That was the other thing about him. He was naturally cautious, a rational individual, a man not given to emotion. His was a need for cold appraisal, moderated, without heat or passion, which was why Gaziev wanted to see the man in the flesh, to look him in the eye, if at all possible to draw near. He thought that by studying the man at close quarters he might learn something new, something illuminating. Would Ivanov's words, he asked himself, reveal a different, more moderate side, someone whom he could do business with?

Ivanov thanked his host and, after brief preamble, launched into a speech about the increase in press freedom. 'Vast changes have occurred in Russia in the past decade. Only a few years ago, we were having this same conversation about the state's so-called control over the media. I said then what I say now, that the number of press assets owned by the state is in decline. Furthermore, there are far too many publications for the state to be able and willing to take an interest—these are of no concern to us.

'As for those Chechen sympathisers demonstrating today, what do their actions say about freedom of speech, freedom of debate?' he said, a withering note in his voice. 'It is not true that there has been a lack of coverage in the Caucasus. For the record, those who wish to cover the emerging conflict are free to travel and report on the rise in terrorist activity—not that they have to stray too far,' he said with a dry laugh. 'You only have to walk out onto our streets in Moscow to see the Chechens in action.' Polite laughter rippled through the hall. 'All journalists, with the correct paperwork from the Kremlin, are welcome to observe the brutality handed out by the rebels to our soldiers. Unrestricted, they can witness for themselves the flagrant disregard for the sanctity of human life in what these fundamentalists call the fight for Islam...'

Gaziev tuned out. He had slowly inched his way towards the stage. The number of tight-jawed heavies at Ivanov's side precluded conversation, but he thought he might be able to deliver a personal letter he'd written earlier, outlining his concerns. The letter was addressed to the President but in his absence he would pass it to the Prime Minister. Not that it would do any good. He could see that now. The intransigence on the man's face was crystal-clear. What did he, Abzo Gaziev, and his wasted life matter to this man? What would Ivanov, the man with the playboy lifestyle, who enjoyed the respect of leaders in the West, care that, as a humble trained medic, he could no longer find work, was actually *forbidden* to practise?

Gaziev, the mild-mannered, cool-thinking individual, shook. As he remembered what the man was responsible for, a part of him twisted inside. Better get it over with quickly, he thought, watching as Ivanov's short, off-the-cuff speech came to a close, the Prime Minister reaching for his chair.

As Gaziev lunged forward, a shot rang out, throwing the hall into commotion. The Prime Minister was thrown down onto the floor, his close protection team surrounding him. As Gaziev craned to see what was going on, he was grabbed and dashed to the floor, blows raining down on him, the letter crumpled in his hand.

Darke again tried to reason with Akhmet. 'We need more men. Why not contact Abdul across the mountains in Vedeno? If we pool our resources, we can still complete our summer offensive.'

It was true, Tallis thought. Their numbers were so depleted the sentries were working double time. This was good. It meant they'd be tired and less alert should he make his escape.

Akhmet said nothing. For two days now he'd hardly spoken except to comfort the bereaved. Tallis was fast running out of patience. He had to get out and get back to civilisation—with Darke.

'If we start at daybreak,' Darke continued, 'me and Tallis can evade the patrols and be with Abdul by nightfall.'

Still Akhmet was silent, his eyes unreachable. Tallis felt a small spark of rebellious anger. All this messing about, trying to finesse the bloke, was getting them nowhere. And he was running out of time. Maybe he already had, he thought grimly.

Finally, Akhmet spoke. 'No. We wait then I will give the orders.'

As day rolled into night, Tallis made his way to Darke's quarters as arranged. Darke had told him to come equipped for flight. The thought of fleeing back down through the mountains left him cold. Coming up had been dangerous, exhausting and physically testing. Going down was a whole different challenge.

This time Tallis's arrival was greeted with no hostility.

'Akhmet's getting suspicious,' Darke said. He was standing next to what passed for a bed, a raised piece of board with a thin mattress on the top.

'Stating the obvious.' Tallis flickered a smile. He'd long come to the same conclusion. 'Now what? You said I stood no chance alone through the mountains.' Although it would certainly minimise any contact with Russian forces, he thought.

'Akhmet has his men watching at all times. I'd give you ten minutes, tops, maybe less. Remember, they're intimately acquainted with the terrain, and determined. They'd track you down like a dog.'

And kill me like one, Tallis imagined. A chill shiver flew down his spine.

'But there is another way.'

'Yeah?'

'Through the mountains.'

Tallis scratched his nose. 'You said that was impossible.'

'I mean literally.'

'There's a tunnel?'

'The Chechens are rivalled only by the North Koreans, who have a bit of a thing for burying their nuclear plants in the sides of mountains.'

'Bloody hell. Why didn't you say so before?'

'Because I wasn't sure.'

'Sure of what?'

'Whether I was coming with you or not.'

'And you are?' Tallis could hardly believe it. Darke had been so adamant about staying.

'Yes.' Darke blinked.

Why? Tallis thought. What had changed his mind? Could it be the suspicion that Akhmet was onto him, or something else entirely? Tallis couldn't quite reconcile the difficulty he encountered in reading Darke's responses. It was as if something was off with the man, something missing from his human jigsaw. 'You sure?' he said, solemn.

'No other way. I want to make clear the Chechen side of the story.'

'That they're innocent?'

Darke hesitated. 'Akhmet's men are guilty of many things but not this. Second, if Ivanov does get bumped off, I don't want to be around for the backlash.'

Sounded plausible. 'When do we leave?'

'Now. Did you bring your weapons with you, like I told you?'

'Fully tooled up.'

'Bet you haven't got one of these,' Darke said, stooping down and reaching under his bed. He took out a Dragunov and handed it to Tallis.

'Think I'll need it?' Tallis said, cautious. He was starting to feel like a character out of a Schwarzenegger film. The rifle had a custom-made leather strap attached so he was able to carry it easily on his back.

'Good for picking off sentries.'

'Right,' Tallis said, lacklustre. Too much blood had been spilt already. Any more had to be on a strictly defensive basis. 'Can we do something first?'

'What?'

'Free those poor bastards in "the factory".'

Any other sensible intelligence officer would have baulked at the increased risk. It wasn't a smart move. The boys were in a terrible state, mentally and physically. They could behave in an entirely unpredictable manner, yet Tallis knew that unless Darke had changed inordinately over the years, it would be hard for him to ignore their plight. Like he'd said, *Think I enjoy it?*

Darke let out a breath. They both knew that with Sultan dead and the remaining men diverted to keeping watch on the south, it was relatively easy to walk in and free them. But then what?

'You mean we take them with us?' Darke said, shaking his head.

'Give them a sporting chance.'

'No such thing. Not here. If we free them we take them. Frankly, it can't be done.'

'Look, I know it's difficult, but—'

'They're collateral damage,' Darke said, edge in his voice. 'Not nice, but that's the reality.'

Tallis tried a different tack. 'That Chechen lad you had freed from the zindan.'

'What about him?'

'You showed compassion.'

Darke's mouth twisted into a sly smile. 'I displayed pragmatism. We're chronically short of men to fight. No point in completely breaking the boy's spirit.'

Tallis studied his old friend, wondering if Darke had been too long in the field. If somewhere along the line he'd detached morally. 'Then I'll take my chances alone,' Tallis said, making to leave. Darke grabbed his arm, stared into his eyes. Tallis felt an inexplicable chill.

'You'll take responsibility for them?' Darke dug his fingers into the sinews in Tallis's arm to make the point.

'Yes,' Tallis said, unflinching.

'Alright,' Darke said, releasing him. 'Let's do it.'

As predicted, the area outside the 'factory' was unmanned. Darke slipped inside first, followed by Tallis. As soon as they entered, the boys stirred. Tallis immediately spoke to them in Russian, telling them they had to be quiet if they wanted to live. Three empty pairs of eyes fixed on him. He then told them that they were to be rescued. All three nodded, their expressions a mixture of disbelief and steely hope. No hurrahs, no howls of relief or joy. They were too far gone for that. Darke reached for the key to unlock their padlocks while Tallis kept a watchful eye for movements outside.

Within minutes, Darke was cursing softly. 'This one's too weak to travel.' Tallis turned to examine the boy, whose name was Dmitri. He looked dreadful. Held the longest, according to Darke, Dmitri had no fingers on his left hand, the more recent wounds red and open. His body was in a pitiful condition and his cheekbones stuck out at such angles the skin seemed as if it might break. He had a dark gush of hair that seemed to sprout from the top of his head like a coconut. His dried-up features and protruding eyes reminded Tallis of a tiny monkey.

'We can't leave him,' Tallis said, meeting the boy's pleading gaze. 'They'll crucify him.' Sadly, it was more than a simple figure of speech, he thought.

Darke exchanged a glance with Tallis, the cool pragmatism in his expression indicating that it would be simple enough to dispatch the boy. One quick twist of the neck should do the trick.

Tallis shook his head. 'Here,' he said, hoisting the boy up onto his shoulder. 'I'll carry him.' He was as a light as a puff of wind. The memory of Ruslan on his back flashed through his mind.

'Madness,' Darke muttered, grabbing a couple of

iron bars that had been used to beat them with, which he now handed to the other two. 'Only use them if you're under attack,' he warned, not that either of them looked strong enough to wield a stick between them. 'Try anything smart and I'll kill you,' he added, casting another sour glance in Tallis's direction.

They left in single formation, Darke leading the way, the other two lads, Sergei and Pyotr, limping behind him, Tallis bringing up the rear. They were heading for the eastern side of the compound, the area that housed the cemetery, the only place that wasn't mined at the border. It was, however, fenced with a concertina of barbed wire unsecured to the ground to deter intruders coming in rather than people going out.

Darke signalled silently for them to stop. After double-checking the fence for booby-traps, he got down on the ground, lying on his back, and lifted the bottom layer of wire with his Kalashnikov, wriggling underneath and rolling down a slight incline on the other side. One by one, the others crossed, the lads using their iron bars to protect themselves. To get Dmitri through, Tallis had to virtually dig a hollow in the ground and roll him underneath, after which he took the Dragunov from his back, using it to pin back the wire, as Darke had done, and edged his way through, taking care to fill in the earth and let the wire bounce back normally into its former position. From there they dropped down onto a rocky path, the descent sheer and twisting. Unaccustomed to the terrain and with no light to guide

him, the night felt like a razor, at any moment threatening to slash him across the face and plunge him and his
cargo several hundred feet down the mountainside.

On they scrambled, down rock and shale and grassy
slope, the lads slipping and sliding in front, constantly
terrified of making too much noise until, miraculously,
Darke pointed to an opening large enough for a man to
crawl into.

'That's it?' Tallis hissed. He had a sudden overwhelming, crushing sensation of claustrophobia. He
could do pretty much anything out in the open, but
underground was a different matter entirely. No wonder
he'd not made it into the Special Forces, he thought.
Holes in the ground were for badgers and foxes, not
human beings.

'It's bigger inside,' Darke assured him, going first,
disappearing from view. The two lads followed. Now
that they were free, they both seemed to have uncov-
ered previously unmined reserves of energy. Tallis
guessed this pointed up the difference between a
fifteen-year-old hostage and a thirty-five-year-old.

Tallis helped Dmitri through the gap where Darke
was waiting to take hold of him then glanced up once
into the starless night, wondering if it would be his last
vision. Something creaked above his head. He looked
and saw nothing except impenetrable darkness then,
taking a deep breath, ducked inside where he was met
by a gust of cold, damp and musty air. Torchlight per-

forated the dark, revealing a chamber and a track running down through it that appeared to twist away.

'We'll rest here for five,' Darke said, squatting, taking a piece of cooked lamb from his rucksack, dividing it up carefully and handing it round, the two more able-bodied boys falling on it ravenously. Both were so skinny it was, at first, hard to tell them apart. Sergei, blond, looked as though someone had put his hair on the wrong way round: long at the front, short at the back. Pyotr, Tallis recognised, was the lad who'd approached him when Sultan had showed him the sights. His thin face and small eyes peeped out from beneath a heavy fringe. Out of the two, he seemed the most spirited.

'Why are you doing this?' Pyotr said, between mouthfuls.

'Because we can,' Darke growled.

'You're not really Chechen, are you? If you were, you'd have slit our throats by now.'

'Shut up and eat.'

Tallis fed Dmitri, bit by bit, in the way a mother nurtured an ailing child, then tipped some of their precious water between his parched lips.

'How on earth did you discover this place?' Tallis said, looking around him.

'By chance,' Darke replied. 'The Chechens are mythically descended from the hero Turpalo-Nokhchuo.'

'The Nokhchii,' Pytor chipped in, chewing vigorously. 'That's what they call themselves.'

'He's right,' Darke said, taking a swig of water. 'The story goes that Turpalo dug a route through the mountains to bring his people to safety.'

'But it's a fairy-tale,' Tallis said.

'A fairy-tale with teeth.' Darke grinned. 'I've been through it several times. Nobody else knows of its existence.'

Tallis briefly turned. Had he imagined the redistribution of air behind him, or was he sensing things that weren't really there?

'Right.' Darke sprang to his feet. 'Let's get moving.'

Revived, Dmitri, with Tallis's help, was now able to stand and walk unaided, fierce determination lighting his eyes.

'Pretty narrow in places,' Darke said, setting off at a fast pace, his shorter frame better able to negotiate the low headroom.

In spite of his initial misgivings, Tallis gazed in fascination. This was the stuff of smugglers and tales of fantasy. Tallis let the light glance off the damp walls. The chamber was about three metres high, two and a half across, the ground beneath his boots stony and steep. A childhood visit to the dungeons of Warwick Castle flitted through his mind as he made his slow descent through the tunnel, bracing at the change in the circulation of air. A weird sort of calm enveloped him the way it had done all those years ago when Graham had been leading him into God knew what. Unused to telescoping his body, he tried hard not to let the narrow space concern him. He was still within earshot of Graham and the lads, who had broken out of their locked-in states and were now talking freely, their voices echoing through the passage. It suddenly occurred to him that without Graham they were screwed. If he lost him down here, he'd never see daylight again. Tallis quickened his pace.

The tunnel oscillated. There was roughly enough headroom. In spite of his best efforts, what he disliked intensely was the proximity of the walls around him. Like in a nightmare, he felt as if they were closing in, the gap getting narrower, the ground underneath his feet more uneven. To quell his panic he pictured each step as bringing him nearer to freedom and light, bringing him nearer to Katya. An image of her beautiful face appeared in front of his eyes. He wondered if she was in danger, if the assault on the police station had led to total clampdown.

And then he remembered Ruslan and how much she'd loved him.

He continued his descent, swinging his torch from side to side, his eyes focused on Dmitri's thin and bony back. The others were moving at quite a pace but Dmitri lagged behind, unable to keep up. Tallis wondered how far they had yet to travel.

They were in a different part now. The way had opened up a little so that Tallis could straighten his back. It smelt different, of vegetation, and there was the sound of water coming from somewhere. He only hoped to God Graham knew what he was doing, that they weren't going to be suddenly swept away by an underground river or onto a ledge, waiting as the water swirled and lapped beneath their chins.

Tallis noticed that there were other tunnels, leading off. They looked less man-made as if it was a part of the mountain's natural topography. He was about to ask Dmitri if he was OK when the boy suddenly let out a shout, clutched his side and pitched over. Tallis called to the others to wait, his voice strange and echoing to his own ears. There was no reply. The boy looked up at him, urgency in his eyes, his face pale and sweating. Something was terribly wrong. His breathing was coming in ragged gasps and there was blood on his teeth. Fuck, Tallis thought, he must have sustained some kind of internal injury, probably during a beating, then he looked and saw that there was fresh blood on his tattered shirt. In less than a second he realised that Dmitri had been stabbed. Fear, in all its twisted splendour, threatened to overwhelm him.

Tallis stood up straight, flashed his torchlight around the cavern. Immediately to his left, there was another tunnel. He let the beam drop to the ground. Fresh boot-marks in the earth, the soles leaving a less than defined impression. This was where the assailant had struck. And that meant Darke was wrong. He was not the only one who knew of the tunnel's existence.

Furious, Tallis drew out his knife, fearing that to use a gun might start some kind of landslide, and headed down the track, the light from his torch bouncing off the rock-faced walls. Here the way was steep and slippery, the smell of dank water strong. He tracked for about fifty metres, cutting one way and then the reverse, one sharp corner after another. Without warning, he caught sight of a movement in black. Tallis lifted his weapon arm up as a figure darted out, knocking Tallis's torch from his hand. He felt rather than saw the blade whip across his face. Fired up, Tallis lunged blindly, feeling his own blade connect with flesh and blood. An ear-piercing cry, like the scream of a fallen angel, rocketed around the stony walls, followed by the sound of running footsteps.

Shaken, Tallis fell back, searching blindly in the darkness for his torch, which had rolled less than a metre away. The cut to his face ran from his temple down to his chin and although it was painful and bleeding it didn't feel especially deep.

Fast retracing his footsteps, he caught up with Dmitri and knelt down. The boy was hardly breathing and his pulse was weak and irregular. At once he saw Ruslan's face superimposed, the expression smiling, his words silently mouthed. *You travel alone.* He knew then Dmitri was done for.

Tallis smiled and gently picked the lad up, holding him to his chest, told him things were cool, that they'd rest for a little while before moving on, that the others were waiting for him.

Raw to his bones, he laid the boy down, closed his

eyes, and left him on his side, curled, his body in a natural hollow. The sides of the shaft were knotted with roots and pitted with holes where animals had tunnelled and made their homes. And now it would be Dmitri's, Tallis thought, feeling a sudden momentary blinding despair.

He had to bend again now because of the reduced roof space. Not much but enough to produce an insane level of anxiety. It felt increasingly airless. The way seemed to be shortening, the shaft narrower. He travelled like this for almost an hour. Tallis wanted to call out, say something, but feared no answer. Something scurried over his foot. He dropped the beam, illuminating the earth, and saw a party of rats skittering away. Had to be a good sign. Then he realised he was lost.

Shit! He stayed for a moment, deliberating whether to continue or flee back the way he'd come. Except he didn't know which way he'd come. He called out. No answer. He called again, astonished by the shake in his voice. Was this it? Had he taken a wrong turn, or was this what Darke had planned all along—to lead him to a lonely death?

Taking a deep breath, he willed himself to be calm and pressed on. At the back of his mind he wondered if there was a less obvious route, dark and unseen. The further he dropped the more insect life was apparent, worms and slugs mostly, and still narrower the space inside the shaft. The air was stale now, less circulated. He dropped down onto his haunches, flashed the torch around, letting the light play on the ground. How stupid of him. He should have done this before. That's when he saw three sets of foot impressions. And they looked recent.

Steeling himself, body bent over, he followed the track, pushing forward in spite of the fact that the sides of the shaft were closing. Where the earth was disturbed and crumbled, old railway sleepers had been erected as protection from landslide. The thought that he could be buried alive hit him with all the savage precision of sudden impalement. He stopped dead, hyperventilating. Jesus Christ, what was happening to him? He wanted to run but there wasn't even the room to turn around. He'd heard of potholers who'd got stuck because, in a tight corner, their muscles had swelled rather than constricted: raw fear superseding experience and skill. He peered ahead into the rank darkness, wondering if the next bend would deliver. And what choice did he have, he thought with an ironic smile, but to move forward?

Bit by bit, he inched ahead, his reward a sharp bend in the tunnel leading to light, an open chamber of rock and stone, and Graham Darke grinning from ear to ear.

'What took you so long?'

Then he noticed that Tallis was alone and bleeding. The smile vanished. Their eyes met.

'You stupid fucker,' Tallis cursed, angry, relieved, despairing. 'Somebody followed us, killed Dmitri and took a pop at me. I've wounded him but he managed to get away. How long before he raises the alarm?'

Sergei and Pyotr sat mute, looked at each other and cast their eyes to the ground.

'Have something to drink,' Darke said, icy cool. 'Then we move on.'

Fear-fuelled speed aided their flight. Tallis could hear the sound of water, the ground beneath his feet giving way to pebble and slate. To walk upright was a welcome relief. The air felt and tasted cleaner. Not only could he hear water, he could see it, probably a tributary of the Argun, he supposed. Wasn't deep. After coming through the mountain tunnel, they'd crossed several tracks in the open, dodging under culverts to cross roads, a risky procedure as many were mined. But the further away from the mountains, the safer Tallis felt, at least from the threat of reprisals. It was shortly after they passed through Shali that they spotted a Russian military transport vehicle, the trundling gait of the truck suggesting that the occupants were in no particular hurry. In roughly three minutes, Tallis estimated, it should pass the ditch in which they were all hiding. He looked across at Darke, who looked back, already reading his mind.

'Journey's end, lads,' Darke said, 'your time to say goodbye.'

Pyotr and Sergei exchanged looks, glanced back at the men who'd helped them escape. Both were incredulous. Tallis wondered if he'd find them later in a Moscow subway, off their faces on booze and drugs. It was Pyotr, the self-appointed spokesman, who answered for both of them. 'We will say nothing but we won't forget you,' he said, grabbing Sergei by the arm. 'Good luck,' he cried.

'Think they'll turn us in?' Tallis whispered as he watched the boys scramble out of the ditch and onto the road, waving their arms, shouting at the tops of their voices, the vehicle slowing.

'Fuck knows,' Darke said.

Tallis pulled out his Kurtz.

The truck pulled up. A sleek-looking officer got out, his weapon raised, suspicious at first then, as the boys gabbled their story, astounded. Calling to the driver, he asked the boys to repeat what they'd told him, which they did enthusiastically and with lots of hand gestures. They also told the officer that they were terrified of the rebels catching up with them.

'No problem,' the officer said with a smug glance over his shoulder. 'They'll be licking their wounds for a long time. You're safe with us.'

'Come on, you two,' the driver said with a jovial laugh. 'We'll give you a lift. You're in luck, we're heading back to Moscow.'

As the truck rumbled off down the road, Tallis and Darke scooted across and to the other side, their destination a plain on the outskirts of Kurchaloi, one point of the triangle of death, according to Yuri Chaikova.

CHAPTER SIXTEEN

THEY didn't stop to rest. They didn't stop to eat. Sleep was a stranger to both of them. Senses strained to the limit, their journey was one of watching and waiting and moving in quick bursts. By the time they covered the relatively short distance to Kurchaloi, the sun, a high shimmer in a sky of deepest metallic blue, had been and gone, the road behind and ahead a mass of checkpoints and military manoeuvres. Tallis got a bad vibe. Something serious had taken place to result in this much bellicose activity.

With Grozny in their sights, less than twenty miles away, they moved off again. From the capital they planned to make contact with the security services, if possible, and find a route out. But Tallis had other more pressing reasons—he needed to see Katya, he had to tell her about Ruslan's death.

Finally, they found themselves in a remote stretch of land on a lonely track, fields as far as the eye could see, with farm machinery and isolated barns and huts dotting the evening landscape. If this had once been a village, Tallis thought, there wasn't much left of it. Up ahead lay the road and the familiar sound of helicopters, and, tempting though it was to bed down for the night, they decided to keep advancing and take their chances. Tallis was glad. In spite of the desolation, there was something not quite right with the place. It had an air of sacrifice about it as if there might be human bones in the soil.

'Got company,' Darke muttered out of the side of his mouth.

Tallis narrowed his eyes, making out a white vehicle, no number plate, with four men inside watching their approach across the track with sinister interest. They were parked next to a lodge—though that was probably too extravagant a description—on the edge of a road behind which nestled a number of barns and farm buildings. Tallis glanced to his right, caught sight of a stretch of ground where the earth had been dug up in piles at various intervals, revealing what looked like ponds of thick green water. To his left was an orchard of apple trees. But the air was not scented with either fruit or foliage. It stank of oil. Then he tumbled to it. The ponds were not ponds at all. At the same time as he made the connection, a tanker started to rumble down the road towards them. The noise of the approaching helicopter grew louder. And they were totally exposed.

Then everything went into slow motion.

Four vehicle doors flew open. Four swarthy armed

men got out, Tallis hard-pushed to tell whether they were cops or gangsters. Two darted towards the tanker and alerted the driver, the stance of the remainder clear: weapons raised, signalling hostile intent. Tallis let off a round, killing one man, wounding another. Darke, meanwhile, bounded forward. Then, without warning, a helicopter appeared, lights blazing, swooping danger-ously low. It wasn't a federal helicopter—smaller, no armour-plating, Tallis thought. Two men were hanging out and let rip a salvo. Tallis threw himself to the ground and watched as bullets spat stone and earth on either side of him, the chatter of automatic fire punching his ears. He looked up briefly. Darke had also dived for cover. Couldn't tell if he was injured. Next came a long burst of machine-gun fire zipping over their heads.

Got to get out, Tallis thought, rolling to one side. The tanker was backing up into the field now. He could hear the engine revving. Nothing must stop it. Men were running towards them, firing, and the helicopter was coming back for another attack. With a gasp, Tallis watched as Darke stood up and, with metal-plated balls, lined up the men and dropped them with two single shots. Exultant, Tallis leapt to his feet. The sky was il-luminated as the helicopter made its deadly approach so low he could see the pilot. Tallis swung the Dragunov round, looked through the telescopic sight, the helicopter showing up like the Empire State Building through the image-intensifying night sight. Cool, he made the necessary adjustments, his concentration on the biggest piece of human surface area: the pilot's torso. Keeping the crosshairs dead on target, he fired straight into the helicopter and hurled himself to the ground.

There was an almighty sound of shattering glass, followed by roaring as the helicopter dropped out of the sky, tilted and ploughed into the earth. Above his head a rush of heat and air like he was caught in a tornado. Seconds later, a desperate, ear-blasting explosion with pieces of metal and shrapnel flying in all directions.

Tallis warily raised his head, hardly able to believe what had occurred, and looked behind him at the burning wreckage, and charred remains of human beings.

'Come on,' Darke said, dragging him to his feet. 'Let's get the hell out of here.'

They ran across the field and onto the road. The tanker, lights ablaze, was slowly going about its work, the driver seemingly unperturbed, determined and without fear. Tallis thought it strange until he saw what lay ahead: a military convoy filled with soldiers, several of whom were out of the vehicle and heading their way. These were no callow youths, or young men on the wrong side of puberty, Tallis thought. These were older, experienced, venal-looking individuals. They had the surly, fuck-off expressions of lifers with no chance of early release.

'Leave this to me and follow my lead,' Darke muttered, striding calmly towards them, keeping a close hold of his AK.

Wish you luck, Tallis thought. To all intents and purposes, they were Chechen rebels who, only days before, had fought these very same soldiers and killed their mates. Christ knows what they planned on doing to them. And if Darke told them the truth, revealed their real identities, the outcome would be cataclysmic. Watching Darke, Tallis was reminded of years ago when Graham had tried to explain to Tallis's irate dad why he was late home. Graham talked a good talk. Tallis's dad had calmed down and become quite reasonable—a rare event. Hadn't lasted long. Tallis had received a hell of a beating once Graham had gone.

'Throw down your weapons. Hands on your head,' the lead officer said. He had a thin face, poor skin and long bones with legs that walked with a twist and swagger as though he were on stilts. The head honcho clearly fancied himself, Tallis thought. Not that he was about to express that view. With several pairs of weapons trained on them, there didn't seem much point in opinion let alone argument. He wanted to stay alive. God knew what Darke had up his sleeve, but he hoped it was something.

'You know who we are, soldier?' Darke said, speaking fluent Russian. The officer stared back with steely disdain. 'We're officers in the Federal Security Service.'

'What?' The colour drained from the man's face, giving him a sickly green sheen.

'And we don't take kindly to being shot at,' Tallis said, adopting his most stony-faced expression.

'So get the hell out of our way and let us get on with our job,' Darke said, waving the barrel of the AK to make the point.

Some of the soldiers began to shuffle and move out of their way. It should have worked brilliantly, but a short crackle and burst of information on the soldier's radio changed all that. Tallis sensed immediately that the tables had turned. He watched the man's face, saw his expression morph from humiliation to surprise to fury. 'Seize them,' he raged.

With so much overwhelming firepower ranged against them, they had no option but to comply and go quietly. As soon as they were disarmed, they were pushed onto the road, faces ground into the dirt by several pairs of heavy boots.

The familiar demand for papers was made.

'They were destroyed when we left our village,' Darke said, staying calm, speaking Chechen, a huge miscalculation, Tallis thought.

'Destroyed?' The officer spat into the dust, turning to his sidekick, a bloke with a shaved head and jowelled features. 'You're rebels,' he said, kicking Darke viciously in the face. Tallis heard the crunch of cartilage snapping.

'We're shepherds,' Darke moaned, blood spurting onto the officer's boot. The man kicked him again, wiping his boot on Darke's trousers, and let out a high-pitched laugh. 'Does a shepherd carry a Dragunov?'

'It's to protect ourselves. Our herd were killed by

rebels,' Tallis explained, for which he, too, received a kick in the face that made his teeth rattle and lips bleed.

'You know where you are?' the officer squatted down, dragging his hand through Tallis's thick mane of hair, yanking him up.

Tallis shook his head, mainly because talking was too painful. However, he was beginning to get a rough idea. They'd just stumbled into an illegal oil complex.

'You are on privately owned land with important commercial interests, which is why it is patrolled by security forces, forces which you have just eliminated.'

'It was in self-defence,' Darke protested. 'We—'

Tallis saw it coming: one heavy swipe with a rifle butt at the back of Darke's head, knocking him out cold. Next it was his turn.

Tallis came to, feeling groggy. He sat up a bit and gingerly touched the back of his head, which felt as though someone had thumped it with a hammer. In other words, it hurt. The floor on which he was sprawled was concrete, as were the walls. It was damp and dark and the only light was through a narrow metal grille high up. The measurements were tight. At six-two, he reckoned he had about three extra feet around him. He was reminded of an ancient cell he'd visited in Sparkbrook Police Museum in Birmingham, except the Midlands piece of Victoriana was more welcoming.

He didn't have long to appreciate the distinction. There was a rattle of chain and key outside. The bolt flew back. Two soldiers stepped in and hauled him out, dragging him roughly down a corridor to another room where the bloke who'd hauled him up by his hair was waiting. Tallis still hadn't quite worked out why the soldiers hadn't just killed them on the spot. Neither had he worked out how they'd got their information. The thought that Pyotr or Sergei had betrayed them was not something he wanted to think about, but it had to factor as a possibility. And did he blame them? Not really. The boys had suffered too much to get moody about their actions.

So what did these guys want from him? he asked himself. Information? An icy chill swept over his body. This is where they'll put a bag over my head, electrodes to my genitals, and beat the living daylights out of me. Instead, he was treated to a sly smile. 'You are being transferred and moved to more appropriate quarters.' Tallis got the picture. Money had changed hands.

'Just me?'

'You and your friend,' the officer said, glancing at his watch. 'In ten minutes.' Nice of you to keep me up to speed, Tallis thought. And that's what bothered him. 'We are turning you over to the department you said you represent,' the officer added, with malignant hostility.

They were handcuffed, blindfolded and forced outside to a warm day spitting with rain, and pushed into the back of a military truck. It was made clear that they would be shot should they try to escape. Tallis somehow thought it unlikely. To kill them would mean welching on the deal. Not that he had any intention of testing his theory. The journey took, he estimated, no more than fifteen minutes, which meant they hadn't travelled that far. Next, they crossed a checkpoint. The truck rumbled along again for a thousand metres or so then pulled up. The tailgate released, Tallis and Darke were hurled out into the dust. That's when the pain started.

Nobody spoke. Although he hadn't seen a face, or heard a voice, everything about the exercise suggested serious player. From the direction of the blows, he reckoned there were three of them. Armed with batons, they knew exactly where to hurt—kidneys, groin, ears, ribs. And they hadn't even got them inside yet. This was no more than a kick-about in a yard.

Muzzy and on the point of passing out, Tallis felt two sets of hands grab hold and lug him through into a building that stank of disinfectant. He cursed as his knees and feet were dragged along a concrete floor. Compound chic was starting to seriously piss him off. In his head, he wanted to call out to Darke, make sure they hadn't overreached themselves and killed him, but his words got tangled in his brain somewhere and the resulting noise that came out of his mouth was a low, incoherent groan.

Doors opened and closed. Steps down. More doors. Must be some sort of detention centre, he thought, before being yanked into a room, one shoulder colliding painfully with the doorframe, and dumped. Cold, thirsty, exhausted and in serious pain, he lost consciousness. Hours or minutes later, he awoke to the sound of a man screaming. Sweat coated his body. Dream or for real? he thought, trying to re-create the noise in his head. Could he distinguish Darke's voice in the agony?

Then they came for him. He paid careful attention to the layout this time, working out the distance of each corridor with the number of steps taken, and counted the number of doors they opened and closed. Moving stiffly, but still moving, he became aware that his injuries were less serious than he'd thought—for now.

At last he was brought to a room and swept into the centre. Some kind of silent, mimed charade took place before he was secured to a low wooden seat. He was aware of at least one other person in the room, if only because of the acrid smell of a newly lit cigarette. His heart sank. Was he to be tortured? Essentially, he was a terrorist and, in general, terrorists in that part of the world rarely came to trial. They didn't usually survive long enough.

'Good morning, Paul.'

The voice was hauntingly familiar. The man was Russian but spoke English.

'Remove the blindfold, please,' the voice said, reverting to Russian. 'Then you may leave us.'

Tallis blinked, one eye so swollen he could barely focus. At first he saw a plain table on which rested a telephone and a lamp, a window, blind open, with a view of a brick wall. There was a swivel chair behind the table on which a man perched, his rear resting on it. Jesus, Tallis thought, he'd know those urbane if not downright thin and effete features anywhere. At once he was transported back to Orlov's party, to the balcony where he'd engaged in a toxic exchange with the man from the FSB. For a second Tallis swore his heart stopped beating. Fear in all its guises came to visit him: fear of not knowing what was to come; fear of what he might reveal, and fear of what had already been revealed. Strangely, he had a sudden urge to laugh. 'So this is what you do for the State, Timur.'

'Amongst other things.' Timur snatched a cold smile. 'But this isn't fair, Paul. You have the advantage.'

That's not how it looks to me. 'How do you work that out?' he said, trying to sound game.

'You know where I work and for whom I work. But I haven't the faintest idea who you serve.'

Tallis opened his mouth to reply. Timur got in first. 'Do not insult me by saying you are employed by a helicopter company.'

'I wasn't going to.'

'Or that you are employed by the State,' Timur said with a dead-eyed expression. 'You almost got away with that tale you told the *kontraktniki*. It is an offence, I think, in your country to impersonate a police officer.'

Tallis swallowed, said nothing. Timur blew out a fine plume of smoke. 'Perhaps I'll let you into a secret.'

'Please do.'

'Your brother-in-arms…' Timur paused, and tapped out some ash, then fixed on Tallis's face. 'He has already admitted his involvement in the murders in Moscow.'

No, it wasn't true. Impossible. Darke wouldn't have cracked, Tallis railed inside. Darke was stronger than that. This was gamesmanship, trying to get him to confess to something he had no part in, unless…

'But as for the attempt on the Prime Minister's life, a plot that failed, I might add, sadly he could not help us.'

'Attempt? What?' Tallis felt as if his veins ran with acid. The conference, he realised. Asim's fears had very nearly been realised.

'Very good,' Timur said. 'Your surprise is quite authentic.'

'No, I—'

'Know nothing because you are going to tell me that you have been up in the mountains these past few days, fighting with the Chechen rebels, the rebels, I seem to recall, for whom you have a touching sympathy.'

'Sympathy, yes, but it doesn't make me an assassin.'

'You think not?' Timur elevated a curiously thin eyebrow.

Fuck, Tallis thought. Timur knew a lot more than he was letting on. How the hell did he know?

'Let me refresh your memory,' Timur said, his eyes hard. 'You engineered a meeting with our Prime Minister, Andrei Ivanov.'

'I did not. I was an invited guest.'

'You pursued him.'

'On the contrary. I had a short conversation with him, which he initiated.'

'During which you brought up the Chechen problem.'

'It's not a crime.'

'Yes, it is. Furthermore, you're a firearms officer.'

'Not any more.'

'Which means you have the necessary skill required for assassination.'

'Ridiculous.'

'And is it ridiculous that you were seen outside a prison where an FSB officer had his throat cut? Is it hilarious that a man answering your description was seen in a café in Rostov-on-Don where two security officers were shot dead and their bodies concealed? Did you yourself not take part in an attack on a military convoy only days ago? Did I imagine that you and your friend killed four Chechen police officers as well as a team of security experts?'

'Look,' Tallis said, conciliatory, 'let me tell you something.'

'No, let me tell you something,' Timur said blackly. 'I know about people like you. I recognised it the first time we met. You're arrogant. You're superior. You think you can come into our country and treat us like children.' Tallis was on the point of protest when Timur reached inside his jacket and took out a mobile, punching in a number, letting it ring twice. Seconds later, the door flew open and Sprite, or Aslan, strode inside, one arm heavily bandaged. So it was Sprite who'd tracked them through the mountain, Sprite who'd killed Dmitri, and who'd tried to kill him. It was also Sprite, Tallis realised, who had betrayed Akhmet and his men at the police station, leading to dozens of deaths on both sides of the divide.

'And something else, Mr Tallis,' Timur said, with a slow look, 'you and your friend are spies.'

In novels and movies, torture either became a blur or a catalogue of voyeuristic and explicit horror. In real life, Tallis registered every second, every minute, every hour for the simple reason that it wasn't simply his pain to endure. Within minutes of Sprite's arrival, Darke was flung into the room. They'd worked him over fairly badly. His hair was matted with sweat and blood and his eyes looked worryingly empty. It was, Tallis realised, quite possible that he'd talked.

They were clever. All the usual—stuffing bags over their heads, half-drowning them, more tamely known as water-boarding, as if it were some brilliant outdoor adventure activity, followed by a series of physically agonising manoeuvres that left no marks on the body but were no less painful and debilitating. Each was subjected to watching the other's torment. That's what did Tallis in. There was nothing like the scream of another man in pain.

The questions were all the same. Who are you? Who

are you working for? Confess, confess, confess. The answers were also the same: We are Englishmen sympathetic to the Chechen cause. We work for no one. Nobody was buying it, least of all Sprite, who was allowed to watch and satisfy his lust for cruelty. And that suggested to Tallis, even as he was hallucinating and swallowing words that threatened to retch and erupt from his throat, that the FSB had more than a single source of local information. Was it possible someone had blown his cover in the UK?

'Fuck you,' he said, as Timur crouched down after choreographing a particularly vicious assault. 'And fuck you, too,' Tallis snarled through bloodied teeth, his half-closed eyes glancing in Sprite's direction.

'Unfortunately, Aslan has already been fucked, many, many times. It was part of our programme for turning him,' Timur said. 'Sometimes it is necessary to break a spirit before you can re-create it.'

'In your own sick image,' Tallis muttered, passing out.

Two days later, they were still being dragged in and out of consciousness until, finally, both of them were told that they were being taken to Moscow for more intensive interrogation, whatever the hell that meant, Tallis thought, feeling sick. So far, he was pretty sure he'd sustained two broken ribs and there was blood in his urine. Darke had fared as badly. Sustaining a broken nose in the initial assault, he'd now got a fractured cheekbone, broken fingers on his left hand and God knew what internal injuries. Timur, clearly unhappy with the decision, stepped up his methods, the psycho in him viewing the lack of a confession as confirmation of personal failure. Good, Tallis thought. He hoped it gnawed away at the bastard and limited his chances of promotion.

After a last gruelling stint, sweaty and bloody, they were chucked into a windowless room that they assumed was bugged. The place in which they were held appeared to be a disused canning factory, their present room a storage area. Preparing for their final leg of the journey, they both knew what they were facing. On the up side, a further attempt on the Prime Minister's life seemed unlikely—security would be as stringent as if he were a nuclear power plant, and Tallis realised they would go to the grave with their secrets intact. They'd be simply executed as Englishmen serving the jihadist cause. It would make news but not plunge the world into war.

'Can't say I planned to die like this,' Tallis said.

'Me neither.'

'You alright?'

'Spot on.' Darke gave a husky laugh.

'God, that takes me back,' Tallis said. 'You always used to say that when things went tits up.'

'Particularly useful around your father, as I recall.'

'And the PE teacher.'

Both of them laughed then lapsed into silence. Perhaps he'd been wrong about Darke, Tallis thought. Perhaps the tough carapace was nothing more than an elaborate disguise.

Tallis fancied he could hear birds singing. He thought of Katya and how much he'd give to see her again, to gaze into those wonderful bright blue eyes and hear the soft lilt of her voice. He wondered how Darke had lasted all this time without a woman in his life. Or maybe he had. Funny, Tallis thought, when life seems limited, affairs of the heart roar to the forefront. 'Lula,' Tallis burst out.

'What about her?'

'She fancies the pants off you. Well, she did. Might change her mind if she could see you now.'

'Thanks very much. Anyway, she'd be wasting her time.'

'Not your type?' Tallis attempted a smile. Ouch, that hurt. 'I think she's quite nicely put together, but I guess with Akhmet breathing down… What?' Tallis stopped. He knew that Darke was in pain but he was giving him the weirdest look ever.

'You didn't suspect?'

'Didn't suspect what?'

'Why I went away?'

'You left with your dad.'

'I left with my lover.'

'Your lover? Which lover?'

'A bloke called Toby Symes.'

'What?'

'I'm gay, Paul.'

Tallis was stunned, not because of Graham's homosexuality, that didn't matter a damn to him, but because he hadn't known. He'd had absolutely no idea at all. It made him feel a complete fool. *How* could he not have known? They'd done everything together, fought together, mucked about together, talked for hours on end. But it did explain something. Darke was adept at deception. It made him a terrific liar and that made him the perfect spy.

'You never came back.' It wasn't an accusation. It was Tallis saying that he'd missed him, that his best friend could have confided in him, that he would have understood, that it would have been alright.

'Nothing to come back to.' Darke smiled, cool with it.

They heard the sound of an armoured vehicle. Bit over the top, Tallis thought. He was hardly going to take to his heels and run. Neither of them was up for another fight. Too much had been beaten out of them, which was probably why Timur and his team had got sloppy with security measures. Having dispensed with blind-folds days ago, they hadn't even bothered to cuff them. Why bother when you could hold a pistol to a man's temple?

They were taken out into a yard. Ahead, a set of open sheet-metal gates, beyond which stood a station-ary truck, behind this an empty British Land Rover Discovery. Sunshine bathed the earth, the walls, sur-rounding tree-lined landscape, and there wasn't a whisper of wind. Perfect weather, Tallis thought, wistful. He glanced across at Darke, who appeared to experience difficulty with walking but failed to catch his eye.

It was quite the farewell party. Timur on the prowl, overseeing the operation, two FSB thugs either side of the prisoners, and Sprite. Soldiers of indeterminate rank looked on with disinterest. All were armed, although they weren't exactly at the ready. They could afford to be blasé against two beaten, defenceless men.

The doors of the truck opened and soldiers began to alight from the vehicle. Suddenly, everyone stopped. Everyone listened. Tallis heard it, too, the tell-tale whistle of a round coming in. He counted one, two, three, and automatically braced himself for the *crump* as mortar landed, which it did, totalling the truck and Land Rover in a double strike. Next came a burst of automatic fire, a storm of bullets ripping up the ground around them. Timur began shouting orders for his men to retreat with their prisoners, but it was already too late. Artillery was flying through the air. Akhmet and a phalanx of men had emerged from the woods, from where they'd been lying in wait, and were advancing at speed in a hail of gunfire.

'Shut the gates,' Timur yelled, but it was no good. The soldiers, panicked, ran all over the place, letting off rounds in a haphazard way, the sound of small-arms and heavy fire surrounding them. Instinctively, the FSB guys, taken by surprise, released their prisoners, their focus diverted to the incoming attack. Big mistake. As the officer next to Tallis drew his weapon, Tallis felt a surge of life-saving adrenalin pump through his body. He lifted his elbow high and jabbed it straight back into the man's throat, felling him. Picking up the man's weapon, he shot his other captor through the neck then swung round to see Sprite lifting his gun. Oh, God, Tallis thought, too slow, responses blunted, not quick enough. Then, as if by a miracle, Sprite dropped to the ground, dead from a single sniper shot to his head, an expression of surprise and shock on his face.

With a burst of wild energy, Tallis darted forward, ignoring the searing pain in his side; everywhere a clamour of sound as bricks and stone flew off the building behind him under the weight of heavy machine-gun fire and RPGs. Darke, similarly pumped up, was struggling to overpower one of the FSB men. Tallis came in close and dropped the Russian with a single shot. Handing Darke his gun, Tallis turned and, out of the corner of his eye, saw Irina standing just inside the yard, lining up to strike. He yelled for Darke to get out of the way and, suffused with another adrenalin spike, ran to where Sprite's body lay, grabbed his AK and, spinning round, belted back towards her, spraying gunfire. He'd only ever killed a woman once before, and that had been under orders. It felt terrible then and it did now, but survival was stronger than guilt.

The Chechens were pouring into the yard. Of Timur there was no sign. Picking over a dead soldier's body with the same intent as a magpie, Darke snatched two grenades then grabbed Tallis. Without uttering a word, they sprinted back to the building, entire strips of wall disintegrating before their eyes, accompanied by a horrendous pounding sound. 'Dshkes,' Darke gasped, 'they mean business this time, and they've got Abdul's men fighting with them.'

They flew inside the building and were immediately pitched into a killing zone of hallways and corridors. Anyone who got in their way they killed either by fire or grenade. Tallis felt like a character in an X-rated video game. None of it felt real, though the blood and noise was real enough.

At last, hugging the walls tight, they made it towards the front of the building. So far, the Chechen attack was focused only on the rear. Presumably the manpower wasn't organised enough to cut off an escape route, Tallis thought, but that didn't mean using the door for an exit was a great idea.

'What do you reckon?' Tallis said to Darke as they peeped out onto a car park.

'I'll go first, you cover,' Darke said, bursting outside, using the vehicles to hide behind. 'Right, what do you fancy?'

'Nice Mercedes over there, tinted windows, the works. Hang about,' Tallis said, squinting. 'Isn't that Timur?'

'Looks like he's got the same idea,' Darke said. 'Come on, let's nail him.' He flicked a grin, crouching low and scurried towards the C-class saloon, Tallis bent double and, cursing, behind him. With the pressure temporarily off, his body was letting him know how much trouble it was in. Physiology was a weird thing. Young men, stabbed in the back and dying, could still manage to walk to the end of a street before collapsing. Tallis wasn't taking anything for granted.

Creeping up close, they watched as Timur, his back to them, thrust in the keys and went to open the door.

'Hold it,' Darke said, pressing the point of his gun to Timur's left ear.

'Throw down your weapon,' Tallis ordered. 'Slowly.'

Timur complied. 'You'll never get away with it.'

'You disappoint me, Timur,' Tallis said. 'I thought an educated man like you could come up with a better cliché.'

'And here's another,' Darke said. 'Open the boot.'

'What?'

'You heard,' Tallis said, giving Timur a vicious swipe in the ribs that must have cracked at least two. Christ, that felt better. He'd yearned to do that for days.

While Darke frogmarched Timur to the rear of the car, Tallis got inside the driver's seat, ready to go. Something out of the corner of his eye made him look up. Lula was standing on the roof of the building in an excellent position, sniper rifle in hand, lining up. From that range it was impossible to tell whether her target was Timur or Darke. Tallis wrenched the car door open and shouted a warning, too late. A shot rang out. Both men went down. Shaken, Tallis started and gunned the engine. The passenger door burst open. Tallis looked across as Darke threw himself inside.

'Drive,' Darke said.

Tallis did. As he glanced in the rear-view mirror, he saw the strangest sight: Lula, bereft, slowly waving them goodbye.

CHAPTER SEVENTEEN

THEY abandoned the car a couple of kilometres from the M29 and made the rest of the way on foot. Effectively, they were operating behind enemy lines. They kept low, avoided open spaces, moved fast and tried to stay alert. Having holed up in a ditch, they waited until night to travel the relatively short distance to Katya's house in Grozny, taking a parallel route to the road. It wasn't ideal. Both of them were suffering from dehydration and exhaustion. By the time they reached Katya's it was two in the morning. The street was eerily quiet. There was no lamplight. It felt as if the place was under curfew.

Tallis tapped at the door, nervous of making too much noise, hoping to God that Katya slept lightly. At first there was no response. He wondered whether she, too, had fled, and her home was empty.

'Could break in,' Darke murmured, his face silhouetted in the moonlight.

Then they heard the light tread of footsteps on a stair, the sound of Katya's voice, low and clear. 'Who's there?'

'Tallis.'

At once the bolt was shot, the door opened. Rarely had Tallis felt such a rush of emotion. A myriad of images flooded his mind—Katya, blue eyes shining, her feet bare, the nightshirt, open slightly, revealing honey-coloured skin, hinting at the curves of her body, her expression serene and beautiful. He almost fell inside.

'Dear God,' she said, staring at both of them. 'How did you get here? Since the assassination attempt the country's been in lockdown, checkpoints everywhere, security forces, army and police all called in.'

'When did this happen?' Tallis said.

'Five days ago. The Prime Minister was standing in for the President at a meeting of journalists. They're blaming a Chechen doctor, but I'm not so sure. Anyway…' She frowned. 'Never mind all that. What happened to you? Are you badly hurt?' she said, putting a cool hand to his face, which was burning. 'Is this the man you went to find?' she said, glancing at Darke. Seeing how wretched he looked, she told him to sit down. 'Please,' she said. 'I will get you water and something for your wounds.'

'Somewhere to sleep and I'll be fine,' Darke said, gruff, slumping into the nearest chair. Now that they'd reached sanctuary, neither had a trace of energy between them.

'And Ruslan,' Katya said, standing on tiptoe, looking beyond as if he might materialise out of the night. 'Where is he?'

Tallis swallowed. He'd broken this kind of news before, not often but enough to remember how dreadful it felt. But this was different. This was a woman who'd touched his heart, a woman he'd failed. She must have read it in his eyes for her hand slipped from his face and fell to her side. 'Katya,' he said, touching her arm. 'I'm so sorry.'

'What?' The knuckle of her hand flew to her mouth, her expression wary and confused.

'He didn't make it,' Tallis said.

'He's dead?' Her voice was incredulous.

'Yes.'

'How?' Her eyes filled with tears of helplessness and fear. He so much wanted to reach out and comfort her, but that wasn't what she needed. Instinctively, he understood that Katya wanted information, cold, hard facts, not soothing words or bullshit about how Ruslan hadn't suffered.

'He was shot at a checkpoint. I tried to bring him back down the mountains, but…'

She turned away, running her fingers through her hair in distress. 'I warned him not to go. I told him it was foolish.'

'Yes, I—'

'You should have sent him back.' She whipped round, her eyes flaring with sudden anger. Her small fists balled. He thought she might hit him.

'I tried.' Had he? Exhaustion was playing tricks on him. He really couldn't remember. Hadn't it been more a case of using the boy to aid his cause? And what cause would that be? He felt crushed by guilt.

'And will you avenge his death?' The words were spat, not as a challenge but with facetiousness, as though she were alluding to the inevitability and point-lessness of the game that men played the world over. She stood tall, her arms crossed, her blue eyes pale and cold.

'Katya, believe—'

'Believe what? That you are innocent? That you have not killed? That your mission here is a peaceful one?'

'It's not what you think,' Darke said, his voice small and tired.

'I think I'm the mistress of my own thoughts,' she said with a searing glance, heading upstairs. 'You may stay here for the night. In the morning I want you out of my home.'

'That went well,' Darke said with a twisted smile.

'I'll find us some blankets,' Tallis muttered.

'Sure she won't mind?'

'Graham?'

'What?'

'Shut up.'

He was laden with bedding, poised at the top of the stairs, when he heard a noise. Creeping across the landing, he put his ear to her door, listened to her crying. Raw, he dropped his load and tapping gently on the wood, went inside. Katya had his back to her, shoulders shaking, face in her hands. Without a word, he slipped his arms around her, drew her close, felt her body freeze and tense under his touch. He became painfully aware of the state he was in—unwashed, unkempt and dirty. She half turned and pushed him away.

'Get out,' she cried, her voice thick with grief.

'Please, Katya,' he said, stepping back, spreading his hands.

The blow when it came took him by surprise. It was sharp, across his face, making it sting. Still he stood there. He reached out to her once more as if she were a frightened filly, trying to calm her, fearing that in her anguish she'd hurt herself. She hit him again, this time in the chest. Pain shot through his body. She was crying, harder now, raining blows, blaming him for Ruslan's death and the shambles that her life had become. Her face was a mess of tears and crying. This was what conflict did to ordinary people, he thought grimly. It crushed them, sapped their spirit, and made even the most reasonable individual insane. It also made good people bad people. As she raised her hand again, he caught it, looked into her eyes, saw the defeat and shame and utter vulnerability; saw something else, something basic and human. When Tallis pressed his mouth to hers, Katya didn't resist.

They both stared at each other in wonder. He was lying naked in Katya's bed, her fingers lightly tracing the bruises on his body. It was as if a storm had passed.

When Katya asked about Ruslan's death, he told the truth.

'And you left him where?'

'In a lean-to, out in the open, between Vedeno and Mahketi. Katya, I'm sorry.'

She gave a sad smile. 'Ruslan is in good company. The Ossetians have a tradition of leaving their dead unburied in mausoleums, the poor among them left in stone huts.'

'Unburied?'

'Entire families are piled one on top of the other so that their mummified remains and clothes mould together, become as one. The huts are guarded by gate-keepers, usually women,' she added. If this was some attempt to make him feel better, it wasn't working. Macabre and strange seemed characteristic of the region. She stroked the side of his face. 'Ruslan was always headstrong. Not like his father at all.'

More like Lena, Tallis thought, dreading how he was going to break the news when he finally returned. Suddenly England hurtled back into his mind, and with it the mission. He could hear Darke moving about downstairs. Whatever their injuries, whatever his feelings, they had to get back to Moscow. 'The assassination attempt,' he said, perching himself up on one elbow.

'What about it?'

'Have they detained anyone?'

'Why, yes, a Chechen by the name of Dr Abzo

Gaziev. I knew him. It's unbelievable that he wished the Prime Minister harm, even if Ivanov is personally responsible for thousands of deaths and abductions that have taken place over the last decade,' she said, a bitter note in her voice. 'Abzo was a pacifist. He was well respected. The type of man who would treat wounded Russian soldiers and Chechen fighters without discrimination. It was reported that a letter was found on him declaring his intention to kill the Prime Minister, but I don't believe it.'

'Never mind the letter. Did they find a weapon on him?'

'They didn't need to.'

'But, surely, with all those people in attendance, someone must have seen something.'

'Confusion and panic do not generally reveal the truth.' She shrugged and gave another sad smile. 'But there were alternative reports from foreign news agencies that suggested a single shot was fired from a different aspect. Whoever it was got away, which in the Kremlin's eyes means that there's no tangible evidence. It suits them better. That way they can blame us and get the Russian people behind them.'

It had the ring of authenticity about it, but it wouldn't stop the men in the FSB from investigating, not when Andrei Ivanov's life was at risk, Tallis thought. The Kremlin would be unrelenting in its pursuit. 'Katya, I have to get to the Embassy.'

'Impossible.'

Nothing's impossible, he believed, reminded of Grigori Orlov's opinion of life in Russia. 'Is there any way you can get to a phone?'

'Maybe, at school.' She wrinkled her nose, which made her look cute.

'Right.' He flicked a smile. 'This is what I want you to do.'

That morning, Tallis told Darke that they could stay.

'Kind of gathered that,' he said with a teasing smile. 'Don't worry, I found my own blankets.'

They washed and shaved for the first time in days. Darke was almost unrecognisable. The scarring to his face had seen to that. With great care Katya splinted the fingers on his left hand and bound them together.

Later, after Katya had gone, and they'd feasted on bread and cheese and bottled fruit, Tallis told Darke of his plan. 'Think it will work?'

'Don't see why not,' Tallis said. 'It worked coming in so why not going out?'

'Things were different then.'

Yes, they had been. Ruslan was alive and he hadn't met Katya. The idea of leaving her behind struck him with a clarity that made him wince. The thought was inconceivable. He glanced out of the window. Outside the birds sang, the trees were in leaf, sun sent a shimmer of gold across the neighbouring streets. Beyond lay the rest of ravenous Russia. 'Graham?'

'Yeah?'

'How the hell did you get to be an intelligence officer?'

'Could ask you the same.'

'Long story.'

'Got plenty of time.'

'You go first.'

So Graham Darke did. He told Tallis that, abandoned and penniless after his disastrous love affair, he'd joined the army where he'd served with the Marines, becoming a sniper. Coincidentally, while Tallis had served in the army during the First Gulf War, Graham had gone to Bosnia as part of a UK team to protect UN convoys. 'Fucking madness,' Graham said. 'After the peace agreement was brokered, I stayed on, was quite happy, but a visit from a bloke in a bar changed all that.'

'You were head-hunted?'

'Yeah. To be honest, I didn't think I was the right kind of material. I'd always thought SIS blokes were sons of diplomats, like you had to go to the right school, know the right people, but they seemed pretty keen to have me on board. Looking back, I wonder now whether they always had me in mind for this mission. I mean, the bloke knew more about me than my own mother did.'

'That wouldn't be difficult.' Tallis laughed.

'Yeah.' Graham grinned, getting the joke. 'I suppose she's still trundling on. You ever see her?'

Tallis studied him. How had Graham managed to

excise his family from his life? What mental gymnastics did you perform for something like that? Again, he had that odd feeling about Darke's ability to morally disconnect. 'No.'

'And your old man?' he asked Tallis.

'Died last year.'

'You sorry?'

'Not really.'

Darke nodded in understanding. 'Mean sort of a bastard, wasn't he? And what about you? They didn't recruit you just to find me, did they?'

Tallis smiled and gave him a potted version of what he'd been up to for the past three years.

'Jesus! You certainly get around in your tea break. So what's your take on the current situation?'

'Apart from the fact it stinks?'

'Definitely looks like someone gave Christian Fazan dodgy information.'

'Which is why we have to get you out and prove your innocence. One look at your ugly mug should do the trick.' Tallis flashed a smile.

Katya returned. 'It's all arranged,' she said, cool. 'The pick-up's tomorrow night.'

'That soon?' Impossible, given the current situation, Tallis thought. He was standing by the stove. Darke was upstairs, having a sleep. The truth was, Tallis didn't want to leave.

'Fly to Mozdok, collect a car there, and drive

straight down. Go back via the same route. It's a good plan.'

'Right.' He could feel the tension in the room. He knew she felt it, too. The way she was standing, at a distance from him, gave the game away. It revealed a facet of her personality for which he was unprepared.

She bit her lip slightly. 'You are worried?' She reached out, lightly touched his arm. It felt as though he'd been hit with an electrode.

'It's not that.'

'Look, what happened last night…'

'Are you going to say it was a mistake?'

'No,' she said with an awkward smile.

He'd never felt so gauche or full of injured pride. This wasn't like him at all. 'Come with me,' he blurted out. 'I could take you to Lena. I know people,' he said, thinking of Viva and Rasu. 'They could help you with finding asylum. Failing that, we could…'

She smiled, looked up into his eyes, cupping his chin in her hands like she'd done with Ruslan. 'Hush,' she said, shaking her head. 'I can't.'

'Why not?' He'd never felt so disappointed in his life. It was bizarre. He didn't know this woman and yet the thought of leaving her was totally abhorrent to him. Had he been infected with madness while in the mountains?

'I'm needed here. This crazy state of affairs won't last for ever.'

'It will. You know it will.'

'It might,' she conceded, 'but if people like me run away, there's no chance for peace. Teachers are vital to prevent our children from turning to the gun, essential to countering the hatred.'

'But if you come with me—'

'It wouldn't work.' She smiled sadly. 'This is my home. That's what I told Ruslan.'

'Then I'll come back.'

'No,' she said, resolute. 'We're different people, you and me. You believe in the power of the gun. I believe in the power of words.'

So that's how she saw him, he thought, destroyed.

'You're a good man, Paul Tallis.'

'But—'

She pressed a finger to his lips then kissed him.

CHAPTER EIGHTEEN

THE Land Cruiser pulled up sharp, tyres spitting rubber and dirt. Two men got out and strode into Katya's with a flourish. Chaikova took Katya's hand and kissed her on both cheeks. 'Sorry to hear about Ruslan,' he said, his craggy face expressing genuine sympathy. 'I really liked the boy.'

She dipped her head, thanked him, and looked awkwardly at Tallis. His face burnt with shame.

'Tallis.' Chaikova beamed, striding over, hugging him and making him wince. As Tallis looked over his shoulder he saw Orlov standing there, cigar plugged into his mouth.

'Isn't this a bit outside your comfort zone, Grigori?'

Orlov flashed a grin. 'My dear fellow, I'm safeguarding my investment.' The helicopter he'd promised him, Tallis remembered. 'Anyway, I like you, Tallis, and when Chaikova said you needed a little help, I thought, Why not?'

'And you.' Chaikova turned his massive head to Darke. 'You must be Tallis's friend.'

'Sorry for dragging you out here to get us,' Darke said.

'It's alright,' Orlov said with an ironic smile, sending a cloud of smoke into the atmosphere. 'Chaikova enjoys adventures.'

'So how do you propose we get through the checkpoints?'

'Piece of cake.' Orlov lapsed into colloquial English with a grin, drawing himself up to his full height, puffing out his chest a little so that his gold necklace and wristband rattled expensively. 'We have plenty of vodka and cigarettes on board.'

Darke exchanged a look with Tallis that suggested Orlov was cracked. 'It's fine,' Tallis assured him with a relaxed smile. 'Grigori is a most persuasive man. He has a lot of contacts.'

'Getting out of the country may prove more difficult,' Chaikova said. 'Some flights have been suspended. Communications are not good.'

'If we can get to the Embassy, we'll be fine,' Darke said.

'I wouldn't bank on that,' Orlov said, less lively.

'There's a problem?' Tallis frowned. He could feel Katya's eyes on him. The tension between them was unbearable.

'You have a lot of enemies. Timur Garipova came sniffing round, asking a lot of searching questions.'

Tallis shared a complicit smile with Darke. 'He won't be searching any more.'

'Mother of God,' Chaikova said, part fear, part admiration. 'No wonder the country's in uproar.'

Orlov was more sanguine. 'Never liked the creep anyway, but we've also had, or rather Kumarin has received, some strange calls from your firm.'

That would be Asim trying to make contact, Tallis thought. 'What sort of strange?'

'Wishing to know your whereabouts.'

'It's fine,' Tallis said, dismissive.

Grigori shrugged and looked at Chaikova. 'OK,' he said, looking around at everyone. 'Are we ready?'

The others went on ahead. Tallis hung back. He wanted to look at Katya and make one last attempt. 'Still time to change your mind.' He sounded upbeat. He felt in despair.

'I know,' she said softly, opening her arms, letting him hold her, clinging to him as if her life depended upon it. His shirt became wet and he knew that she was crying. He drew away a little, smoothed a lock of gold behind her ear.

'Come with me, Katya,' he whispered, nuzzling her neck.

She said nothing, seeming to hesitate. Hope briefly blossomed inside him.

'You're entitled to a life, too,' he pressed.

She looked at him intently, staring right into the heart of him then, shaking her head sadly, she let her arms fall to her sides. 'Go now. Go quickly.'

Choked, he turned on his heel and walked to the waiting vehicle. He did not look back.

Chaikova was decent enough not to pass comment, simply handed him a bottle of Stoli. Darke remained silent. Orlov, alone, oblivious, talked about his favourite subjects—Svetlana, his latest art acquisitions, and the state of a recent building project. A thick fug of smoke built up around them. After a while, even Orlov dried up. Tallis was glad of the vodka. Like an anaesthetic, it dulled his physical senses. His intellect, however, remained pin-sharp. To relieve the hurt he felt, he turned his mind to work. He'd done the job, completed the mission, averted conflict, yet still the mystery remained. Who was the lone assassin? Who was responsible? How had Fazan come by what had proved to be clearly false intelligence? Not that he was a stranger to such situations. False intelligence had been responsible for Tallis's original decision to quit the police three years before.

He glanced across at Darke—asleep, face slumped against the glass—wondered, not for the first time, who exactly he'd spirited away.

After negotiating two checkpoints without incident, they drove through Mozdok and turned off the main road and down a dogleg, past a small truck company with a yard and mesh fencing where they abandoned the Land Cruiser.

'It's fine, I know the owner,' Orlov assured them.

They walked a short distance past a sewage works then

down a dirt track with high hedges and fields to a gateway, beyond which the Agusta 109 was waiting, rotors running. The pilot, a young Russian with blond good looks, wore a Panama hat, light linen suit over a navy shirt. Reminded of an old TV advertisement when he was a kid, Tallis thought the man from del Monte had turned up.

They all climbed in, putting on headsets to communicate, Orlov in front in the passenger seat, giving the orders. As Tallis was lifted into the air, he briefly fell asleep.

Their first port of call was Chaikova's dacha. Dawn was breaking, sunshine falling in vertical bars giving the impression of mullioned windows. As soon as they touched down, Chaikova insisted they eat. While he prepared breakfast, Tallis called Asim, waited for the call to be routed, Darke at his side, listening in.

'Mission accomplished,' Tallis said.

'I thought we'd lost you.'

Not a chance. 'Understand you've been trying to get hold of me.'

'Only by telepathy. I didn't know where the hell you were, remember.'

'Right,' Tallis said, making light of it, feigning that he was too knackered to worry about that now. 'I've got Darke with me.'

'Good,' Asim said, clipped. 'And?'

'He's innocent. I can personally vouch that I was with him when the killer attempted to murder Ivanov. Whatever intelligence Fazan's received about Darke, it's wrong.'

Silence.

'Asim, you still there?'

'Sure, look, can I call you back?'

Tallis pulled a face, gave the number. 'One other thing, Darke wants to speak to Fazan. Is he at the Embassy in Moscow?'

'Already taken up his post in Berlin. Don't worry, I'll make the necessary arrangements for you both to come in.'

Come in? This was starting to feel like they'd done something wrong, that they were fugitives. Tallis was getting a really bad vibe. 'Fine,' he said, breezy. 'You'll get someone to pick us up?'

'Sure, give me your co-ordinates.'

'What? Sorry, can't hear you…line's breaking up… Have to…' Tallis put down the phone and stared at Darke.

'What's the matter?' Darke said.

'Something's off. Asim's not acting normally.'

'Think he's under pressure?' Darke said.

Tallis thought and shook his head. 'I don't know.'

'OK, let's think this out. Fazan approached your guy and asked him if he could borrow you to find me because he thought I'd turned rogue.'

'And to avert international disaster.'

'Understated, but I get the drift.' Darke flashed a smile. 'And who had the intelligence?'

'Fazan.'

'Who supplied the intelligence to Fazan?'

'Source unknown. What are you suggesting?' Tallis

said. 'That Fazan set this whole thing up as a smoke-screen? Why? To discredit Asim, or you?'

Darke scratched the side of his face. 'Rather an exotic way of thinking.'

'And who the hell is carrying out all the hits?'

'Supposing Fazan is responsible…'

'Is he capable? I mean, you've got to be good.'

'Not that good. Anyone with the right expertise can set a bomb, cut someone's throat, punch someone in the leg with a hypodermic.'

'You've got to be young and fit. Is he?'

'I heard in his day he was pretty good in the field.'

'Alright,' Tallis said. 'So say Fazan is doing the killing for reasons we haven't even begun to work out, but would he seriously have a crack at the Prime Minister?'

Darke let out a sigh. 'No, I agree with you. That doesn't tally. Besides, he'd be easily identified at such a public gathering.'

'Which brings me to my next question,' Tallis said. 'Why go to Asim in the first place, why involve me?'

'To make it look good. Puts him on the side of the angels.'

'But he didn't need to. He could have orchestrated the hits and simply left it at that. The Chechens are always getting the blame. By sending me to find you, he was actually drawing attention to you and taking a risk of exposure. He must have known there was a chance I'd actually defy the odds, find you and bring you back.'

'And point the finger in his direction.'

'Precisely. Back to square one.'

'Do you think your contact, Asim, is on the level?'

In this business, you had to trust someone, and Tallis trusted Asim implicitly, which was why he felt as if Asim were sending some kind of coded message when he talked about them *coming in*. Then there was the whole business of those mysterious calls from Shobdon. Had the operation been compromised right from the start? His thoughts went immediately to Blaine Deverill, the spooky Walther Mitty character who'd quizzed him in the canteen.

'Know how to pilot a helicopter?' Tallis asked Darke.

'No, why?'

'We're flying to Berlin.'

Orlov wasn't happy. Since Tallis had proposed the idea he'd been chain-smoking cigars like a laboratory-tested beagle. 'What if you don't come back?'

'I will, I promise,' Tallis said.

'What if you don't? What about my helicopter?'

'I'll have it delivered.'

Orlov blew another gust of smoke into the atmosphere. They were in Chaikova's large sitting room, maps and military paraphernalia on one wall, iconic pictures of 1950s starlets on the other. Tallis, Darke and

Orlov's pilot were bent over a map, working out a route. Orlov cast Tallis one of his curious smiles. 'I think you're really James Bond, Tallis.'

James Bond, Jason Bourne, how come I don't get the girl, then? Tallis wanted to say. Katya's luminous face briefly materialised in front of him. He bent over the map again, redoubled his thinking. The distance from Moscow to Berlin was approximately a thousand miles. Taking into account a wind speed of twenty knots, travelling at one hundred and fifty miles an hour, he reckoned they should average three hundred miles in two hours. If they could refuel with the rotors running, they'd arrive in Berlin in roughly eight hours, and if he radioed ahead to Asim, transport from Reinsdorff to the British Embassy could be laid on. However, he was still feeling jittery about making an approach.

'Where can we pick up Av-Gas?' Tallis asked Orlov's pilot.

'Minsk, Brest, Warsaw.'

Darke glanced up at Tallis. 'What about a flight plan?'

'We'll fly outside the zones—means dropping to a lower level. I've done it before. It's not a problem.' Except last time he'd been refreshed and healthy and rested. Last time it had been a bit of fun.

'Here,' Chaikova said, striding towards them, looking like Rambo. He'd spent the last ten minutes rooting in the armoury. 'In case you run into trouble,' Chaikova said, dumping a cache of weapons on the table in the middle of Poland.

'My God, what sort of trouble?' Orlov coughed, obviously alarmed his nice expensive helicopter was going to be turned into a sieve.

Nobody took any notice of him.

'Bloody hell! Is this what I think it is?' Darke picked up a gun, handed it to Tallis who studied it with professional interest and handed it back.

'Heavy sniper rifle,' Darke said, weighing it in his hands. 'And the cartridge is a brute. My guess it's a silent semi-automatic.' He looked up at Chaikova. 'Val Silent Sniper. Good to blast through body armour even at ranges of four hundred metres or more.'

Chaikova grinned, his eyes disappearing into one of the seams in his face. 'And for you,' he said, picking out a Heckler and Koch MSG90 military sniping rifle and passing it to Tallis. In common with its close cousin, the PSG1, the rifle was outstanding for its accuracy. It had a range of settings to twelve hundred metres.

Orlov let out a groan and bit down hard, almost severing his best Havana.

Clean, fed and watered, and starting to feel slightly more human, Tallis and Darke took to the skies shortly before eleven. The weather, which had started that morning with crisp clean sunshine and puffy white clouds like dandelion clocks quickly deteriorated to a universal grotty grey.

'Visual is critical so keep a lookout,' Tallis said, rubbing his eyes, red-rimmed from lack of sleep.

'What, in case you nod off?'

'If I do, give me a prod, but make it gentle,' Tallis flicked a smile. 'No sudden movements.'

They were sixty miles north of Smolensk, flying over the Przhevalsky National Park when Tallis clocked something to his port side. Fuck, he thought. Wasn't a transport helicopter, or the search-and-rescue model, this was the real deal—armed, armoured and fitted with built-in machine-guns and six external weapons racks with S-5 rockets. These guys weren't out for a jolly. 'Spot on,' he let out, praying that they hadn't detected him. Jolted into action, Darke reached for his rifle as Tallis manoeuvred the helicopter into cloud cover. Perhaps they'd simply go away, Tallis thought. Perhaps they were looking for someone else. If they'd seen him, or picked him up via his transponder, and already launched a missile they were doomed. Probably too late, he quickly flicked off the transponder.

'What do you reckon?' Darke said, alert. For safety reasons he'd been travelling with the safety catch on. Now he depressed it for fire. 'Any way I can take a shot at them?'

'Only if I get up on the blind side. I don't want to risk it unless they have hostile intent.' No point trying to attack simply for the hell of it, he thought. They had overwhelming firepower on their side. The best course of action was outrun and outrange.

'Might be too late by then.'

Tallis privately agreed. He thought about radioing

them to see what their game was but was reluctant to blow his cover. Emerging from the cloud, he decided to drop low, making him a more difficult target. As soon as he did so, the Russians exploded from behind a bank of cloud, hot on his tail.

'Shit,' he cursed, sweat erupting from his brow. Seeing the missile launch, he peeled off and turned in sharply so that he was facing his attacker and flying at a perpendicular angle towards the enemy. The missile hit where they had been rather than where they were. Hanging out of the machine, Kumarin was bellowing orders. So that's where it all went pear-shaped, Tallis realised. Kumarin, Grigori Orlov's engineer and the guy responsible for negotiating the helicopter deal, had been in on the act right from the very start. With a dull shudder he wondered about Orlov. It would be rational to suspect his involvement, too, except Tallis didn't quite buy it. Orlov had bent over backwards to help him.

Darke let off a round, forcing Kumarin to dodge back into the cockpit, singed, maybe, but unharmed.

'Motherfucker! Might as well be armed with a pea-shooter.'

'Hang on. I'm dropping low.' At least there was no sunshine to reveal their shadow, Tallis thought, and even though the enemy helicopter was swooping down after them, it would have more difficulty with locking onto a low-flying target. His idea was to get as much terrain between them and an incoming missile. Failing that, they'd have to get sneaky. And lucky.

'How far to the border with Belarus?' Darke said.

'About a hundred and twenty miles.'

'Pity. If we can fly there, the military will soon sort them out. They might be more Soviet than Stalin, but they're fiercely nationalistic even against the Russians.'

'What makes you think they won't *sort us out*?' Tallis said, tracking along the river Dnepr at less than six hundred feet, temporarily vanishing inside some low-lying mist. Good, he thought, no sign of the enemy. 'Looks like a gully ahead,' he said. 'We'll land, wait for them to pass over and get behind them.'

He switched off the engine, allowing the helicopter to glide down gracefully, quiet and serene, before switching it back on, the engine immediately kicking into life as the helicopter went into a hover. On landing, Tallis kept the rotors running.

'I'm climbing in the back,' Darke said. 'It will give me more manoeuvrability.'

Sure enough, a minute later the Russian helicopter flew overhead. Tallis counted to twenty then took off again, raising the collective control, increasing the power and pitch on the blades so that enough air was pushed downwards to lift the Agusta.

'Fuck me, where are they?' Darke let out, scanning the skies, his finger light on the trigger.

Playing cat and mouse, Tallis thought. No sooner had he climbed to two thousand feet than he saw the Russians behind him on his starboard side. In seconds they'd be above and on six o'clock. Curtains, he thought, then watched with amazement as Kumarin, his face blown away by a silent shot from Darke, tumbled out of the open door and plummeted thousands of feet. The attack helicopter immediately began a tight turn in response.

It was the diversion he needed. Spotting the forest of Katyn ahead, he moved the collective control once more to decrease altitude and let the Agusta plunge down towards the trees. Like most of Russia, the forest had an unsavoury history. The earth was saturated with the blood of thousands of Poles shot by the NKVD, predecessor of the KGB, and Russian prisoners of war massacred by Nazis.

'What the hell are you doing?' Darke shouted out.

'Playing chicken,' Tallis called back. Let's see who's got the biggest balls, he thought.

As predicted, the Russians, having peeled away, also dropped down. Gritting his teeth, Tallis increased speed and headed for a narrow country road on the edge of the forest, forcing the helicopter down almost to ground level, the rotors skimming the tops of hedges. The enemy was playing the same game, except that the machine wasn't as responsive as it ought to be. It was dipping and rising dangerously, like a bucking bronco. Either too old, or too knackered, or, Tallis thought, hope rising, with his passenger decorating the landscape, the pilot had lost his bottle. If it came to it, a well-flown fully operating helicopter was every bit a match for a badly piloted wreck of an attack machine.

He turned minutely and glanced at Darke. Neither of them spoke. Nerves had taken over.

They were at the entrance to the forest. The path ahead was roughly the same width as the rotors. If that suddenly narrowed, Tallis knew he was done for. Bracing himself, he flew into the sea of green, the Agusta's paintwork perfect camouflage. With the Russians continuing the pursuit, Tallis adjusted the throttle and increased power, his eyes straining to see a way ahead.

The path widened out into a clearing. Seizing the opportunity, the attack helicopter speeded up, lining up for a kill shot. Tallis blinked, taking his last breath, waiting for a fast single fare to eternity. But nothing happened. Something was wrong. The system must have jammed or bust. Suddenly the trees began to close in, the path ahead funnelling. When Tallis abruptly rolled sideways, peeling up and away, the Russians' rotors clipped the trees. The pursuing helicopter seemed to buck one last time before ploughing straight into the ground, where it exploded in a ball of flame.

They were refuelling at Warsaw when Asim's voice suddenly crackled over the radio. His tone was dry and cynical.

'You wouldn't happen to know anything about a Russian attack helicopter coming down over Katyn, would you?'

'Whatever gave you that idea?' Tallis said, cool.

'The undeniable fact you were in the vicinity?'

'Coincidence. What happened to you earlier? You sounded a bit odd,' Tallis said, deftly changing the subject.

'I was in a meeting with C.' The head of the Secret Intelligence Service? Tallis ignored a worried glance from Darke. 'There's been a fresh development.'

'Yeah?' Tallis said.

'Where are you heading?'

'Berlin.'

'The Embassy, I trust.'

'Yes.'

'Good. I'll have you collected soon as you touch down on German soil.'

Tallis gave the co-ordinates.

'Darke here,' Graham burst in. 'Like to tell us what the hell is going on?'

'Good afternoon,' Asim said smoothly. 'A Russian professor by the name of Dr Turpal Numerov was scheduled to give a series of lectures in Berlin at Humboldt University. This morning he walked into the Embassy, claiming political asylum. Apparently, he says he worked for the FSB.'

CHAPTER NINETEEN

THEY were collected in a lithe black Mercedes-Benz
S-class. Two officers got out, searched and disarmed
them: standard procedure. Tallis sank back into the
huge interior and closed his eyes. Darke, preoccupied,
sat beside him. He must have dropped off for, in what
felt like no time at all, they'd pulled up outside the bol-
larded entrance to Wilhelmstrasse, where German
police minutely examined the driver's credentials. Their
papers in order, the bollards were electronically
lowered and they were waved on.

The Embassy was a modern construction designed,
to Tallis's mind, by a three-year-old. The outside was
big yellow sandstone blocks. It had a blue glass
frontage and part of the building was a bright purple
curve.

Following another search, Tallis and Darke were
shown into a meeting room with cameras in all four
corners. Christian Fazan was waiting to meet and greet
them. He was bigger than Tallis had expected and could

easily pass for a Russian, he thought, watching Fazan's genuine pleasure and relief at seeing Darke while also observing shock in those dark brown eyes at the scarring on Darke's face. It seemed to Tallis, in that moment, that Fazan's emotional make-up was tempered by something else, though what he couldn't say. Fazan obviously hadn't forgotten the intelligence with which he'd been supplied, even though it had been wrong.

'Good to have you back, Graham,' he said, shaking his hand and clapping Darke on the back. 'Sorry for springing you so unceremoniously.'

'We need to talk about that,' Darke said coolly.

'We do, indeed.' Fazan smiled, breaking the tension, turning his attention to Tallis, who he shook warmly by the hand. 'Fantastic job. Asim was absolutely right about you. 'Drink?' he said, moving with agility towards a cabinet from which he took out a bottle of Chivas Regal and three glasses. He was left-handed, Tallis noticed. No wedding ring on his finger. Tallis glanced across at Darke, almost expecting him to refuse the alcohol—for the best part of a decade he'd lived as a devout Muslim—but Darke accepted, raising the glass, and took a healthy gulp. Darke was right about where his loyalties lay, Tallis thought—to the security service first and foremost.

'I'm not sure whether you're familiar with the drill,' Fazan said, looking at Tallis.

'You want to debrief both of us,' Tallis said, feeling the alcohol throbbing pleasantly through his bloodstream.

'And separately.'

'What about Numerov?' Tallis said, recalling Asim's conversation and his revelation about the Russian professor who'd claimed asylum.

Fazan issued a smile, short and businesslike. *You're new to the spy game, aren't you?* his expression implied. 'How did you come by that information?'

Tallis felt himself flush. He hadn't wanted to drop Asim in it. With no convincing way out, he told Fazan the truth.

'I see,' Fazan said, curt. 'Despite what you may think, a genuine turn-coat from the former Soviet Union is extremely rare. It will take many months in a safe house to see whether he can be trusted. The Russians place a great deal of importance on agent infiltration. They have a well-documented history of sending their people over feigning a desire for Western ideology and disillusionment with the current regime.'

'And supplying misinformation,' Darke said, a slightly surly note in his voice.

Fazan said nothing. He knew what Darke was getting at, Tallis thought, but wasn't going to apologise until after the debrief. The fact was, Tallis didn't envy Fazan one little bit. Basically, the man had made the wrong call. He should have been more cautious regarding the quality of information supplied about Darke. Still, he couldn't help but feel a measure of sympathy. It wasn't very nice to have one's professionalism called into question at such a high level. 'I thought all that finished with the fall of the Berlin wall and break-up of the Soviet Union,' Tallis said, trying to lower the emotional temperature in the room. It suddenly occurred to him that Fazan and Darke had something in common: both were proud men.

'The focus has switched from Eastern Europe to the Middle East,' Darke admitted. 'But assets are still cultivated, agents recruited, betrayal their currency.'

'The world hasn't changed so very much,' Fazan agreed with a smile, looking pointedly in Tallis's direction. And none of this is your concern, was what he meant, Tallis thought, studying the man over the rim of his glass. 'So, if you've finished, gentlemen,' Fazan added with what appeared to be old-school charm, 'let's get started.'

Tallis didn't think they had the facilities, but he was wrong. He was escorted one way through the building, Darke the other. In a room with padded walls and without a window, he gave a full and calm account of his time in Russia to two colourless intelligence officers with Home Counties accents. He spoke of his dinner-party conversation with Andrei Ivanov, his foray into Chechnya, where he'd stayed, with whom he'd stayed and who he'd travelled with, his meeting with the rebels and his part in the attack on a Russian police station. He talked of his flight back through Chechnya and his interrogation and torture by a wing of the FSB. He passed on Darke's intelligence about Akhmet's intended meeting with Hattab, more to corroborate Darke's story than to gain any brownie points.

He did not tell them about Ruslan or Dmitri's death. He did not tell them that he was sickened by the cruelty he'd witnessed on both sides of the divide. After that, they left him. Ten minutes later he was escorted to a room with a bed and en suite facilities. Having never been to university, he imagined this was what a room in a hall of residence would be like—apart from the plainclothes officer standing outside with a loaded Glock.

Stripping off, he washed and slipped between the sheets. Exhausted, he thought he'd fall asleep immediately. He didn't. His brain refused to shut up. He was thinking about Katya. Spilling his guts to the security service officers had disturbed his feelings. Every time he turned over he saw her eyes, her face, that smile. Try as he may, he could not get her out of his head or from under his skin. He doubted he would. Next, he started thinking about Graham Darke, wondering how he would adjust to being a British citizen again, considering how weird it must be to be back among billboards and technology, the cult of celebrity, women with make-up and careers, modern living with all its joys and hardships and temptations. How different it would seem from life in the mountains where life and death co-existed in such close proximity.

He must have fallen asleep because the next he knew someone was knocking at his door. Scrabbling into his clothes, he called out that it was okay to come inside. A sweet-faced brunette walked in, carrying breakfast:

full English with a pot of tea. He could have kissed her. When he asked her the time, she answered in German.

'I don't understand.'

When he tried again in German, she smiled and closed the door behind her.

He ate like a starving wolf then made use of the bathroom facilities. He spent a long time under the shower. Dressed again, and with Teutonic timing, the door opened and Fazan walked in. His expression pale and grave, he asked Tallis to accompany him. Tallis's immediate concern was for Darke. He voiced it.

'He's fine. Nothing to worry about,' Fazan said crisply.

Tallis followed him down a light and airy corridor, nice prints on the walls, to a small room decked out like a waiting room in a private hospital. There were chairs, a low table with German and English magazines, a water dispenser in the corner and a fish tank with lots of electric blue fish haring about. The only thing that was missing was piped music. Darke was already inside, sitting down on a squashy leather armchair. He looked up as Tallis entered.

'What did you reckon to room service?'

'Not bad,' Tallis said, taking a seat next to him. 'So what's happening?'

'Looks like we're being spirited away.'

'This going to be a rerun of *Funeral in Berlin*?'

Darke smiled one of those smiles that don't quite match the expression in the eyes. Fazan, Tallis noticed, ignored the remark. A nerve in his face was pulsing slightly. He wondered what had happened to upset him.

'We're flying you to London,' Fazan said. Good news, Tallis thought, and probably the reason Fazan was out of sorts. Up until that moment he'd thought it was his show to run. The man had, in effect, been upstaged. 'Along with several intelligence officers, Numerov will be travelling on the same flight,' Fazan added.

The Russian professor claiming political asylum, Tallis reminded himself. He envisaged Learjets flying in the dead of night from private British or American military airbases. With the Russian embassy round the corner, it was probably necessary to move Numerov with speed. If the Russians could brazenly bump off a Russian dissident in the middle of a London street, they'd have no problem with popping round the corner and doing the same in Berlin. Tallis sensed the change in temperature. Suddenly the atmosphere had altered as if there was static in the air. This was getting interesting. He began to consider what, if anything, Numerov had disclosed. He glanced at Darke but his expression was vacant and unreadable.

'Needless to say,' Fazan said, 'the details and circumstances of your trip will not be discussed. You will, to all intents and purposes, be ordinary British passengers.'

As it turned out, it was more ordinary than even Tallis had imagined. Having been driven to Tegel airport, Berlin's nearest and busiest airport, they boarded a scheduled British Airways flight in broad daylight, the avoidance of passport control and easy passage through what seemed to be a VIP lounge the only major irregularities. Numerov, who arrived separately with his minders, was ushered into the same suite. He was tall by Russian standards, late fifties with ascetic features. On his nose, which looked as though it had been broken at some stage in his life and reset badly, he wore a pair of spectacles. He had dark hair with very little grey. Similarly, the stubble on his chin was also dark. He looked more Eric Clapton than an academic, Tallis thought, wondering what was travelling through his mind at that moment. Had he fallen out with his superiors, and with Ivanov? Did he have strong ideological objections? Was he an agent sent to infiltrate? And how high up the food chain, are you? Tallis wondered, unable to judge anything from the man's demeanour, which seemed calm, cool and untroubled. And if you are who you say you are, what have you left behind? A wife, family, lover, friends, everything you've ever known?

Their flight was called. Nobody spoke. Nobody made eye contact. They boarded in silence. Rather than coming across as normal and ordinary, they must have seemed a socially inept lot to their fellow passengers, Tallis thought. In a bid to lighten the tone, he muttered to Darke about their host's unstinting generosity. Darke flicked a smile and told him it was connected to cuts in funding. Same old.

As soon as they landed at Heathrow, they followed the same outgoing procedure in reverse except, this time, there were three cars to meet them.

'End of the road,' Darke said. 'You go your way. I go mine.'

'I don't think—'

'Sir,' one of the blokes assigned to Tallis cut in. 'It's time we left.'

And with no time for Graham Darke to answer or say goodbye, all Tallis could do was look over his shoulder and watch helplessly as Darke, without so much as a backward glance, and Numerov were driven away.

They took him to a safe house, a modern executive home on a mid-range housing estate outside London. Asim was there. He smiled warmly. 'I'm sorry about all this cloak-and-dagger stuff. Not really my style.'

'I can tell.' Tallis smiled back. 'This isn't how we normally do business.'

'I know, and I apologise.'

'I guess this is what happens when I get lent to other agencies,' Tallis said, sanguine.

''Fraid so. I know it's a bore, but we need to run through everything.'

'I already did that in Berlin.'

'I know. If it's any consolation, your debrief is with me this time.'

Tallis laughed. 'No consolation at all.'

'How did you find Fazan?' Asim said. His eyes

were level with Tallis's. There was no trace of guile in his voice, yet the slight tic in his left eyebrow raised Tallis's suspicion.

'Is this a trick question?'

'Not at all. I just wondered how he measured?'

Measured in what way? Tallis thought. By comparison to you? That surely wasn't what Asim had meant. 'Asim, is there something you're holding back, something you think I'd like to know?' Tallis's smile was nimble. He knew how to play his handler. The guy was not immune to humour.

Asim flashed a mischievous grin in return, looked at his watch. 'Think we should start, don't you?'

For three days he was questioned. For three days he revisited old ground. He told Asim everything, including the fact he'd gone off piste to search for Ruslan Maisakov. Asim listened quietly for the most part, his expression unchanging, giving no indication what was of interest to him and what was not. Tallis imagined that Asim would match his account with his previous one and see if there were discrepancies in his statement. After he finished, Asim returned to the subject of Darke, for whom Tallis only had praise.

'Think he'll be able to adjust?' Asim said.

'People do.' Tallis shrugged. The last thing his friend needed was the security services breathing down his neck, worrying if he was about to either top himself or go off on a crime spree. And yet it was a good question.

A proportion, admittedly mostly soldiers, went off the rails when returned to civvy street. Was Darke in the same league? However hard Tallis tried, he couldn't shake off the feeling that Darke was not the individual he'd thought he was. 'Best thing for him would be take a break and get back in the field.' With a face so badly scarred it wouldn't be that easy, he suddenly realised. 'He's committed to the service,' he said, clearing his voice slightly. 'I saw that for myself.'

'It's alright, Tallis,' Asim assured him. 'We no longer consider Darke a suspect in the Moscow killings.'

'Glad to hear it.'

'Neither do we suspect Fazan.'

'What?' Tallis was astounded.

'You seriously think I'd go along with that type of information, unquestioning, allow one of my best people to put their life at risk without checking out my source? Thing is, when I did, I got rather more than I bargained for. It's no accident that Christian Fazan was, for many years, stationed in Moscow.'

'Yeah?' Tallis felt bewildered.

'Twenty-six years ago and five years before the fall of the Berlin Wall, Fazan was a lowly intelligence officer on his first mission. Using the assumed name of Edward Rose, his brief was to befriend a Russian journalist by the name of Malika Motova. Motova moved in what was considered dissident circles, artists, playwrights, and the kind of people that get a bullet in the head at the first sign of revolution. Motova was important to MI6 because she was in a relationship with a KGB officer considered to be on the up.'

'She was being used?'

'She was. Unfortunately, Motova got sussed. As I said, she was entirely innocent and had no idea that she was a pawn in a dangerous game. Most unfortunately, the Russian authorities didn't see it that way. To cut a long story short, Motova died of a heart attack in a transit prison. Fazan was not happy.'

'And let me guess,' Tallis said. 'The young KGB officer was none other than Andrei Ivanov.' That's why Asim had harboured suspicion, he realised.

Asim agreed with a smile.

'But setting aside the fictitious name, surely Ivanov would have recognised Fazan?'

Asim slipped a photograph from the file in front of him and handed it to Tallis. 'Would you?'

'This is Fazan as a young man?' Tallis was taken aback. The photograph showed a smooth-skinned, heavy-boned, almost plump-looking individual, hand-some featured for sure. The dark blue eyes were more startling and there was tranquillity in his expression, serenity even, something that had been clearly eroded over the years and replaced by a certain predatoriness.

'Fazan was taken out of circulation for a decade before being sent back to Moscow,' Asim said.

'So Fazan had every reason to exact revenge? Is that what you're saying?'

'Not quite,' Asim said, a cautious light in his eyes.

'Fazan is a professional, dedicated to his career. He has never once strayed from his brief. As a man he may have harboured murderous designs, but as an intelligence officer he recognised that this is not the way we get things done.'

Tallis arched an eyebrow. Next, Asim would be telling him they didn't kill people. He'd laughed his socks off when he'd heard a former head of the SIS saying exactly the same at the inquest of Princess Diana. 'Your point?'

'It was something I had to factor in and explore. I can assure you Fazan is clean.'

'So who carried out the murders, who tried to assassinate Ivanov? Please don't tell me it was a Chechen hit squad.' Although, come to think of it, nothing would surprise him any more.

'If I told you, I'd probably have to kill you.' Asim was smiling, but that didn't mean he wasn't serious. Tallis felt vaguely unsettled.

'I guess we've upset a lot of people.'

Asim leant back in the chair, stretching his legs out, cracking his knuckles. He was enjoying the thrill of the chase, Tallis recognised. 'One in particular. Think I need to catch some fresh air,' Asim said, suddenly standing up. 'You might want to listen to some music while I'm gone, help you relax. There's a CD over by the player, if you're interested.'

As soon as the door closed, Tallis got up and retrieved the CD, which was in a plain transparent case with no writing or label attached. Tallis switched on the player, put the CD into the drawer, and pressed Play. At first there was nothing but scratchy silence and then a voice, a curious hybrid of Russian-accented English with a hint of American.

'We have always maintained special departments, as you know, departments dedicated to technology and surveillance, abduction and assassination.'

'And you are stating that the murders that have taken place in Moscow, including the attempt on the Prime Minister's life, was the work of a special department?' an English voice cut in.

'Why, yes.'

'It wasn't a rogue outfit, or made up of old diehards loyal to the former KGB?'

'An irrelevant question,' the Russian said, testy. 'A change of name does not denote a change of operation or tactics. Once you become an agent, KGB or FSB, you have a job for life. And the FSB never abandons its operatives.'

'I'm not quite clear on this,' the English voice cut in again. 'Are you saying this was a legitimate operation, that the State was aware of the plan?'

'I tell you this was a project that was fashioned within the walls of the Kremlin itself. The orders came from the very top. The murders of fellow countrymen were all part of a well-orchestrated plot.'

'I'm confused. Are you saying that the orders came from the new President?'

Numerov burst out laughing. 'The very top, I said. Just because we have a new man at the helm does not mean there's been a change in the power structure. Ivanov is still in charge.'

'Alright,' the questioner said smoothly. 'How do you explain the attempt to kill Andrei Ivanov? If as you say the orders came from Ivanov, why would he order his own death?'

'He didn't.' The Russian let out another raucous laugh. 'It was bluff, never designed to happen. The bullet was a blank. The "shooter" was never found.'

'And Dr Gaziev?'

'Nothing more than, how do you say, the *fall guy*? It was happy coincidence that certain wings of the press were demonstrating about the Chechen crisis, and the fool doctor was a gift, which was spontaneously exploited.'

Tallis heard the interviewer cough and clear his throat. Numerov began speaking again.

'Why do you think the President was so unexpectedly taken ill? It meant our larger-than-life Prime Minister was able to step in and become the so-called target. That way, as well as engendering outrage, he won universal sympathy. When he left the country for a recuperative break after his ordeal, he had all the good wishes and blessings of the Russian people.'

'Alright, but help me out with the motivation.'

'You are asking me to explain Andrei Ivanov's thinking?'

This was followed by a marked pause. 'To his mind, Ivanov believes he is making Russia strong again, imbuing it with a sense of national pride, diverting democracy to dictatorship. Notwithstanding his recent foray into South Ossetia, he has already lost Georgia and Belarus. As for the Ukraine, they have a pro-Western stance. Who will be next? Dagestan? Added to that, he has the West, as he sees it, clamouring at his borders. To have another troublesome state flexing its muscles and claiming independence was a step too far.'

'But the Russians have only recently ended their operations in Chechnya.'

Numerov let out another laugh. 'Work there will never be ended. Ivanov's plot was specifically designed to stir up political unrest and hatred so that a third and final assault on Chechnya would go unopposed, not simply by his own people but by the West.'

'Since when did Ivanov care about the West?'

'He cares very much, and the West has made it easy for him. Your so-called war on terror plays nicely into his hands. If you can attack the Muslims, why shouldn't he? And, believe me, his repugnance for the Chechens as a race, as a creed, is of psychotic proportions.'

Another pause.

'Tell me about Lieutenant Ilya Simaev again.'

'Musa's contact?' the Russian said. He was referring to Darke's contact, Tallis registered. 'He was arrested eight months ago. That's when Musa's true identity was discovered. In spite of the revelation, it was decided to sit on the information and use it at a later date. It is good, is it not, as you English say, to keep one's powder dry?'

'They didn't think to put Simaev back in the game, let Musa, or rather Graham Darke, run?'

'Too late for that. One cannot send a corpse into the field.'

'Simaev was killed?'

'He died under interrogation.'

'For what purpose does the Kremlin intend to use the information?'

Again the Russian laughed. 'They already used it.'

'How?'

'By telling your man, Fazan, that Musa had gone rogue, that he was responsible for the killings in Moscow.'

'You mean the intelligence passed on to Christian Fazan?'

'Absolutely. The so-called forensic evidence for one of the hits was entire fabrication. I think you seriously underestimate Ivanov. Something you should know…' The Russian broke off to sneeze and blow his nose. 'It's a little known and unreported fact that when Ivanov was a young officer he had a serious relationship with a woman who turned out to have a Chechen mother. He once boasted to me personally that he'd used her to try and entrap a suspected British agent and had her arrested on a trumped-up charge. She was interrogated at Lubyanka, usual treatment—sleep deprivation, physical and mental abuse and the forced use of drugs, including Haloperidol. It has a nasty side effect of inducing cardiac arrest. As a result of her treatment by the State, she, too, died. That's how much he hates the Chechens, and he will use anything he can to silence opposition to his policy towards them.'

The CD petered out into silence. Tallis sat alone, taking it in, fearing for the Katyas and the Lenas and even the Akhmets of the world and, yes, fearing for what might be disclosed and the fallout of such a revelation. He wondered if this was the reason Fazan had seemed so stricken the last time he'd seen him—he'd sustained not only a professional attack but also a personal one. He wondered whether Graham Darke knew that his own cover had been blown months before, and how close he'd come to being betrayed, both men played for fools. He was so lost in thought, he didn't even notice that Asim was back in the room. And then it came to him.

'You know what this means, don't you?' Tallis said.

'Apart from the obvious fact British Intelligence sent one of its own to play fast and loose with the Russians, which of course we'll strenuously deny?' Asim said, laconic. 'From where I'm sitting I'd say the scales are evenly balanced. We have dirt on them. They have dirt on us.'

'That's not what I meant,' Tallis said.

'No?' Asim frowned.

Tallis leant towards him. 'Don't you see?'

'See what?'

'Now would be the perfect opportunity to assassinate the Russian Prime Minister, and I can think of two people who'd be happy and willing to do it.'

CHAPTER TWENTY

IN ANSWER to Asim's startled look, Tallis explained. 'What would happen if you went public?'

'About the Russian security service killing its own civilians? It would be denied. The most we could hope for would be that the Kremlin admitted there was a rogue agency at work over which they had no jurisdiction.'

'As in the Litvinenko case?' It had been suggested that the Kremlin, although not exactly issuing the order to assassinate the former FSB officer, had turned a blind eye to some over-zealous former members. No surprises that the main suspect, whom the Russian authorities flatly refused to hand over for questioning by British police officers, had subsequently risen to an elevated seat in the state duma and had then been given a key security role.

Asim hiked an eyebrow, clearly uncomfortable with the comparison. 'Your point?'

'Who are the people who know about Numerov's admission?'

'What admission?' Asim blinked.

Tallis felt a nerve pulse in his jaw. 'The people in the know, how many? Ten? Twenty?'

'Less. Aren't you forgetting something? Who and why?'

'I was coming to that. Fazan was a changed man the last time I saw him.'

'Shocked, stunned, not changed,' Asim snorted. 'Don't be too influenced by what I told you.'

'I'm not. It's what Numerov revealed on the CD. You said Fazan used Malika Motova, but what if it was more than that, what if he fell in love with her? It was bad enough that she got caught but now he discovers that Ivanov set her up and was personally behind her death. More critically, that Ivanov was onto him long before he knew it. That kind of thing dents a man's pride.'

'Paul, you're speculating. It was over twenty years ago, for God's sake.'

'So what? Fazan went back to Moscow, didn't he?'

'Proves nothing.'

'Did he ever marry?'

'What's that got to do—?'

'So he doesn't really like women?'

'On the contrary, he—'

'Guilt does strange things to people.' He should know.

'Guilt is not an emotion with which Fazan is familiar.'

Tallis wondered if the same applied to the man

sitting in front of him. Did that come with the job description, too?

'Look, Paul,' Asim continued, 'for Fazan to suddenly decide to have Ivanov killed now doesn't make psychological sense. Fazan came to me asking for my help to avert an international crisis.'

'Based on false information. Not only has he suffered personal injury, his professional expertise has been called into question. He fucked up, Asim. He should never have fallen for the information he was fed.'

'Fazan is a proud man,' Asim conceded, 'but I don't think he'd let something like this cloud his better judgement. He'll settle into his post in Berlin, lie low and forget all about Russia and Ivanov.'

'You're right. You know him. I don't,' Tallis said, curt. 'But I know Graham.'

'Graham?'

'You asked me how he'd adjust. The truth is I don't know. If I'm honest, I don't think slotting back into modern life is something that will come easily to him. And what's he going to do now he's back home, sit at a desk and push a pen around like Fazan?'

'Not necessarily,' Asim said, looking troubled.

'One of the first criteria for being a spy is the fact you blend effortlessly into the landscape. You haven't seen his face. He wouldn't last five minutes out in the field. And remember, he's spent years in the most basic of conditions, fighting, living on the edge, witnessing acts of extreme cruelty. What I do know is that he could swear black was white and have you believe it.'

'Aren't you forgetting something? Graham Darke is loyal to a fault.'

'Making him the best man for the job.'

Asim pulled a face. 'You're seriously telling me that Darke would follow an order to kill a head of state?'

'Not just any head of state.'

'Alright, suppose he does it. Then what? Where is Darke supposed to go? What happens to him afterwards?'

'Wherever the loner in him takes him. I'm sure Fazan could provide safe passage. It's in both their interests for him to succeed.'

Asim thought for a moment, exploring the possibilities. 'With careful handling, stories leaked in the right places, we could allow Ivanov to become a victim of his own policy.'

'You mean what was supposed to be a bluff actually takes place?' Asim was prepared to let it happen, Tallis thought, quietly appalled.

'It wouldn't be the first time someone screwed up, exchanging a blank for a live bullet.'

'It won't make the problem go away,' Tallis said, insistent. 'If Darke kills him, believe me, the story of an SIS officer fighting against Russian soldiers isn't going to die with him. The Kremlin will see to that.'

Asim's expression darkened. He said nothing. 'Wait,' he said sternly, getting up, taking out his phone.

Punching in a number, he asked for a status report on
Darke and Fazan. Tallis watched Asim as he waited and
was given an answer. Asim nodded, his expression in-
decipherable.

'Fazan is in Berlin, Darke has been released, destination unknown.' He went to make another call.

'You won't find him, if that's what you're doing,'
Tallis said.

A pulse tensed in Asim's jaw. He closed the phone.
'If, and it's a big if,' he warned, 'there was an intention
to strike the Prime Minister, where would it be?'

'France. He has a home there and my guess is that's
where he's fictionally taken refuge, except, of course,
the threat to his well-being is entirely real.'

'And the last thing he'd expect would be an attack.'

'You're getting the picture.' Tallis smiled. 'Having
said that, he's a high-risk target whatever his current
threat level, and high-risk targets are rarely caught in
ambushes. If he's going to be taken out, it will be when
he's at home.'

'Impossible. The Russians are meticulous. They'll
have the place locked down—dogs, state-of-the-art
technology, armoured doors, armed security. For Darke
to even attempt to get inside would be suicidal.'

'Who said anything about attempting to get inside?'

Asim raised one eyebrow, thought for a moment, let
out a long slow breath. 'Go on.'

'Darke will do what he's best at. He's a sniper. If we
can find the layout of the house we have an advantage,

we'll discover the target area. If I know the target area I can work out where Darke will position himself for the hit.'

'It will take time.'

'No, it won't. One phone call should do it.' Tallis swallowed. Would Orlov play ball? Would he give him the information he needed? Could he trust him? Had Kumarin been using Orlov, or, like Kumarin, had Orlov been in on it from the start? Tallis briefly closed his eyes. This was his call, his decision. If he got it wrong, the consequences were unthinkable.

'I know the bloke who constructed Ivanov's house. He'd have the plans.'

'And he'll just calmly hand them over to you?' Asim's tone was as incredulous as it was cynical.

'Doesn't need to. I simply need him to talk. Served up in the right way, saving the nation blah-di-blah, I think he might crack.'

'And what if you're wrong about this? It won't look good for you to be stalking about the French countryside with a gun in your hand.'

'Certainly won't do much for the entente cordiale even if the French aren't too keen on the Russians.'

'Not too keen on anyone at the moment, but I'd like to think they'd stop short of having a head of state assassinated on their soil,' Asim said dryly. 'I don't need to point out that if you're caught…'

I'm on my own, Tallis knew. 'What if I'm right?'

Asim gave him a long hard look. 'Do you realise what you're saying?'

Tallis met Asim's eyes. 'I have to stop Darke before he gets to Ivanov.'

'Are you out of your mind?' Orlov wasn't playing ball.

'I wish I was. Look, Grigori, I'm not asking you to disclose the security arrangements.'

'I don't know the security arrangements,' Orlov bellowed, his voice reverberating down the line like a trumpeting elephant.

'But you know the layout.'

'Which I'm not going to tell you. You want me to be sentenced to thirty years' hard labour?'

'Look, I wouldn't ask, you know that, but I think Ivanov is going to become the next victim.'

'Absurd. You see how the man is protected.'

'Any killer only has to get lucky once. We live in strange times, Grigori.'

'Certainly since I made your acquaintance,' Orlov muttered. 'And how the hell do I know I can trust you? That Chechen girl might have turned your head. Maybe it is you who wants to hurt our Prime Minister.'

'I assure you that isn't the case.'

'Assurances come cheap.'

'Alright, how are you going to feel if Ivanov is assassinated?'

Orlov said nothing. Maybe he didn't give a damn,

Tallis thought. Time to apply some pressure. 'Heard from Boris Kumarin lately?'

'What has Boris to do with all this?' Orlov said, testy.

'He worked for the FSB.'

'That's ridiculous. He—'

'Used you.'

There was a brief, stunned silence. Tallis could almost hear Orlov's brain making the connections. 'Worked, you said? You mean he is no longer with us?' Orlov spluttered.

'Sadly, he took a bit of a fall.'

'Mother of God, Paul!' Orlov exclaimed, clearly shocked. 'And now you expect my help?' His astonishment bordered on awe. If there were two things Tallis had learnt about Orlov, he was a man of inconsistency, a man who always had an eye to the main chance. Bugger loyalty.

'Think of it as doing your bit for the motherland,' Tallis persisted. 'There might even be a medal in it for you,' he said, appealing to Orlov's sizeable ego and ignoring the ferocious warning look Asim was giving him.

The silence that followed was for so long Tallis thought Orlov had gone off the line. He imagined him puffing away, sitting in a fug of cigar smoke, jewellery jangling. 'What would I get for this information, apart from the honour of serving my country?' Orlov said, his voice a low burr.

That's my boy. Tallis beamed inside. He looked at Asim who slowly but firmly shook his head.

'It's not the agency's style to reward Russian gangsters,' Asim murmured in his ear.

'Businessman,' Tallis hissed back. 'Let's see, Grigori, apart from the Agusta—' Tallis began.

'Which I bought fair and square,' Orlov cut in.

'And which is being flown back to Moscow even as we speak.'

'And my Robinson 22?'

'Delivered any day now.'

'Why the hell are we horse-trading when there are matters of international security at stake?' Asim barked in his ear.

'I'm sure we could come to a mutually agreeable arrangement,' Tallis said to Orlov, smiling. 'What would you be looking for?'

'A house, Queen Anne, anywhere in Britain.'

'Done,' Tallis said, ignoring Asim's shocked expression. 'Now tell me what I need to know.'

Early the next morning, after Asim called in a favour from the French and secured safe passage, Tallis was flown to Hyères in a Cessna Citation 501. From there he travelled by helicopter.

It was a beautiful spring day, high cloud, little wind, and the sun shining bright and clear. The light was every bit as intense and luminous as he'd been led to believe, which was why, he guessed, the Côte D'Azur was such a hit with artists. From his vantage point, Tallis had a fantastic view of contrasting terrain—beach and palm trees, forest with sprinklings of eucalyptus and acacia, and hard rocky peaks. Down below he could see the Massif des Maures, extending over sixty-five kilometres, a compressed, entangled wilderness of pine and oak, dark and forbidding, and a strange reminder of the mountainous regions of Chechnya.

Sidestepping the flowering hilltop village of Gassin, and its near neighbour Ramatuelle with its winding streets and ancient-looking houses and ruined wind-mills, they travelled north over a profusion of lavender fields so dense and vivid he could almost smell the scent. Minutes later, losing altitude, they cleared the small and unspoilt agricultural town of Aups and tracked the road north, touching down near the western end of the Gorges du Verdon.

Tallis thanked the pilot, and got out, walking clear and turning only briefly as the helicopter ascended and flew off in the direction of Nice. If Tallis made it, the pilot would be back at 15.15 at the planned pick-up point on the outskirts of the town of Castellane. If he didn't, no doubt a clean-up squad would be dropped in to bag and remove his body.

He was standing on a sheer slab of rock, deeply hewn into a rugged rust-red valley, the holly-coloured river Verdon flowing from the top of the gorge and dis-appearing into fathomless tunnels below. Lifting the telescope to his eyes, he saw a mass of hairpin bends and largely uninhabited countryside that in a couple of months' time would be packed solid with traffic and holidaymakers. Using the zoom facility on the scope, he scrutinised the surrounding area in more detail—the mountain villages, the Pont de l'Artuby, a magnificent curved bridge that spanned the gorge with its hair-raising drops to lake and river—but it was of no intrinsic interest. He was looking for one man only: Graham Darke.

He began to climb, ignoring the designated walking routes, carefully calculating which path Darke had taken. Each step taking him higher than the last, the land was a mixture of twisted rock and heath. Automatically he searched the ground, looking for proof of Darke's existence, but the hardened stone obscured any trace of a trail. The only give-aways would be some movement, a noise, or silhouette in the late morning sun. That Darke had travelled that way was almost of no consequence to him. He sensed he was there, *knew* it.

On he walked, boots hitting the stubbled earth, travelling light, no backpack, no compass, his binoculars and the holstered Glock his only weapons. He'd insisted on it. How much firepower do you need to stop a man? he'd said. How much to prevent an old friend from committing a criminal act of calamitous proportions? That he could not stop him had never occurred to Tallis. Failure was not an option. He, too, had his loyalties. If that meant that one of them had to die, so be it. Beyond all doubt, he knew that Darke was not a man to give in or give up; along with his pride, it was the essence of his character.

And did Tallis feel regret? He'd once fondly thought of them as blood brothers. Now, in his heart, he thought they were different creatures. Events and circumstances had seen to that. If he could stop Darke without killing him, if he could somehow win him over, he would. If he couldn't…

The rock had given way to hills and woodland, thick, dense and unkempt. From the sky it would look like a massive sea of dark green. Heat from the midday sun fastened like a dark spot in the middle of his shoulder-blades, moderated only by the sudden approach of a bitter mistral wind blowing cold through the trees. The narrow streets of the town of Castellane beckoned from less than nine kilometres away. Maybe Darke was already on its outskirts, already in position. As a seasoned sniper, he'd wait for days, if necessary, to get the perfect shot. Patience was key and another of Darke's more recently acquired attributes, but Darke didn't have days. If Orlov's information proved correct, he only had one window of opportunity.

Tallis had already worked out that there were two possible vantage points for a sniper: the fourteenth-century clock tower and the massive rock that rose abruptly above the town and had once served as a natural lookout. He discounted both. Apart from being blatantly obvious and checked by the Russians regularly, from his conversation with Orlov, neither presented a view of the outdoor pool in which Ivanov was so fond of swimming come summer or winter or spring.

With the smell of tree in leaf heavy in his nostrils, he forged a way through the woods then, taking a sharp left turn at a pile of white stones, exactly as Orlov had described, dropped down a little into a valley. Below lay the remains of Hôtel de la Fôret, now a Jacobean-styled residence belonging to Andrei Ivanov.

Tallis lowered himself to the ground and crawled through the undergrowth to where the earth shifted and fell away. Lifting his binoculars to his eyes, he smiled. Orlov hadn't been joking, Tallis thought in amazement. With its gargoyled figures over the entry gates, leaded-light mullioned windows, enormous oak doors and beams, the house could have been lifted straight out of the county of Hereford and Worcestershire. Given a free rein, Orlov had indulged his obsession with British architecture to the full. Tallis was too far away to glimpse an inside view, but it was easy enough to picture the oak panelling, stone fireplaces, the great hall that Orlov had described and the gallery overlooking it.

Satisfied that he was where he ought to be, he got up, kept low, moving forward in a high crawl, conscious that every step on twig and leaf would create a sound distinct from the blanket of birdsong. By moving in a radius of almost ninety degrees, he reckoned to be in direct line with Ivanov's outdoor pool. Along that same continuum, Darke would be holed up lower down the valley, tracks concealed, probably in a hide, his view of the target narrow and limited. It would be a difficult shot but doable. Tallis wondered on the choice of weapon. If it were his decision to make, he'd go for a Swiss-made SSG550, a heavy-duty gun with bi-pod and telescope and anti-reflective screen to cut down air disturbance, but it would be a bastard to carry so maybe Darke had selected something lighter and more portable. Tallis estimated that whatever weapon Darke was using, he'd need to be within a range of five hundred metres.

Tallis arced swiftly round then dropped right down onto his hands and knees, slowing the pace, moving with extreme caution and in silence. A quick glance at his watch told him he had twenty minutes to make the deadline. Painfully slow and covering only a short distance, he took the Glock from his holster and, keeping his eyes fixed ahead, saw a silhouette on the ground. Either it was a bird spotter or Darke had broken an elementary rule: he hadn't factored in the sun's movement or the change of light behind him.

Tallis edged forward again, a mental clock ticking in his head like the countdown to a bomb going off. Sweat was pouring off him, even though a biting wind blistered through his body, a definite disadvantage for the sniper. He was on the point of taking another look through his binoculars when he sensed a presence and froze. As the chill of cold steel connected with the base of his skull, he knew that his fortunes had been reversed.

'Graham,' he said, without moving. 'This isn't a good idea.'

'What? Killing you, or killing Ivanov?'

'Both.'

'You're right,' Darke said calmly. 'Put down your gun and crawl slowly to the left.'

Tallis did.

'Good,' Darke said, squatting down next to him. He was wearing full camouflage, with a soft green cap on his head to give a blurred outline of his head. The dark glasses on his face gave him a sinister appearance. 'How did you know I'd be here?' There was no challenge in his voice, no animosity. It sounded more like a friend talking. Except a friend doesn't normally address you with a pistol in his hand.

'Something happened to you out in the mountains. One moment you were hell bent on staying, the next you wanted to come back. I think you knew then that you wanted to exact revenge, and when you found out about what was really going on, how you'd been betrayed, and then, of course, there was Fazan and his damned order.'

'He told you?' Darke frowned.

'Didn't need to,' Tallis said, eyeing the gun, a SIG-Sauer with, using firearms speak, a moderator. Using layman's language, a silencer. 'I worked it out from Numerov's account.'

'Always were the smart one,' Darke said almost fondly.

'Strange. You always called me a fool.'

Darke's smile was chill, as if it were of no consequence. 'This isn't personal, you understand?' Killing Ivanov, or me? Tallis thought. He said nothing. 'I've got my orders,' Darke insisted.

'From a man who has intimate reasons to have Ivanov removed,' Tallis pointed out.

'You know Fazan was the British agent in the Motova case?'

'The Chechen journalist who happened to be Ivanov's lover? Yes, I know, and *crime passionel* is as old as these hills, Graham,' Tallis said, glancing around, 'but usually the aggrieved party carries out the killing. The job isn't normally handed out for someone else to fulfil.' Unless you worked for the security services. He supposed that's what spies were really all about.

'That's not why I'm doing this,' Darke protested, sounding mightily offended. 'And you, of all people, should understand. You saw those FSB guys in action, how they behave—like animals.'

'And the Chechens? What about Akhmet and his men, their treatment of Russian soldiers, teenage lads, their cruelty?' And yours, he wanted to say.

But Darke was not to be persuaded. 'Don't you get it? Throughout Ivanov's reign of terror, twenty-five thousand Chechens have either lost their lives or gone missing. As for native Russians, the State has eliminated any number of journalists and even detectives, to say nothing of ordinary people who get a knock at their door in the middle of the night.'

'And the State has waged a silent war on its own people in order to create hatred and distrust,' Tallis cut in. 'Come on, Graham, that's no reason for you to take the law into your own hands. What are you going to do next, turn your attention to the despots of failed African states?'

'If I have my orders,' Darke said, glacial, a resistant look in his eye.

Orders were all Darke had left, Tallis realised. 'You never used to do as you were told.'

'I do now.'

'Because of your loyalty, or because you're a washed-up nobody without prospects?' Tallis ground his jaw, watched as Darke's expression flared with anger, half expecting a bullet in the head. Recovering with mercurial speed, Darke flickered a smile.

'Seeing as you're here, I have an idea.'

Let's hope it means I get to stay alive, Tallis thought.

'I'm prepared to spare you, to give you a sporting chance,' Darke said, a glittering light in his eyes. 'In the spy game you have to be constantly flexible and ready to adapt plans on the hoof.'

'I didn't think being merciful was part of the strategy.'

'It isn't usually.'

'So is this for old times' sake?'

'It's because you're a better shot.'

Tallis felt the colour bleed from his face.

'Your call,' Darke said, indicating for Tallis to move. 'Either you kill Ivanov, or I kill you.'

Tallis stared at him, half-stunned, seconds ticking by like a slow drum-roll in his head. What sort of a choice was that? Kill or be killed? Except he doubted that Darke would spare him and even if he did, what future would he have after carrying out such a monstrous act? 'Alright, fair trade,' he said, sounding eminently reasonable. 'I guess I didn't much like the bloke anyway.'

'Thought you'd see it my way.'

Darke motioned Tallis forward to where he'd set himself up. Tallis crawled slowly along on his belly, Darke's gun trained on him, his mind racing. There was a sheet of green scrim netting on the ground designed to break up any physical outline. The gun was the deadly Soviet Dragunov, effective to a thousand metres. 'Fitting, isn't it? From Russia with love,' Darke said with an icy smile. 'Ivanov is due to take the air in roughly three minutes. The range isn't great but, with luck, you should be able to slot him.'

'You know as well as me that I'm not going to be able to take the shot if I think the next second you're going to blow my head off.' It was critical he have a steady reliable yet relaxed shooting position, and he needed to be able to breathe without hyperventilating.

'I'd love to say fair point but, frankly, not my problem.'

'Your problem if I miss.'

Darke gave him a hard-edged look. 'What do you suggest?'

'Lower your weapon, shut up, and don't sit on my tail.'

'Two out of three, best I can do. You'll have to put up with me standing behind you. I could spot for you, if you like.'

Tallis hesitated fractionally. With Darke guiding him, the shot would be more accurate. 'No,' he said. 'I'm alright.'

Rather than using the netting, Tallis pulled it away. The last thing he needed was to get entangled in the weave.

He took the gun, lay prone and spread his feet comfortably apart then rolled down slightly on his left side, putting his elbow forward and placing his left hand well forward, the rifle resting in the natural V formed by his left thumb and forefinger. With his right hand, he grasped the stock, thumb over the top, his right elbow lowered to the ground so that his shoulders were in line. Next, he adjusted the setting of the sight. This was when he was at his most vulnerable. Any hint of the Dragunov's barrel and exposure to the Russians, and it would all be over.

He looked through the sight again. The distance between him and the swimming pool was roughly six hundred metres. A body viewed by the naked eye at that distance appeared wedge-shaped, but to Tallis it would seem as if the target was up close and very personal. But that didn't mean emotions came into play. It was

important to be focused, determined and without fear—
in sniper-speak, *in the zone*.

The aquamarine-coloured modern fence around the
perimeter, although transparent, was made of bullet-
proof material, unlike the gap through which the bullet
was to pass. Narrow in the extreme, it was double the
width of a slit in a medieval castle. To target Ivanov,
Tallis needed him to be near the pool's edge, or about
to get in, a shot in the water too difficult to pull off.

Seconds ticked, Tallis aware of Graham Darke
standing right behind him, within easy reach of a
weapon should he decide to change his mind or trick
him. Bang on cue, two thick-set men, part of Ivanov's
close-protection team, judging from the earpieces,
stepped outside, fully dressed, followed by Ivanov who
was wearing an open towelling robe over a pair of
skimpy, skin-tight white swimming trunks. Tallis took
a deep breath, ensured the cross-hairs were level, that
the butt of the rifle was close in, resting in the hollow
of his shoulder, his body ready to absorb any recoil, and
that his right cheek was fixed on the spot formed by his
right thumb. Around Ivanov's neck was a thick gold
chain with a St. Christopher hanging from it, the me-
dallion lying against his breastbone, presumably to
protect him yet in reality providing the perfect bull's-
eye. Ivanov was sharing some joke with the others then
another man stepped out of the house bearing a bright
green inflatable, already blown up in the shape of a
chair with a holder for a drink. He rested it down on the

water, holding it while Ivanov disrobed, exposing his muscled torso, and climbed aboard like a Chinese emperor mounting an eighteenth-century sedan. Beads of sweat broke out on Tallis's brow as he zeroed in—the further a bullet had to travel, the higher the trajectory.

Ivanov pushed off a little from the side of the pool, floating silently towards the killing zone. As Tallis watched, a roll-call of the damaged and the dead drummed through his head—Ruslan, Asya, their father, Dmitri, the countless numbers of Chechen and Russian soldiers, the Vladimirs and Viktors, the Lenas and Katyas, the children made orphans, the wives made widows, and all the people in between. It would be so easy to kill him, he thought, this man with blood on his hands. He took a breath, released it a little, holding the rest while he took aim, knowing that in less than ten seconds it would be finished.

With the cross-hairs over the target, he touched the trigger and fired, Ivanov toppling down into the water at the same time as Tallis rolled and instinctively grabbed the netting, literally pulling the ground from underneath Darke so that his premeditated shot missed him by millimetres. That's when he recognised the true nature of the man, the emptiness in the eyes, the moral detachment, the dreadful toll the mountains had taken on him. As Darke lifted the Sig to fire another round, as fast as a viper Tallis shot Graham Darke in the face at point-blank range.

As Tallis got up to run, he could hear all hell unleashed behind him as the Russians dragged their prime minister, cursing and shouting orders, out of the pool, the tattered remains of the inflatable already sinking to the bottom.

When, fifteen minutes later, an RAF helicopter swooped low, Andrei Ivanov had no idea that the man who'd rescued him was on board, or that the man had shot his oldest friend in order to save him.

CHAPTER TWENTY-ONE

Thames House, MI5 Headquarters, London

'THE Russian Prime Minister sends a personal message of immense gratitude.' Asim beamed.

It was two days after Tallis's trip to France. When he returned he reported back and slept the clock round in an expensive hotel near Bayswater. He thought about calling home on a couple of occasions to talk to Lena but feared she would ask about Ruslan. Unless essential, breaking that kind of news should never be done on a telephone.

'I'm touched,' Tallis said, unsmiling. He hadn't enjoyed saving him, still less killing Graham Darke to do so. 'And Fazan?'

'I'm flying out to Berlin tonight.'

'To hear his side of the story? I told you Darke was adamant he was following Fazan's orders.'

'And Fazan is equally adamant that Darke was acting off his own bat.'

'He denies everything?' Only idiots denied everything.

'He doesn't deny that from a human point of view he won't be sorry when Ivanov fades from power. He thinks it would be healthier for both Russia and international relations.'

'Clever,' Tallis said. 'He's admitting to some kind of motivation but giving it an interesting slant.'

Asim tipped the palm of his hand up.

'You believe Numerov's testimony triggered Fazan's response?' Tallis knew that he was shamelessly fishing, but what the hell.

'Let's put it this way,' Asim said, his eyes hooded, 'there is absolutely no need for you to worry about it.'

Worry? That was hardly the word he'd have used to describe a whole host of feelings he hadn't even begun to process, but Tallis felt too knackered to argue. 'Which brings me to another question. Does Ivanov know it was Darke?'

'Naturally. He was quite relieved to hear that Musa is dead.'

Tallis met Asim's eye. And so are you, he thought. At a stroke it devalued the story of the SIS agent fighting alongside Chechen rebels. Tallis knew that he'd had no choice but to kill Darke but it still made him feel shoddy. 'And what did the French make of it? It's one thing to allow free access, another to have assassination attempts on their doorstep.'

'Franco-Russian relations may stall for a while. As

far as the French are concerned, Darke was an Algerian national with excitable views.'

'You swapped bodies?'

'It happens,' Asim said airily. 'You may be interested to know,' he continued, looking like a lion fed a huge chunk of wildebeest, 'that as a mark of the Russians' desire to form a better relationship with us, they're prepared to wind down their current programme of assassination.'

'What about Ivanov's obsession with the Chechens?'

'Miracles take a little longer, but I think you'll find Ivanov's near-death experience has had a suitably salutary effect. I think he'll quit messing, at least, in the short term.'

Probably do no more than get that gap in his fence fixed, Tallis thought. He asked about Grigori Orlov's contribution.

'Fulsomely recognised by the Prime Minister. I gather Orlov is in line for some sort of presentation as a mark of his loyalty to the motherland,' Asim said, clipped. Tallis smiled. Orlov definitely played on the wrong side of the tracks, but he was no pawn of the state and Tallis still harboured a sneaking admiration for the man, if only for his sheer originality.

'And what about that lead I gave you?'

Asim smiled. 'Wondered when you'd get round to that. It gave us another bit of leverage, I must say. Would you like to do the honours?'

'Hasn't the bird already flown?'

'Only as far as Shobdon.' Asim glanced at his watch. 'We've a helicopter on standby. You could be there in forty minutes.'

Shobdon, Herefordshire

The airfield was buzzing with activity. Tallis had never seen so many people. Aside from mechanics and pilots out in force, dozens of punters were standing around, waiting patiently for their turn to take to the skies. Serious buyers were easily distinguishable from enthusiastic visitors. Came down to the cars they drove: Astons held sway over Astras.

A number of helicopters were waiting to take off while a couple took their turn to come in to land. Tallis couldn't help but stare at an impressive Eurocopter EC 155, a beautiful twelve-seater beast of a machine costing millions, with four fuel tanks, the noise from the helicopter shrouded by a low-vibration main rotor and a specially designed Fenestron tail rotor. The contrast with two-seater planes, swathed in tarpaulin, snoozing silently in the afternoon sun couldn't have been more apparent. A very British scene of excitement and geniality, Tallis thought, dragging himself away and crossing purposefully towards Tiger's offices.

And he was about to ruin it.

Reception was no less busy. Phones were ringing. Smoothly dressed thirty- and forty-something males were vying for attention from two attractive girls manning the desk whose job was to note potential clients' details and book test flights or appointments with sales staff. The atmosphere was hard-edged and slightly frantic. About to walk upstairs, he caught sight of Ginny Dodge, dressed in a dark navy flight suit. She was ushering two men into a suite, presumably to close a deal. Tallis returned to Reception and, politely apologising to a tight-faced man with a petulant manner, more used to interrupting than being interrupted, asked to be informed when Ginny was free.

Upstairs, he was given a decent cup of tea, helped himself to the free food on offer and made himself at home. It soon transpired, as if he hadn't already worked it out, that he'd arrived in the middle of an open day. Two hours later, his mobile rang. Ten minutes following that, and after making a single call out, he made his way back outside, heading for the bar adjoining the canteen.

Tallis thought he'd stumbled out of the Tardis and fetched up in World War Britain. The bar, small, dark and clubby with brown leather chairs and sofas, heaved with people. Images of moustachioed blokes in Bomber Command, pipes clenched between their teeth, tumblers of single malt at the ready, preparing to go into battle, flashed before his eyes.

As he cut through the swathe of early evening drinkers, conversation was dominated by the blinding success of the open day. Blaine Deverill, Tallis noticed, was in full flight, Ginny Dodge, immaculately turned out in a pure white shirt and tailored trousers, looking bored beside him. As Tallis walked towards them, both turned, each face registering astonishment then forced pleasure. He reckoned Ginny had the edge by about half a second.

'Good God, thought you'd left the country,' Deverill said, half getting up.

'Did you now?' Tallis smiled, nodding hello to Ginny who nodded hello back.

'So what have you two been up to in my absence?'

'This and that,' Deverill said. ''Course, when you're used to a high-powered existence, it's not easy adapting to a slower pace.'

'High-powered existence?' Tallis frowned, exchanging a grin with Ginny who was suddenly hugely enjoying herself.

'Well, yeah, did I ever tell you I was in the Special Boat Service?' Deverill said.

'Thought it was the Hereford Gun Club. Actually, Ginny, I will have that drink after all,' Tallis said. 'Single malt, please.'

'Really?' Deverill coloured, unused, it seemed, to having his fantasies punctured. 'My mistake.'

'Odd error to make. There's quite a difference.'

Deverill let out a shaky laugh. 'No, really, it was a long time ago, naturally, but I was definitely in the SBS. Lived down in the South-West, you see.'

Tallis didn't see. What the hell did that have to do with anything? Deverill was floundering and he knew it. Under Tallis's icy gaze, Deverill decided to down his pint and cut and run. 'Anyway, must be getting on,' he said, pushing his chair back.

'So soon?' Tallis clamped a hand over Deverill's arm, glancing up as Ginny returned with his whisky, her expression altering from one of good humour to mild concern. 'What surprises me, Blaine,' Tallis said, smiling warmly, Deverill's arm still manacled to the table, 'is that you come out with all these fibs like some blundering fool, yet you never tell us what you really did.'

'Well, I—'

'You worked in the defence industry, isn't that right?' Tallis said, aware that the noise in the room had dipped and others around them were glancing their way,

'I'd prefer not to talk about it,' Deverill blustered.

'Because you're not allowed to, I understand, and also because you're embarrassed that, after your nervous breakdown, your employer was less than happy with your performance,' Tallis said, looking at Ginny, whose smile had vanished like frost in sunshine. 'Which was why when you left you took off, like many escapees from life, to the South-West, but by then, of course, you were well acquainted with certain classified designs in the aeronautical market.'

Deverill paled. His fingers gripped the table, nails digging into the wood. 'How did—?'

'Which explains why Miss Dodge here…' Tallis switched his gaze '…thought it worth hanging out with you.'

'What?' Ginny said, her blue eyes standing out

sharply against skin that had turned an odd shade of grey.

'But I've never said a word,' Deverill protested. 'Not to her, not to anyone. I wouldn't. I signed the Official Secrets Act. I believe in Queen and country,' he burbled. He looked mortified.

'Which was why you got suspicious of her apparent interest in you.'

'What the hell…?' Ginny began.

'Isn't that why you were in her office a few weeks ago, searching for clues?' Tallis persisted.

Blaine looked from Tallis to Ginny, spreading his hands, mouth gaping open.

'It's alright. I understand,' Tallis said kindly.

'Understand?' Ginny burst out. 'Have you had a blow to the head or something?'

'Many.' Tallis smiled sweetly. 'But, then, you'd know about that, wouldn't you? Did you have a direct line to Timur Garipova or did you use Boris Kumarin as your go-between? I know you approached Orlov under some pretext to find out if I was still alive—bum move, if I might say so—but I suppose if you have no concept of loyalty and trust, you fail to recognise it in other people,' he said, calmly taking a sip of whisky. 'I'd no idea you were a member of the Communist Party in your youth.'

Conversation in the bar was so non-existent it was possible to hear the hunger pangs of the man standing next to you.

'It's not a crime,' she said, the accompanying smile lacking conviction.

'But spying for another country is.'

Ginny appealed to Deverill, who was staring open-mouthed, then burst out laughing. 'Paul,' she said, looking around her. 'This is ridiculous. This is—'

'True,' Tallis said, his voice granite-hard. He glanced out of the window and saw the black saloon draw up outside, two men stepping out.

'I don't have to listen to this,' she said, getting up, darting him a venomous look before storming out of the bar where two intelligence officers, waiting in the wings outside, prevented her flight.

'Like another drink?' Tallis winked at Deverill.

He nodded blindly. For once Blaine Deverill kept his mouth shut.

Berlin

Christian Fazan stared at the unfamiliar surroundings of his office and drained his glass of whisky, and wondered if he'd got away with it. Asim seemed to buy his account but appearances were deceiving. Asim was not an easy man to fool.

Fazan got up, walked a little unsteadily to the window and looked outside to the quiet street below. Will I ever get used to Berlin? he thought sadly. In some ways, it was similar to Moscow, especially the older parts that had not yet been knocked down, yet in other respects, the people in particular, it was a different world. Whatever the truth, he would miss Russia, and his last link to Malika Motova.

Reaching for his coat, his mind reeled back through the decades to a shabby Moscow apartment on Leninsky Prospekt that had exuded more life and glamour than he'd experienced before or since. How he'd enjoyed those thrown-together late-night meals, downed with vodka, the terrific conversation, the ebb and flow of ideas, the rebelliousness and courage of people motivated by art and words, and, of course, with such a fabulous woman, an older woman, at his side. That it had been his first and only foray into entrapment he chose to forget. He'd never meant to fall in love, and hadn't been certain that Malika had felt the same, although as the years had rolled by his memory had become smoothed and refined and prettified by time. Yes, he believed that she had loved him, too. Thing was, he'd never found anyone to replace her and the guilt of what he'd done, what he'd exposed her to, weighed heavily on his soul. But he was a professional and to carry out a job like his it was essential to separate emotion from intellect, and he had. For years, and to the very best of his ability, he'd compartmentalised and detached the personal from the career. In fact, his job had been the saving of him. He put on his coat, light and expensive cashmere, and frowned heavily. In the end, even his work had betrayed him.

Opening the door, he walked outside into the corridor

and down the stairs to the entrance, issuing a series of goodnights along the way. The evening was cool but not unpleasant and, wishing to clear his head, he decided to walk in preference to taking a cab, taking the scenic route back to his apartment by walking along the river Spree.

When he'd first heard about what he believed to be Darke's rogue status, the intelligence officer in him had taken over. At least, he thought so. Certainly, his approach to Asim had been honest and above-board, sanctioned by C. himself, but now, looking back with the aid of several glasses of finest malt, he wasn't so clear in his mind. Perhaps, even then, he'd secretly entertained the unconscious hope that Darke would succeed in his so-called mission. Then when he'd found out that not only was Darke innocent of the allegations but on his way back he'd realised the depth of his disappointment. Maybe that had been the moment the seed already sown had blossomed. Next had come Numerov's account. It had proved to be the deciding factor.

Fazan felt a chill so strong he rolled up the collar of his coat even though it was not particularly cold and wished *guten abend* to a young pair of lovers strolling past, the only people on the riverside. He glanced at his watch: shortly after seven. Most would be at home, or eating dinner in one of the many restaurants in the capital.

Apart from feeling duped, what enraged him most was the racism and callousness of Ivanov's behaviour. His attitude to Malika had not been born out of her alleged treachery but her cultural roots, her creed, everything that had made her different to him. It had been in that moment he'd known he had to act, to get rid of this smiling tyrant, and to hell with world peace. That Darke, a loyal if damaged collaborator, had failed was a personal tragedy for both of them.

Footsteps behind him. Fazan turned and smiled. 'You two again,' he said in German. They smiled back. As he stepped aside to let them pass, he never realised his mistake. Neither did he spot the outline of a man watching with interest from a distance, a man he knew only as Asim.

The expert blow to the back of Fazan's neck rendered him unconscious immediately. As he tumbled into the ice-cold river, his clothes and the whisky he'd consumed that afternoon did the rest.

Tallis did not leave the airfield immediately. He went back to his office, cleared his desk and called in at the village pub to consume a pint of their best ale. He was stalling. The thought of going back home filled him with dread. It was awful enough breaking bad news about Ruslan to Katya. The thought of telling Lena, who had already lost so much, appalled him. He'd tried to call Viva to see if she could come round to provide emotional support. Neither she nor Rasu were picking up the phone. All he could do was leave a message to the effect that he would be back in Birmingham within the next hour and please could she contact him.

Eventually, and undoubtedly over the drink-drive limit, he drove back in silence. Images of Katya floated to the forefront of his mind. When he pictured her, she was smiling, her face lit up with a radiance that was only matched by the light in the Côte D'Azur. Then he thought about Lena, dark-eyed, anxious, waiting. He expected she'd looked after the bungalow beautifully in his absence. On his arrival, she'd probably burst into a great litany of how she'd kept house, washed his curtains, spring-cleaned and polished the furniture, wanting to please him, and then she would notice the fear and despair in his eyes and guess that something terrible had happened.

He pictured the scene. A hand covering her heart, her eyes welling with tears, and he would put his arm around her shoulder, lead her through to the sitting room and sit her down and say those words that, however much you switched them around, however painstakingly you chose them, the message was the same: raw and bleeding and final.

The bungalow looked as homely and welcoming as when his gran had lived there, he thought, pulling into the drive. The grass was cut without being too short. Spring flowers, narcissi and crocuses, peeped through the borders. Lena had given the front door another coat of paint. It sparkled in the evening sun. By the time he parked the Porsche in the carport, he'd run through what he would say a dozen times. He knew that what he finally told her would be nothing like his prepared speech. The best he could offer would be to provide a roof over her head, to look after her, to see if a fresh appeal could be made to the Home Office.

Putting the key in the lock, he turned it and let himself inside, dropping his bag on the floor, calling Lena's name, his own voice hollow in the silence. There was no smell of mustiness or neglect. Perhaps she'd gone for a walk he thought, walking through to the kitchen to check the phone for messages. That's when he saw a note with his name on it, propped up by a jug of yellow tulips. The writing was in Viva's strong hand. Tallis picked it up, already sensing its contents, and took it through to the sitting room. He noticed that it was dated the day before.

Paul,

So sorry to inform you that Immigration officials came for Lena this morning and, despite my strong protestations, put her on a flight back to Moscow. Although clearly upset, she seemed to accept what was happening with weary resignation.

Lena asked me to thank you for all that you've done for her. She said how much she'd enjoyed your company and that she would never forget you, or your kindness. She also said something about you looking for her son, Ruslan—was that the real reason for your trip? Anyway, she said that if you had any news, a message could be left for her at the Cathedral Mosque in St Petersburg.

As you can imagine, we're pretty upset and disappointed. No doubt you'll feel the same.

Hope you're OK. Perhaps we could get together soon and you can update me.

With love,

Viva

Tallis let out a breath, sank into the nearest chair and briefly closed his eyes. Inexpressibly sad, he stayed there until the light finally faded from the sky.

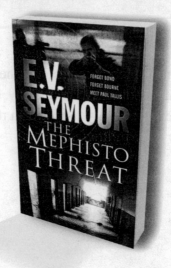